THE HOLTS
An American Dynasty

A BOLD FAMILY OF BREATHTAKING SPIRIT AND DARING IDEALS, THEY FIGHT FOR WHAT THEY BELIEVE IN—WITH PASSION, COURAGE, AND HEART.

SHARE THE EXCITING ADVENTURES OF THE HOLTS, THE THIRD GENERATION, AS THEY CONTINUE THE STRUGGLE FOR JUSTICE, RISKING THEIR LIVES—AND LOVES—IN A RUGGED, TEMPESTUOUS LAND.

FROM THE STORMY WATERS OF A CONFLICT-
TORN WESTERN ISLAND TO THE SPIRITED
SHORES OF AMERICA, THE HOLTS CREATE
HISTORY AS THEY FIGHT FOR THEIR COUN-
TRY'S HERITAGE AND STRUGGLE TO FREE
ITS PEOPLE—EVERYWHERE.

MIKE HOLT—

Now grown to manhood, powerful Toby Holt's
adventure-seeking son accompanies the brilliant, ec-
centric moving-picture pioneer Thomas Edison to the
primitive coast of Florida—where he is determined to
become a moviemaker. But he is haunted by the
memory of exquisite runaway Eden Brentwood, the
beauty who has captured his heart.

EDEN BRENTWOOD—

Nearly eighteen now, caught in the crossfire of Hawaiian revolution, she is torn between fear for the life
of her brother, Sam, and her desire to leave the island
to find the man she cannot forget.

SAM BRENTWOOD—

Dangerously embroiled in his adopted land's revolt,
he leaves his family behind and sacrifices all he
cherishes for a cause he passionately believes in. But
when the empire falls, the royalist rebel finds himself
in deadly peril—and no one, not even his wife,
Annie, can save him.

ANNIE MALONE BRENTWOOD—

Left alone to run the Brentwood sugar plantation while her husband suffers hard labor on a chain gang, she welcomes her old friend Dallas McCall as her farm's savior . . . until the ruggedly handsome drifter begins stirring all the wrong emotions within her.

DALLAS McCALL—

A hard-living, hard-drinking wanderer who is finally ready to settle down, he is determined to run things in Sam's absence . . . and seems just as ready to take Sam's place in Annie's heart.

DICKIE MERRILL—

The wealthy New York womanizer comes to Hawaii at Sam's invitation—and uses the lavish Brentwood home as his own private playground. Attracted to lovely Eden, he finds his most passion-filled delights in the smoldering embrace of a sultry Hawaiian servant.

JANESSA HOLT LAWRENCE—

Heavy with child, she returns with her husband, Charley, to New York. But it isn't until she begins her heartbreaking work as a doctor on the legendary Ellis Island that she encounters her greatest challenge: a haunting young Russian immigrant named Rachel.

RACHEL POLIAKOV—

Exotically beautiful, she barely escapes the murderous cossack pogroms. Torn from her family by the harsh realities of disease, she starts her new life alone—until she is transformed by the vision of a daring film pioneer.

LOT KAMAHAMEHA LANE—

The son of a hot-tempered, territorial Irishman, this possessed rebel introduces Sam to the heady perils of revolution. But with the queen and her loyal factions crushed by the ruthless Provisional Government, together Sam and Lot face execution.

Bantam Books by Dana Fuller Ross
Ask your bookseller for the books you have missed

THE HOLTS: AN AMERICAN DYNASTY
VOLUME FIVE

HAWAII
HERITAGE

DANA FULLER ROSS

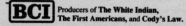

BCI Producers of **The White Indian,**
The First Americans, and **Cody's Law.**

Book Creations Inc., Canaan, NY • Lyle Kenyon Engel, Founder

BANTAM BOOKS
NEW YORK • TORONTO • LONDON • SYDNEY • AUCKLAND

HAWAII HERITAGE

A Bantam Domain Book / published by arrangement with
Book Creations, Inc.

Bantam edition / November 1991
Produced by Book Creations, Inc.
Lyle Kenyon Engel, Founder

ISBN 0-553-29414-8

Published simultaneously in the United States and Canada

Bantam Books are published by Bantam Books, a division of Bantam
Doubleday Dell Publishing Group, Inc. Its trademark, consisting of
the words "Bantam Books" and the portrayal of a rooster, is
Registered in U.S. Patent and Trademark Office and in other
countries. Marca Registrada. Bantam Books, 666 Fifth Avenue, New
York, New York 10103.

PRINTED IN THE UNITED STATES OF AMERICA

OPM   0 9 8 7 6 5 4 3 2 1

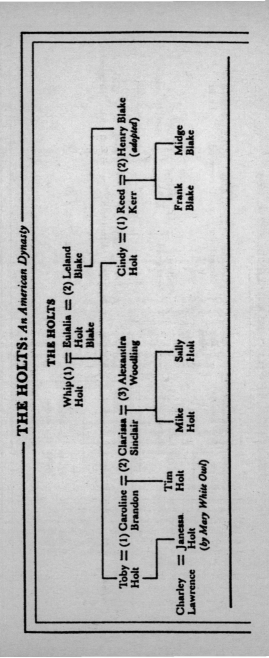

THE HOLTS: *An American Dynasty*

THE HOLTS

THE BLAKES, THE MARTINS AND THE BRENTWOODS

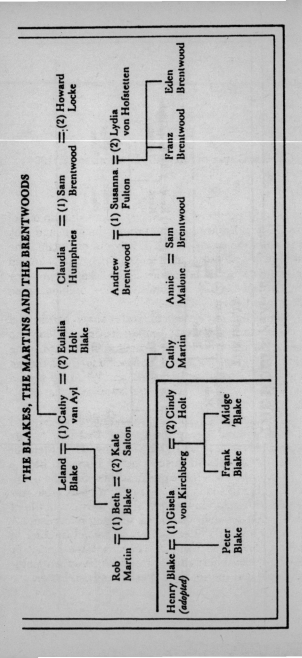

I

An outrigger, dragged by two men, came up out of the surf. Sam Brentwood ran through the foam and took his place in the canoe, which swiftly put out again. The first time he had been out in one of these vessels he had nearly drowned, but he had learned a thing or two since then. In fact he had, in some people's opinion, gone native to a disgusting degree.

Sam could see a steamer, just a shape against the sky, bobbing in the dusk, waiting for him. It bore no running lights. Aboard it, someone blew a piercing whistle, and a rope ladder was let down. Sam shook the salt spray from his eyes and climbed up. When he turned around, the outrigger had melted away into the indigo waters.

The steam engine began to thud to full speed, and the boat pointed her prow up the coastline for its eventual destination of Oahu, dogging the lantern-lit wake of the interisland steamer out of Honuapo Bay.

"Come below," the captain invited, and Sam followed William Davies into his cabin. A chart table was overlaid with maps and weighted down with a bottle of whiskey that someone had been working on already. A tall, big-boned man lifted a heavy-bottomed tumbler in greeting. Lot Kamehameha Lane, a *hapa-haole*, or half-white, had inherited the size of his Hawaiian mother's people and the reckless eyes of his Irish father.

1

"How's tricks, Lot?" Sam picked up an empty glass and filled it for himself.

Lot smiled. "Pa's fighting mad. Bob Wilcox told him he was too old to come with us. So he made us a fine speech: 'Go, my sons, and fight for the rights of your people. Spill your blood if necessary on the soil of your mother's land—and never forget that there flows in your veins the blood of the Careys and Lanes of County Cork!'"

Sam chuckled. The six Lane boys were all more than he would want to take on, but old Pa Lane was the biggest firebrand of the batch.

"Sit down and look here," Captain Davies said.

Sam drew up a chair beside Peter Aikanaka, who had once been one of the deposed queen Liliuokalani's cabinet ministers. Lot moved the whiskey bottle off the charts, and Peter snagged it as it went by. He tipped some liquid down his throat.

They were a piratical-looking crew, dressed in colorful *malos* wrapped around their waists and not much else. Their hair was dark and sleek with the salt water. Except for Sam, who was an American, all the conspirators who passed the whiskey bottle among them were Hawaiians—Polynesian, *haole*, or white, and hapa-haole—and they knew full well what they were doing. The last revolution had been bloodless, but this one would not be unless their efforts were perfectly timed. A great deal rode on the timing.

A month before, William T. Seward, the tough old Civil War major who had fought with Ulysses Grant through the Wilderness campaign and later settled in the islands, had gone to California and bought rifles and ammunition. Rumor had it that Claus Spreckels's son Rudolph had paid for them. Spreckels lived on the mainland and, despite large sugar plantings in Hawaii, had iconoclastic political views. In a fit of pique, the ruling Downtown party, the provisional government that had deposed Liliuokalani, had tried to have him assassinated but hadn't been able to bring it off. Spreckels was a wily bird.

But whoever had footed the bill, the important thing was that guns for the revolution had been bought and were coming in that night on the schooner *Wahlberg*. The little steamer, the *Waimanalo*, would take on the weapons in the waters near Oahu, then off-load them inconspicuously at points along the shore.

"Here." Davies stabbed a callused finger at a point on the chart. "We rendezvous with the *Wahlberg* here, take on the cargo, and anchor here, off Diamond Head."

"What for?" Lot Lane was ready to wade ashore, rifle in hand, and get things started.

"For orders, you damn crazy Irishman," Peter Aikanaka said. "We'll anchor off the Head opposite Henry Bertelmann's place and check in with Bob Wilcox. See what the PGs are up to." PG stood for provisional government, and even though the force that had overthrown the queen now considered itself duly appointed, no Royalist thought it necessary to update the nomenclature.

"Captain!" A whistle shrilled from above, and a young sailor poked his face down the stairs. "Signal to port. We got 'em!"

"Or somebody's got us," Davies responded. "Don't signal back till I get up there." He rose and hurried above, with Sam, Lot, and Peter following.

A thin light winked in the black band where the sky met the water. It was like a star-spangled curtain of ink above, flowing with the pale lines of combers below. There was no moon. Davies studied the signal light and, satisfied, nodded curtly. "Reply."

An hour later the steamer was tied alongside the schooner, and the Royalists were passing wooden crates of ammunition and rifles packed in grease down into the hold. The schooner was the bigger vessel, and the ladders between the ships swayed like kelp along the schooner's side.

"Look out!" someone yelled below as Lot came down too heavily. Lot tried to swing back up the ladder and off the fallen man. Then Sam's bare foot came down on Lot's wrist. Sam slithered on wet skin, and the crate in his arms lurched dangerously.

"Watch what you're doing!"

The crate was heavy, and the corners dug into Sam's bare chest. "I can't watch anything," he grumbled. "It's as black as the inside of a billy goat."

The steamer bumped the schooner and then drifted a few feet back from it, riding on its tether. The ladder moved again, out and back, slamming Sam against the schooner's side. He clasped both arms around the crate and held on with the tenuous grip of one hand on wet rope.

"Get the crate down!" Lot yelled.

Sam tried to turn slowly, to lower the crate, but he was sliding, overbalanced. In another moment he lost his grip, and the crate plunged to the deck of the *Waimanalo*. Sam was upended in the rope ladder, his ankle tangled and his hands flailing at the air. The ship's motion slammed him hard into the schooner again.

Swaying upside down above the *Waimanalo's* deck and the narrow crevice of seawater between the ships, Sam tried to reach up and grasp the rope; but it danced just beyond his fingers. Above him, it dug into his ankle, slowly searing his skin. He thrashed, terrified of coming down headfirst or being pinned between the ships if he fell.

"Look out above!" Lot yelled.

Faces peered over the rail of the schooner. Hands reached out for the ladder. The steamer bumped the bigger ship again, and Sam smashed face first into the schooner's side. He could feel blood running down his face. It was warmer than the salt water. The men above tried to pull the ladder up but stopped when Lot shouted at them.

"No! You'll lose him!"

Sam could feel the rope's stiff fibers scraping painfully across his ankle. Lot, a knife in his teeth, had climbed the ladder beside Sam's. Peter Aikanaka, standing on the deck below, leaned out and caught the loose end of Sam's ladder. He had scrambled through the broken crate to grab the rope, which he held straight until Sam could get his hands around it.

"Hang on good," Lot grunted. "I'm going to cut you loose up here."

Sam gripped as hard as he could, trying to hold back the light-headedness that was overwhelming him. Suddenly he was falling, flipping over, his heels coming down as his hands remained clenched around the ladder. The drop jerked his arms nearly out of their sockets, and he let go, landing in the broken shards of the ammunition crate. He hunched on the deck and gasped from the pain while Peter patted him solicitously. The captain of the *Waimanalo* yelled at the men above to get moving. The longer they took, the more danger there was of a PG cutter intercepting them.

Sam stood up and wrapped his malo back around him. Now that he was safe and relatively unharmed, the indignity of his previous position struck his shipmates as grimly amusing.

"You should try out for a trapeze act," Lot hooted. "But better wear more than a malo. You'll catch a cold in your privates."

"You're lucky there weren't no ladies. You'd have been famous."

Sam gritted his teeth, his dignity seriously offended.

"Get those guns unloaded, Brentwood," Captain Davies said. "This isn't vaudeville."

Sam turned, snarling, ready to punch him. But after Lot handed him the whiskey bottle and Sam took a drink, he thought better of it. The hoots and laughter subsided, and Sam finally managed a rueful grin. It was tense work, and if anyone could find a joke in it, then let him. There would be little enough levity once they began using these weapons they were loading. The crate he had dropped had broken open, and paper boxes of shells, heavy and ominous, spilled out of it.

As the *Waimanalo* steamed away from the *Wahlberg,* Sam leaned against the railing and thought about the fact that he had never fought in a war—unless he counted a certain difference of opinion between miners and mine owners in Virginia City. He had taken one side, and his courtesy cousin Tim Holt had taken the other. Sam still had a chipped tooth to show for it. This situation would be different, he thought. The Hawaiians were a notoriously gentle and peaceable people, but their relatively recent history included Kamehameha I, the warrior-king who had united all the islands at spear point before his people caught both religion and civilization from the missionaries. Pushed too far, the descendants of Kamehameha were as capable of bloody violence as the next man. Suddenly a shiver ran up his spine, and the gentle air of paradise that clung to the islands seemed to Sam to be wholly illusion.

Sam Brentwood slunk down the teak-floored hallway from his wife's bedroom into dawn's first pool of winter sun. Cursing the plank that creaked, he flattened himself against the wall and eyed his grandmother's door.

Hell of a thing, he thought, trying not to get caught making love to your own wife. But since ending their separation, Annie still had him at arm's length half the time, and she wouldn't let him into her bedroom unless she thought nobody in the household would notice. She didn't want everyone thinking everything was jake when she still had him on probation. That was part of her terms: public pillory.

Still, he had to admit, their marriage was on the mend. He had been courting Annie with champagne and flowers, rubbing her feet, and reading her poetry for over a year now, and she wasn't made of stone. Sam chuckled. Annie liked to make love, which made it difficult for her to hold out on him. He heard no noises from his grandmother Claudia's door, so he straightened up and slid past his younger half sister Eden's room and down the stairs to the breakfast room. Annie's maid, Koana, was just bouncing up the stairs from outside with a load of clean towels in her arms.

"Good morning, Mr. Sam," she caroled. A hibiscus flower was stuck behind her ear.

"Good morning, Koana." Through the etched glass of the front door, he could see a pair of loungers—Koana's beaux—on the porch take note of him and depart hastily. Koana indiscriminately encouraged all men, so Sam ignored them unless they were actively trying to cut out one another's liver.

In the breakfast room, he discovered that he needn't have been so quiet when passing Claudia's room. She was already at the table and drinking tea.

"How it can smell like this in December . . ." she murmured. She flicked a finger against the bowl of fresh flowers, strange and unnameable to her, on the table. Her hands were paper white and wrinkled, like thin tissue. Her green eyes, sunk beneath thin white brows, still held the spark of shrewd intelligence, however. She watched while Sam poured himself a cup of coffee.

"I tasted that," she remarked. "The cook brews it up like mud. You'll poison yourself."

Sam bent to kiss her cheek. "Too late to stunt my growth. I like it like this—coffee you can get your teeth into."

"Literally," Claudia said, amused.

"It's unpatriotic to drink tea here, Gran. This coffee is homegrown, whereas that"—he pointed at her teacup—"is imported from sinister Oriental climes." He chuckled ruefully. "As are half my field hands, so I buy a good deal of tea, actually. The Chinese don't like coffee. Aggravating of them."

"You ought to plant tea," Claudia suggested. "Everything seems to grow like weeds here."

"Weeds grow like weeds here, too, unfortunately," Sam said. "You should see what comes up between the cane rows before it 'shades.'"

"What does that mean?" Claudia asked.

"Before the cane's thick enough to choke out anything else. Some planters have been trying tea, but the labor cost is pretty high. Tea is persnickety. No, Gran, sugar's where the money is. I plant a little coffee just to hedge my bets, but sugar owns this place."

"From what you've told me, sugar owns Hawaii," Claudia commented.

"Sugar planters do," Sam agreed grimly. "I'm a renegade. The Downtown party doesn't like me much, and my factor tolerates me only because I bring in a good crop. If I ever needed an advance, I think he'd be unaccountably short of funds."

"You don't seem particularly concerned about it, you devil," she said. "From the light in your eyes, I'd say that you're about to make trouble for someone."

He filled a plate with bacon and eggs and sliced mangoes from the dishes on the sideboard. "You never know, Gran," he said noncommittally. "You just never know."

After buying the plantation, Sam had aligned himself on the side of the other sugar planters when the McKinley Tariff destroyed Hawaii's favored status in the American sugar market. The solution, in the planters' eyes, had been the annexation of Hawaii by the United States.

Annexation had not been achieved, but revolution had. The annexationists—otherwise known as the Downtown party or the Committee of Safety—had, with the connivance of the American minister in Hawaii and the muscle of a shipload of U.S. Marines from the cruiser *Boston*, overthrown Queen Liliuokalani and set up a provisional government in her palace—all the while piously declaring that finances had nothing to do with it. The revolutionaries were largely descendants of the white missionaries who had brought Christianity and voluminous clothing to the islands. They took a moral stance; the queen, they said, permitted heathenism to flourish.

Under the presidency of Sanford Dole and the behind-the-scenes machinations of his right-hand man, Lorrin Thurston, the provisional government demanded loyalty oaths, jailed journalists who spoke too critically, terrorized the deposed queen, and spread nasty and blatantly untrue rumors about her personal life. In Sam's estimation the members of the PG were behaving like school-yard bullies. Feeling that he had been deceived and used, Sam, furious, bolted to the other side. He was not alone. The native Hawaiians had finally lost their collective temper, and many of the white and half-white citizens were outraged as well. Annie had been among Liliuokalani's friends from the first.

By this December of 1894, a coterie of Royalists regularly frequented Washington Place, the queen's private house, set spies among the government men of the Downtown party, and plotted an armed revolt. Sam was up to his neck in it.

Now, over a forkful of mangoes, he contemplated his grandmother. He and Annie had been at pains to tell neither Claudia nor Eden what was afoot, but Sam wondered how much they knew anyway. Eden was in the throes of adolescent love, and it might have rained toads without her noticing. Claudia was another matter. He did not think she would try to discourage him; he didn't want her frightened for him nor in possession of any knowledge that the government might find useful. The authorities had taken lately to hounding citizens who they thought might inform on one another, and Claudia was too old to withstand harassment.

Just then Annie came downstairs in a yellow silk wrapper. Her rose-gold hair was neatly pinned up and fluffed over her forehead. She eyed Sam with the look of wary affection that she had accorded him since they had made the disconcerting discovery that they were in love. Sam had been under the impression that he had married Annie, eleven years his senior, for her money, the fruits of her Virginia City boomtown silver days; Annie believed that she had married him for his dark and rakish good looks and his family's social status. It had been a shock to them both to find love lurking in the equation, and they hadn't handled it very well.

Sam kissed Annie's cheek and let himself go just

enough to hug her tightly for an instant. She was so damn beautiful, he thought, and she wasn't wearing a corset under that wrapper. Usually she felt like a beetle in a shell. All women did, except for some of the Hawaiian ones who hadn't grasped the concept of underwear. In this climate only haole women insisted that respectability triumph over comfort.

"I'm not sure when I'll be back," he said. "Probably in time to celebrate the New Year."

"You be careful you don't see the year in through iron bars," Annie whispered. "Where shall I say you are, if anyone wants to know?"

"I'm going to the south camp," Sam said. "Maybe I'll catch the packet to see Niall Tevis." Tevis was Aloha Malihini Plantation's factor, the agent who arranged for the sale and shipment of Sam's sugar crop. "That's all you know."

"Tevis'll tell them you weren't there," Annie whispered, casting a guarded look at Claudia. "Tevis is a weasel."

"Don't take your politics so personally. Tevis's livelihood depends on us, or he thinks it does."

"So personally? Sam Brentwood, no one but a frozen flounder could be detached about what's going on. This is not some game. If you—"

"Got to go." Sam ducked out the door, leaving Annie to glare after him. It had been his intention to rile her. Maybe now she wouldn't sit and stew, worrying about him.

"What got Miz Brentwood worked up?" Hoakina, the ranch's foreman, was already mounted and waiting to go. He handed Sam the reins of a pony he had led from the stable.

"Oh, you know women, Hoakina. They get . . . worked up." He waved a hand at Annie's form, which appeared vague behind the door's etched glass.

Hoakina nodded sagely. "Women are like that," he agreed, then added under his breath, "especially if they are older than you and act like they are your mama."

As soon as Sam swung into the saddle the foreman drummed his heels into the flanks of his own beast. "We go stir up that south camp," he told Sam. "They go to sleep; no one watches them."

Hoakina was the big *luna*, the first boss. He was dressed in a bandanna, serape, and red-fringed Spanish sash. His name, like his clothes, proclaimed his Mexican grandfather. There was less cattle ranching on the islands now than there had been, but to dress like a *paniolo*, a cowboy, was fashionable.

Sam was dressed in cotton-duck trousers and a full-sleeved shirt. A wide-brimmed panama was pulled over his dark hair. He was browned enough by the sun to appear Hawaiian himself.

The sun was fully up over the nearest cane fields, and Sam gazed around with satisfaction. Aloha Malihini, which meant "Welcome Stranger," had been neglected when Sam bought it, and it had not welcomed Sam Brentwood. After much effort on Sam's part, the ranch was thriving, and he had a sense of belonging that no other place—certainly not his father and stepmother's cold, dreary house in Missouri—had ever given him.

Aloha Malihini's house sat beneath a monstrous flame-colored bougainvillea. The kitchen garden grew every fruit and vegetable that anyone might dream of eating: strawberries, peach-fleshed melons, green peas tiny and perfect enough to eat raw, asparagus, and lettuces. These were ringed with more exotic species: bananas, avocado pears, tamarinds, cherimoya with its overlapping scales like smooth pinecones, and pomegranates with their tiny ruby-colored seeds. Beyond these the *hala-kahiki*, the pineapples, shot up in bursts of spear-shaped leaves, and the taro patch showed bright green crowns that caught the slanting sun and turned the crop to emerald. Groves of oranges and Kona coffee climbed the lower slopes of Mauna Loa above the plantation. Everything grew with a lushness that made even food plants as mysterious and exotic as flowers.

Except for the kitchen garden, the terraces above the house, and the sugar mill, the cane covered everything. Mature cane, ready for harvest, waved well above their heads like a forest of gargantuan grass. The wind-blown tassels, like the feather *kahilis* of old Hawaiian warriors, whispered in the air while the cane stalks, mysterious and impenetrable, rustled beneath them.

Sam unslung a cane knife from his saddle and lopped off the top half of a stalk. He threw the soft tasseled top section away, peeled back the thick green skin in strips, and bit the end of the bare cane. He twisted his head to yank away a fibrous strip with his teeth, then chewed it and spat the dry fibers on the ground.

"Damn near!" he shouted at Hoakina. "It'll be ready on New Year's Day!"

Hoakina was peeling his own stalk. He bit off a strip and, gazing skyward in thought, chewed it. "Maybe," he allowed. "Maybe day after."

Sam laughed. "New Year's Day, you opinionated paniolo. I'll bet you."

Sugarcane required anywhere from eighteen months to two years to mature. It grew year round, so the planting was staggered to bring fields to ripeness at different times and keep the sugar mills working. As soon as Sam and Hoakina pronounced it ripe, the field hands would set a backfire into the wind, then set the cane itself alight, burning off the dry leaves.

As soon as the fire was out, the harvest gangs would cut the stripped, juice-filled stalks and bundle them into railway cars, which wound along a narrow-gauge track through the edges of the cane fields. The little railway increased Sam's sense of ruling a private kingdom. This was a world of his own, where he belonged and could put down roots like the cane's, which lived beneath the soil after harvest. Aloha Malihini had caught at him so completely, he felt as if he might be like the cane ratoons—if you buried him there, he would grow up out of the ground again.

In the south camp the planting gangs were putting in seed cane. Yield dwindled if cane was allowed to ratoon too often. The camps were villages within the self-contained kingdom of Aloha Malihini. Each had barracks and a small store stocked with soap, tooth powder, and such native food as the field hands might want and was not supplied by the camp cook. A chapel provided a pulpit for circuit-riding preachers of various denominations. They all preached much the same gospel and were listened to solemnly by the Chinese and Japanese, who understood not a word of it, and by the Hawaiians, who understood it perfectly, sang hymns loudly and enthusiastically, and then did what they wanted to.

A preacher was there this morning, unloading a bundle of tracts from his mule. He wore a black suit and a wide-brimmed, low-crowned black hat that sat a little too low on his ears. He was a full-blooded Hawaiian, which was not unheard of but was not all that common, either.

"Shoo! You go away! Come back Sunday! We got work to do," Hoakina shouted at him, flapping his hands.

The preacher stood unmoving, holding his bundle of tracts by their string. When he caught Sam's eye, his brown face split into a grin.

"Let him pass his tracts out, Hoakina," Sam said, "since he's come all this way. But no preaching on my time, understand?" He drew rein by the preacher and stifled a laugh.

"I bring God's word," the preacher said solemnly.

"You've got crust, Peter, and you're too muscular to pass for a man of the cloth," Sam murmured. "Anyway, I'm more interested in what God has had to say to Bob Wilcox."

"Wilcox confers directly with Him, I believe," Peter Aikanaka said. "But he can tell you what they've both had to say, if you would care to accompany me on my return journey to Oahu. At approximately four o'clock this afternoon?"

"I shall be charmed to escort you off the premises at that time," Sam agreed. "Meanwhile, go pass out the

Word on Harvey Sessions's place. Just don't let him catch you."

"Harvey objects to the gospel?"

Sam snorted. "He'll object to *your* gospel."

Harvey owned the farm next to Aloha Malihini. Having helped foment one revolution, Harvey was petrified of a counterrevolution.

Sam watched while Peter mounted his mule and rode between the furrows, distributing his pamphlets among the field hands. The Hawaiian laborers were more interested in them than were the other hands, and Sam saw Hoakina, brows knitted, read the folded four-sheet tract.

Sam opened one and smiled. The Royalists had become very adept at communication and propaganda since the government had declared any criticism to be treason. This pamphlet spoke in impassioned terms of doing God's will, of respecting the land that God had provided, and of resisting the sinful ways of the big city and the sinners downtown. It was allegorical in the extreme, but the Hawaiians, who had not yet lost their tribal myths to civilization, were good at deciphering allegory.

Harvey Sessions wouldn't like it at all, Sam thought gleefully, but his field hands would.

Peter finished distributing his tracts, shamelessly laid a blessing on the forehead of an ailing worker, then turned his mule and moved up the valley. He would be back at four o'clock, Sam knew, lurking in the cane somewhere on the road to Pahala. The overnight packet for Honolulu put out from Honuapo Bay, but an outrigger would be waiting for them somewhere between Pahala and the dock.

When the mule and its black-clad rider were out of sight, Sam unsaddled his horse and tethered it to a banana tree beside the bungalows where the workers slept. They were coming in from the fields already in ones and twos, as Hoakina and their Portuguese luna gave them permission. On these visits to the camps, Sam acted as a circuit judge of complaints large and small.

Just now he found himself confronted by a Japanese worker and a Hawaiian twice his size.

"He break my fiddle," the Hawaiian said, aggrieved. "Just this morning." He exhibited a ukelele with a snapped neck. The strings waved like tendrils from their pegs.

"He play it at dawn. Laughing and shouting. He have a woman in there," the Japanese accused.

"No women in the barracks," Sam said automatically.

"I never did! Well, just a little . . ."

"No women in the barracks." The men always violated this rule, but if Sam condoned such behavior, the barracks would be overrun with females. "But why did you break his fiddle?" The ukelele, popularly known as the taro-patch fiddle, had become so popular that nearly every Hawaiian owned one.

"Too loud. *Some* people want to sleep."

The brawny Hawaiian made a sour face. "He's just jealous," he confided to Sam.

"Well, why didn't you stop him?" Sam asked. "You're bigger than he is. How did he get the fiddle away from you in the first place?"

The Hawaiian studied the toes of his boots. "I put it down for a minute," he said finally.

"And then he took it? Why didn't you chase him?"

"He wear no pants," the Japanese said.

Sam laughed. "Hey! Alfonso!" he shouted, and the Portuguese luna came across the yard, coiling his black-snake whip onto his belt. Sam pointed to the Japanese. "He buys this man another fiddle." He pointed at the Hawaiian. "He gets fined an equal amount for having a woman in the barracks." He looked at the whip. "And don't you use that thing so much."

"Sure, boss." The whip was a luna's badge of office, and the foremen liked to show off with it. They weren't allowed to use it on the men, but most considered that a rule meant to be broken.

"Next!" Sam said.

By three-thirty he had assessed the fines for a

drunken brawl, settled a contested poker game (six jacks had materialized from the deck) by donating the pot to a fund for the lepers on Molokai, given a young Chinese worker two days off to get married and the promise of a cabin to his bride and himself, and warned the others who were looking interested that marriage was permanent, and two days off and a cabin weren't necessarily worth the price.

Sam resaddled his horse and told Hoakina he was catching the last packet for Oahu. Hoakina nodded without comment.

The last of the seed cane was going in, in the field nearest the road to Pahala. Sam watched the men bending to the rhythm of the cane, themselves looking like live stalks, swinging up, swinging down. They sang as they worked, not because anyone in his right mind enjoyed planting seed cane but because singing made the work go easier. The Hawaiians, it seemed to Sam, sang all the time anyway, and the other nationalities picked up their songs and mimicked them or added tunes of their own, strange and high-pitched to American ears.

The Hawaiians were in the minority now, both in the cane fields and in the general population of the islands. The haoles had brought to the islands Christianity and diseases to which the Polynesians weren't immune.

Sam let his horse clip-clop at a moderate amble down the Pahala road and waited for something to happen. The silver-mounted saddle made faint clinks and jingles. Hawaiian horseflesh was notoriously underbred, but the Hawaiians made up for it with the glory of their accoutrements. Most haole planters sent to the United States for purebred horses and sober tack, but Sam had simply gone native.

The pony snorted and threw up its head when Peter Aikanaka's mule poked its bony nose from the creeper-hung banana trees that lined the road.

"Hee-yup." The mule emerged farther, and its rider

grinned at Sam. He doffed his black parson's hat in a sweeping gesture.

"You'll be struck by lightning, you old reprobate," Sam warned.

Peter chuckled. "Never. The Lord knows that ours is a good cause. But we'd better get a move on."

II

"Is Sam back? Has the post come?" Eden Brentwood bounced through the door onto the veranda, where Annie was trying to coax the honeycreeper that lived in the bougainvillea onto her finger.

"Drat!" Annie said as the little bird backpedaled in a flurry of yellow feathers and flew off. "No, dear, Sam's not home. I don't expect him until late. And the post has come, but you didn't get anything."

Eden's face drooped. "You're sure?"

"Dear, Mike writes to you once a week, and you just had a letter from him."

"I know, but I was wondering if he'd left Florida yet."

Annie took a deep breath. This seemed as good a time as any. "Are you sure you aren't getting just a little silly over him? There are a lot of men in this world, and you're awfully young."

"'Awful' is slang. Miss Potts says that ladies are not to use it," Eden told her. "And I'm nearly eighteen."

"Aged," Annie agreed. "And please follow Miss Potts's instructions, not my example. She is far more reliable." Miss Potts was Eden's governess.

"Well, you're more interesting," Eden said. "When you forget to pay attention." Annie was a railroad man's daughter. Her formal education had stopped after the third grade. The rest had been acquired directly from life.

"Interesting and proper aren't the same thing," Annie responded. "Be glad you won't ever have to stop

18

and pay attention to your speech for fear you'll make a fool of yourself in some swell's fancy-pants parlor."

Eden laughed.

"And don't repeat that, either," Annie said. "We want to send Miss Potts away happy." Eden was considered "finished" and had mastered everything a lady was supposed to know. Miss Potts was leaving soon to take charge of younger, unmolded material on a plantation at Hilo.

Eden picked at the bougainvillea. Her gold hair, piled in a high pompadour, glowed almost the same color as the honeycreeper, which had perched among the vine's fiery petals.

"Dear, about Mike . . ." Annie ventured.

"I love him," Eden said stubbornly. "Nobody is going to change my mind. Nobody."

"No one wants to change your mind," Annie pointed out. "Just try not to be quite so—impassioned. Mike's health isn't good."

"His heart hasn't given him any trouble in years."

"But it may at any moment. Rheumatic-fever damage is like that." Annie's face was pleading. "Just think twice before you tie yourself to a man with a bad heart. You and Mike are young. Neither of you has any idea what it would be like to deal with disease every day."

"Neither do you," Eden said.

"No, but I watched what your mother's illness did to your father. And indirectly to you and Sam."

Eden's lips compressed. "My mother was crazy, not sick."

"That's a form of sickness. Lydia swallowed up all of his time, his life, until he had nothing outside the four walls of that house."

"Mike wouldn't be like that!" Eden protested.

"You don't know what Mike would be like, and neither does he. Something could go wrong. He could be bedridden for the rest of his life."

Eden's eyes shot sparks. "I wouldn't care. I want to be with him." As she stomped back through the veranda doors, she sailed past her grandmother. "You don't understand what it's like to be in love!" was the girl's parting shot.

"Oh, heavens, who does?" Claudia came out to the porch.

"Lord knows I don't," Annie muttered. "But unlike Eden, I'm old enough to admit it."

The elderly woman settled herself in one of the white wicker chairs and smiled. "And how are you getting along with my grandson these days? I know that's a rude question, but I've been wanting to ask it ever since I got here at Christmas. Besides, one of the privileges of old age is asking unsuitable questions."

"I don't mind telling you," Annie said, "but I don't know the answer. It's been over a year since he promised to behave, and it seems like he means it. Not so much drinking, and no more . . . well . . ."

"Tarts," Claudia supplied.

"Well, no more of them." It was all right for Claudia to say "tarts." She was a lady born and bred. Annie Laurie Malone had to be more careful. "I worry that he can't make it last. He's trying to prove something to me right now. If I forgive him, will he still feel that he has to behave? If he starts playing the tomcat on me again, I don't think I could bear it."

"There's only one way to find out," Claudia said. "I'm not trying to pretend Sam's perfect." She raised her eyes heavenward. "On the contrary. But he does love you. Just figuring that out has been hard on him."

"It hasn't been a fish fry for me, either," Annie said. "I hadn't counted on being in love. I never was in love with Joe, my first husband. We just kind of took up together. I thought it would be easy being married to Sam. Then when he started bringing women home under my nose . . ."

"You don't have to be in love to wish not to be humiliated," Claudia told her. "But I suppose that's when you realized that you *were* in love with the wretch."

Annie nodded agreement. "I can't fault him his past." She had some past of her own and was uneasily aware that Claudia might have guessed as much. "I just want to be sure he doesn't go back to acting that way."

Claudia smiled. "It's New Year's Eve. That seems a highly appropriate moment for a new start—if you want one."

Annie decided that maybe she did.

Sam got home late, wearing a pious expression that fooled nobody.

Dinner was over, and Davy, the Hawaiian house-boy, had put a tray of coconut macaroons and rum punch on the veranda. The night was only faintly cool, and the night-blooming jasmine growing by the front steps enveloped the porch in a fragrant cloud. The honeycreeper stirred in the bougainvillea and whistled sleepily. The moon was up now, nearly round and hanging just over the peak of the roof. It was all very seductive—far too seductive for Annie. She slipped her arm through Sam's and leaned her head against his shoulder.

"Happy New Year," he whispered, faintly startled but not willing to ask questions and take any chances.

"Auld lang syne," Annie murmured, "hasn't been so hot so far. Maybe we ought to take the cup of kindness for the future."

"To the future then." Sam clinked his cup of rum punch against hers. "The cargo is waiting off Diamond Head," he whispered. "Orders are to take it into Honolulu on Thursday. We're to stay home and act innocent until then." He slipped an arm around Annie's waist and looked over at his sister, who was curled in the porch swing. Claudia had gone to bed long before. "Two minutes to midnight, Pudd'n," he said to Eden.

She got up. "Don't call me Pudd'n. I'm not five."

"You're cranky enough to be. Maybe I should have let you have some rum in your punch. It might have improved your mood."

"Davy put some in anyway," Eden informed him. "And I'm not cranky. It's just that everybody treats me like a child."

"Maybe if you could be a little less irritable, they wouldn't do that," Annie remarked sympathetically.

"'I want my dress with ruffles, and I want my new straw hat—'" Sam quoted.

"Stop it," Eden said, but her lip twitched as Sam continued.

> "And I haven't got the snuffles,
> And I ain't a fussy cat,
> And I will not mind my daddy
> And I do not want my doll,
> And no one can get me ready
> To go anywhere at all!"

Eden burst into laughter as the tall clock in the house struck midnight. "I'm not that bad, am I?"

"Entirely," he said.

"Maybe I'm fate's revenge on you for all the trouble *you* caused everyone," Eden suggested, her eyes sparkling.

"You aren't nearly wicked enough," Sam said. "Go to bed."

"Poor kid," Annie said after Eden, yawning, had gone upstairs.

"Phooey," Sam said. "She's just a baby. She'll forget about Mike Holt and be mooning over someone else in a year. We'll toss her a coming-out party this spring that'll make her the envy of every wahine in the islands, and the boys will be lined up down the road to carry her prayer book."

"Mmmm . . ." Annie wasn't convinced.

Sam, now that they were alone, was nuzzling the nape of her neck.

"I haven't finished my punch," she said halfheartedly.

Sam stood and picked up the pitcher and the plate of macaroons. "We'll take them with us." Before she could protest, he had gone inside and started up the stairs. As she followed he turned into his own bedroom and set the refreshments on the dresser. "You are moving back in," he announced. "Tonight."

Annie stood motionless, and he came toward her, his face hungry, his dark eyes gleaming in the faint glow of the gas jet. There was something less predatory and more pleading about him tonight. He took her hands in his, then stood for a long time just looking into her eyes.

In the morning when Koana came in with the coffee tray, Annie buried her head and shoulders under the quilt to disguise the embarrassing fact that she wasn't wearing a nightgown. There was a half-finished glass of punch on the windowsill.

"Thank you, Koana," Sam said gravely, accepting both cups. He didn't have a nightshirt on, but since half the men in the islands went around in only a malo, Koana wasn't shocked. Koana wouldn't be shocked anyway.

"You want some fruit for breakfast, Miss Annie? Or waffles maybe?" Koana inquired. She was plainly fascinated to have found Mistress in bed with Master for the first time since she had come to work for them. She would undoubtedly inform the rest of the servants immediately.

"Tell Cook I'd like fruit and toast," Annie said from under the pillow.

"Up here, Miss Annie?"

"Certainly not. I'll come down to breakfast. Tell Cook half an hour."

Sam's hand moved exploringly along her thigh. "Tell Cook an hour."

"A gentleman is below to see you," Koana said to Sam. "He came quite early. But I will tell him you will be down in an hour."

"Don't you dare," Annie said, horrified. Probably the preacher or one of the queen's gentlemen-in-waiting. *Mr. Brentwood can't receive you right now. He is in bed with his wife.* Koana was perfectly capable of saying that.

"We'll be down immediately, Koana," Sam said. "Did he leave his name?"

Koana handed him a calling card, somewhat crumpled from being stuck in the pocket of her *holoku*, the loose-fitting garment favored by Hawaiian women ever since the missionaries had informed them that a small skirt of *kapa* cloth was not sufficient.

When Sam saw the name of the caller, his eyes widened in surprise.

"He is very nice," Koana said, smiling brightly. She departed, her long, abundant black hair swaying behind her, and the concealing folds of the holoku doing nothing to disguise the swish of her hips.

Annie sighed. "I wish I could get her to quit doing that. No wonder she has so much trouble with the men."

"Koana doesn't consider it to be trouble," Sam said. "I warned you not to hire her. She was engaged to two men at the same time and cheating on them both because some third fellow had promised her a gold necklace. She nearly caused a riot." His hand crept down Annie's thigh again. "You already have a gold necklace," he whispered into her ear, "but I can offer you a very nice lei of *wiliwili* flowers."

Annie wriggled away from him. "Quit that. Who on earth is downstairs?"

"Dickie Merrill," Sam said. "Lord knows what he's doing here."

"Well, he might have written first." Annie struggled to sit up. She didn't approve of Dickie Merrill, a companion of Sam's unreformed days, and she wasn't going to let Sam talk her into making love again while Dickie sat in the parlor letting Koana tell him all about them. "New York to Hawaii's a long way just to drop in."

"Not if you're Dickie. He's probably on a grand tour and was too sozzled to know what boat he got on."

The suave visitor awaiting them in the parlor, however, was spruce and chipper. He bent gallantly over Annie's hand, assuring her that he was a cad not to have written and that he did hope she would forgive him.

Dickie Merrill was a dapper young man close to Sam's age, and at twenty-eight his round, well-scrubbed face was still unmarked by lines of either age or character. His light brown hair was stylishly slicked down, and the expression in his blue-gray eyes was genial. He wore a glen-plaid traveling suit and spats and carried a gold-headed cane, with his derby hat balanced upon the end.

"We're delighted to have you," Annie said, and managed to sound as if she meant it.

"Absolutely, old man," Sam agreed, slapping him on the back and towing him toward the breakfast room.

"Amazing place," Dickie said. "I rode out here in a kind of rickshaw, pulled by a couple of Hawaiians."

"That's the custom," Sam told him.

Minutes later, as Dickie tucked into bacon and eggs and a fruit compote, he leaned across the table toward Sam. "I say, old fellow, that little filly who let me in—are all Hawaiian girls like her, or did you just snare the prizewinner?"

Annie gave him an icy eye. "Koana is my maid."

"Oh. Oh, well. She certainly is charming. Very friendly." Dickie beamed at Annie, then winked at Sam.

Annie clenched her fruit spoon a little more tightly. Dickie obviously suspected Sam of carrying on with Koana. Annie's pride was not soothed by the knowledge that Sam was not. She was angry and humiliated that Dickie should assume it. Her irritation was redoubled because she could hardly take up the subject with Dickie and set him straight.

By the time Eden came down to breakfast —languishing over star-crossed love—Annie was in no mood for Eden's vapors. Dickie, however, appeared to have been struck dumb—momentarily, at least.

"You can't be little Eden," he said, chortling, when he had gotten his breath back. "Not little Eden with the pigtails! My girl, you've turned into an absolute corker!"

"Thank you, Mr. Merrill," Eden said demurely.

"Oh, pooh, now you're old enough to call me Dickie. Favorite uncle and all that. Isn't she, Sam?"

"Favorite uncle, my left hoof," Sam said, but he grinned, amused to see his worldly chum falling all over himself because of a seventeen-year-old. "It's about time someone married you off, Dickie, before you get to be a silly old bachelor, pinching girls' cheeks and not being quite able to remember why."

"No fear, old man. Absolutely no fear."

When Dickie wasn't looking, Eden rolled her eyes at Annie to indicate that she thought Dickie was a dope and practically geriatric. After breakfast he tried to convince her to show him around "your pretty little farm" but settled reluctantly for Sam when Eden pleaded that she thought she was getting a cold.

As the men went down the steps to the stable, Eden's and Annie's laughter caroled like bells behind them.

"I don't think your missus quite likes me," Dickie said ruefully. "Sorry I made eyes at the little hula-hula girl. Sore subject around the domestic fire?"

"Not at all," Sam said. "I've reformed. Koana would be too rich for my blood anyway. She's a walking sexual crisis and will do nearly anything with anyone who promises her a present."

"My kind of gal," Dickie proclaimed. "And so, on an entirely different level of intentions, is your little sister."

"You mind your manners around my little sister," Sam warned, "or I'll cut your balls off."

"Samuel! My intentions regarding Eden are of the utmost propriety. You yourself said it was time I got married."

Sam hooted in amusement. "Are you serious? You just met her at breakfast. You have my permission, but I have to warn you she's mooning after some eighteen-year-old kid with a bad heart who's too sick to marry. Eden fancies herself as Florence Nightingale, I think." He turned away from Dickie long enough to shout at a groom to bring out two horses. "It makes her feel spiritual."

Dickie nodded knowingly. "Girls that age all do it. My older sister wanted to be a nun when she was fifteen. She's married now, has three children. Husband's a banker. Hell of an unpleasant fellow, now that I think about it, but he keeps her in style."

The stable boy appeared after a few minutes, leading the horse that Sam had ridden to the beach with Peter Aikanaka, now mysteriously restored to its stable, and a second animal for Dickie. Dickie, who was used to riding Thoroughbred horseflesh in Central Park, eyed his mount askance. It was a piebald with one blue eye and ears that swiveled like semaphores.

"You steal these from the iceman?"

"Naw, his are uglier," Sam said. He swung into the silver-mounted saddle and waited for Dickie to do likewise.

Dickie settled himself and bounced a bit in the seat. "Comfortable. I rode one of these out west. Learned not to trot, though. Walk or gallop—don't trot."

"You get used to it," Sam said. Sitting a trot was a bone-jarring experience for anyone trying a western saddle for the first time.

"Amazing little place here," Dickie approved. He watched a steam engine chuff by, pulling three cars filled with cane. "All the comforts."

"It's a working farm," Sam retorted. "Nobody wants to ride that train but the engineer and the brakeman."

"Pity. The Astors have a private car. Mrs. A. threw a gala on it. I was invited."

"This track doesn't go anywhere but around the cane fields, you idiot."

"I suppose no one would want to take a ride, then," Dickie conceded. "What's that over there?"

"Sugarhouse. It's where we mill the cane." Its stack poured smoke into the clear blue sky. A thick smell of sugar syrup hung around it. The boiling vats created little heat shimmers in the air.

"Do you really know what you're doing out here?" Dickie asked, curious.

"I've learned," Sam said. "I can't say it was easy, but

I'd hit the point where I had to do something worthwhile or I was just going to roll up my life and stuff it into the end of a bottle."

"Lots of things to do besides turn into a farmer," Dickie pointed out, smirking. But something in Sam's expression kept him from commenting further.

They dismounted, and Sam led Dickie into the sugarhouse. The temperature inside was very like that of a Turkish bath, and Dickie ran his finger around his starched collar. The sweet, sticky air was almost viscous. A steam-driven crusher rumbled and bellowed as shirt-less workers fed cane into immense rollers with inter-locking corrugated teeth. Dickie edged away from them.

"Anyone ever lose a finger in those?"

"Lose a hand if you aren't careful," Sam said.

The sugarcane fibers came out of the crusher as a moist, flat layer like jute padding. The extracted juice ran down a trough, into the first of a set of tanks. From the crusher the pressed cane passed through the mills proper, a set of nine grooved rollers arranged in triangles of three that extracted the last ounce of juice. Gigantic, relentless, and altogether impressive, they turned slowly.

"The mills of God," Dickie murmured, "that grind so exceedingly fine."

He looked a little green.

"Come outside," Sam said. On a shelf near the door was a tin of shelled pecans and a small spool of thread. Sam took them with him and tied a strand around a nut. He handed it to Dickie. "If you want to win Eden's heart, dip one of these in the syrup until the sugar builds up a good thick layer. Like dipping a candle. Eden loves them, but she hates standing over a hot vat."

Dickie looked as if he wouldn't care much for it, either. Even in the wall-less, outdoor boiling shed, the bubbling syrup gave off rolling clouds of thick, sweet steam until everything he touched felt sticky. Dickie felt as if he himself had been dipped in sugar, an unpleasant sensation, and was finally beginning to understand the adage about killing a cat with cream. But he stood stoically over the last of the vats where the sugar was closest to being crystallized and dipped a dozen pecans for Eden. He was soaking wet by the time he was through, his shirt collar wilted and his hair plastered over his forehead. Sam folded the pecans in waxed paper when they were dried, and Dickie gamely picked a spray of plumeria with which to wrap them.

Eden was appreciative in appetite if not in sentiment. She accepted Dickie's present gravely, then retired to her room with it, where she nibbled pecans and started a letter to Mike Holt. The Holts and the Brentwoods were courtesy cousins. The families' assorted grandparents had gone west together years before on the first wagon train to Oregon.

She had gotten as far as writing "Dear Mike," and was staring dreamily at the wallpaper, conjuring up his image, when her grandmother knocked on the door.

"Come in, Gran." Eden held out her hands to Claudia.

"Koana said that you were looking for me, dear."

"Dickie dipped these pecans for me this morning, and I wanted to share with you. I know you love them."

"Dickie?" Claudia raised an eyebrow.

"Sam says I'm old enough to call him that. And he asked me," Eden said nonchalantly.

"Well, be careful not to encourage him, dear, if you don't mean it." Claudia settled herself into the wing chair beside Eden's writing desk and accepted a nut.

"Encourage him?"

"The young man is courting you, dear." Claudia chuckled.

"Well, I'm not courting him!" Eden said indignantly. "He's as old as Sam!"

"That does not exactly indicate one foot in the grave." Claudia nibbled a pecan. "He went to a great deal of trouble over these. You know how *you* hate standing over those hot vats."

"Maybe he likes the heat." Eden shrugged. "Anyway, I think he's silly."

"But you're willing to eat his pecans."

"Certainly." Claudia and Eden both laughed. Eden leaned her chin in her hand. "Gran, you know I'm not interested in anyone but Mike."

"You haven't been courted by anyone but Mike—except for this Dickie Merrill, and frankly I don't blame you for not falling into *his* arms. He *is* silly. But the world is full of men who aren't."

Eden looked at her sideways. "You aren't going to change my mind, you know."

Claudia smiled at her. "You make me sleepy, child, with all your certainty. I'm going to bed. Don't sit up too late."

"I won't. Here, take some with you." Eden scooped five nuts into a handkerchief.

After her grandmother left, Eden picked up the pen again and dipped it purposefully into the inkwell. She had been in love with Mike Holt since she was twelve, and nobody had ever taken them seriously. They would soon enough, though. Eden's birthday was in February, and she would be eighteen. That was the age of majority in New Jersey, where Mike lived. Once Eden arrived at that magical age, she would take charge of her life.

She refrained from detailing her plans prematurely to Mike. He had declared his own independence a year before in similar fashion but might frown on Eden's doing likewise. For one thing, Mike was working for Thomas Edison as a kind of combination slave and apprentice, and he didn't make much money. He had a room in a boardinghouse that couldn't possibly be as miserable as he said it was, but it certainly was not palatial. All in all, Eden thought she had better present Mike, along with everyone else, with a fait accompli.

She gave him the week's domestic news, including the happy departure of Miss Potts and the arrival of Dickie Merrill, of whom she painted an unflattering picture. Eden chewed the end of her pen for a minute, thinking about what else to say. The trouble was that nothing ever happened on Aloha Malihini. The sugar-cane grew, laborers chopped it down and boiled it, and all the time more was growing. The island that had so enchanted her upon her arrival was now a constraint upon her. Years before, Mike had been to visit, and when he went away again, he had taken all her pleasure in the island with him. But she couldn't say that for a whole letter. It would only make him feel bad.

She tried to envision his face. Mike was slim and his face thin boned, the gray-green eyes deep set, the wide mouth always either talking or laughing, his russet hair usually falling over his forehead. He was not very tall—not nearly as tall as his father, Toby, or his brother, Tim. But he was strong, with the compact muscularity of a range pony, and his movements were concentrated, as if some suppressed intensity existed within them. He burned in a room, Eden thought, and then she blushed. She couldn't write about that.

The physical sensation Mike produced in her was tangible even when experienced only in memory, but it was not something she could speak of. It was just there, part of the equation, part of the sum total that was Mike and her. There would be more to it, too, she knew, but that would have to wait. What would making love be like? she wondered. Having lived in the country, she knew certain things from the way animals behaved. But that was only theory. Practice might be altogether different.

Restless, she got up and went to the window. It was nighttime now, but about two-thirds of a moon sat fat and lopsided in the sky. Eden pressed her face against the cool glass pane, and then her eyes narrowed with interest. Someone was moving in the garden just below her window—someone who acted as if he ought not to be there or didn't want someone else to know he was. Eden wondered for a moment if Dickie Merrill was going to play the mandolin under her balcony the way boys in books did. She giggled at the notion and then saw that it wasn't Dickie. It was Sam.

If he was stepping out on Annie again . . . Eden's fingers clenched into fists. She would fix him. She took the inkwell from her desk, then eased up the sash and

bent out cautiously. He was right below her, and he was
with a woman! It was Koana! She came quietly on bare
feet out of the shadows along the side of the house and
put her hands into Sam's. The holoku she wore did little
to disguise a languorous walk and hourglass curves.

Eden gritted her teeth, and her fingers tightened
on the ink pot. She took the stopper out, stretched her
arm deliberately, and upended the inkwell.

There was a very satisfactory trickling noise and a
kind of *sploosh,* followed by a startled murmur and then
a scream of outrage. Eden closed the sash again and,
humming, sat down at her desk. She could still hear
expressions of consternation and shushings in the garden
below.

In a few more minutes, Eden heard the heavy tread
of footsteps marching up the stairs, and her door was
whipped open. Sam confronted her, fists clenched, head
down like a charging bull's, and his shirtfront liberally
splashed with ink.

"Goodness, what happened to you?" Eden asked
him.

"Someone," Sam growled, "tipped her ink pot out
the window."

"My word, were you down there?" Eden gave him
a bland look. "I just thought I'd empty it and make up
some fresh. It was getting thick. I certainly didn't expect
anyone to be lurking in the garden at this time of night."

Sam advanced on her. "It's only eight o'clock, and
nobody was lurking."

"Well, I'd like to know what *you* call it," Eden said
indignantly. "Down there canoodling with one of your
poppets under *my* window! Shame on you, Sam Brentwood."

"Then you *did* know I was there." Sam lifted a hand
and looked longingly at Eden's backside. "It may interest
you to know that was no poppet, and there haven't *been*
any poppets in quite some time."

"That was Koana. And if she isn't a poppet, I don't
know who is."

"That was not Koana." Sam folded his arms and

considered his sister. "That was someone with a message, which you don't need to know about. And I'd appreciate it if you would just keep your mouth shut and your thoughts to yourself."

"You just don't want me to tell Annie." Eden sniffed, but she looked intrigued.

"I don't care in the least if you tell Annie," Sam retorted. "But I don't want you to tell Gran or your new admirer. Dickie's not discreet. And when he's been drinking he has no common sense at all."

"He said you gave him permission to court me!" Eden fumed. "And that's your opinion of him?"

"Well, he's an old pal," Sam said, "and I didn't want to insult him." His expression softened. "Anyway, I didn't figure he was going to get anywhere. There are fresher fish in the sea than Dickie. But he'll do for you to practice on."

"You're trying to distract me," Eden said. "You're changing the subject so I'll forget about what you're up to." Sam was right—she didn't want Dickie. But if a gentleman was courting her, she preferred not to hear him described as having no sense. Such criticism didn't reflect well on her as his choice of a mate. "I still think you were down there in the garden with Koana. I want to see if there's ink on *her*."

Sam threw up his hands. "All right. This is probably against all the rules for raising delicately minded young ladies, but come with me." He took Eden by the hand and towed her down the hallway to the landing window, which faced the back of the house at a right angle to Eden's view. "There," he said. "*That's* Koana. As you can see, she's too preoccupied to be meeting with me—or anyone else. You didn't want Dickie anyway," he added as Eden's face froze.

These subjects of discussion were entwined upon a stone bench beneath a romantic backdrop of trumpet vines. Eden drew in her breath sharply, and a picture crossed her mind of another amorous couple, in a book of Indian statuary. Except that Dickie and Koana had clothes on, they were fully as entangled in each other as those fascinating and unsettling statues. Something sinuous and urgent in their movements made Eden flush. But she stood there, reluctant to turn away.

"Good God," Sam said, taking her arm. "I didn't know they'd gone quite so far. Come away from that window."

Eden turned and looked up at Sam, puzzled. "Are men always like that? So rough?"

Sam's lip twitched. "It won't seem rough with the right fellow, I promise. Now go back to your letter. I've corrupted your sensibilities enough for one night."

Eden raised her eyebrows regally. "I am not as much of a baby as you think. And I'm not going anywhere until you tell me what you were doing in the garden."

"Playing spy and counterspy," Sam answered, exasperated. "And I *won't* tell you more, so forget it."

"Was the woman who met you from the queen?" Eden asked breathlessly.

"Will you shut up?" Sam hissed. "Indirectly, yes. Now are you satisfied? I'm not telling you any more."

"Oh, all right," Eden said. Deep in thought, she drifted back down the hall to her room. If Sam was involved with the Royalists, he would be too busy to notice whether she was around, maybe even for a day or two. That would be plenty of time to go through with her plan. The only problem was Dickie. If he decided to dog her footsteps all day, she would never manage anything. Yes, Eden decided, Dickie definitely had to go.

III

"Dickie was out in the backyard kissing Koana last night," Eden remarked chattily to Annie and Claudia at breakfast the next morning. "I saw them."

Annie and Claudia bent simultaneous reproving stares on Eden, who was busily buttering her toast so as not to notice.

"A lady does not gossip about the things she sees," Claudia said. Her eyes met Annie's over the top of Eden's head. "However—"

"Most certainly however," Annie said angrily. "I will not have him making false promises to poor Koana. Heaven knows what might come of it."

"Lots, I would guess," Eden said, "if he promises her a silk dress."

"Eden!"

"Well, she wants one, and you know what Koana is like."

"I do," Annie replied grimly. "And I know what that Dickie is like. He's not even down to breakfast, while Sam's been out in the fields for over an hour. Eden, you're not to have anything further to do with Dickie Merrill."

"Too late for that," she said. "I've made plans to elope with him." She speared another piece of toast with her fork.

"Eden!" Claudia passed her the plate of toast. "How could *all* your manners vanish so quickly? Do we need to invite Miss Potts back?"

"No, Gran. Sorry."

"Well, just try to hang on to the rudiments."
Claudia's eyes met Annie's again over Eden's head, and
the women's lips twitched against smiling. Eden had
blossomed in the last few years once she had been
removed from the mausoleum that her mother and
father, both now dead, had called a house. She still had
no idea of how very pretty she was. She looked quite
ethereal, every man's fairy princess, but her relatives
knew better.

Dickie Merrill breezed down to breakfast. His hair
was neatly parted in the center and slicked down, and
his blue eyes, a trifle bloodshot, were otherwise as
innocent as a parson's.

"Ah, good morning, ladies. What a bevy of beauties
to find about a fellow at the breakfast table. Eden, you
look just like a buttercup in that yellow dress."

A buttercup with a spine of steel, Annie thought,
listening to Eden gravely ask Dickie how he had slept as
she poured him a cup of coffee. Deciding that Koana
probably needed more protection just now than the
buttercup, Annie rose and went in search of Sam. She
found him, filthy and covered with grease, wrestling
with a recalcitrant drive-wheel rod on the Aloha Malihini
steam engine.

"Some damned fool left a handcart on the track," he
said, grunting, "and the rod got bent just enough to
stick. Damn it! Get in there, you bastard!"

"I want to talk to you," Annie said.

Sam looked up. "Not the best time," he said.

"When you're through. And don't swear."

The engine driver, who was standing just behind
Sam, snickered. Sam growled something unintelligible
and smacked the rod hard with a wrench. Annie backed
off a little. It was plainly not the ideal time for a
discussion, but she was too irritated with Dickie to wait.

Finally Sam came over to her and wiped his face on
his sleeve. Both were as black as soot. They were, in
fact, covered with soot—that is, the areas that weren't
smeared with engine oil. Annie backed away a little
more.

Sam leered at her. "Give us a kiss, honey."

"Don't you touch me. Sam, your pal Dickie's flat gone too far. He's been chasing Koana, and I won't have it."

"Koana's about as vulnerable as lava rock," Sam said. "What's thé harm?"

"How can you say that? He's asked to court Eden. I won't have him going after Eden and Koana."

Sam shrugged. "Eden doesn't want him. And she wouldn't come to any harm with him anyway. He's not that sort."

"I see. He's only that sort with housemaids. Charming."

"He's harmless, Annie."

"He's a layabout. He gets up at ten, and he's probably never done a lick of work in his life."

"He's never had to," Sam said. "Okay, he's a lay-about. But he's an old friend, and he's good company. Koana seems to think so, too."

"Sam, how can you defend him?" Annie was indignant. "We don't know what kind of lies he's telling Koana. Eden saw them kissing in the garden last night."

"Eden's being discreet." Sam chuckled. "Kissing wasn't all they were doing."

Annie balled her hands into fists. "He's got to go."

"Now hold on." Sam started to put his arm around her, but he looked at his shirt again, then glanced at her spotless linen and thought better of it. "Just stop a minute here. Dickie is my guest. This happens to be my house. Yours, too, of course, by courtesy, but before we came to the island, you insisted that we risk my money, not yours."

"I remember," Annie said stiffly. "But I don't recall specifying that your male guests could molest my maid."

"Then," Sam inquired, "do you recall my telling you—quite loudly, in fact—not to hire this particular maid? Koana has the habit of climbing between the sheets with every fellow who gives her a box of choco-lates. It's hard to fault Dickie's behavior when the 'victim' is already flat on her back in an indecent posture of anticipation."

"Sam Brentwood, don't you be vulgar with me!"

Sam's eyes flashed. "I *beg* your pardon, Miss Annie Laurie, but when did you get to be so blasted moral? When I met you, you could outswear a sailor. And, if my memory serves me, you invited me into your bed considerably before the wedding."

"Don't you dare throw that in my face! You think it was acceptable for you, but *I'm* an immoral woman? That's the way men always think. That's why you're blaming Koana and not the jerk who's sitting at your breakfast table right this minute trying to court your sister!"

"Would you stick to one subject, you hellcat?" Sam tried to sort out her various accusations. "Be reasonable. I don't think you're immoral. You're no more immoral than I am. Well, less actually . . . I mean— Oh, the hell with it. You know I wasn't throwing that in your face. I just meant I don't see how you can be two-faced about it—"

"Two-faced! You're calling me two-faced!" Steam seemed to rise from her red-gold hair. "I spent years trying to learn not to swear or talk country, just so I could live up to your precious snooty family and your uppity friends like Dickie Merrill. He thinks it's just fine to climb into bed with my maid because he's so genteel and I'm not!"

"Well, you aren't being very genteel now," Sam said when she ran out of breath. "You're screaming like a fishwife." The engine driver was listening with interest from his cab. Sam pointed at him and yelled, "Get out of here!"

The train started up with a hiss of steam and a toot-toot of acknowledgment on the whistle.

"You sure gave old Bill an earful," Sam commented.

"I'll give *you* one," Annie said, stabbing a finger at him. "You tell that randy parasite to stay away from Koana. Is that clear?"

"As clear as a bell, but I'm not going to do it. Koana

can take care of herself, and I'm certainly not going to try to make *her* stay away from Dickie. That would be like trying to defy gravity."

Annie glared at him. "And just how long is your delightful guest going to be staying with us?"

"As long as he pleases. I'm sorry if he's in your hair, but I don't see any way to get rid of him without being rude. He's been a pal when I needed one, and for all I know, he's lying low over something in the States."

"He's lying low because he's too shiftless to move," Annie snarled. "He was a pal when you needed someone to get drunk and chase chorus girls with. That doesn't endear him to me."

"You probably haven't endeared yourself to him either, you shrew."

Annie looked as if she might explode again, but she got a grip on her temper. "I will not broach this matter to Mr. Merrill," she said icily. "That would be vulgar and indelicate. I rely on you, as my husband, to handle it."

"And what makes you think you can do that?" Sam inquired genially.

Annie fixed him with a haughty eye. "Because the *Ladies' Home Journal* says that's what you ought to do. It's full of good advice for genteel ladies."

"Maybe you ought to give up on this," Sam suggested, retreating a step, "and just let Koana have a roll in the hay with whomever she wants."

"I can move out again," Annie warned through clenched teeth. "You'd better remember that."

Sam blew her a kiss, which infuriated her further. Annie knew his tactics: He clearly wasn't going to give in on this one, but he figured that if he stayed playful, she wouldn't get mad enough to leave him.

"I won't be home tonight anyway," he told her. "Watch out or I'll crush you in a manly embrace right now. Isn't that what the *Ladies' Home Journal* would call it?"

"I thought you weren't leaving until Thursday," Annie said, ignoring his last remark.

"We're unloading the guns on Thursday," Sam said,

his voice low. "But I want to meet with the other men beforehand. This is getting too tricky. Her Majesty keeps blowing hot and cold. First she writes to all the foreign governments and says she's resigned to her fate unless they will step in and help her. Next she encourages the Royalists here to get all worked up. Then she shakes her finger at us and tells us not to be bad boys and riot or anything dreadful like that."

"She's an old lady," Annie reminded him. "And she's frightened. The PGs have bullied her terribly."

"I know, I know. But she's got to be solidly behind an overthrow of the PGs and stay that way, or all our plans will come undone. I think she's realized that now. I had a message last night that she's come around to warning the Royalists that it must be outright revolt or nothing. She's right, of course. If we just riot and yell slogans, the PGs will lock us all up and our momentum will be lost. We've been telling her that for months, but now she's telling *us*. I just hope she stays committed."

Annie looked at him uneasily. "Are you sure it has to come to armed rebellion?"

Sam snorted. "How do you think the PGs got where they are? You can't make an omelet without breaking eggs—and you can't have a transfer of power without breaking a few heads."

Annie sighed. "Well, I hope yours stays in one piece."

Sam smiled, reassuring and affectionate. "I have a cast-iron skull, I assure you."

"I expect so," Annie said. "I wish you'd let me see her."

"Too risky. You're known to be a friend of the queen's, but this isn't the time to be seen hanging around."

"But you do."

"I don't. I slink in and out, and my involvement isn't generally known."

Annie crossed her arms and regarded him stubbornly. Sam folded his and stared back at her with the same expression.

"All right," she said finally. "But I warn you, Sam, if I catch Dickie slinking anywhere *he* shouldn't while you're gone, I'm not going to be understanding about it. You just put a flea in his ear before you leave."

She turned on her heel, and Sam looked after her, still stubborn. He wasn't going to let her have the upper hand forever. True, he had been unfaithful and a drunk when they lived in New York, but no atonement was ever enough for Annie. As far as he was concerned, things were square now—and he was *not* going to talk to Dickie.

Sam also walked toward the house, staying some distance behind Annie. He wrestled with the important fact that he was joining an armed revolt against men who would most certainly be armed, too, and very probably better so. Sam had never been a crusader; his heartbeat had never quickened with outrage for the downtrodden. So why was he mixed up in this now? he wondered. Once he had realized that he was serious about his involvement, he had thought about his motivation from all angles and could come only to the conclusion that he was fed up with the PGs. They seemed small-minded to him in their treatment of the citizens under their rule, and Sam was no longer willing to be one of those citizens, kowtowing to their petty meanness.

Within the hour he had bathed, packed a carpetbag, kissed the females of his household good-bye, slapped Dickie on the back with the comment that he would be home in a few days, and mounted the horse that Hoakina had saddled for him. Hoakina looked through narrowed eyes at his boss. *He knows something is up,* Sam thought.

Sam caught the interisland steamer for Oahu and managed to sleep fitfully during the ten-hour trip. It was nighttime when the steamer docked at Honolulu, so he took a room at the Royal Hawaiian Hotel and, not at all sleepy, occupied himself for the evening with the symbolic act of cleaning his pistol.

It was a ragtag army he was joining. The Royalist faction consisted of *kanakas,* the Hawaiian "man in the street"; Hawaiian and haole statesmen and businessmen; and a handful of planters who, like Sam, had gone against their own kind. The Royalists still mingled freely in business and socially with the PGs, so the game of spy and counterspy continued to be played.

The conspirators who met for lunch the next day were a mixed bag. Sitting under the banyan tree that shaded Robert Wilcox's beach house was the hapa-haole Wilcox himself, a fire-breathing insurrectionist and reformer whose wife had grown up in the court of Kamehameha V. With him were Major William Seward and Thomas Walker, a former British army officer who, with Seward, had worked out the plan of attack: Lot Lane, Wilcox, and the hapa-haole Samuel Nowlein, captain of the Queen's Guards, were to close in from Diamond Head and the country districts. Meanwhile, Thomas Walker and Sam would take charge of the guns unloaded in Honolulu and of the downtown forces—mainly foreigners dissatisfied with the way the PGs were running things.

A part of the *Waimanalo*'s cargo weapons and ammunition had already been unloaded and hidden in Henry Bertelmann's garden on Diamond Head, and Bertelmann, a Royalist sympathizer, was now nervously sitting on them. The rest of the cargo was awaiting the run into Honolulu harbor before being off-loaded. Sam could just see the *Waimanalo*'s silhouette offshore.

"A toast, gentlemen." Major Seward raised his glass of claret. "Confusion to the enemy."

"For the Lord's sake, let's get on with it," Lot Lane muttered. "This is no time for a decorous lunch with white linen and cut crystal."

"All right, you hothead," Walker said. "Brentwood, Nowlein, and I will ride in and scout the harbor. Try to contain yourself until you get word."

"I'm coming with you," Wilcox said. "Lane, you can go to Diamond Head and hold Bertelmann's hand for him until I get back."

"That's not necessary," Walker said to Wilcox. "We can manage without you."

Wilcox rose abruptly and walked behind his chair, then restlessly tipped it back and forth. Its wrought-iron legs rang against the flagstones. "Damn it, Thomas, I don't know what you can manage. None of us knows what we can manage. But I *do* know it's my neck if we don't manage, so I'll ride with you."

Thomas Walker shrugged. "Suit yourself."

They threaded their way along the path that ran through the banyan trees. Banyans were as magical and mysterious as anything on the islands. A banyan's spreading branches dripped roots downward. When finally they touched the ground, they sank beneath it and became new trunks, so that a banyan tree walked outward in all directions on these legs and became a forest in itself.

We're like the banyan trunks, Sam thought. *We came here out of thin air and rooted ourselves*. It was an absurdly sentimental thought, he realized, and most unlike him. Until the group rode into Honolulu, Sam pondered the transformation that kept working within him. He could not grasp what metamorphosis he was undergoing in Hawaii, but he was not at all the man he had been. Then there was no more leisure for philosophy. All hell was about to break loose.

Orders had been given for a small, secret force of Hawaiians to meet the *Waimanalo* at the waterfront and off-load the guns. But word had spread—no one knew how—and everyone wanted to claim that he had been in on the action from the beginning. Instead of fifty men, there were hundreds milling in the darkness, talking, growing indiscreet, becoming very obvious to the increasingly alarmed PG police. There were too many people on the waterfront. They were orderly now, but a mob's mood could shift in split seconds.

"Damn it!" Wilcox exploded, reining in on his horse.

Nowlein leaned to put a restraining hand on his friend's arm. "Steady, Bob."

Shouting erupted from the docks across the street. A troop of PG police on horseback went by them at a trot. The policemen pulled their truncheons from their belts. Sam's horse snorted and began to rear as a policeman got too close.

"Get out of here! Move out, or I'll arrest you." The policeman's face was frightened under his helmet.

"Arrest me for what?" Sam demanded. "For trespassing on the public streets?"

"For interfering with the police," the man snapped as he dismounted.

Another policeman went by on foot, dragging a protesting Hawaiian, and the first officer spun around and caught the prisoner around the neck, helping to heave the Hawaiian into a waiting wagon. As the man landed in a flurry of arms and legs, Sam saw a nightstick rise and fall and heard the crack of bone.

The waterfront was chaotic. The acrid smell of human fear and fury cut through the salt-laden breeze. Lanterns swung wildly and made strange arcs before the waterfront warehouses. More men were pouring down the alleyways and spilling out along the wharves. The police, grossly outnumbered, panicked and caught everyone they could lay hands on. The prisoners, thrown into police wagons, were then beaten senseless as the authorities succumbed to their own fears.

The policemen's fury was directed mainly at the Hawaiians, whom they could abuse with little fear of retribution, unlike the haoles, who had the ability to make trouble if victimized by the police. Sam, who was sunburned and looked nearly as dark as a Hawaiian, felt hands clutch at his boot to drag him off his horse. He kicked out sharply, and his foot made contact with a lawman's chin. The shadow of a nightstick fell across him, limned by lantern light, and in a steadily rising temper Sam was making ready to deal with that, too, when Nowlein reached down from his horse to grab the lawman's arm and bark, "Back off!"

The PG policeman, eyes as wide as Nowlein's thrashing horse's, looked up dubiously. As captain of the Queen's Guards, Nowlein had wielded certain authority among the protectors of law and order.

"Go home!" he shouted. "All of you, go home!"

"Captain!" The Hawaiians, recognizing Nowlein, now clustered around him, pushing past the police. "Captain, what should we do?"

"Go home!" Nowlein hissed under his breath. "Go home and wait for some word." He gestured abruptly at the police. "*These* fellows aren't going home tonight."

Sam thought of the *Waimanalo* getting ready to put in. He spun his horse around and knocked someone flat—he hoped it was the PG cop—and drove his heels into its flanks. He glanced over his shoulder and saw Bob Wilcox on horseback just behind him.

"Don't look back!" Wilcox shouted. "Just ride like the devil!"

A shout from behind them made it clear that the PGs had noticed their flight. Hoofbeats thudded on their heels.

"Down here!" Sam swung his reins around hard, and his mount slithered and skated into a narrow alley littered with wooden grocery crates. With a splintering crash the horse stumbled into them and out again and began to buck. Sam balled up his fist and smacked the top of the animal's head, and it straightened into a flat-out run.

Sam and Bob came out of the alley and went into another. Clouds of steam were billowing from a Chinese laundry into the night. The hot, white fog swirled up the balconies. The hoofbeats were still behind them. Sam swung down a third alleyway, then wrestled with his writhing horse after it ran head-on into a set of sheets hung out to dry. It bumbled like a ghost in the streets, and before Sam could rip away the damp cloth and throw it aside, Wilcox's horse skidded to a dead stop at the sight.

A kitchen window opened on the alley, and a woman shrieked, "Get out of my sheets with your dirty horse!" A mounted PG policeman rounded the corner. Sam saw the lawman's hand rise against the golden glow slanting from a window—a dark silhouette extending into the outline of a pistol. Sam wrapped his terrified horse's reins tightly around his left hand and snatched a flowerpot off the window ledge with his right. He drew his arm back and heaved.

The flowerpot caught the pursuing policeman squarely between the eyes, and as he tumbled off his horse, his pistol discharged into the air.

Windows popped open up and down the alley and created sudden squares of light. The dwellers shouted back and forth.

"Murder!"

"Revolution!"

"Chicken thieves!"

Sam pulled his hysterical horse's head around by sheer force. Wilcox had swung his own mount around and with a well-placed smack on the rump was sending the riderless PG police horse galloping off into the night. The lawman was supine on the cobblestones.

"Let's get out of here!" Wilcox shouted.

Sam reached down, scooped up the sheets, and shoved them at their owner through a window. "A thousand pardons, madam." He tipped his nonexistent hat, then kicked his rearing horse forward. The woman goggled at him as they clattered around the corner.

They dodged in and out of narrow streets, staying off the main roads of Honolulu. But no one else came after them. After a few more turns they were on the coastal road to Waikiki. Robert Wilcox and Sam let the reins out until the horses flattened out into a dead run, burning off their own fright.

It was no more than a few miles to Diamond Head. Sam and Bob pulled lathered horses up to Henry Bertelmann's front door and pounded on it.

Bertelmann, in a smoking jacket and a fez-shaped nightcap, opened the door and stared wide-eyed at them.

"Quick, Henry, your canoe!" Wilcox pushed him back through the door, then followed him inside.

"My canoe?"

"Everything's gone to hell at the harbor."

Bertelmann blanched.

"We've got to tell Davies not to put in there with the guns."

"My canoe's in the shed."

Sam and Bob brushed past him and sprinted for the opposite door.

Bertelmann followed, eyes uneasy. "What about the guns you've hidden in my garden?"

"Leave them planted for the time being," Bob called over his shoulder.

"But what if someone finds them? What if the police come?"

"Then say you don't know how they got there," Sam said. "There are revolutionaries everywhere. You can't know everything that goes on at night."

They found the canoe in its grass-roofed shed just above the tide line, ran it into the surf, and clambered over the outrigger bars and into the shell. The *Waimanalo* sat on the black, diamond-pointed water ahead of them, with just one bow light burning. The long, rolling combers moved under the canoe as the men paddled.

Sam remembered his first outrigger ride. A drunken Harvey Sessions had nearly drowned him, but Peter Aikanaka had picked him up on a surfboard and drained the water out of him. Peter was one of the disenfranchised now—a pure-blooded Hawaiian who had seen his land divided again and again among adventuring haoles. His sisters and aunts had taken haole husbands, so even the Royalist leaders were half-bloods. What would Peter get back? Sam wondered. Not the power of Kamehameha's day, certainly—no government could give his people back their bloodline—but at least a government that didn't force him into second-class citizenship, a government that gave him a voice again.

"*Waimanalo! Hoi!*" Bob shouted.

A face peered over the bow rail.

"Let down the ladder. Where's the captain?"

The ladder bumped the side of the steamer, and Sam and Bob climbed it. In a moment they stood dripping on the deck before Captain Davies.

"The waterfront's guarded," Bob managed when he had his breath back. "There was trouble—a near riot. We'll have to put them ashore here."

"Where?" Captain Davies stared, incredulous.

"We'll have to bury the crates in the sand," Sam said wearily.

They spent a nightmarish several hours digging holes. They heaved damp sand out of trenches along the foot of Diamond Head and ransacked every beach house of every known sympathizer from Diamond Head to Waikiki for oilskin in which to wrap the crates. They lowered an endless number of wooden crates into the sand, then looked up to see the ship's boat beaching with still more.

Lot Lane, stripped down to a malo, heaved crates onto his shoulder and, like a figure of oceanic myth, strode across the sand with apparent ease. Sam followed him, too proud to complain but painfully aware that he wasn't in as good shape as he had thought. Soon his hands were blistered raw, and he limped from a crate that had fallen across his instep. His wet boots, more painful than bare feet in the moving sand, were long since discarded.

When the work was done, Sam collapsed in the sand and immediately fell asleep. With the horrible clarity of a nightmare, he dreamed he was being chased across the sand, sinking as if through water with each step, while his pursuer floated above him, squawking among the gulls, pecking with bullets at his head and neck.

He awoke with a start, gasping, and sat up.

"You all right?" Lot Lane peered at him.

A vague recollection of having gone to sleep the night before crept back to Sam. The sun was just coming up over Diamond Head, and he saw that Lot, too, had been lying in the sand. In the rosy light he saw that all the trenches were filled in, and the *Waimanalo* was gone from the horizon.

Sam stood up stiffly. He couldn't remember feeling this sore since he had mucked silver ore in a Virginia City mine. And last night's toils had been voluntary!

"Jesus," he muttered. "I feel as if a horse fell on me."

"Walk it off," Lot suggested cheerfully. "Let's go eat poor Bertelmann's breakfast."

"If he's not hiding under the bed," Sam said.

"Even if he is. I'm hungry. Also, you mustn't blame Bertelmann. He's a Royalist by temperament, but he moved to the islands for the quiet life. He didn't plan on rebels hiding guns in his hibiscus."

Henry Bertelmann appeared to have rallied in the night. He greeted his coconspirators at the door, offered them towels and a change of clothes, and when they had bathed, led them into his dining room, where Robert Wilcox, Seward, and the former British army officer Thomas Walker were arguing strategy over coffee and waffles.

Lot snorted in disdain. "I never heard tell of such a civilized rebellion. And what are we going to do now?"

"Patience, you bloody Irishman," Walker said. "We're going to lie low a day or two, that's what."

"And give the PGs time to get ready for us!" Lot protested.

"And give the PGs time to decide that nothing is happening," Seward said. "They arrested fourteen men last night at the waterfront, and we need the authorities to think that it was just a spontaneous riot."

Lot cut a forkful of waffle and jammed it into his mouth. "And I'm tired of being patient," he complained around it. "I want to break some heads."

"It seems to me," Sam said, "that Lot may have the right end of it. The longer we wait, the greater the chance that somebody'll spill the beans. Remember, we ended up with four times the number of men at the waterfront than should have been there. And Lot's not the only one who wants to break some heads *now*. You don't have a well-disciplined military force here, Tom; you've got civilian volunteers, and they'll get away from you."

Thomas Walker nodded glumly in agreement. "But I'm not ready to go off half-cocked," he said. "Preparation. That's the key."

Lot Lane made an exasperated noise.

Seward stepped in. "We'll move on Sunday. That is final and not to be argued with. Get word to the kanakas that they'll be given their arms here at Diamond Head on Sunday morning. Tell them to act as if they've come to fish. After everyone is armed we'll march on Honolulu. Thomas, you and your foreign contingent will be waiting to join us. As planned, we'll attack the police station first and then occupy the key points in the city. Brentwood, I want you here with Lane, Nowlein, and Wilcox. We'll have more troops on Diamond Head than downtown, at the start."

Sam nodded. "I don't suppose I could slip back home to see my wife?" he inquired. "Just to mention the change in plan?"

"Don't be an idiot," Walker growled. "If you poke your nose out of this house, you'll probably be arrested. Go read a book."

Sam poured himself more coffee. He grinned at Bertelmann, their enforced host. "At least you have a good cook, Henry."

On Saturday night the Hawaiians in the country, too excited to wait, eager to be ready for the morning, set out in droves for Diamond Head. Any attempt at subtlety was sacrificed because they had enormous faith that their cause was right and that God would be on their side.

A PG policeman, out for a Sunday-morning carriage drive with his wife, noted the unusual number of fishermen. Suspicious, he followed them to Kapiolani Park, on the beach between Waikiki and Diamond

Head. He didn't like what he saw. Within half an hour his alarm resulted in guards being posted at the Waikiki entrance.

"Damn! They're turning the Hawaiians back!" Nowlein paced the floor of Henry Bertelmann's living room. "Brentwood! How many have gotten through?"

"No more than thirty," Sam answered. "They're still trickling in, though—" He broke off and looked through the living room and the lanai beyond it to Bertelmann's banyan tree. It was an even larger specimen than Wilcox's, its twisted corridors gray-green and mysterious at midday. "Hold on a minute."

He prowled through the living room and out to the lanai and stared at the banyan. Something moved in its shadows. "Henry!" Sam called more loudly than necessary. "Didn't you say something was getting your chickens? I think it's out here in the banyan. Bring me your shotgun."

A hasty scrabbling in the banyan answered him. Sam chuckled.

"It was Sam Brentwood. I saw him. And he threatened to shoot me!" The PG spy was outraged.

"For chicken thieving?" President Sanford Dole put a hand across his mouth.

"They're up to something," Lorrin Thurston insisted. The PG spy was his agent, handpicked, and Thurston glared at him. "Just give us your information and don't act like an ass."

"There's a big gathering at Henry Bertelmann's," the agent said, aggrieved. "They're up to something."

"They may just be up to a poker game," Dole said.

"There's thirty of them!"

"A luau then."

Lorrin Thurston made an irritated noise with his tongue and his teeth.

"Brentwood knew I was out there. He said he'd shoot me," the agent said.

"That may have been just devilment." Dole sighed.

"All right, I agree it looks fishy. Keep as many Hawaiians as you can from getting through to Bertelmann's, but *don't* do anything unless they start it. I don't want a repeat of last night."

Thurston threw his hands in the air. "This isn't a picnic."

"Don't push me, Lorrin," Dole said angrily. "We are not despots, nor will we act as if we were. Just keep hauling them out of the park, and we may defuse whatever's going on before things get carried away."

By twilight eighty Hawaiians had eluded the PG police to assemble at Henry Bertelmann's. Another eighty men were posted along the shoreline.

"A hundred sixty men!" Lot Lane fumed. "We should have had a thousand!"

"The rest may get through yet," Nowlein said. He peered into the dusk as if he didn't really have much hope of it.

Outside, eighty faces turned with optimism to Sam. "Any orders yet, Mr. Brentwood?"

"Not yet," Sam replied. "Hang on to your weapons and stay well out of sight."

The Hawaiians moved restlessly in the shadows of the banyan and banana trees and in the open door of the canoe shed. They were eager to accomplish something. This standing around was getting to them—and Sam could feel their restlesness. He knew when a scheme was going sour. His wilder days had taught him how to get a sense of runaway events, and his perceptions were almost always reliable.

He walked up to the house and hunted up Walker. "If we don't move now," Sam said bluntly, "we might as well give up and go home. Someone will inform the PGs, then half of us will get arrested and the PGs'll confiscate the weapons. We'll never get the momentum back to try it again. These are civilians, damn it, not a trained army. You have to *do* something with them."

"I am not entirely unaware of that," Walker said dryly. "Word's just come. We'll attack the key points in the city at two tonight with all the men we've been able to gather by then. You'll move from here under Nowlein."

The men continued to feel restless, but at least the waiting was easier to endure now that they had the word: They would fight. Excitement spread down the beach road, touching those stragglers who had managed to slip around the police in Kapiolani Park, urging them on toward Henry Bertelmann's. The ripple in the air moved outward and felt almost tangible, like a mild electrical current. It raised the hair along their forearms and caused those in its path to rest uneasily. The PGs, their alarm growing, sent a patrol down to Diamond Head under Captain Robert Parker, and the lawmen carried with them the same aura of electricity.

The patrol caught up young Charles Carter and two of his college cronies, who were spending the weekend at the Carter beach house on Waikiki. When the patrol turned into their driveway, the three young men came tumbling out of the house. Their faces were taut with excitement.

"What's going on, Captain?" Charles Carter was nearly bouncing on his toes.

"Just a routine patrol," Parker answered. "We've had a report of some suspicious activity."

"They've been all over the place all day!" Carter said. "Are you going after them? We'll come, too."

"I don't think that will be necessary," Parker said.

"We want to help." Charles was a big boy but flabby, not muscular. He exuded the confidence of the overprivileged, and his eyes gleamed with anticipation. "We know the area, don't we, fellows? We know who you should be looking for, too—that German fellow Bertelmann, for one. He's not a right 'un."

The other two boys chimed in.

"We can show you where he lives!"

"I heard he's a friend of Robert Wilcox!"

Parker gave up. It was easier to take them along than to argue with them to stay.

"You wait right here!" Carter raced for the house and strapped on a pair of six-guns, then passed two more of his father's pistols to his cronies. "All right, fellows, let's go have some fun with the kanakas."

The PG patrol was just pulling out as the young men ran back toward the stables. Carter and his friends saddled their horses and caught up to the police.

"Give us our orders, Captain!" Carter hooted excitedly as they trotted into Henry Bertelmann's drive.

"Scout the beach," Parker said, thinking to keep them out of trouble. He had had second thoughts about his decision to bring the boys along. He stood watching as Carter and his pals slipped around the house toward the beach. They stumbled once or twice and giggled in the darkness. Then they grew silent.

Parker turned and went up the steps of the lanai. Through the lanai, Henry Bertelmann could be seen, reading in innocent isolation by a kerosene lamp.

Parker turned toward Carter again, hopeful that the boys were staying out of trouble. Just then a faint movement flickered in the shadows, and as the police captain watched in horror, Carter jumped and pivoted, hands on his pistol grips. The young man drew both guns and fired into the banyan tree. Pistol shots cracked the silent darkness, splitting it open into chaos.

Then Captain Parker spun around and watched helplessly as gunfire flowered from the darkness of the canoe shed and surrounding shrubbery. Charles Carter fell, clutching his stomach, and Parker's patrol returned fire. The shots went wildly across the yard, screaming overhead toward the shrubbery from the lanai, where Parker's men had taken cover. A man spun out of the banana trees, hands to his chest.

"Stop! Stop this! For the love of God, stop it!" Henry Bertelmann was on the lanai, waving his hands at Parker.

"Cease fire!" Parker roared. His men lowered their rifles. Another shot spat from the shrubbery, and then that gun was still. One of Carter's pals stood gaping over his friend's moaning body while the other stared dumbly at Parker. At last he found his voice.

"They shot him!" he cried, outraged.

"Get them in the house," Henry Bertelmann said furiously. "All of them. What are you doing firing guns in my yard? This is disgraceful!"

"Get the kid!" Parker snapped at his men. He could deal with Henry Bertelmann later. Carter was bleeding like a stuck pig and needed immediate attention. Two wounded Hawaiians—one with a bullet in his lung, the other with a thigh wound—were also brought into the house. When Parker saw that Carter had bullets in his shoulder and abdomen both, he swore.

Outside in the darkness, the Hawaiians were frozen into immobility again, watching Henry Bertelmann standing up alone to the police. As he shook his fist in Captain Parker's face, his tasseled fez quivered with fury.

"I don't think they can arrest him," Nowlein whispered to Sam. "They can't prove anything. Some idiot of theirs fired first."

A PG trooper ran from the house and slung himself into his saddle. Hoofbeats spattered into the night and were gone.

"That idiot was a civilian," Sam whispered back. "That's Carter's kid. I recognized him. I hope they can get a doctor back here in time."

"I don't care if it was the Virgin Mary," Nowlein said. "We have to get out of here now, before the PGs send reinforcements."

Lot Lane dropped down on one knee beside them. "Pass the word: Move out quietly to the beach, then skirt around the patrol until we hit the road. We're going up Diamond Head."

Sam stood, melted into the banyan, and tapped men on the shoulder, bending low to whisper. Silently he rose. Above them, lifting over the feathery tops of the date palms that fringed the beach, rose Diamond Head, mouth of an ancient volcano, steep and craggy and unrelenting, pushing itself into the sky. With luck they could hold out there until the contingent of foreigners could be rallied from Honolulu to come to their aid.

At the Central Union Church in Honolulu, the congregation was singing the last hymn of evening worship when the courier shoved open the heavy doors and ran breathlessly up the aisle. He whispered in the pastor's ear, and the latter held up his hands urgently, stilling the organ into a last fitful squall and then silence while his congregation bunched against one another, whispering.

"Fighting has broken out on Diamond Head." The words came short and clipped, and the pastor watched his congregation stare around uneasily. Confusion etched their faces: If this was a revolution, who exactly were the revolutionaries?

A civilian captain jumped onto a pew and waved his arms. "Citizens' Guard, follow me!"

Those who knew they *weren't* revolutionaries and didn't want anyone to mistake them for revolutionaries followed him at a run out the wide doors to gather at the armory.

Among those left behind were the wives of the guard, frightened and gathering up children and prayer books, and those citizens who did not belong to the guard—who might perhaps be rebels. These latter exchanged glances among themselves. Their expressions said: This was not how it was supposed to have been begun. What had happened? Where were the Hawaiians from Bertelmann's?

They slipped from their pews and went outside to learn whatever news they could on the street. But the avenues were crowded with PG militia. The rebels, muttering among themselves of bungled tactics, decided to cut their losses and lay low.

IV

The doctor, feet planted wide and unmoving on Henry Bertelmann's rug, stood glaring at Captain Parker. "The kid's dead," he said.

In the corner Bertelmann groaned. He sat with his head in his hands, his fez on the table beside him. Dawn was just coming through the windows.

"He bled to death," the doctor explained grimly. "Gut wounds do that."

"He wouldn't stay away," Parker said defensively. "*I* didn't tell him to tag along."

"He thought he'd be a cowboy," Bertelmann said. "He fired the first shot, you know."

Carter's friends had come white-faced out of the back bedroom. Their eyes were red and puffy. "We just wanted to have some fun with the kanakas," one of them said. "And they killed him! It's murder. Someone's going to pay for this."

"You were all ready to shoot kanakas," Bertelmann accused. "So how does that make you any better? Because they were only kanakas?"

"This is your fault, old man! You're a traitor!"

"There are libel laws," Bertelmann threatened.

"Go home!" Captain Parker abruptly told the two boys. "Get away from here and stay away. I'll be the one to tell Mr. Carter what has happened."

"And if it's of interest to you," the doctor said, "those two kanakas you shot are going to live."

"I'll send a police wagon for them." Parker stood up

and looked at Bertelmann. "I'll deal with you later—after I've told Carter that his son is dead."

"I'm not going anywhere," Bertelmann said heavily.

"Here, lady. Read all about it: Bloodthirsty rebels attack citizens!" A newsboy shoved the Honolulu *Star* into Annie's hands as she stepped off the interisland steamer. After five days with no news from Sam, she had been unable to stand it any longer and had come to Honolulu to see what she could find out. The dock area appeared to be in total chaos. Policemen were everywhere, and troopers of the Citizens' Guard stopped and questioned every male who disembarked.

Annie gave the newsboy a nickel and, her stomach tightening into a sick knot, sat down with the paper on a public bench. The fact that something had finally happened was plain from the front page.

The *Star* had wasted no time in turning Charles Carter to the government's use:

> Charles Carter fell a martyr in a glorious cause. . . . His patriotic death will ever be an inspiration to all who battle for liberty against oppression and wrong. . . . His leadership was as brave, courageous, patriotic as ever rescued a country from a despot's rule. His death adds increasing luster to the courageous bravery and statesmanship of the founders of the Hawaiian Republic.

With shaking fingers Annie folded up the newspaper. She managed to find a cab at the hack stand and set out along the Waikiki road for the Wilcox house. If anyone knew what was happening, Theresa Wilcox would, Annie thought. There was no point in trying to see Liliuokalani. Washington Place would be surrounded with PG agents now.

So was the Wilcox house, Annie discovered upon arrival. A man in the buff uniform of the Citizens' Guard stood on the lanai, his arms folded across his chest.

"State your business here, ma'am."

Annie squared her shoulders. She was nearly rigid with rage. "I am paying a social call on Mrs. Wilcox. What is *your* business here?"

"Mrs. Wilcox is under house arrest."

"Oh, an excellent idea," Annie said acidly, "seeing as how she is extremely dangerous. She has threatened you, I am sure. Don't you think you ought to be wearing a pistol?"

The guard, looking irritated, stood his ground. "I got my orders, ma'am."

"Well, I'm not trying to get her out, you silly man. I'm trying to get *in*." Pausing only long enough to lower her parasol at the front door, she swept past him before he could protest. A frightened Hawaiian maid escorted Annie in.

With the air of a lioness getting up from its nap, Theresa Wilcox rose from the chaise where she had been reading. She was a big woman, tall and broad shouldered, with a grand manner and a theatrical air. She had been born Theresa Owana Kahekelani, and her father had been Kamehameha V's chamberlain.

"Annie! How nice of you to come." Her voice was rich and deep. "I trust you had no trouble getting past the toad at the front door?"

"Not much," Annie said. "How dare they?"

"Because they don't know where Robert is—or your Samuel either, for that matter—and that's making them irrational. If you lived on Oahu, you would have had them around your head all morning, too. They're like a plague of gnats."

"I just came across on the steamer. I couldn't stand it anymore. I can't believe what the *Star* has printed." She held out the newspaper, tightly gripped in a gloved hand. Her glove was filthy from the ink.

"Of course you can't believe it," Theresa said. "I knew Charles Carter—he was a fat young lout who gave himself airs. He went where he shouldn't have been, started shooting like a silly ass, and made a great deal of trouble."

"I'm sorry he's dead, poor thing," Annie told her.

"Well, so am I," said Theresa. She flicked a disdainful finger at the *Star*. "Wouldn't have to deal with all this nonsense if he wasn't. Sit down, dear, and Leilani will bring us a pot of tea. It will give her something to do—she's petrified because her young man is off with Robert. I'm not sure whether she thinks he's going to get killed or she's going to get arrested. Both are very likely, of course."

Annie sat down and took off her gloves. Theresa's attitude was bracing if scarcely soothing. "Where are they?" she managed to ask.

A heavy boom that sounded like thunder answered her. It shook the floor.

"The PGs have field artillery in Kapiolani Park," Theresa said acerbically. "They're shelling Diamond Head— hoping to knock the Royalists off the ledges, I suppose. The police haven't the nerve to go up after them."

"What are our men going to do?"

"I expect they'll try to recruit reinforcements in the country. No one in the city's going to stir to help them now, that's for certain. I'm only guessing, mind you. I haven't seen Robert in days, despite what the idiots watching my house believe. They seem to think that people conducting a rebellion come home for a sandwich in the middle of the day so they can be arrested."

The maid brought a plate of lemon-iced cakes and set them on the wicker table. "There is a boat offshore, with big guns on it," she said fearfully.

"I heard the PGs had put cannon on a tug," Theresa said.

"To shell Diamond Head!" Leilani wailed, and buried her face in her skirt. "They'll all be killed!"

"Stop that right now," Theresa said, and Leilani departed, wiping her eyes on her hem. "Her beau's our gardener," she told Annie in a low voice. "I wonder if he's been planting more than he ought to. Still, if she's pregnant, the police probably won't arrest her, so there's always some silver lining."

"Would they arrest her otherwise? Without proof of her involvement?"

"Annie, the guards have been arresting everybody in sight all day, without the slightest reason. 'Somebody heard that somebody said that he was friendly to Royalists.' It's disgraceful. The PGs have declared martial law, and nobody's safe except those louts in the Citizens' Guard. They're bound to pick you up, you know, if you stay around here."

Annie bit her lip. "I've left Eden alone with Sam's grandmother, who's eighty-something. And a Yankee houseguest I wouldn't trust to defend me against a field mouse."

"Then you'd better get back on the packet before the police realize who you are."

Annie bent her head toward Theresa. "You truly haven't heard anything from Bob?"

Theresa shook her head. "If I had, I would have told you. They're on Diamond Head, and there isn't a thing we can do for them except pray for their safety."

Praying did not seem to Annie a particularly useful venture since the government supporters were no doubt praying also, but she did it anyway. On Theresa's advice she also stocked up on bandages, morphine, and carbolic soap. If Sam came home wounded, calling a doctor would be out of the question.

A Citizens' Guard who had stationed himself at the pharmacy counter peered at her suspiciously. "What's that stuff for?"

"For nothing, I hope," Annie answered. "But I run a farm on the Big Island, and laborers do get hurt."

"Hoarding's not patriotic."

"It's not against the law yet, either," Annie snapped. "So I'll just buy these things before it is." She paid for her purchases and dumped them into her basket.

She visited another pharmacy, this one mercifully free of guards, and doubled her purchases, then tripled them at yet a third. She packed her goods carefully into the bottom of her basket. If it came to outright war, medical supplies would be scarce. Memories of Annie's girlhood, when everything had been scarce, were always just under the surface, and she took no chances.

She caught the last packet to the Big Island and arrived home bleary-eyed the next morning in a hired cart, to find her farmyard full of soldiers. Annie narrowed her eyes. No, not soldiers . . . They were the Citizens' Guard, that ubiquitous organization that apparently could be joined by anyone who wanted an excuse to bully his neighbors. Eden was arguing furiously with the captain.

Annie climbed down from her cart, paid the Hawaiian who had pulled it, then sent him on his way before the guard decided to snatch him up, too. She pushed her basket and carpetbag at Koana, who had run over to greet her. "Take these in the house." Then Annie swung around to face the captain. "What are you doing on my property?"

"They want to arrest Hoakina!" Eden said tearfully.

Annie saw the Aloha Malihini foreman standing stolidly in the grip of two uniformed guards. They appeared to love the way they looked in their uniforms.

"We have information that he's been associating with Royalists," the captain said.

"Associating!" Annie sniffed. "What kind of kangaroo court arrests people for 'associating'? Hoakina is my foreman. He's been here all week."

"He was seen in Pahala with known Royalists. I'll have to ask you for the whereabouts of your husband as well, madam."

"I have no idea where he is."

"I tried to tell them he's gone to Honolulu," Eden said. "They just won't listen."

"Gone to Diamond Head, more likely," the captain said, "with the rest of those murdering scoundrels. But we'll round them up soon enough. How would you like to spend a night in prison, miss? Just to refresh your memory?"

"This is too much!" Annie, fuming, moved between Eden and the captain. "You're a disgrace! Dressing up in silly uniforms and terrorizing young girls. Neither one of us knows where my husband is. He's in some bar in Honolulu probably, or worse. I would have preferred to shield his little sister from that," she added grimly.

Eden moaned and covered her face with her hands. Her shoulders shook, presumably with sobs of disillusionment.

"Now see what you've done!" Annie accused.

The captain looked doubtful.

"Animals," Annie seethed. "All men are animals."

Eden wailed loudly, and a few of the guards snickered.

"All right, but we'll be back," the captain said angrily. "And we're taking this one." His men dragged Hoakina forward and roughly tied his hands behind his back.

"I promise you he's no Royalist," Annie said quietly. "And I desperately need him here."

"It is my duty to inform you that any further argument will result in your falling under suspicion yourself," the captain said. He made a stiff military gesture with his riding crop, and the troop clattered away with Hoakina tied to his horse in their midst.

"Of all the—"

Eden cried genuinely now. "Annie, where's Sam?"

"Right where that man thinks he is," Annie answered. "Dug in on Diamond Head. The PGs shelled it all night—I could see the fire from the boat." She gave Eden a terse accounting of events.

"What will they do to Hoakina?" Eden asked tearfully.

Annie sighed. "Put him in jail, I suppose. I'll try to get him out."

"But he hasn't done anything."

"In this case, I think he probably has," Annie said. "He disappeared right after Sam left, and I took pains not to ask where he was. That tin-horn captain doesn't know that, but I'm afraid it won't make much difference. Theresa Wilcox says the PGs have been dragging people off in *chains* and throwing them into horrible, dirty cells." There were worse rumors, too, but she wouldn't go into them with Eden. *Torture* was the word that had surfaced.

Koana came out of the house and looked fearfully down the road. "I put those medical things in the bottom of the blanket box, Miss Annie."

"Good. Make sure Miss Claudia knows where they are. Where is she?"

"She just woke up. She had a bad night, so she slept late, but those men they woke her up. Miss Annie, will they let Hoakina go?" Hoakina was Koana's cousin.

"I don't know, dear," Annie said.

"Miss Claudia wants to know when is Mr. Sam coming back," Koana said.

Annie put her hand to her head. Everyone seemed determined to ask her questions to which no one could possibly know the answers. "I'll go up and talk to her." Another thought struck her. "Where on earth is Mr. Merrill?"

"He's having breakfast," Koana told her.

"He said he didn't feel he'd be any use in a matter of local politics," Eden said. "*I* think he was afraid of the guards."

"Oh, no," Koana assured her. "He said he wasn't."

Eden rolled her eyes.

"Koana, would you please tell Miss Claudia I'll be up there directly." When Koana had gone, Annie put her arm around Eden. "Are you all right, dear? You aren't going to faint on me?"

"No," Eden said. "I thought you were wonderful, talking to those men. But—Annie, have you ever been in a war before?"

"Well, I was six when the Civil War started. But I don't remember much about it, except for a lot of men in blue uniforms marching around. There were speeches and so on in town. My pa fought in the war, but it was more of a relief to get him out of the house than not. I haven't rightly been *in* a war."

Eden's eyes darkened with concern. "I wish I knew what was going to *happen*!"

"You can brace yourself for anything if you know in advance what it will be, eh?" Annie asked.

Eden nodded. "I suppose."

"Well, I'll tell you one thing we've got to do."

"What?"

"We've got to learn to run a sugar farm. It's just you and me now, because your grandmother's too old."

"Aren't you worried about Sam?"

Annie closed her eyes. "If I stay busy and keep this place from going under, I won't have much time to worry. I'm not about to let this farm rot—Sam loves it too much. I think it flat saved his life."

Her face and throat felt tight from trying not to cry. The place was too big. And she didn't know anything about sugar. . . .

The whine of the shells coming in was like the shrill wail of fear that every man on Diamond Head wanted to give vent to but wouldn't. The sound was more terrifying than the thunderous boom of their launching by the big guns in Kapiolani Park or on board the *Eleu* offshore, because it meant that the shell was about to strike—to smash into the mountain and spew upward everything around it, including rocks, trees, men, and parts of men. And wherever the missiles struck, shards of glasslike rock would spray outward, impaling men where they lay wedged into the crevices that split the ancient crater's sides.

Sam flattened himself still further into the minimal shelter of a stone outcropping and listened to the shrieking shells falling around him. At first it had been an adventure to scramble up Diamond Head in the night. The Royalists, with their guns on their backs, dug in, glad to be doing something at last. But now, after spending two days on Diamond Head, they realized that there would be no reinforcements from the city, that there would be no quick coup. Instead, a long, bloody war—one they might not win—stared them in the face.

The men, particularly the young ones, had plunged from high spirits to uncertainty. For two days they had watched while their comrades were blown into pieces or left to writhe on the slopes in the broiling sun because the PG shelling never stopped long enough to get to the injured. The rebels had begun to understand that the next shell might strike them; there was no good reason—justice, fairness, common sense—why it should not. This realization had descended upon the cocksure young in the same nightmarish fashion as the falling shells. Through experience the older ones fared better. They had already come to an acceptance of chaos as a pattern in itself, as possibly the grand design. They were scared, too, but they were not surprised about it.

There was silence for a moment, and Sam lifted his head cautiously and peered through the palmetto scrub. All around him heads lifted, and someone whimpered, a reedy sound that cut like a thin knife through the murmuring of other voices.

Samuel Nowlein crouched beside Sam in the trench that they had dug with their hands behind the outcropping ridge. Nowlein was bearded and hollow eyed, and his lips were blistered and swollen. His face was purple with bruised patches caused by stumbling into the rock in the night, and his hands, which cradled his rifle, were gloved in bloody, shredded leather that had split at the fingertips.

Sam wondered if his own face looked as bad as Nowlein's. He imagined that it must. When he put his hands to it, it felt strange, as if it might have been someone else's.

He allowed himself a small sip of water through parched lips. The water was warm and murky and almost made him vomit. They had had no food except for a few wild bananas, nearly green.

"What are they doing?" he whispered to Nowlein when the silence lengthened and no more shells came.

"Waiting to see if we come out," Nowlein said.

Peter Aikanaka half crouched just behind them. His shirt and trousers were split and filthy, but there clung about him a few vestiges of his usual air of being on the way to a party. "We must try to bring the wounded in,"

Peter said, smiling. "Since the troops are taking a break."

"No!" Sam grabbed Peter as he started to climb from the trench.

"I'm going to get to that man there." In the silence the whimpering was agonizing to listen to. It was the voice of pain, all reason gone out of it.

"That's what they're hoping for, damn it," Sam said. "Stay down!"

On the slope below they could just see the wounded man's hand, the fingers splayed and clenched, grasping dirt.

Peter slid forward, leaving his rifle. "They won't shoot a medic. And not even the PGs would shoot at the wounded."

"I know them better than you do," Sam said. "I know my own. Now get down, Peter. Nowlein's right—they're just waiting for someone to move."

The whimpering rose to a wail, and the hand beat at the ground. Someone below them could stand it no longer, either. He rose and began to scramble up. A dull boom rattled the mountain. The whimper was overlaid with the shrill scream of a falling shell, and both men exploded together—the wounded fellow and the man who had stood up to help him.

Peter Aikanaka turned around and vomited.

"They're waiting to spot movement," Nowlein said grimly. "It makes the best target at this distance and in this light."

The sun, flaming crimson, hung behind the western edge of Diamond Head. It turned the water below to bloodred. Then like a gas jet turned down, the huge round orb faded.

"Going, going, gone," Sam murmured as it dropped below the crag, hung an instant on the edge like a bloody flag, and went out.

From below, from where the PG troops were positioned, the mountain face would now be draped in deepening darkness, colors impossible to distinguish—shades of gray flowing swiftly into black. The first night

the Royalists had assumed that the shelling would stop at
twilight. Now they knew better.

Another boom and crash drowned the constant roar
of the surf and pounded it to a whisper. In the dusk the
rebels could see the fire from the cannons' mouths. Then
the shells shrieked and whined, shaking the earth as
they hit. The men tensed and held their breath until
their grateful discovery that this missile had also missed
them. The air was filled with quick gasping for breath.
What would it be like, Sam wondered, when one *didn't*
miss you?

A hand touched his ankle, and he twisted around,
squinting in the deepening darkness. It was Lot Lane,
bending over him, seemingly as heavy as the rock.
Wilcox was with him, and they slid into the trench.

"We're moving out," Wilcox announced.

A shell screamed and exploded beyond the outcrop.
Choking dust and needles of glasslike rock rained down
on them. Something warm spattered Sam's left hand. He
put his right hand over it, then recoiled, gagging.
Another man's hand, severed completely at the wrist,
was lying on his, fingers spread along his knuckles as if
asking his attention. Beneath it, Sam's own hand felt
numb. He thrashed in the trench, lifting the thing and
flinging it outward.

No one spoke until Wilcox said again, "Moving out.
Tonight. Nowlein, you will take ninety men to Moiliili
and through the foothills, recruiting on the march. I'll
take sixty into Manoa Valley. Lane wishes to stay here
and try to bring up the wounded." He looked at Lot
Lane as if they had been arguing about it.

"I'll stay with Lot," Sam heard himself say.

"I won't give a direct order against it," Wilcox told
him. "I don't like it, but I couldn't bring myself to say
no."

"I'll stay, too," Peter Aikanaka offered.

"You're crazy," Sam snarled.

"You're staying," Peter pointed out.

"I like being crazy." Sam thought of the severed
hand and brought his front teeth down hard on his lower

lip to chase the image away. Maybe he *was* crazy, to have sold a perfectly good shipping business and come here to this primitive paradise, only to find himself seduced by it into developing a conscience. He had never wanted a conscience. It was a hell of a nuisance.

Nowlein and Wilcox pulled out that night, taking part of the battered force with them. Other men stayed to help with the wounded. The PGs shelled the mountain relentlessly, oblivious to the rebels' departure. At night the PGs simply fired randomly and kept it up till dawn.

At first light, when the night had barely begun to thin, Lot Lane took stock of what was left to him. With whispered orders, the youngest and most agile of the Royalists began to slide down the creviced slopes and wriggle their way toward the wounded who lay among the rock. The PG shells went off around them, but still aimlessly. The rescuers left the dead where they were and dragged the wounded upward, killing more than one in the process. There was no other way.

Sam bent over a man whose breath was coming in shallow, intermittent gasps. He had a ragged wound in his groin, which was black with dried blood and thick with flies. An overpowering stench rose from it. The man's eyes were half-open and unfocused, but when Sam touched him, his lips formed a word: *water*. Sam held his canteen to the man's mouth, and a trickle of water ran out the sides. But Sam thought the fellow might have swallowed some of it—although not enough to do him any good.

He put his hands under the man's shoulders and tried to move him up the mountain. There were no trails here, only what footholds could be found among the rock and palmetto. The man moaned once, and the wound in his groin opened, spilling a thick liquid down his already encrusted trouser leg. He made no sound at all, and when Sam bent over him again, he saw that the shallow breaths had stopped.

Sam closed his eyes, wearily relieved that now he didn't have to choose between tormenting this man further or stilling the breath with his own hands—a thought that had crossed his mind. He left the corpse in the shadow of whatever otherworld, if any, might open for its spirit, then crawled back up the mountain.

He climbed into the first fiery sun, as accusing as a spotlight. The shelling from below, which had been erratic all night, increased and narrowed in on the rebels. Sam took the legs of the man whom Peter was dragging, and together they staggered farther up the mountain and then around toward the other side, angling as far as they could onto the north face while the guns in Kapiolani Park swung around to follow them. The *Eleu*, meanwhile, steamed up the coast, dogging their flanks.

In many places the volcanic rock was fine and sandy, and their ankles sank into it and twisted under them. The man that Sam and Peter carried was wounded in the chest but unaccountably tenacious. Behind them, Lot Lane carried a man over his shoulder and grasped a rifle in his hand.

Another shell whined down, and the trail below was filled with trees catapulted into the air and clods of earth blown skyward. Lizards, fleeing from the explosions, darted under the men's feet. A rabbit rocketed across the trail, and a flock of birds lifted, squawking in alarm, from the tangled branches of a *hau* tree as if blown on the shock wave of the blast.

Another boom and then yet another rocked the mountain above them now. Dirt and branches rained on their heads. One of their men fell, his leg streaming blood, and two others picked him up. They staggered and stumbled into the green thickets at the foot of the mountain. But their retreat was followed always by the shelling, by the sudden bursting of the earth as if some long-buried demon was waking and emerging from beneath their feet.

When they came finally to water, they halted and

dropped on their faces at the stream's edge, gulping. Lot filled his canteen and began to walk among the wounded with it. They had no medical supplies. They could do nothing except make bandages from whatever filthy clothing could be torn into strips.

Sam hung his face in the cold, clear water, swallowed, held his breath, and just let the water wash over his cheeks and chin. When he had to surface, he took only a breath and then put his face back in the water. The coldness of it gave him assurance that he was still alive, that he was not delirious and waiting to die somewhere back on the rocks on Diamond Head's face.

When he had swallowed all the water he could, he emptied the last foul dregs from his canteen and remembered the wounded. He filled the canteen and went to help Lot.

"Where are we taking them?" he asked Lot, bending stiffly over a Hawaiian boy who couldn't have been more than fifteen. It was the first time he had thought to ask, as if reality had come rippling in on the cool fingers of the water.

"Farmhouse," Lot answered. "First one we come to."

"How do you know the owners'll take them?"

"Because I will tell them to," Lot said simply. He looked more than ever like some being of an oceanic myth, some god's child, muscular and intractable. His eyes glittered like the sunstruck water.

"The PGs will know that's where we're making for," Sam said. "What if there's an ambush?"

"Then we will fight," Lot said.

"Without catching up to Nowlein or Wilcox? With only fifteen men?"

"God is with us," Lot said. The boy at his feet murmured something, and Lot stroked his forehead. "*Our* god," he whispered.

Lot Lane was a Catholic, the son of an Irish father and a missionary-schooled mother; but just now Sam was not at all sure what god Lot was praying to. He looked up at the scarred slope of Diamond Head and thought that it didn't matter. A man with Lot's kind of faith could put a serious dent in the enemy. But Sam had never heard it claimed that God—anybody's god—had ever personally fired a rifle. He stretched and wearily picked up his weapon.

V

Sam and Lot Lane's ragtag band did not hear until afterward what had happened to Nowlein and Wilcox. The world very quickly narrowed to keeping their own skins safe. At the head of the Palolo Valley they were met by a Chinese farmer and his wife, who gave them melons and water and such news as they had.

"The soldiers are out with the dogs, sir," the farmer said. "If you listen, you can hear them. You have to go after you have eaten," he added stubbornly.

"I must leave my wounded here," Lot insisted.

The farmer's wife spoke to him urgently in Chinese, shaking her head, making pushing motions with her hands at the wounded men.

"The government will put me in prison," the farmer protested.

"They can't go with us," Sam said around the piece of melon he was gulping down. Juice ran down his chin, and he wiped his hand on his filthy trousers. "They can't stand any more jostling. They need to be kept still. Otherwise they'll die."

"No!" the wife said. "No, no, no. The soldiers will come with dogs and take us away if we hide these men."

"Don't hide them," Sam suggested gently. "Just look after them. If the soldiers come, they'll take the men to a hospital. You can tell the soldiers that we made you take our wounded. Here." He dug into his pocket and found a few coins and his gold pocket watch. He pressed them into her hand. "To buy the things you need."

Lot Lane produced his own watch and a silver

pocketknife. The wife stared as he added them to Sam's offerings and curled her fingers around them.

The farmer calculated the value of the watches and came to a decision. "Bring the wounded to the barn. But we will not fight the PGs. If they find these men, we will not interfere." He repeated that over and over, trotting beside Lot as they carried the wounded through his melon patch. The wife followed.

Finally Lot swung around, glaring at him. "Damn and blast you for being a quivering coward who lets other men buy your rights for you!" he thundered.

The farmer would not give ground. "I won't be responsible. Not responsible."

Sam clapped a hand on Lot's arm. "Settle down before he changes his mind." In the distance they could hear the clear belling of a hound. "Just worry about our making tracks."

They laid the wounded out on straw in the barn while a pair of plow oxen eyed them curiously. The woman knelt in the straw beside the most seriously wounded man and began to cut away his shirt with the silver pocketknife Lot had given her.

"We are not bad people," she said, eyes lowered, refusing to meet Sam's. "We are very afraid."

"You get gone," the husband said. "Before the dogs track you here!"

Lot ducked through the barn door, then lifted his head to scan the hills. It was already late afternoon. They wouldn't get very far before nightfall. "Come on!" he called, and set off at a trot up the valley.

Two hours later they stopped, exhausted, and robbed a farmer's orange grove for food. They had knocked on the farmhouse door first, but there was only stillness inside, windows turning their blank, shuttered eyes inward. So the men stole oranges, then dug themselves a den in the jungle canopy that grew beyond the farm.

After he had eaten, Sam lay with his head buried in his forearms and tried to sleep. A nightjar kept calling, drilling through the stillness. Lot Lane turned and turned, revolving like a wolf in his sleep.

Palolo Valley proved to be a washout. A few more farmers, Hawaiian as well as Chinese, had given them water and a calabash full of poi, but they kept one eye on the trail and their ears cocked for barking dogs.

"Captain . . ." One of the rebels, a fisherman with a broad, worried brow, sat down beside Sam and pulled his sleeve. "Captain, when do we meet up with the reinforcements?"

"Manoa Valley," Lot, who lay nearby trying to sleep, said. "Tomorrow we'll push into Manoa. Nowlein and Wilcox will have the reinforcements waiting for us there."

Sam sat up. His head throbbed, and he was ravenous. Morosely he dipped his fingers in the calabash. Poi was the staple of the native diet. It was made from taro root, mashed and slightly fermented. It was nutritious, nearly a complete diet in itself, but Sam loathed it. He stuck his fingers in his mouth and forced himself to eat a few more bites. By the time he had, the urge to tell Lot Lane a few home truths had subsided: In his opinion there weren't going to be any reinforcements.

Over the last few days, Sam had found himself growing steadily angrier with the universe, until by now he was little more than a boiling temper. The rebels, he believed, had lost their chance, proved themselves to be fools, and were now going to be hunted down with dogs. Sam wanted no part of it—neither surrender nor flight. He wanted to go back the four days and do the thing over, but correctly this time. That he couldn't frustrated him into near madness. What *was* keeping him sane, he thought, was the growing suspicion that Lot Lane might not be—not at the moment, anyway.

The next morning, with a ground mist wreathing like smoke all along the river valleys, they staggered up, ate the last of the poi, then filled their canteens at a stream. They set out over a track that wound upward and then down again into the Manoa Valley. Only half-visible above the mist, the men looked to Sam like the spirits of the night marchers—dead warriors who were supposed to wander these mountains—caught unaccountably by day, limned against the dawn's pale light before they faded entirely.

As they stumbled down toward Manoa, the mist burned off. The red-earth road up the valley glowed wide and easy and enticing against the swaying green grass—too enticing. Lot halted the column above the road and slipped into the tangled branches of a hau tree to have a look around.

The haus grew in a demented fashion. Their branches trailed to the ground, reached upward again, doubled back, and arched down. They made an impenetrable thicket in which a man could hide while the enemy passed by within ten feet.

Sam slithered in beside him. He didn't like the look of that road, either. He stretched himself out on a limb and contemplated the horizon. Something was out there. The only trouble was, he didn't know what. Was it possible that Nowlein and Wilcox might actually be awaiting them?

"There's a farm just around the bend," Lot whispered. "That's where they'll be. The owner is a Royalist."

"I'd feel better if Samuel and Bob showed themselves."

"They are waiting for us." Lot's eyes flashed. In his world it was not possible that the rebels were going to lose.

Sam's shoulders itched as curiosity overrode wariness. He wanted to know—*had* to know—what was out there, where that road would go. The urge to know and be done with it was stronger than the inclination toward caution. Exhaustion, uneasy sleep, and bad food had all taken their toll. His perceptions were skewed, and he felt as if he had entered some altered dimension where the usual rules might not apply. Sam tried to get a grip on his own reality, to catch it by the neck, drag it back, and make it sit with him like a properly trained dog. But in the face of so much that was unknown, his driving force became the simple act of wanting to know. Was that, he wondered, what was driving Lot Lane?

"We're going to move!" Lane said, and jumped from the hau tree, to land in a crouch on the road. "Follow me, boys!"

Sam didn't argue; he didn't even want to anymore. He jumped down, too, and the rest fell in behind them, slithering and stumbling, their shoes worn through and their bare toes caked with blood. They picked up the pace into a semblance of a march and swung off down the road.

Lot began to sing. "'Onward, Christian soldiers—'"

The rest took it up, ragged and hopeful, defying any outcome but the victory they had counted on, the success they had been promised, the one that was *right*.

> "Marching as to war,
> With the cross of Jesus,
> Going on before!"

They had gotten to the end of the first verse before the bullets started. Peter Aikanaka, marching beside Lot, dropped wounded in the road. The column turned, firing wildly into the tall grass across the road as it sprouted armed and uniformed members of the Citizens' Guard.

The guard howled and rushed at them. "Get the traitors! Rebels!"

Both sides fired wildly. Lane's column staggered back toward the farmhouse where they had expected to find Nowlein and Wilcox waiting. Instead, there was only an old man reading his newspaper on the porch. He jumped up and fled into the house, and a stray bullet smacked through the glass after him.

Sam flattened himself against the side of the old man's barn and fired into the ranks of the guard, attempting to pick off officers systematically. There were nearly thirty soldiers all told. A bullet whined past his head, and Sam retreated farther, at last stretching flat in damp grass to put an iron horse-trough between him and the attacking troopers. He leveled his rifle and fired, and a captain dropped. That seemed to discourage the guard. There was a brief moment of confusion while all the troopers tried at once to drag their wounded captain away but fell over one another. With enormous satisfaction, Sam put a bullet into the buttocks of the nearest.

A bullet pinged back into the horse trough, and the metal reverberated with a sound like angry bees. In the yard another of Lot's followers, trying to reach the rear of the house, was shot down. He spun and fell, clutching his throat, while blood poured out between his fingers. There was a cry of anguish from the dead boy's brother, crouched in the shadow of a hayrick.

"Cease firing!" a lieutenant of the guards shouted from a position by the wounded captain. "Cease firing! Surrender, and you'll not be harmed!"

"Go to hell!" Lot bellowed back.

"The rebellion is over! You're alone! Think about your families!"

There was a shifting among the men hidden by the barn and hayrick. Their families had had no word from them for a week. What if wives and children were sick or starving? What if they had been arrested?

"We want to see our families!" one of the rebels shouted.

"You have my word!" the lieutenant called back.

"Don't trust him!" Lot yelled. "They're PG liars! They'd sell their grandmothers! At them, boys! Now, for Hawaii!" Lot stood and fired, then ducked around the corner of the house as the guards fired back. "At them!" he shouted again, but no one moved.

Finally a hand holding a tattered scrap of cloth appeared above the hayrick.

"Come on out, son," the lieutenant called.

The Hawaiian crept from his hiding place, hands in the air. He looked over his shoulder at Lot. "I'm sorry, Captain. I got to."

One by one they rose to surrender, hands holding shirts and handkerchiefs, expressions pleading.

"I'm sorry, Captain."

"We're sorry, Captain."

"I got to see my family."

"I got to go, Captain."

The Citizens' Guard gathered them in gently, with elaborate care, beckoning kindly as the next man and then the next came out from their hiding places. Sam lay low and watched. A moan of anguish sounded from the tangle of creepers and wild banana trees behind the farmhouse. Lot Lane turned and ran, thrashing through the unterraced hillside above the farm, stumbling through the hau trees and wild cane. A rifle shot followed him.

"Let him go," the lieutenant of the guard said. "He'll come down when he's hungry enough." He looked around him, and then questioningly at the prisoners. "Now, you—is that all of you?"

They looked at their feet. Sam held his breath. He didn't know why he wouldn't surrender, only that something in his gut told him, as he had told Peter Aikanaka, that he knew his own kind. These haole citizens playing at war were unreliable. They were a mob with uniforms.

Peter had been recognized and brought up from the road where he had fallen. He lay propped against a cart. The lieutenant prodded him with the toe of his boot.

"Well, is that all of them? Aren't you the senior officer here?"

Peter nodded stiffly. "I expect so."

"All right, then, move them out! Anyone who hasn't turned himself in will be shot on sight." He pushed Peter again. "Here, you, get up. You aren't hurt too bad to walk."

The men who had surrendered stared wide-eyed, frightened now. Sam squeezed his lids shut to still the pounding in his head. It didn't work. He lay, growing stiffer and sicker until the troop was out of sight, driving its prisoners along before it. The boy who had been shot in the throat was still lying in the yard.

Sam stood up, his back protesting as he straightened it, and went to bend over the boy. It was too late for anything but to bury him, and Sam was too tired to do that. He walked to the farmhouse door and looked in. The old man was on the floor, bleeding but not dead.

Goddamn it, Sam thought, and went inside.

The old man opened his eyes at him. By the look of him he was a hapa-haole, with thick beetling brows and a balding head. "You dimwits shot me," he grated.

Sam pulled the man's shirt away and found that the bullet had gone clean through the shoulder and out the front. "We didn't shoot you," he muttered. "We're the good guys."

"You don't know who shot me," the old man said. "You sons of bitches got the aim of a bunch of Sunday-school kids."

"Just shut up and hold still," Sam told him. He limped to the stove and found that mercifully there was a fire going in it. He put a saucepan of water on to boil and found a whiskey bottle in a cupboard. After the water boiled and then cooled a bit, Sam washed the old man's shoulder with it, then poured some whiskey on the wound for good measure while the patient swore at him.

When he was through, he ripped down the kitchen curtains and tied the old man's shoulder up with them.

"Them's my good curtains!"

"Your tablecloth isn't clean enough to use as a bandage," Sam retorted.

"Hmmph! And where do you think you're going now?"

Sam was ransacking the pantry cupboard for something to eat, not bothering to ask for permission. "I'll find Nowlein and Wilcox if I can." He glared at the old hapa-haole. "They were supposed to be here."

"But they ain't. I'd of let them, mind you. I always been loyal to the queen, poor old lady, but we're finished now. The best we can hope for is that the United States will take us on. We won't get the PGs out any other way."

"You're a pessimist, aren't you?" Sam found a pie tin with a slice of stale apple pie in it. He ate it.

"I had rats before," the old man observed. "Couldn't

get 'em out without blowing up the shed they was living in."

Sam took a drink out of the whiskey bottle and handed it back to its owner. "If you don't think you'll get arrested on suspicion, go see a doctor for that."

"And where are you going?" the old man asked him again.

"Damned if I know. Mind if I raid your garden on the way out?"

"Naw, help yourself. And good luck."

Sam climbed the hillside behind the barn, where Lot Lane had gone, hoping to find the man. In his present state, Lot wasn't hard to track. He had blundered through the thickets, trampling young banana trees and fern and hacking vines out of his way with his belt knife. In an hour Sam came on him, high in the mountains again, sitting on a rock.

"I hope the PGs haven't sent a detail back to look for you," Sam informed him. "You could have just painted some red arrows on the ground."

"The PGs will be too busy fighting in the city," Lot predicted.

Sam stood looking down at him. "Nobody is fighting anybody. If I'm not mistaken, Nowlein and Wilcox have either been rounded up or have surrendered."

"There is still firing," Lot insisted stubbornly. In the distance, far below them, they could hear the faint crack of gunfire. "Our comrades are still fighting. The foreigners in the city will have joined with them by now."

"You've lost your marbles," Sam said. "Those soldiers are after us." He gave Lot a handful of peas from the old man's garden. "Here, eat something."

"Then why didn't you surrender?" Lot growled. He ate the peas, shells and all.

"I'm damned if I know," Sam said morosely. "I didn't trust those guards. Maybe I can get around to Kaneohe Bay and take a boat home from there."

"The PGs will check everyone's credentials," Lot

told him. "You don't have but two choices, Brentwood—surrender or fight."

From below them, and not very far below, they heard a deep yelping bay, rising in a triumphal quaver. They barely had time to flatten themselves in the grass before a bullet sang over their heads. The hounds began to clamor wildly.

The men stumbled to their feet again and fled, higher onto the rocky green slopes of the Koolau Range, which ran like a spine down the northeastern side of the island.

Sam lost all track of time, of everything but the effort to put one foot in front of the other, to climb, to shut out the belling hounds below him. His shoes lasted out the day, but rain fell during the night, and at dawn he couldn't get the shoes on again. He tried to beat them into suppleness, but the leather split in his hands and fell from his fingers in sodden fragments. His pants were ribboned now by the sharp rock that jutted upward in sheer escarpments, his shirt hung in rags, and the hat in which he had gathered vegetables was long gone, blown away by the howling gale that formed from the trade winds as they hit the towering slopes of Nuuanu Pali.

Lot and he had made their way northwestward behind the city, out of the Manoa Valley, and into the Nuuanu Valley. They fled upward into the mountains. The dogs were always behind them. Their pursuers never came nearer but never backed off. Bullets whirred past their heads when Lot and Sam showed themselves on the skyline, but they stumbled on. Torrential sheets of rain poured down the mountain, soaking the men to the bone, and they huddled into crevices at night and shivered against each other with very little but the other's body heat for warmth.

Sam had ceased asking himself, *Why are we doing this?* What drove them was not explicable and had very little to do with the practicalities of the rebellion, which, Sam admitted—even if Lot did not—was over and done. All he knew was that surrendering would end the struggle and his commitment —including something moral and ethical within him—before it was allowed to come to its natural conclusion.

Sam lay huddled against the wet, mossy rock and looked up at the high, sickening shadow of Nuuanu Pali, immense and omnivorous in the moonlight. Kamehameha I had driven his enemies to the edge of the Pali and watched as they spilled like lemmings over the side. Was that what he was climbing for? To drop from Nuuanu Pali, to fall screaming into oblivion? Tonight he wasn't sure.

In the morning it was raining again, and the Pali was sheeted in gray mist. The dogs below them had lost the scent and were quartering up and down the trail for it. There was a road up Nuuanu Pali to Kailua, but Sam and Lot had long since abandoned it in the hope of shaking off their pursuers. They climbed among the rock and soft lichens, the fern and tangles of creepers that caught at their ankles. The trade winds whispered, *Stay, give up, rest here.*

There was nothing to eat on the high slopes, and Sam began to feel the floating sensation that was the second effect of starvation once the first—hunger pangs—had stilled. He pulled a handful of young fern, chewed it, and swallowed. In a minute it came back up, leaving him doubled over and retching.

A hound barked below them. Sam straightened and walked on. His feet left red prints of blood in the wet moss, marks that stayed a moment, then were washed clean.

Queen Liliuokalani sat with her plump hands clenched on the arms of her chair as she listened to the shouting and the bursts of gunfire outside in the streets. "There is no one to shoot at," she said, miserable. "The police just like to fire those rifles."

Her companion, Mrs. Clark, a lady-in-waiting of long standing, said nothing because there was nothing to be said. The short-lived rebellion had been botched, and now the queen and her companion were waiting at Washington Place while the PGs decided what to do next. The authorities would be certain to assume—or pretend to assume—that the queen had been behind the uprising. And she certainly hadn't tried to stop it, Mrs. Clark thought.

There was a knock at the door. Deputy marshals strode in. They hadn't waited for the maid to announce them.

"We have a warrant for your arrest, madam," the elder of them said portentously to the queen.

Liliuokalani stood up. "Very well. But I have already told the police that I know nothing about this."

The officers clearly were not interested. They bundled her and Mrs. Clark into a carriage. Looking back, the lady-in-waiting saw the chief justice of the supreme court striding briskly up the steps of Washington Place. Then the carriage lurched forward, to take the women to the Iolani Palace, now in the PGs' possession.

"The chief justice," Theresa Wilcox informed Annie the next morning, "proceeded to ransack the house, top to bottom—the queen's desk, her private safe, her bureau drawers! It was disgraceful! Then the PGs terrorized all her servants, trying to get evidence out of them. Her private secretary, poor old Joseph Heleluhe, is by all accounts lying stark naked in an unlighted cell in an attempt to persuade him to disclose treasonous information."

"Did your husband tell you that?" Annie asked. "How is Bob, dear?"

"Not a bit better than you might expect under the circumstances," Theresa said grimly. "He got word that they had detained me at the police station, so he was on his way to surrender when he was captured. He is sick and heartbroken, and Samuel Nowlein isn't any better. You heard that he had surrendered, too, didn't you?"

"Yes." Annie bit at a fingernail.

"You shouldn't even be on Oahu," Theresa observed. "If you'd just stay holed up on the Big Island, the authorities would be more likely to leave you alone. They want your Sam, you know."

"I don't even know where he is." Annie's face was taut, very carefully controlled. The harsh afternoon light gave definition to the lines around her eyes and mouth. She looked her age and on the verge of tears. "What will happen if they catch Sam?"

"I don't know," Theresa said tightly. Her deep voice carried none of its usual confidence. "They've arrested everyone they can lay their hands on: Seward and Walker and Will Davies. William Rickard—he footed the bill for a lot of the uprising, did you know that? And Charles Gulick—while searching through the queen's papers the PGs found the constitution he drew up for the new Royalist government. Scores of other people have been arrested on no grounds at all: the Ashford brothers, Arthur Peterson, Charles Crighton—they all had government positions. The PGs are eating their own young now."

"I heard they put Edmund Norrie in jail," Annie said.

"Well, he might have expected it." Norrie, a Dane, was editor of the outspoken *Holomua* newspaper. "The charge was 'speaking disrespectfully of the government.' He's been doing that for years. They picked up the rest of the Lane brothers, too, and some poor German who was overheard to say that the natives were the true lords of the islands. Informers are all over, selling one another out for a fee or just to be spiteful."

"It's disgraceful. I'm ashamed to be a haole."

"I wouldn't take it that far," Theresa commented. "Half the people arrested are haoles, and thank God for it, too. The British government and the United States won't stand by if the PGs start hanging British and American citizens."

"Will it come to that?" Annie's hands tightened. No one knew how far the PGs would go. Their reputation wasn't good since Queen Liliuokalani's overthrow had been repudiated by President Cleveland. Would that make them cautious or vengeful? Once Sanford Dole had been persuaded to arrest the queen, his men had acted with unseemly haste, probably to avoid letting the kanakas get wind of it. The people in the street would surely have made a fuss and embarrassed the government.

"They're being very spiteful at the moment," Theresa said, considering. "Further, they are torturing prisoners. I've heard stories of beatings and of men being immersed in ice water for a day at a time. And other things I don't want to contemplate. . . ." Her voice faltered. "I don't know what they've done to Robert. He's refused to turn state's evidence. But Nowlein has done so, and poor Captain Davies, and they're strong men."

Annie stood up abruptly. "It's possible Sam may try to come home. I want to be there if he does. Please send me word by packet if you hear anything. His grandmother is desperate for him, and she's very old. I'm nearly as worried about her as I am about Sam."

"Listen." Lot Lane cocked his head at the dark valley below Sam and him.

The moon illuminated a silvery mist that slid down the peaks of the Pali and floated into the lowlands. It was ethereally beautiful, Sam thought, like something from the otherworld. "I don't hear anything," he said. Maybe they *were* looking into the next world, given sight but no sound.

"Correct," Lot agreed. "They've stopped firing."

Sam's perceptions had split and shifted because of his profound weariness, so anything might come into his head. Lot's, however, had grown concentrated, focused only on the revolution that everyone but him acknowledged was over.

"They've stopped firing," he said again. "In the city. The foreigners have come to our aid."

"The PGs have won," Sam said flatly. "Nobody's coming to our aid."

"Listen, Sam, listen. No guns."

A shot rang out below them.

"Except those," Sam said acidly.

"They don't know. They just haven't gotten word yet. We must get to the city."

"You aren't thinking straight, Lot. Don't do it."

Lot stood and looked down at him. "There are times when a man must act on faith. I am going down."

"Faith won't make it so, you damn fool." Sam refused to budge from the nest of trampled fern he had created, wolflike, for himself among the rock and underbrush.

Lot's eyes glittered. They caught the moonlight and bounced it back. Whatever thoughts existed behind his eyes were unreadable. Maybe Lot was beyond all ability to reason, Sam thought. And maybe he himself wasn't any saner, but he wasn't going down the mountain tonight. He curled himself into a ball among the ferns, drawing as much of his own warmth around him as he could. "Go on then, you damn idiot."

He heard Lot's footsteps moving down the mountain, then heard the baying of the dogs and another shot. Maybe Lot would draw them off. It would be Lot's own fault if he did. Sam huddled in the fern, afraid to sleep and too weary to move on if he didn't have to. He cursed himself for joining Lot after leaving the old man's farmhouse. The guards hadn't even realized he existed until after they were chasing Lot.

It was almost dawn when Sam realized that Lot had not drawn their pursuers away—nor had the pursuers left. The guards were determined now, tired of the chase, and surely as footsore as was their quarry. They would push on without stopping until they got him.

Sam struggled to his feet and began to climb again, up the silvered face of Nuuanu Pali. Slowly the white sheen of the Pali turned pink and then golden, and he dragged himself onto the plateau at the top just as the sun spilled over it. The flat crest was magical in rose-gold light, veiled in a mist as diaphanous as gauze. The creepers that twined the stones shimmered with dew. This beauty stretched away beneath his feet to the edge, where, soft-lipped with moss and grasses, the Pali ended in a sheer, dizzying drop back to earth, plummeting through limitless space into a caldron of cool mist.

Sam stood on the edge of the cliff, his arms spread like wings, and imagined himself flying, soaring out into the air as Kamehameha's vanquished foes had done. Would those few seconds of freedom, suspended hundreds of feet above the mist, be worth his death? Some seductive voice whispered to Sam that the flight would be worth its price. He balanced on his toes as a hound bayed low behind him.

"There he is!"

Sam spread his arms wider, then turned to see the dogs and men charging across the plateau through the eddying mist. A shot went over his head.

"You're under arrest, Brentwood!"

"Christ, he's going to jump!"

They surged toward him while Sam stood poised to leap. His mind, cut loose by exhaustion and lack of food and spun by the altitude, floated somewhere beyond the Pali and half into the next world already. The mist shone like an inviting silver web below him. He moved his arms again, leaned outward toward the web, then collapsed on the brink of the precipice just as his pursuers reached him.

A captain of the guard grabbed Sam and yanked him away from the cliff's edge. "You're under arrest. Tie him up, boys. Don't trust him."

The body in their hands was inert, but they handcuffed Sam anyway.

"He ain't moving, Captain."

"Is he dead? He looks dead."

"Hell, no, he's breathing. He's gone and fainted on us."

"Well, that was the damnedest thing I ever saw. He's lucky he didn't go over the edge."

A burly trooper slung Sam over his shoulder.

"I think he was trying to," the captain mused. "You know that? I think he was trying to."

* * *

After dusk that same night Lot Lane gave himself up. His faith in the rebels' victory had been short-lived—at the head of the Manoa Valley a friend had met him and told him that the queen was under arrest. With dogged determination, he walked the rest of the way into the city and presented himself—an unshaven, nearly naked, belligerent apparition—to the Honolulu police.

They hustled him into the office of the attorney general, who nervously pulled a gun from his drawer and set it within easy reach on the desktop.

"All right, name the men who agreed to help you with this idiocy, and I'll see what I can do for you."

"I won't be wanting anything you can do for me," Lot growled.

The attorney general bristled. "You realize you can be executed as a traitor?"

Lot leaned his massive hands on the attorney general's desk, a little too close to the pistol for comfort. The attorney general snatched it back. "Isn't that like the pot calling the kettle black?" Lot inquired.

"Put him in a cell and let him think about it," the attorney general snapped. The guards towed Lot down the stone hallway and with visible relief shoved him into a cell.

Lot took stock of the room. The cell was barely large enough for twenty prisoners, but more than a hundred men were crowded inside. Most of them were Hawaiians, although he saw Sam Brentwood, wearing prison garb, curled into a ball, sleeping in the corner. The floor was greasy with dirt, and the acrid odor of the slop jars made Lot gag. A pile of tin plates and cups was stacked by the door. Lot inspected them suspiciously.

"What have they fed you?" he asked.

"Hardtack, Captain," one of the prisoners replied. "And coffee."

"That's *all*?"

"Near all. There was some meat once, but it was rotten."

Lot drew back a bare foot and sent the stack of plates and cups flying. As they clattered and banged into the bare walls, they made a racket as deafening as gunshots. The cell doors slammed open before the last reverberations had died away.

Guards with drawn guns stared around wildly. They all spoke at once, their faces taut with nervousness.

"Lie down on the floor!"

"Get your hands up!"

"Face the wall!"

Lot folded his arms across his chest. He had apparently become a legend in the last ten days, capable of reducing the PG guards to incoherent terror that he might do . . . something, anything. He was larger than life now. The opportunity wasn't to be wasted.

"Get these men some food!" he roared.

One of the guards got a grip on himself. "They've been fed. It's too late at night. Get your hands up."

"They haven't had anything to eat but hardtack for ten days! They haven't even been convicted of anything!" Lot lifted his hands in a gesture that made the guard think better of his order. "Get some *food!*"

The guards looked warily at one another. If they didn't feed these men, it might be as much as their lives were worth to venture into the cell next time. But the warden wasn't going to like it. . . .

"Food!" Lot bellowed again. His voice filled the stone-walled cell, echoing across it like the tin plates had done.

In his corner Sam Brentwood sat up and looked around. His eyes were glazed, dull, as if there were a coating of dust across them. At Lot's howl he shook his head, clearing it of sleep. His hand stroked the filthy ticking of his mattress, almost caressing it. A rat, disturbed, sat up just beyond Sam's hand and *eek*ed at him. Sam's hand shot out and caught it by the neck. He stood and advanced on the guards.

"Get us some food," he said quite distinctly, although his eyes were enough to unnerve the guards. He held out the rat, ignoring the cocked pistols. "Get us some food, or the next time you come in here, we'll feed you this rat."

"We have guns," the guard threatened.

"That's true," Sam allowed, "and you might shoot me. But there are a lot of us, so you're still going to eat the rat."

The poi the guards brought within the hour was stale, and the meat was barely edible, but like starving dogs the men in the cell fell on the food. The guards watched stolidly throughout. When the poi and meat were gone, six armed lawmen stationed themselves around Lot Lane's mattress as if he were either a royal personage to be guarded or a dark magician who might turn the night to some subversive use.

Lot purposely tossed and raved all night and left the guards as unstrung as possible. Sam kept the rat in his pocket and began to tame it, watching the guards to gauge the effect. A different kind of war had now begun.

Liliuokalani's hand shook over the document: "After full and free consultation with my personal friends and legal advisers . . ."

There had been no consultation, only the bald statement from the PGs that the queen and six of the imprisoned rebel leaders were to be shot for treason. The authorities had left her to think about that for three days, and then they had reappeared with an abdication decree. Should she sign it, they told her, then everyone who had been arrested, herself included, would be released immediately. There would be no need, they said, for anything so drastic as firing squads. She could save all the Royalists by her abdication. They assured her of this very earnestly, and a number of PG lawyers appeared to help her to her decision and congratulate her on her wisdom.

"How shall I sign it?" she whispered.

"Liliuokalani Dominis," a lawyer answered.

That seemed no more real than the rest of the proceedings. Liliuokalani was the title by which she had been proclaimed queen. Dominis was her married name. She had been Lydia Dominis with her beloved John, never Liliuokalani. None of it made sense, she thought, grappling with this discrepancy. She felt a petulant urge to argue with them about it, then shrugged and put the pen to the paper. It didn't matter. *Liliuokalani Dominis*.

Eyes overflowing with tears of sympathy, the lawyer took her hand in both of his.

"Crocodile tears!" said a lady-in-waiting as the door closed behind him.

The following morning, the government, having obtained the queen's abdication, announced that it would try all imprisoned rebels—plus any more that it could get its hands on—and seek the death penalty for six: Seward, Gulick, Rickard, Walker, Wilcox, and Sam Brentwood. Despite the lawyers' promises to the queen, haoles who had gone against their own kind were not going to be forgiven.

Foreign journalists, in flocks nearly as thick as the foreign diplomats, descended on the islands, as they had for the revolution that had overthrown the queen two years before. Everyone had some stake in the outcome of these volcanic islands' latest eruption.

Tim Holt, owner/editor of the San Francisco *Clarion*, appeared among the reporters, checked in at the Hawaiian Hotel, and then went to make a nuisance of himself at the Honolulu jail. Now he sat in the office of the attorney general.

"'Military Tribunal of the Republic,'" Tim said, nodding, taking notes. "That's what it's calling itself? Doesn't sound much like a republic to me."

"We didn't ask what you thought of it, Mr. Holt," the attorney general said. "What precisely do you want here at the prison?"

"I want to see my cousin," Tim said. "Embarrassing to have your relatives in jail." He didn't appear embarrassed. His clean-shaven, handsome face bore a broad grin, and his felt hat was set at a jaunty angle. His white duck traveling suit looked as if he had slept in it, which he had.

The attorney general shrugged. "It's not allowed."

"I see. 'Prisoners are allowed no visitors, including family members,'" he murmured as he jotted it down in his notebook.

"Damn it. Prisoners aren't allowed to talk to reporters."

"*Mmm-hmmm*. 'Government worried about allowing prisoners to speak to foreign press.' Understandable. The American government's very interested just now in how these people are being treated. I believe Hawaii is still hoping for annexation, isn't it? Did I mention that my father is a senator?"

The attorney general glared at him. "All right, all right! But you can only see him for half an hour."

Tim stood in the doorway of Sam's cell and blinked. The stench was so bad that it made his eyes water. He supposed the men inside must have gotten used to it. "Magnificent accommodations," he said sarcastically to the jailer who had brought him. "Almost the Waldorf."

The jailer gave him a disinterested glance. "Bang on the door when you're ready to leave. I'll let you out—if I'm around."

The pupil's of Tim's eyes dilated in the gloom until he could see Sam sitting on a disgusting piece of mattress ticking in the far corner. He had what looked like a rat in his lap. Tim went over and sat down gingerly, wishing he hadn't worn white trousers.

"How are you holding up?"

"I'm taming a rat," Sam said. He put it in his pocket. He didn't seem surprised to see Tim. His face looked odd, Tim thought, all sharp planes and angles. He was thin and unshaven, and his hands and face were filthy. His dark hair was plastered to his face. The rat was cleaner than he was. It was a wonder Sam didn't have typhoid, Tim thought, furious.

"Is there anything I can do for you?"

"Go see Annie," Sam said.

"I will. I'm catching the boat tonight."

"She's been here, but she can't leave the farm that much. There's no one else to run it."

"How's she managing?"

"God knows. She doesn't know sugarcane from bamboo. If they don't hang me, I'll have lost my shirt by the time I get out of here."

"I gather shooting is what they're planning," Tim said. "Firing squad for traitors and all that. How the *hell* did you get into this?"

"I got mad," Sam said. "The PGs just got to be too much."

"Well, there's enormous pressure on them not to be vengeful," Tim said. "The American and British ministers have been haunting the PG Government House."

"Nasty place," Sam said. The rat stuck its head in Sam's hand, and he scratched its ears. "You here for the trial?"

"Yep."

"I thought you owned the business. Sat around on your butt in your offices and smoked big black cigars."

"I can't afford the cigars if I sit on my butt." Not to mention the fact that the only reporter available to send had been Hugo Ware, and since Tim had fallen in love with Hugo's wife, he had been reluctant to send Hugo as far away as the corner grocery store. Tim didn't quite trust himself, and every time he had found himself alone with Rosebay Ware, his instincts had proved well-founded. "Besides, I picked up some kind of ailment or other," he said, alluding to this difficulty only in slant-wise fashion. "I thought I might shake it off out here."

"Tropical paradise," Sam murmured.

Tim looked around the filthy room. The Hawaiians regarded him curiously but didn't interrupt. Sam was the only haole in the room. "What are you doing in here? I thought they had all the ringleaders in isolation."

"I wouldn't go," Sam said.

"You had a choice?"

"Not exactly. But I make them nervous for some reason."

Tim could understand why. There was an expression in Sam's eyes that Tim had never seen before. Sam reminded Tim of some newly invented machine that might blow up, shattering itself into oblivion.

"I don't suppose you brought any food?" Sam asked.

"I didn't think," Tim said, stricken. "What're they feeding you?"

"Hardtack and coffee unless we make a fuss. A fuss only works about once a week."

"Jesus." No wonder Sam looked on the edge of madness. "I'll bring you something. A lot," he said, regarding the ring of dark eyes watching him. Tim reached into his coat pocket and found half a bar of chocolate. "Eat this now. All of it. There isn't much, and if you share it, it won't do anyone any good." He sat and watched to be sure Sam ate it.

The rat stuck its head out again. Sam gave it a morsel and ate the rest.

"I'll bring you some fruit. And clean water. And meat. I'll make sure it gets here."

Sam's grin was as fleeting as it was sardonic. "Get us some poi," he said. "You don't get scurvy if you eat poi."

VI

New York, January 1895

Janessa Lawrence laid the newspaper in her lap. "I can't imagine Sam Brentwood having any convictions at all, much less the courage of them," she said, bemused, to her husband. "But apparently he's neck deep in this. And the *Tribune*'s picked up Tim's story," she added. "That's a compliment, isn't it?"

"Absolutely," Charley confirmed. "West Coast newspapers are viewed with scorn by the *Trib*. If it's picking up your brother's pieces, the *Trib* is impressed." He peeled off his coat and hung it on the back of a chair. The shirt underneath was rumpled and stained. He stretched luxuriously, and a button popped off. Charley made a dive for it before Janessa could get up. "Lord, I'm tired," he said, dropping the button into a candy dish. "How are you holding up?"

"Okay. I hemmed sheets for the nursery today." Janessa got up anyway and transferred the button to a wicker sewing basket. "I'll never remember what you did with it if you leave it there. I put new shelf paper in the kitchen and polished all the brass on the icebox. Oh, and I organized the bookcases." She glanced at the glass-fronted shelves by the parlor fire. "All the novels are on the bottom shelf now, with the medical books above them so I won't have to bend to get them."

"Splendid," Charley murmured.

Janessa stood, hands on hips, and looked around the

96

parlor as if in search of something else to do. "Do you think we ought to reupholster all the chairs?"

Charley jumped. "God forbid," he said. Every time he came home, Janessa had moved something else or changed its color. He liked the chairs the way they were.

"Maybe just slipcovers . . ." Janessa murmured.

Charley didn't answer. He thought she was talking to herself anyway. Warily he eyed her thickening waist. The baby was due in three months, and Janessa, in enforced idleness, was about as relaxed as a hyena. Dr. McCallum, the head of the Marine Hospital Service in which Janessa, like Charley, was a commissioned officer, flatly refused to allow her to practice. As a consequence, Janessa had gone from the rigors of epidemic fieldwork to a tea-cozy domesticity, and it did not agree with her. She was making the best of it by refurbishing their rented house, throwing herself into the work with the same energy she had given to medicine. Once past the first three months, when she had slept all the time, Janessa seemed to have boundless energy. She read *Harper's* and the *Ladies' Home Journal* and met Charley at the door with bolts of material and plans to stencil the parlor walls.

Charley hung his uniform cap on the coat tree. "Couldn't you just sit down for a few minutes?" he asked. He was bone tired.

"You sit down," Janessa said. "I'm not the one who's exhausted. Why can't you sit down unless I do?"

"Because you're pregnant. I feel as if I ought to be rubbing your feet or something."

"I don't want my feet rubbed," Janessa muttered. "I want to be working. Sit down, blast you. You look like a fresh corpse."

"Thank you, dear."

"You're entirely welcome."

He watched Janessa pace over to the hall-tree mirror and peer into it. Physically, pregnancy agreed with her. Her light brown hair had developed more sheen than it usually had, and her complexion glowed a pinker shade. At the moment the Holt family characteristics in her appeared to be superseding any resemblance to her Cherokee mother, so that she looked . . . well . . . *fluffy* was the only word Charley could think of. She had never looked fluffy before. But the broody-hen image vanished as soon as she began to pace again, and a fluffy wolf was not a restful creature to live with.

Janessa turned sideways and studied her reflection. "I never should have told McCallum I was pregnant. He'd never have guessed."

"He'd know," Charley said. Her profile wasn't exactly gargantuan, but it was not the shape it had been, either in the bust or the waist. McCallum was no fool. "You know you can't take a chance of catching something," Charley said wearily. "There's no telling what those people are carrying."

"Well, tell me about it," Janessa said, settling back in her chair. "Tell me about a nice disease." She tossed the newspaper to the floor.

"You don't seem unduly worried about poor old Sam," Charley commented.

"I'm worried about him for Annie and Eden's sake," Janessa said. "And for his, too, I suppose, the feckless idiot. But I can't do anything about it. And right now I feel like I'm in jail, too. Charley, I'm so lonesome."

Her blue eyes spilled over with sudden tears, and Charley pushed his irritation and weariness away. Janessa never cried. "All right. You *are* desperate, aren't you?"

Charley searched his mind for something to tell her. He had requested a hitch as an immigration doctor at Ellis Island rather than being sent out on assignment and leaving Janessa alone. The misery he saw there daily made him long for fieldwork again. He didn't want to tell her that.

"I delivered a baby by myself today," he said, grinning. "To a Polish lady who startled everyone with it. She was pretty hefty to begin with and dressed in layers like one of those round wooden dolls. When she suddenly doubled over, Hotchkiss called me to help, and he and I went through layer after layer of skirts and shawls

and petticoats just trying to find bare skin. By the time
we finally got down to flesh and realized what was going
on, it was too late to move her. She had a boy right there
on the registry room floor. The people in line kept trying
to move around her, and we kept pushing them back.
Her husband was terrified of losing his place in the
queue. I think he was afraid we'd send him back to
Poland if he did, poor devil."

"Mike wants to go down there with you one day,"
Janessa said. "He's in New York on some business for
Mr. Edison. I invited him to dinner so he could talk to
you about it."

Charley just barely managed not to groan. The last
thing he wanted tonight was company, and the last thing
he wanted to talk to anyone about was Ellis Island.

"He wants to make a moving picture of the immigrants coming through."

"They're not a raree-show, Janessa. These are people."

"He's not making a kinetoscope strip," she explained. "He's got this notion to make a moving picture
that tells a story, like a pantomime. In any case, he's
been reading the newspapers, and he's frantic about
Eden's safety. He telephoned me from some warehouse
to ask if I had heard any news from Tim. I told him I was
sure that the fighting was confined to Honolulu and
pretty much over now, anyway. That soothed him a bit,
but he sounded as if he needed his hand held."

And Janessa hadn't seen her younger brother in
months, Charley thought. Anyway, she was starved for
company. It would have been horribly rude not to invite
Mike. Charley heaved himself out of the chair.

"I'll go wash, then."

Maybe that would wake him up enough to get some
work done before dinner. On his desk in his and
Janessa's bedroom lay the notebooks from two yellow-
fever epidemics. He stared at his scribbling nightly,
convinced that if he stared long enough he could extract
some answers from them.

Charley had willingly withdrawn from field research

to examine the flood of humanity that poured daily through the three-year-old immigration station on Ellis Island. It was the practical solution to impending parenthood, not only for himself but for Janessa as well, once the child was born. But he couldn't force himself to find any satisfaction in the work. He hadn't joined the Marine Hospital Service to screen terrified peasants for pinkeye, he thought sourly. Epidemiology was to have been his life's work, and Janessa's. It was what they took their satisfaction in: Janessa, in the act of stemming the tide of the disease, of containing the beast before it devoured more victims; Charley, in the knowledge gained, the research that might ultimately neutralize the disease, erase it. It had been knowledge dearly bought sometimes. He had caught yellow fever and nearly died two years before in North Carolina.

But as a result he was immune to "yellow jack" and therefore the ideal doctor to send to each fresh outbreak. *So here I am,* he thought as he stripped off his shirt and collar and poured water in the basin on the washstand. *Putting chalk marks on men's coats as they go by, as if they were cattle. This one fit for admittance. This one suspected of hoof-and-mouth disease. I might as well be a veterinarian.*

Charley washed his face, slicked down his hair—his cowlick declined to conform to the prevailing fashion—and inspected himself in the mirror. He had gray eyes, a wide and mobile mouth, and ears that he had always thought stuck out too far. All in all, though, he had always been reasonably satisfied with his appearance. Just now, however, he seemed to be ossifying, growing sleek but unbendable. Beneath his dissatisfaction with his work, under the boredom and the depression, he knew that his was a comfortable job. He went off in the morning; he came home at night. No one shook him awake in a panic in the middle of the night; no one's survival depended upon his medical skill. On the other hand, there was never any end, any victory.

"We didn't think this thing through, you know that?" he told the mirrored face. Once the baby was old enough to be left behind with a nanny or with family, could Janessa and he go back to fieldwork? Was his current depression due to the suspicion that they might not? That once the baby was born, they would have no right to risk their lives?

The idea that *he* might go back in the field and leave Janessa to pursue a safe, domestic practice in pediatrics—professionally as well as maternally—crossed his mind, then was pushed away. When they married he had assured her that his ideas of fatherhood were not defined by the convention of giving the baby over to its mother's sole care.

Besides, despite the fact that Janessa seemed to have turned her restless energies to a form of nest building, she would hate a humdrum, comfortable practice as much as he would. "We could wear spats and be swells," she had once put it, with a disdainful sniff for a former medical acquaintance who was doing just that.

Charley stepped out of his uniform trousers and, clad in long johns, hurriedly inspected the contents of the oak wardrobe. It was as cold as the devil in January, and the coal fire in the potbellied stove in the parlor did little to heat the bedroom. If they did decide to wear spats and become swells, they would be able to afford a better house, of course.

Charley used to wonder if financial security was important to Janessa. She had lived the first years of her life in poverty with her mother, but her father, Toby, had money. He wasn't exactly rolling in it, but the Holts were a power in Portland, Oregon. Since Toby had been elected senator, however, he had managed to annoy nearly everyone who contrived to put him up for election. Charley chuckled and fished a pair of tweed trousers off a hanger. No one could accuse Toby Holt of being a party man. It was very doubtful that he would be able to hang on to his Senate seat. Unfortunately, senators in Oregon were elected by the state legislature and not by popular vote.

The Holt children were currently outraged about his probable defeat, but as far as Charley could tell, their reaction had nothing to do with losing whatever social status they derived from their father's being a senator; instead, their indignation was based on his not being properly appreciated.

None of the Holts had seemed inclined to rest on their father's money. Janessa had let Toby pay her way through medical school, but any support had ended there. Tim had made a newspaperman of himself after a short-lived attempt to get rich by digging silver in the played-out Comstock Lode. Mike, who was chosen to inherit the Madrona, the home ranch in Portland because of his supposed frail health, had rebelled and gone to work for Thomas Edison, for a salary approximately equal to the lunch money he had been allotted in school. Now everyone was hopeful that Sally, the only child left at home, would marry a country boy who wanted to ranch. But Sally showed every sign of developing into a Washington princess, and the family was expending considerable energy trying to squelch those pretensions. The Madrona had been founded by Toby's father, Whip, who had led the first wagon train over the Rockies to Oregon. It was utterly unthinkable to everyone that the ranch should pass out of the family. The only trouble was that nobody seemed to want to live on it.

Charley had the uneasy suspicion that Toby was keeping his fingers crossed that once the baby was born, Janessa would want to settle down to a practice in Portland. She was pushing thirty-four, no spring chicken for a first baby, as the females in the family kept pointing out. She would want to rest, they predicted.

The hell she would, Charley thought, buttoning a clean shirt.

The door knocker thumped in the hall, and Charley abandoned this line of speculation. He had been over it in his mind many times before. What it boiled down to was that Janessa and he didn't know what they were going to do, and they were both afraid to admit it.

He knotted his necktie and, with only a wistful glance at the yellow-fever notebooks, went back into the parlor. Mike was sitting glumly on the settee. Noises from the kitchen announced that Janessa was doing something to dinner. Mike stood and shook Charley's hand, and they inspected each other.

"You don't look too chipper," Charley said.

"I have spent the day," Mike informed him, "arguing with a Japanese gentleman who was largely unintelligible to me. The bill he submitted for three tubs of bamboo was a lot more than Mr. Edison had bargained for. Now I have to baby-sit for the bamboo and get the tubs on the train back to Orange. It's a new strain, which Mr. Edison has decided will make better filaments than the variety in use now." Mike made a face indicating his total disinterest in bamboo filaments of any variety. "He's planning to plant it at his winter house in Florida, and *I*, O joy, get to make sure it doesn't die of the cold between now and then. The tubs are sitting in your hallway," he added, "with my suitcase."

Janessa, wooden spoon in one hand and an apron tied over her dress, stuck her head around the door from the kitchen. "Mike's going to Florida next week. To— where is it?"

"Fort Myers," Mike said morosely. "As far as I can tell from the other fellows' descriptions, it's in the middle of a swamp and accessible only by barge—once a week."

"What does that do to your moving-picture project?" Charley asked him.

"Plays merry hell with it," Mike replied.

"Come tell us about it in the kitchen," Janessa said. "I want Charley to look at the chicken. I don't know what I think about it."

Mike went to peer into the oven. "I think it's a chicken," he judged.

"I think it needs another fifteen minutes," Charley said, "if that's what you're asking."

"It is," Janessa said, giving her brother a squelching glance.

"Still can't cook, huh?" Mike asked her, unrepentant.

The men sat down at the kitchen table, and Janessa put a kettle to boil on the stove. The stove, a cast-iron monster that took up one-third of the room, gave the kitchen a cheerful warmth. The copper pans that had been a wedding present hung from a circular rack above it, and glass-fronted shelves held a set of blue-willow china. Janessa lifted the lid off a pot of applesauce, and the smell of cinnamon mingled with the scent of roasting chicken.

"It so happens," she said haughtily, "that I have learned to cook."

"I like kitchens," Mike said, settling contentedly at the table. "I'd like to do a whole film in just a kitchen— move the camera around past all the boxes and jars and pans, watch someone's hands making a pie."

"What kind of progress are you making with Edison?" Charley poured a cup of tea out of the pot that Janessa had set on the table.

Mike shook his head. "Nothing consistent. He keeps interrupting me with new projects. I just get into a picture, get it all set up, and—*bang*—he's thought up an idea for making an electric toasting rack or an electric storage battery or electric bed socks for all I know, and I'm set to working on that. I can't figure him out."

"He's a very famous man," Janessa mused, staring into her tea. "Maybe he thinks moving pictures are frivolous."

"Maybe," Mike allowed.

Charley reached for the whiskey decanter that sat on the kitchen counter and poured a dollop in his tea. "We need frivolity," he declared. "It's a necessary component of life—certain puritans' opinions to the contrary. Are you old enough for whiskey in your tea?"

"I'm eighteen," Mike answered. "That's old enough if my sister isn't looking."

"I'm not looking," Janessa murmured. "If you're old enough to run away from home and give everyone fits, I suppose you're old enough to drink alcohol."

"Thank you very much. I'll probably be a rum-soaked disgrace by the time I get back from Florida," Mike informed her gloomily. "It doesn't sound as if there's anything else to do but get drunk. I don't know why the old man insists on going down there. Mrs. Edison probably thinks it will keep him from working so hard. All very well for Mrs. Edison—she has her husband for company. The rest of us are stranded. He's agreed to let me build a studio to make pictures in, though," he added, brightening.

"That sounds as if he's interested," Janessa said.

"Either that, or he doesn't want me to quit just when he's got me trained. Laboratory assistants who are intelligent enough to meet his standards but stupid enough to put up with him aren't all that easy to come by. Is that chicken done yet? I didn't eat lunch. Maybe whiskey and tea aren't the best hors d'oeuvres."

"Certainly not," Janessa said. She got a pair of pot holders and took the roasting pan out of the oven. "Let's eat in here, since we're family."

After removing a stack of newspapers to the floor, Charley and Mike set the kitchen table, while Janessa produced a pot of peas and carrots from the back of the stove and then ladled applesauce into a dish. They joined hands and bowed their heads. "Lord, make us thankful for our blessings," Janessa said. She sounded as if she was trying to be.

It had been an odd year for all of them, Charley thought. Nobody had achieved exactly what they wanted, but they all had what they had *thought* they wanted: he and Janessa were set on having a baby; Mike had been determined to go to work for Edison. Even Janessa's brother Tim had something under his skin that his family hadn't been able to nose out yet—although not for lack of trying. It was odd, Charley thought, how annoyed he, Janessa, and Tim all were when life didn't work out properly, considering that they were all old enough to know that it never did. Mike was at the point of discovering that now.

"I can't figure out if Mr. Edison really believes there's no practical use for a motion-picture camera," Mike was saying, "or if he just doesn't want me to be the one to develop it. Maybe he's saving it for when *he* has the time."

"Hard to say," Charley murmured, listening with one ear to the dogs barking outside in the street and to the high, shrill voices of children playing. What would it be like to have children?

"But I've got to stick with him until I've learned everything I can. No one else has the equipment. I've got to be able to support Eden. If I don't find out what's going on in Hawaii, I'll go crazy. Why don't we have a Pacific cable? There's been an Atlantic one for thirty years."

"Because very few people feel the same urgency about knowing what's going on in the Hawaiian islands as they do about what's going on in Europe."

There was another outburst of barking in the street, louder this time. Charley got up and went toward the front of the house. Before he could look out the parlor window, someone banged on the door. Charley pivoted to answer it, ducking through a cloud of bamboo. A telegraph boy stood on the porch. He wore his Western Union cap at a jaunty angle, and his bicycle leaned against a telephone pole.

"Janessa Lawrence?"

"That's my wife." Charley held out his hand.

"Two of them," the boy said, then waited expectantly.

"But you only made one trip," Charley said, digging into his pocket. He gave the messenger half again the normal tip anyway, then went inside with the envelopes. He felt some trepidation.

"Never talk about telegrams," he told the two in the kitchen. "It makes them come home to roost." He handed the envelopes to Janessa and watched somberly over her shoulder while she opened them. Telegrams were generally not good news.

"Oh, Charley . . ." Her eyes spilled over with tears. "It's from Gran. Dr. Martin died. The funeral's at the end of this week."

Charley laid his hand on her shoulder. "I'm sorry, darling."

She leaned her head back against him and let the

tears flow. "He was my first friend. When I came to Portland he let me tag around with him on his rounds. He trained me to assist him before I ever went to medical school."

"Over the protests of the hospital, as I recall," Charley said. "He was an amazing old man."

"I remember him," Mike said. "The last time I saw him was at Dad's election victory party. Mrs. Martin was pushing the doctor in a bath chair, but he was alert. He would have been nearly a hundred this year, wouldn't he?"

"Ninety-seven," Janessa said. "Charley, I want to go to the funeral."

"Not on your life." Charley stopped rubbing her shoulders and came around to the other side of the table, where he could look her in the eyes. "No."

"It's not right not to go." Janessa picked up her fork and poked at her chicken with it. "I owe it to his wife."

"Your grandmother will take good care of Mrs. Martin. They go back together a lot longer than you do," Charley said. The Martins had been part of that first wagon train, on which Janessa's grandmother Eulalia had met her grandfather Whip Holt.

"But what will people say if I don't go? I don't want to seem disrespectful."

"No one will expect a woman who is six months pregnant to travel across the country," Charley said gruffly. "Janessa, I'll tie you to the bedstead if you even think about it."

Janessa's eyes flashed. "I'd like to see you try."

"You will," Charley said as he sat down.

Embarrassed, Mike went on with his dinner. He had never seen Janessa and Charley argue before, and it unsettled him.

Janessa and Charley glared at each other across the applesauce. "I'm the one who's pregnant," she said.

"I'm the one who'll be left alone if you miscarry and die," Charley retorted.

"What's in the other telegram?" Mike asked.

"I forgot it!" Janessa ripped the envelope open. "This is from Gran, too."

"That's getting to be an expensive habit," Charley said. "And if she's asking you to come home, I'll have a thing or two to say to—"

"Oh, no!" Janessa fixed a furious gaze on Charley. "Dad lost the election! Those back-stabbing low-life *politicians* elected Ephraim Bender!"

"What?" Mike sat upright in his chair, fork gripped in his right hand as if he were going to use it on the interloper. "That *crook?*"

"As I recall," Charley offered, "no one could prove he was a crook."

"Well, Dan Schumann's in jail for his part in Bender's scheme," Janessa retorted. "So tell me how that matches up with his *not* being a crook."

"Oh, he's a crook, all right. I just said nobody could prove it in court. So officially he's *not* a crook."

"He's a land-grabbing, swindling, opportunistic son of a bitch," Mike said.

"Watch your language, Michael," Janessa said automatically, but her heart wasn't in it. "I can't believe Dad lost. That's what comes of being an honest man." She was incensed.

"It might have come from your father's conscience," Charley said, putting in his oar on the side of practicality. "Supporting that Federal Elections Bill didn't make him popular."

The bill had been designed to ensure the vote for the Negroes in the South. As a side effect it would also have given the same right to the Chinese in Portland. Prevailing sentiment there had held that Negroes, of whom there weren't many in Portland, should have their rights protected, but the Chinese were another matter. As a southerner, Charley took a certain sardonic amusement in that.

"It's also what comes of running up against a snake like Ephraim Bender," Mike said, still frothing. "He and Schumann took advantage of Gran. They tried to swindle a helpless old woman and then make it look as if she'd been a willing partner."

"Your grandmother's about as helpless as a mountain lion," Charley said.

"Well, Schumann did manage to get her power of attorney," Janessa said. "Just to have her name linked to something like that makes some stupid people think she must have been part of it. Gran's convinced she created a scandal that hurt Dad politically. The last time she wrote she said that Cora and Dora Langley had somehow gotten hold of the idea that Gran had been a defendant instead of a witness at Dan Schumann's trial. They were surprised to see her in church."

"Being under the impression that she was in jail?" Mike chuckled. "Cora and Dora Langley have about enough brains between them to make a jaybird fly crooked. Cora and Dora Langley are why no one will give women the vote."

"Michael Holt, if you want to start counting imbeciles we know, you'll find just as many men," Janessa seethed from between clenched jaws.

"Sorry. Thoughtless remark." Mike backed off quickly. He had been raised in a suffragist household, and he knew when he had put his foot in it. "I just meant no one pays any attention to the misses Langley."

"Gran thinks people do," Janessa said. "She's bound to be blaming herself for Dad's defeat."

"A waste of energy," Charley said gently. "And so is getting in a rage over the election. Your father's known since his first year in office that he might not get reelected. He conducted his affairs in exactly the way he warned his backers he was going to. He voted for what he thought was right, and he probably expected his party to be angry that he didn't support their special interests." As a politician, Toby Holt was something of a miracle. It was also a miracle he hadn't been lynched.

Janessa stabbed her fork into her applesauce with a force more appropriate to a side of beef. The sauce splattered the tablecloth, and embarrassed, she put her fork down. "Sorry," she said curtly.

Mike looked at Charley and raised an eyebrow. Charley gave Mike a look back that said plainly that any remarks about pregnancy and nerves would be most inadvisable. All the same, Charley thought that Janessa's irritation stemmed from more than her father's defeat or even her desire to go back to Portland and pay her last respects to Robert Martin. Being cooped up in the house was the real issue; it was more than she could bear. Charley took a bite of his own dinner and wondered sympathetically how long *he* would be able to stand it, if in the same position.

Washington D.C.

"Well, Alex, I'm afraid that's it." Toby Holt looked at his own telegram and crumpled it slowly.

"And we aren't entirely surprised," Alexandra said placidly. She was seated at the breakfast table of their big rented house on Connecticut Avenue. Alexandra would turn forty this year, but so far her red hair, pinned up in a knot, contained no more gray than could be removed with careful scrutiny and a pair of tweezers.

Toby sat opposite her and smiled ruefully. "No, I suppose we aren't." Toby was nearly fifty-four, and his sandy hair had considerable gray in it. He was clean shaven again; to his wife's relief the fashion for handlebar mustaches had passed. He was dressed in striped pants and a morning coat, preparatory to taking his seat on a committee called to consider the possibility of a revolution in Cuba and what the United States might do about it.

"Is it a little soon to start packing?" Alexandra inquired.

"*Packing?*" An outraged wail erupted behind them. Sally, aged eleven, appeared, framed in the doorway.

"Dear—"

"Father has lost the election! I had a premonition!"

Sally cast her eyes heavenward in a tragic pose that resembled Bernadette of Lourdes.

"Dear—"

"I shall die!" She looked, however, unlikely to succumb at the moment. With her rose-gold curls and delicate complexion Sally appeared ethereal. Behind her looks, however, lurked a core of steel also found in Janessa. "We'll have to go back to Portland!"

"You were brought up in Portland, young lady," Alexandra said with asperity. "Furthermore, you had an excellent time."

"That was when I was a baby," Sally said scornfully.

Toby polished his spectacles on his napkin. He put them on and regarded his younger daughter. "Plenty of legislators do not bring their families with them to Washington," he informed her, "to avoid the effect of unwholesome influences. Turning into a snob is among those."

Sally sniffed. "I am not a snob. But there's nothing to *do* in Portland. Alice feels the same way every time her parents drag her back to Oyster Bay." Sally folded her arms across her chest and stuck her chin out. "When we're grown, we're going to make our come outs in Washington."

"You're a little premature," Alexandra said dryly. "And it is my opinion that Alice Roosevelt has been premature all her life. That child is a menace. Why are you two in such a hurry to grow up?"

"Because it's boring being eleven." Sally struck another pose. "I shall waste away before I'm fifteen for lack of intellectual stimulation."

"I wouldn't let her read *Arabian Nights*," Alexandra explained to Toby. "The Burton version."

Toby's eyes widened. "I should think not," he agreed. "Young lady—"

Alexandra laughed and held up a hand before Toby could argue. "When you're sixteen, darling." There was a popular myth that only gentlemen scholars read Sir Richard's wicked literal translation. "You can read Kipling for now," she told a pouting Sally. "He's quite as romantic and not nearly so, er, frank."

"Kipling," Toby said. "That's the ticket." He thought that Alex was laughing at him gently, and he flushed. He was not a prude, but he had the same urge that his father had had—to protect just a shade too much the women he loved.

"And you can stop the fuss you're making over this election," Alexandra told Sally. "We haven't left Washington yet, and it is reasonably likely that we won't have to, if I read your father correctly."

"What do you mean? Daddy, can we really stay?" Sally flung herself at Toby.

"You're kissing the wrong man," Toby said. "You'll have to go kiss President Cleveland if you want to know right now. But he has said that he wants me in Washington."

"I believe a presidential appointment has been discussed," Alex said. "But you're not to pry, Sally. You'll be told when we know."

"What kind of appointment?" Sally demanded, ignoring this instruction.

"We don't know," they said together.

"Get your schoolbooks," Alexandra told her.

"You'll be late," Toby added.

When the front door banged behind her a few minutes later, Toby and Alexandra looked at each other.

"Maybe we should devise a code," Toby suggested wryly.

"Or simply not communicate at all when she's in the house," her mother said. "She'll spill the beans if she finds out."

"Worse yet, she'll spill them to Alice," Toby said. "Theodore has no idea of the things I know about him that Alice has told Sally." He laughed. "Theodore says that as a team, Sally and Alice probably constitute a secret weapon. But I particularly don't want to get into an argument with him just now about my appointment to the State Department. I'm supposed to act as a restraining influence—that's why the President wants to stuff me into the State Department over Olney's protests."

"Whom are you supposed to restrain besides Richard Olney?" Alexandra inquired. "For a former U.S. attorney general, that man has the tact of a buffalo. I don't know why the President made him secretary of state."

"Well, I *am* supposed to put a leash on Olney," Toby conceded. "And keep an eye on public opinion. That's why I'm concerned about Theodore. He would just love a nice war. I like Theodore immensely, but he's a hothead."

"A nice war where?" Alexandra asked.

"Pretty much anywhere," Toby replied. "In Cuba, if American planters over there don't stop supplying the *insurrectos* with money. The word we're getting from Cuba is that a revolution is pretty much inevitable now. And we'd better think twice before we get involved."

"The way we thought twice before we got involved in Hawaii?" Alexandra asked.

"That's the point. Our *citizens*, the damn fools, got involved in revolution in Hawaii, but our government hasn't. Where there are financial interests involved—which is the case with American planters in Cuba as well as in Hawaii—I doubt if there's any way to prevent the citizens from pursuing whatever course they think is profitable. My interest is seeing that the government doesn't follow their lead. The price of sugar is not a sufficient reason for war. Or for getting in the middle of someone else's war."

Alexandra sighed. "I expect Sam Brentwood may have come around to your way of thinking by now. Toby, isn't there anything you can do for that poor man? Mike is frantic."

Toby shook his head grimly. "Not a thing."

VII

Eden stared dully at her birthday cake. It was a wonderful cake, covered with pink-icing roses, but there wasn't much of a celebration. The Royalists and the Downtown party no longer mingled socially; none of her friends whose fathers were PG men were allowed to see her anymore. Besides, Sam was in jail, and his trial would be coming up in two days. You couldn't have a party when your brother was about to be sentenced to be shot. His execution was regarded as inevitable by those in the know.

Nonetheless Annie had insisted on a small gathering to mark Eden's eighteenth birthday. In the hope of giving the gathering an air of festivity, Annie had invited Theresa Wilcox and the wives of two other imprisoned Royalists. These latter two wore black as if their husbands had already been executed, but Theresa defiantly wore a scarlet hibiscus in her hair. Dickie Merrill, who was still in residence and showed no signs of going away, and Tim Holt were the sole male guests at a table full of women who might soon be widows.

In better times there would have been a coming-out ball. Eden would have worn a glorious new dress, and Sam would have been her partner for her first official waltz as a grown-up. Then all the planters' sons would have danced with her. Feeling guilty for her disappointment when Sam was in such trouble, Eden reminded herself that she wouldn't have cared for a grand party all

114

that much because Mike couldn't have been there, either.

Dickie Merrill had bought her a book of Mrs. Browning's poetry, although Eden had steadfastly refused to show any interest in him.

Davy, the Hawaiian houseboy, came in with a burning taper to light the candles on the cake, and everyone at the table *ooh*ed and *aah*ed.

"Blow them out, darling," Annie said, and Eden did.

Her grandmother put a hand on hers. "Everyone feels melancholy, dear, but let us try to celebrate the things we have to be happy for."

Davy cut the cake and put a big slice on Eden's plate. "You eat that now, Miss Eden." Davy most likely didn't consider that she had enough flesh on her yet. Hawaiians liked their women plump.

"Thank you, Davy."

He served the other slices deftly, then retired to the sideboard where a cheerful *pop* announced the opening of the champagne.

Dickie fetched a mandolin from a chair by the wall and produced a creditable "Happy Birthday" on it, accompanied by the quavering sopranos of the Royalist wives and Theresa Wilcox's alto bellow. Claudia sang enthusiastically with the rest of them, but Eden thought she looked frail, and midway through the last lines her voice faded into a thread.

"Are you all right, Gran?" Eden whispered.

"I'm just tired, honey." Claudia shook her head at Davy when he came around with the champagne bottle.

"I'll have some," Theresa Wilcox announced, and lifted her glass. "A toast: Confusion to the enemy, and bad luck to the military tribunal. Disgraceful, the way they're trying free citizens." Her husband had already been sentenced to death and a ten-thousand-dollar fine, although, as Theresa remarked acidly, one precluded the other. The only hope for salvation lay in the British and American ministers who attended every day of the trials and made it known that if any executions were carried out, drastic measures might be taken by their respective governments. No one knew how much good that would do if Lorrin Thurston's faction in the provisional government overcame the more moderate element headed by President Sanford Dole.

"To a happy outcome," Tim said solemnly, raising his glass. "And to Mrs. Wilcox, who is a tiger." He smiled at Eden, and she thought she detected a hint of suspicion under his carefully composed expression.

Eden smiled back at him with as guileless a look as she could manage and wondered if his being Mike's brother gave him special powers to read her mind. While the older ladies complimented her on her beauty and poise—all the things that one always told debutantes—her thoughts wandered between Sam and what was going to happen to him, and Mike and the need to be with him. The urge to see him was so strong that she felt it was pulling her almost physically from the islands.

She hadn't seen Mike for a long time. Sometimes she had nightmares that he no longer loved her, and then she would get out his hoarded letters and read them by candlelight to reassure herself that he did. She had been planning to go to him as soon as she was eighteen, but in two days the tribunal was going to sentence Sam to be shot, so how could she leave Hawaii? And how could she be so heartless as to *want* to leave, as to think that she couldn't do him or Annie any good by staying?

Two tears rolled down, one on either side of her nose, and Claudia touched her hand again. "Don't cry, sweetheart. We'll pray every night for Sam."

Eden gave a choking sob and guiltily turned away from Claudia. *I'm a beast*, she thought. *I'm a selfish beast*.

Two days later Sam came to trial. Seward, Gulick, Rickard, Walker, and Wilcox had already been convicted and given the identical penalty. Prince Kuhio, a relative of the queen's, had declared himself guilty and been sentenced to a year in prison and a thousand-dollar fine.

The venerable Anglo-Hawaiian John A. Cummins, who had known nothing of the plot, was sentenced to five thousand dollars and five years' hard labor. In view of his age it was obvious that he wouldn't survive the sentence, so his friends were allowed to purchase his freedom for twice his fine. The six Lane brothers, tried with a group of twenty-five Hawaiians to demonstrate the PGs' contempt for them, got five years' labor. The brothers were brought to trial half-starved and filthy, and rumors flew that they, along with Robert Wilcox, had been tortured in an effort to pry confessions from them.

Sam would have provided the truth about the prisoners' treatment, had Tim been permitted to see him again. After Tim's visit, Sam had been dragged from the cell, hands tied, and dropped into a wooden tank, which the jailers had filled with ice water. He had gritted his teeth, shivered, howled, and complained but confessed nothing, except to call the jailer a name so vile that the man had to be restrained by his fellows from diving into the tank to retaliate.

Sam had given up stoicism when he discovered that if he shivered, the cold was somewhat less painful than if he didn't. The authorities left him in the tank all day, and he passed the time reciting multiplication tables to himself. He was afraid to get numb enough to fall to sleep; that was how people froze to death. He supposed that if he died by mistake, Annie and Tim would make a big stink; but Sam was afraid that his jailers were stupid enough to let him die anyway.

When the horrible grinding pain went clear to his bones and caused him to forget the numbers—and he had run out of names to call his tormentors—Sam started on limericks of the filthiest kind, altered to include the jailers and their female relatives.

Toward nightfall his mind began to drift again, not outward as it had on the Pali, but backward, to an old nightmare. His father, Andrew, had drowned at sea, in the icy waters of the North Atlantic. Sam's stepmother, Lydia, had thrown herself overboard, and Andrew had gone after her—though how willingly, Sam had never been sure. Lydia had been a burden to Andrew for years. Her body had been found, but Andrew's was never recovered. Although that tragedy had occurred more than three years before, Sam still awakened sometimes with phantom waves breaking over his head, and his father's pale face, as translucent and smooth as ice, gleaming just beneath the water.

Now Sam began to see his father again, floating just beyond his own naked legs in the icy waters of the wooden tub. Andrew's dark hair spread out like kelp from his face, and his eyes were strangely white.

Those are pearls that were his eyes . . . Sam thought, then blinked his own eyes, trying to force the hallucination back beneath the water or up into the air to dissipate. But it wouldn't go away. Instead, the apparition seemed to be trying, mouth agape, to speak to him.

"Go away!" Sam whispered. He rocked back and forth, trying once more to loosen the swollen ropes that tied his wrists behind him.

The face made no sound. The mouth closed, but the eyes did not.

Outside in the dusk, church bells began to strike five o'clock. The sound reverberated in the dark, stone-walled chamber and pounded inside Sam's head. He began to hear faint voices. The face in the water opened its mouth again, but the sound came from above him, in the darkening air. *Sea nymphs hourly ring his knell: Hark! Now I hear them—ding-dong bell*. . . . Sam's head fell forward on his chest, and he began to slip beneath the water.

A pair of hands grabbed Sam Brentwood's shoulders. "Jeez, you were supposed to be watching him, weren't you?"

"It's not my fault. I looked at him not ten minutes back. He was right enough then."

"Well, he's gone and fainted now."

"I can't help that. He was awake ten minutes ago. Called me names and tried to spit at me."

"He can't talk if he's passed out, can he?"

They dragged him, naked, dripping, and unconscious, out of the tub and down the prison corridor, then dumped him on the straw mat in his cell. . . .

Sam woke up when the tame rat came out of its hole and nosed him. He was alone because Lot Lane and the other prisoners had been transferred to "the reef," the prison farm built atop a coral ridge on the city's outskirts. He sat up and wrapped himself in a dirty blanket, which was the only cover he could find.

An hour later the jailers came in and, finding him awake, tried to beat out of him what the ice water had failed to produce.

"Go to hell," Sam told them, and tucked his head into his arms and grunted when a booted foot slammed into his ribs.

It seemed impossible to him to become conciliatory now, although he could have confessed his own guilt without implicating anyone else who had not already been tried. A confession would not have materially changed his sentence, but it would have stopped the beatings. Or, he predicted, it would have stopped the beatings for an hour or two, and then, convinced now that compliance *could* be beaten out of him, the guards would have been at him again, to force him to implicate people wholesale. It wasn't worth the respite, he decided as the boot crashed into his ribs again and a truncheon came down on his wrists where they were laced across the top of his skull. He bit his tongue and spat blood.

In the morning his jailers brought back his tattered clothes and took him to his trial. The garments were filthy and smelly, but Sam put them on without complaint because the worse he looked, the louder the foreign journalists would howl with outrage. All the captured rebels were aware that the only factions that might save them were the foreign journalists and the foreign ministers.

In the court, the former throne room of the Iolani Palace, the military tribunal gave the proceedings the air of a court martial. The Military Tribunal of the Republic did not provide or allow any lawyers for the defense. The accused were on their own. The judge and prosecutor were in uniform, and military guards were stationed in all the doorways. The trappings of royalty–the chair of state and the feather kahilis–had been removed, replaced by a long teakwood judge's bench and rows of chairs for spectators. Members of all races living in the islands, except Hawaiians, were in the audience. Sam could see Annie and Eden, ashen and motionless in the back row, next to Dickie. Tim sat with the journalists. *Where is Gran?* Sam wondered, concerned.

"Samuel Brentwood, you stand accused of treason." The prosecutor glanced with scorn at Sam's ragged figure. "Where did you get the weapons for this traitorous revolt?"

"Off a banana tree."

"You would do well to comply with our wishes."

"I'm not going to tell you anything except that I fought for the queen," Sam snarled. "It happens to be her throne room you're barking and scratching in."

"It may interest you to know that that woman has been sentenced to five years' imprisonment at hard labor."

"That ought to ensure notoriety for these islands," Sam responded. He looked pointedly at the row of foreign journalists. "Worldwide."

"Your opinions are not wanted!" the prosecutor snapped. "We want to know where you got the guns."

"And people in hell want ice water." Sam grinned crookedly. "I, on the other hand, have had plenty of that–not to mention other attentions." He quickly rolled up his sleeves, past the livid purple bruises and dark scabs. The foreign journalists craned forward, furiously taking notes.

"Get him out of here!" the prosecutor shouted. He turned to the judge. "Your honor, the Republic of Hawaii requests the death penalty for this treasonous rebel."

* * *

The family council that night was hushed. Upstairs Claudia could hear their voices faintly through the open window beside her bed:

"There's no saying they'll carry it out," Tim stated. "They haven't shot anybody yet."

"I'm afraid they'll do it just for spite," Annie told him. "They're so revengeful, and Sam was a Downtown man to begin with. He changed his allegiance to please me."

"Now don't you go taking the credit for Sam's change of conscience," Tim said. "That was Sam's decision, and he's entitled to have us treat his loyalties as genuine. Anyway, no one's responsible for what someone else does."

Eden was with them, Claudia knew. The poor child was silent and probably terrified. There was no telling where Dickie Merrill was, but Claudia assumed he was trying to lure Koana out into the concealment of the cane field. Only the fact that Eden was absolutely uninterested in him kept Claudia from complete outrage over Dickie's simultaneous sexual pursuit of Koana and courtship of Eden. Dickie had maintained that he couldn't possibly go home now while his friend's fate hung in the balance. *Oh, Sam . . .*

Claudia closed her eyes. Annie hadn't allowed her to go to the trial, maintaining that the trip and the strain were beyond her strength. She supposed that was true, but here, in the big four-poster bed with the sheets pulled up to her chin, she felt weaker than ever. For the first time in years, she thought of Gil Humphries, her first husband. He had been a drunkard and relatively spineless, but still it had been a shock to her when he drank himself to death. Her beloved had been the first Samuel Brentwood, Andrew's father and young Sam's grandfather. After he died, she had stayed a widow for nearly two decades before she made a late-life marriage to Howard Locke. Now Howard was gone, too. Three times widowed, her only son drowned. So many dead! And now perhaps Sam's hours were dwindling.

The others had tried to hide the news from her when they came home. But after one look at their faces, she had known, even without asking. So she had demanded the verdict, and they confessed and then put her to bed with a cup of camomile tea to help her sleep. Young Sam was her heart's darling, her favorite of all of them, from his wild, rebellious babyhood through all the scrapes and wickedness.

The entire family knew that. No one, not even Eden, begrudged it to him. It was as if everyone acknowledged that he had to have some champion, some protector who believed in him, despite his best efforts at self-destruction.

Now? Now he had finally grown up. He had done the right thing. But he was going to die for it.

Claudia turned her face to the wall, away from the voices filtering up through the window. She closed her eyes and in the darkness thought she could see her Samuel. And Howard, standing a little away, because really she was her beloved Samuel's. And Gil . . . was that Gil? She couldn't remember his face, but maybe she should try, in case she should meet him in heaven. And Andrew, her son, Andrew, hers and Sam's. She couldn't quite see Andrew. Someone was there—was it young Sam?

In her sleep she reached out, but he stepped away from her, moving quickly, receding into some light. But her true love, her soul's mate, Samuel was there in a shimmering light, and he smiled and held his hands out to her.

"Miss Annie! Miss Annie, come quick!" Koana's bare feet flew down the hall, silent on the Chinese runner. "It's Miz Locke!"

Annie threw her door open and ran, tying her wrapper around her as she went. "Get the doctor, Koana!" Behind her she could hear Eden's door opening, then footsteps from the guest room down the hall where Tim Holt was staying.

The sunlight slanting through the lace curtains at

Claudia's window gave her still face a glow that almost made Annie think it was still inhabited. But when she touched the frail hand, it was as cool as marble. Its heavy sapphire slipped sideways on the finger.

"*Gran!*" Eden flung herself at the bed and stiffened when she felt the cold skin. "Oh, Gran!" She burst into sobs and buried her face in Claudia's nightdress.

"Eden, darling." Annie put her arms around her. "Oh, darling, darling, I'm so sorry."

Eden looked up, her face blotchy and slick with tears. "She's gone," she hiccuped. She touched her grandmother again. "There's nobody *there!*"

Dickie Merrill, apparently awakened by the noise, had wandered down the hall. When he met Tim, he retired discreetly to his room.

Soon the doctor arrived, and he offered a sedative to Eden, which she rejected, and what comfort he could.

"Her heart just gave out, I'm afraid. She was—how old? Eighty-five? Eighty-six? And she's been under a tremendous strain." He coughed tactfully, attempting to steer his condolences clear of politics.

"We should have kept the news from her," Annie said sadly.

"You couldn't," Tim told her. He held out his arms, and Annie and Eden both clung to him. He looked over their heads, thinking it ironic that these women should find comfort in him when he himself felt so rootless. "I'll stay until after the funeral," he said, feeling helpless.

They buried Claudia in a pouring rain in the first grave of the Brentwood family plot. Her final resting place was on a shaded slope above the coffee groves, where wild creepers climbed the trunks of a stand of young sandalwood trees. Sandalwood had once covered all the islands, but long ago it had been logged off. The fact that Sam had planted these made Annie feel better about Claudia's resting under them. But the thought that immediately followed—that Sam might rest here, too, and within the week—caused her legs to wobble.

Annie and Eden, in muslins dyed a dingy black, stood beneath black umbrellas while Tim and the circuit riding preacher—the real one—lowered the coffin into the wet earth. Dickie Merrill held the umbrellas over their heads while they sang Claudia's favorite hymn. The farmhands, particularly the Hawaiians, lifted their voices melodiously.

> "Amazing grace, how sweet the sound,
> That saved a wretch like me. . . ."

Koana sniffled into her handkerchief, and Annie looked at her with empathy. No one knew what had happened to Hoakina, Koana's cousin. Annie had tried without success to get information about his fate from the PG police.

> "I once was lost, but now am found,
> Was blind, but now I see. . . ."

Eden wept silently. *Poor thing*, Annie thought. The girl didn't see why her grandmother had to die, and she couldn't find any justice in the world.

Annie wept as silently as Eden, but with far more bitterness. While Eden railed against fate, Annie had a direct object to her anger: the PGs. The strain of Sam's sentence was responsible for Claudia's death–that and nothing else. Through her misery Annie wondered, *What is going to happen to us?*

She began to wonder in earnest the next day when Christo, the Portuguese luna who had been second in command to Hoakina, came to her with the planting and crushing schedules for the year. Annie stared uncomprehending at the calendar pages with their neatly squared boxes and indecipherable notations.

"Christo, I just don't know."

The luna wiped his wrinkled brow. His soft straw hat was folded under one arm. "I'll tell you right now, I can't cook sugar, Miz Brentwood. Hoakina, now, he had a good hand for the sugar kettle. And I can't manage all these men unless they think they got a boss that'll know when they're dogging it."

"But I don't even know what they're supposed to be doing in the first place," Annie admitted. She flushed. Feminine conventions about what was man's work had not kept her from getting involved in the workings of Aloha Malihini; it was her determination that Sam would have to make a go of this venture on his own. Those had been her terms for coming back to him: This farm would succeed or not on the virtue of his sweat, his money, his sense of responsibility. Now she would gladly put her own money into it, but that wouldn't help—unless she could buy knowledge.

"We'll have to hire an overseer," Annie decided. "Someone trustworthy who knows the business."

Christo gave her the look he reserved for fools. "Miz Brentwood, you're lucky to have the men you got. Half of 'em are so scared, they're only here because they're too petrified to leave. They're afraid the PGs gonna get 'em."

The bogeyman, Annie thought ruefully. Ghosts in the night. Well, they had a right to be afraid. The PGs arrested whomever they felt like these days, with no regard for proof or even a definite accusation.

"Ain't no sugar man gonna go to work for you, Miz Brentwood," Christo said flatly. "Not anyone from around here. You might get someone from off the islands, though."

And whom did she know who could put her in contact with a competent foreman? Annie wondered wearily. There was Niall Tevis, Sam's factor in Honolulu. But Niall was a government man down to his socks. He was probably busy trying to appear as if he'd never had any business dealings at all with Sam Brentwood. Tim Holt might try to hire her someone when he went home, but Tim wouldn't know a competent sugar man when he met one any better than she would.

"Christo, I just don't know," she said again. "For now go with what's on the calendars and try to keep the men in line. I'll do my best to find a boss."

"Yes, ma'am." Christo went out, unfolding his hat, then pulling it down over his dark curls, and leaving her sitting in the plantation office in the gathering dusk.

Annie put her chin in her hands and stared out the door as Christo's receding figure faded into the sea of cane. She needed a miracle, and it had been her experience that miracles did not drop out of the sky when she called for them.

The home camp crew, cane knives over their shoulders or dangling from thongs, was coming up the twilit road. Christo joined them, and soon the barracks windows flowered into light. The shadows swiftly covered the road, and then, out of the shadows, whistling, came Annie's miracle.

He was forty-three, and his body had a look of having been used hard. His walk carried the rolling gait of a cowboy or a sailor, but was overlaid with the slight limp of arthritis and the wear and tear that a man comes by on the road. He looked as if he had been habitually as loose in his skin as a cat, and age was only now beginning to change that. His shoulders were broad and muscular, his waist thickening just a little. His feet were shod in heavy black boots, and he had on corduroy trousers, tucked into the boots. He wore a blue cotton shirt, collarless and open at the neck, under a black leather vest. His hair was the color of dark terra-cotta salted with gray, and a wide-brimmed hat of sweat-stained leather sat back on his head. His eyes were blue, nearly as dark as the shirt. He carried a canvas seabag, and he was whistling "Who's the Pretty Girl Milkin' the Cow?"

Annie peered into the twilight. His face was in shadow, so she slid her hand into the desk drawer where she kept a pistol. She crooked her finger around the trigger as the whistling stopped and the man loomed just outside the doorway.

"Who are you?" she demanded. "What do you want here?"

"I'm a ghost out of your past, Annie Malone." The man chuckled and stepped through the door, eyeing the pistol. "Now don't you go and shoot me."

"*Dallas? Dallas McCall?*" Annie dropped the pistol on the desk. She stared at him. "Is it really—it is!" Eyes alight, she flew around the desk, then hurled herself at him. He staggered back, laughing, against the door frame. "How did you know I was here? What are you *doing* here?" After hugging him again, she stepped back to let him get his breath.

He grinned at her. "You're looking fine, Annie Laurie, that's for sure. Time's treated you good."

"That's because I don't drink like a fish and spend all my nights in a whorehouse," Annie said. "Unless you're going to tell me that you've reformed."

"Hell, no. Reform ain't no fun." He grabbed her around the waist and swung her up in the air with a howl of delight. "Yow! It's good to see you." He set her down and looked at her. "That's a hell of an ugly dress, though."

Annie smoothed the front of her black muslin. "My husband's grandmother just died. She was a fine old lady. It seemed right to wear mourning for a while. How did you find me?"

"I ran into Vina Perkins in Tonopah. She keeps a boardinghouse there. She said you'd up and married a swell and moved here. I figured that big old house you had in Virginia City would get lonely one of these days. I'd of danced at your wedding if I'd of known about it."

"I'd have invited you if I'd known where you were. What have you been doing?"

"Well, a little of this, a little of that. I never got rich off the silver—not like you and Joe did. But I got a bit put away. I work when I need to. I was punching cows outside Tonopah when I ran into Vina." He sobered. "I heard on the ferry comin' over here that your husband is mixed up in the rebellion and revolution."

"They're threatening to shoot him," Annie said. Her eyes filled. "I'm at my wits' end, Dallas."

"I guess you might be," he said solemnly. "Then it's

a good thing I came visiting. If you have enough other things on your mind you might let me in without shooting me."

"Hell, that's water under the bridge." Annie closed the office door, then linked her arm through his. "You come on up to the house. I'm glad to see you."

She led him through the twilight and up the steps of the veranda. Dallas inhaled. "This is the best-smelling place I ever was in."

"It's paradise," Annie said. "It never gets cold, and it doesn't ever get too awful hot. And anything will grow here. We grow our own coffee, and strawberries year round."

Dallas chuckled. "If it's as good as all that, it's a wonder you don't have friends sponging off you year round, too. 'Course I got a little something to offer to pay my way."

"Now, Dallas, you know you don't need to—" Annie had opened the front door, and she broke off as Dallas whistled admiringly. Dickie Merrill was adjusting his cravat in the entrance-hall mirror.

"I'll be!" Dallas said in awe. "It's a genu-wine silk-tufted, silver-backed dude. You don't see a real one very often."

Annie laughed. "Now, Dallas, you be nice."

As Dickie Merrill took notice of Dallas, his nostrils flared delicately.

"How do," said Dallas.

"Dallas, this is my husband's friend Richard Merrill. Dickie, this is my old friend Dallas McCall."

Dickie extended his hand to shake, but with the appearance of someone about to grasp a cactus. "How do you do? I fear you have come at an awkward time."

"Reckon you ought to know," Dallas observed, "bein' as *you're* here. You help out on the place much?"

Dickie raised his eyebrows.

"Gentleman farmer," Dallas said, nodding in recognition. "Gin and lime on the veranda."

"And what exactly is your line of work, Mr. McCall?" Dickie demanded.

"Well now, that's hard to say," Dallas allowed. "I been a fair amount of things. Kind of got me a wandering foot, you know? But I put in a couple years down by New Orleans once. Me and sugarcane are old buddies."

VIII

"Honey, you are in trouble," Dallas said to Annie the next morning. "Do you mean to tell me you don't know *anything* about cane?"

"I know as much about sugarcane as I do about mink farming," Annie confessed. "And don't you look at me like that, Dallas McCall. I had my reasons."

"What kind of fellow *is* Brentwood anyway? Have you up and married yourself a peppermint drop like that fellow I met last night?"

"Certainly not," Annie said. "And lay off Dickie, will you? It's enough of a trial just having him here."

They were lingering over breakfast, just the two of them. Koana's melodious laughter trilled from upstairs.

Dallas grinned. "I betcha. Keeps the housemaid entertained for you, though, don't he?"

"He's a friend of Sam's from New York," Annie said, as if that explained everything. "I think Sam was starting to get fed up with him, too, but he wouldn't admit it."

Dallas calculated Dickie Merrill's apparent age and applied it to Sam. "Robbed the cradle, didn't you, Annie Laurie?"

"Yes," Annie said. "You got anything against that?"

"Not me." Dallas chuckled. "I like an enterprising woman."

Annie laughed. She never had been able to stay mad at Dallas long enough to work up a good fight—except, of course, the last time she'd seen him. And that reminded her. . . . "While we're on the subject of cradle robbing—"

Dallas threw up his hands. "Not me, not if you mean your little sister-in-law. I swear. I may not have mended my wicked ways, but there comes a time in a man's life when an eighteen-year-old starts to look a damn sight too much like someone who might be his kid."

"Well, you just keep that in mind. I've got a long memory."

Dallas got up, pulled his chair next to Annie's, and threw an arm around her shoulders. "I thought that was water under the bridge."

"It is." Annie rested her head on his shoulder for a moment, enjoying the solid feel of his being there. "You just tell me about sugarcane."

"Well, come on out then, and we'll take a look at it together." He wiped his mouth on his napkin, then stood up and stretched, arms out, joints cracking a little. "You got a mighty good cook. I like that lemon sauce on those eggs."

"It's called hollandaise," Annie said. "Cook is very good with sauces."

"I remember when the only sauce *you* knew about was red-eye gravy," Dallas said. "You've been studyin' to come up in the world?"

Annie put her hands on her hips. "And just what are you referring to? The fact that *I* got rich? You could have, too, if you'd have spent more time digging rock and less time spending what you got. Besides, my being rich didn't bother you the last time I saw you!"

"Last time I saw you, you wasn't trying to talk like a schoolmarm, neither," Dallas said.

Annie sighed. "I try, but it doesn't take when I get around you. You stick around too long, and I'm going to get to sounding like a railroad man's brat who didn't get but through third grade. And after I took such trouble not to."

"How come?" Dallas demanded.

"Because Sam's family and friends would all have snooted me or laughed behind my back," Annie explained. "All but the nicest ones, and *they'd* have been embarrassed by me. Eden can't have a sister-in-law that talks common. And I *like* knowing what to say and do and how to pick clothes that don't look tacky. I *liked* going to Washington and hobnobbing with senators. So there."

"Good for you, then," Dallas replied mildly. "Now come on and show me this old cane."

After Annie changed into a riding habit, she and Dallas walked to the stables. Dallas, dismissing the stable boy's efforts to help him, saddled a pair of horses. Annie and he mounted and turned down the road past the home camp. The sun was out now, brilliantly butter colored in an aquamarine sky. Shreds of ragged, white-gauze clouds drifted by. The air was heavy with water, and the cane shot up through it in verdant exuberance.

"Damnedest thing I ever saw," Dallas said, shaking his head in wonder as they passed from a mature cane field, where the field hands were setting a backfire preparatory to burning the field itself, to a crop of half-grown cane, then another field just beginning to ratoon, and finally a fourth, also nearly mature. "It gets full-grown here, don't it? Down in Louisiana, it never gets but about three-fourths ripe. Then winter comes along, and the weather gets cold, so if you don't cut the stuff, she rots. This is somethin' else entirely." He drew rein beside a mature stand of cane taller than his head and, not having a cane knife, pulled his penknife from his pocket and sawed off a length. He peeled it and stuck a piece in his mouth. "*Mmmm*. Mercy!" He offered a piece to Annie.

She took it and followed his example.

"I'll tell you the first thing about cane." Dallas spat the chewed fibers on the ground. "You can't predict it nohow. You can't put it on a schedule. It just laughs up its old sleeve at you. So you gotta baby-sit it. You gotta come out here every blessed day and talk to it and taste a bite and see how the tassels look and how the leaves feel. And then you just gotta close your eyes and blind guess. It's an art. I spent two years learnin' it as assistant overseer down by Bayou Teche."

Annie cocked her head at him thoughtfully. "When was that?"

"Not too long after I left Virginia City. Hell, Annie Laurie, I had to hide out somewhere."

Annie laughed. The sound was as melodious as Koana's laugh, and it rippled through the cane. She had a feeling of time flowing, running away like water; but with Dallas the stream stood still, cool and familiar enough to wade in.

"My dear fellow, we have to shoot somebody." Lorrin Thurston placed his fingertips together in a little steeple and rested his elbows on his desk. "It is necessary to show that we are masters of the situation."

Albert Willis, the American minister to Hawaii, leaned back in his chair, an elaborate affair of tufted red leather, brass studded. "There are ways to spell it out other than with bullets," Willis observed. "Thank you, I believe I will have some more sherry. This is excellent." Neither his appreciation for the government's sherry nor his Kentucky drawl served to soften his ultimatum. "Bullets are mighty permanent. You shoot somebody, he tends to stay shot. You can't go dig him up again."

"We have no intention of reneging on our decisions," Thurston said stiffly.

"Well," Willis said, "I'd think twice about that. Little bitty island republics such as Hawaii are awfully inviting—kind of like an hors d'oeuvre out there in the ocean, waiting for some big fish to swim by. A Russian fish or maybe a Japanese one. . . ." Willis sipped his sherry and studied the flame-colored trumpet flowers outside Thurston's office window.

Thurston cleared his throat. "We have hoped, of course, for a favorable reception in the States to our proposal for annexation."

"I'm instructed to tell you," Willis said flatly, "that it will be a cold day in hell before the United States annexes the Hawaiian islands if the Hawaiian government executes any of its prisoners." He set his sherry glass on Thurston's desk and watched impassively as

Thurston refilled it. He seemed to have a head as hard as a cannonball for liquor.

"We've already commuted Mrs. Dominis's sentence from hard labor to incarceration within Iolani Palace," Thurston pointed out.

"So I should hope." Willis cracked a smile for the first time. "Not even the most inept among you could fail to envision the international reaction if you set an old lady to breaking up rocks."

"When I was in Washington, I gave President Cleveland my personal assurance that I would do my best to comply with his wishes," Thurston said. "And so we've released that pernicious and degenerate woman from a portion of her sentence. Personally, I wish we had deported her. These Hawaiians are like children. They'll never be capable of a decent society so long as she remains among them."

Willis raised his eyebrows.

"Heathenism lies just under the surface with these people," Thurston explained. "They revert as easily as savages. That woman permitted heathen idolatry and orgies within the palace."

"Spare me," said Willis dryly. "She's an old Christian lady who goes to church on Sunday and knits mufflers for the lepers on Molokai. You couldn't make charges of heathenism stick if you used glue. Now let us get to practicalities."

Thurston glared at him. Albert Willis was as stubborn as a pig, he thought. "I'll take your advice to President Dole," Thurston said.

Willis smiled benignly. "You do that."

Tim Holt brought the news to Annie. "Sam's been given life in prison. The PGs have commuted all sentences." His clothes were salt stained and rumpled. He dropped his satchel on the floor and balanced his hat on top of it.

Annie let out a long breath and closed her eyes momentarily. Then she sat up straight and beckoned Tim to a place at the dinner table. "We have a plate for you. We hoped you'd come back here tonight."

"I nearly didn't," Tim said. "I'm beat, and the Hawaiian Hotel looked mighty good. But I wanted to give you the news." He sat down and began piling his plate with everything in sight.

"Sam will be all right now, won't he?" Eden asked. "They won't shoot him?"

"No, but he's been sentenced to hard labor," Tim answered. "They haven't transferred him to the reef yet, but it's just a matter of time, unless Willis can put more pressure on the government."

Annie set down her fork. How long before a sentence at hard labor would kill a man? she wondered.

"Disgraceful," Dickie Merrill said. "The United States government should be protecting its citizens."

Tim, who had been glued to the front steps of the Iolani Hale, the Government House, the day before and hadn't eaten since breakfast, went on wolfing his food and didn't answer.

"Protecting them how?" Dallas inquired. He had been out in the cane fields all day, getting the laborers back on track, but he had had a chance to eat his fill by now. "You can't just lay down your napkin and lift your little finger and say 'Waiter! Go call the marines to squash these folks.' Not when you're dealing with a foreign government, you can't."

Dickie sniffed. "You can make fun of me if you wish—"

"No one," Annie said firmly, "is making fun of you. *Are* you, fellas? Tim, there's another plate of chops on the sideboard. You don't need to chase down the last cold, gristly slice out of that one."

"Thanks, Annie." Tim grinned his thanks, then got up and helped himself to a fresh chop and, for good measure, another portion of everything else that was there.

"But can't President Cleveland do something?" Eden asked him.

"He can listen to public opinion, honey," Tim said.

"When it gets loud enough, he can swat these boys with legislation instead of bayonets. Works a lot better anyway."

"People in the States are getting pretty riled up," Dallas observed.

Tim chuckled. "It's worse since the damn fools here exiled a bunch of their culprits. The Ashford brothers showed up in San Francisco and gave interviews about a 'reign of terror.' And Arthur Peterson, poor devil, got there just in time to die of pneumonia as a result of being stuck in a tank of ice water. That looked terrible in the papers, I promise you."

"They did that to Sam," Eden said, paling. "Do you think he's all right?"

"Sam's younger than Peterson, and stronger and more bullheaded," Tim said. "All those things help." He didn't say that they wouldn't help indefinitely, not if his captors got too vengeful. There was no use worrying the girl any more than she was already.

"Have you seen him?" Annie asked. "They won't let me in."

"Nor me," Tim said. "But I'm working on it."

Koana, who had come to clear the dirty plates, gave a muffled sob at that. "My cousin Hoakina," she said dolefully. "We have not heard of him at all."

"Our foreman," Annie explained. "I can't even find out where he's in jail."

"Let me try." Tim laid his hand across his plate, still piled with peas, yams, and gravy, and said to Koana, "No, darling, I'll just hang on to this for a while. You can bring me dessert anyway, though."

"Yes, sir." Koana looked at Tim speculatively, and Annie thought, *Oh no, not again.*

When Koana had gone into the kitchen, Annie hissed at Tim, "Don't you dare!"

Tim shook his head and laughed. "Not to worry. I've got enough woman troubles already. Koana looks far too dangerous for my blood."

"She doesn't mean to," Annie said. "It just happens. One of her beaux tried to kill another one with a cane knife." She glanced at Dickie out of the corner of her eye and caught him blanching. She was gratified.

"Femme fatale," Tim said, grinning. "Literally. But I'll see if I can't dig up some information about her cousin."

Eden looked from Annie to Dallas to Tim, apparently realizing that they were all enjoying themselves poking fun at Dickie Merrill even when they were simultaneously worrying about Sam. How could they? She stood up, threw down her napkin, and startled them when she asked, "How can you·be having *fun* when Gran's dead and Sam's in prison?"

"Unfortunately, sitting around like a bunch of buzzards won't do much for either Sam or your grandmother," Tim said quietly.

Eden glared at him. "You're just like the rest of the family! I thought you might be different!" She spun on her heel and fled upstairs.

"She's overwrought," Annie said. "It's all been very hard on her."

"Hell, nobody takes any offense," Dallas said. He grinned at Tim. "And what makes you such a disappointment to her? Why were you supposed to be different?"

"I'm related to my half brother, Michael," Tim explained, "who is a finer, nobler soul, and in all ways a paragon, and with whom Eden is desperately in love."

Dickie Merrill glared at him.

Dallas nodded. "And she thought some of his finer sensibilities might have rubbed off on you."

"It'll never happen, my being in the newspaper business," Tim said cheerfully. A pair of double doors opened out of the dining room and into the entrance hall. Out of the corner of his eye he could see Eden's feet behind the banister at the top of the stairs. "Eden's awfully young." He pitched his voice to carry, feeling avuncular and full of his twenty-eight years. "But she's no fool. It'll dawn on her pretty soon that airs and vapors and languishing aren't required to mourn someone. And that a cheerful nature and attention to the matters at hand are of a lot more use to the living."

Koana came in with a crème caramel custard for dessert. "Miss Eden isn't feeling well," Tim told Koana. "But Mr. McCall and I will be happy to take care of her dessert for you."

Eden's boots and ruffled hem at the top of the stairs vanished.

In her room Eden flung herself across her bed. She took a few deep breaths and then sat up and unbuttoned her shirtwaist and loosened her stays. They were miserably uncomfortable. Annie had let her have a grown-up corset and allowed her to lace her slim waist more tightly now that she was grown. But she couldn't breathe properly in it, and she certainly couldn't cry in it. No wonder grown ladies fainted all the time.

Her mother, Lydia, used to lace herself as tightly as possible all the time, Eden remembered. She had said it was woman's cross to bear in order to be beautiful and feminine. Eden lay down across the bed again and thought about her mother. If her father could have had a choice, she felt certain he would have preferred to have her mother fat and jolly. That certainly would have been Eden's preference. She remembered her mother as a waiflike, trembling creature, rail thin and ethereal, with huge blue eyes that seemed always to be filling with tears. Lydia had had an unhappy first marriage, and her firstborn child, Franz, had been lost to his paternal relatives in Germany. Then the child had died of scarlet fever. Lydia had never gotten over that. She turned their house into a shrine to the lost boy, and Eden had always been conscious that she was not a sufficient substitute.

Was that what Tim had meant by airs and vapors and languishing? Eternally reminding everyone around her how bereft she was? Eternally making everyone feel guilty just for being happy? Was *that* what she was doing? Eden examined the notion with horror. She decided with as much dispassion as she could muster that she was certainly showing some signs of imitating her mother's behavior. It was such an easy trap to slide into. She had watched her mother's hysteria feed on itself enough times to know that. Eden shuddered. Never again.

What was it Tim had said? "Attention to the matters at hand." Eden managed a smile. If they wanted attention to the matters at hand, they would get it. She got off the bed and rummaged in her writing desk for her bankbook. Most of her money, her inheritance from both parents—and now, she supposed, from Gran—was in a trust administered by Sam; but the bankbook held her personal account, her quarterly allowance and such monetary presents as relatives gave her at Christmas and on her birthday. She had nearly a thousand dollars. Surely more than enough for her purposes, Eden thought.

She sat biting her thumb, trying to figure out what things cost. She had no idea of the cost of travel, but she assumed that the price of tickets to the mainland was well below what she was allowed to spend on dresses every quarter. Of course she couldn't spend all her money on transportation—she would need some to live on. Once she left, Sam would be bound to stop her allowance.

It would have been easier to make plans if she knew where Mike was—in Florida or back in New Jersey. But she had not gotten any letters from him, not since Sam's arrest. Annie suspected that the PGs were opening all the mail addressed to the rebels' households. The only correspondence reliably delivered were the bills. The rest the PGs did not bother to send along.

Naturally she couldn't go anywhere while Sam's fate was still uncertain. But she could lay plans. Eden went to open the doors of her cherry-wood clothespress. All her garments were appropriate to the islands' climate— muslins, linens, and batiste, with evening gowns of wedding-ring silk or taffeta. Even her traveling suit was the lightest Irish linen. Eden sighed. Somehow she would have to contrive serges and flannels and a winter coat.

* * *

In a week Tim had managed, by dint of what he called "wriggling and conniving," to wangle permission for Annie to visit Sam in prison. He still had not yet been sent to the reef. Tim said that was because the government was busy with trying to soothe international public opinion and to talk the United States legislature around to their way of thinking. Tim didn't think there was much chance of that. His father had written from Washington to say he didn't think so, either.

Tim had gradually eased into a slot beside Toby as the one the family consulted when they needed advice, inside information, or just a level head. Annie ragged him about it as she pinned on her hat preparatory to catching the steamer.

"When I met him, mind you," she told Dallas, "he was living in a hole in the ground up the side of Sun Mountain, trying to get rich with one pickax and a sorry mule."

"How did you happen to take up newspapering?" Dallas inquired.

"Got drunk in a poker game and won the damn thing," Tim answered. "Excuse my language, Annie."

"They weren't but babies," Annie said, laughing. "Him and Sam."

"I reckon Virginia City growed you up some," Dallas remarked. "Boomtowns got a way of doing that."

"Virginia City wasn't so much a boomtown by the time we got there," Tim said. "But I had my next paper in Guthrie, right in the middle of the Oklahoma land boom. That did a fair job on me."

"I reckon."

Annie stuck a long silver hat pin through her straw hat. "We'd better go."

Dallas hung back. "I ain't sure this is such a hot idea. Chances are Sam may not take to me."

"We've been over this," Annie said. "It's bad enough I've got to tell him his grandmother's dead, without him having to worry about the farm, too."

"I dunno, Annie Laurie. . . ."

He still didn't know when they got to Honolulu, so he hung back at the prison gate.

"I don't know what you're so worked up about," Annie said. "You're a godsend to me."

"This is Dallas McCall, and he's an old friend and a godsend," she told Sam when the jailer let them into his cell. "He knows sugarcane."

Sam stood up slowly, unfolding himself stiffly from the bare mattress. The stench in the cell was overpowering. His clothes hung on him in rags, and his face was thin and bony, with a taut look. His eyes looked very deep set, as if falling into their sockets. His hands were filthy. He held them out to Annie and then tried to pull away again as she came toward him.

Annie ignored that. "Oh, baby, you look awful." She wrapped her arms around him, dirt and all.

"You'll probably catch something," Sam muttered. "I'm not fit to touch. I'd offer you a chair, but as you see . . ." He gestured at the bare stone floor and walls. His eyes settled on Dallas again. "And who did you say that was?"

"Name's McCall," Dallas said. He ambled forward, inspecting Sam, while Sam inspected him. He held his hand out. They watched each other like a pair of circling dogs, hackles raised, and then shook hands slowly.

"Where'd you come from?" Sam demanded.

"Tonopah, lately," Dallas said. "I used to know Annie Laurie in Virginia City."

"Yeah? How'd you happen to leave?"

"Now, Sam—"

"Ran off with a preacher's daughter," Dallas said. "Might as well give you the truth. Trouble was, she wasn't but thirteen. She told me she was older because she wanted to get quit of her old man. Hell, I wasn't thinking."

"Not with your head," Annie muttered.

Dallas looked as if he were about to retort but thought better of it. "Well, I was just transportation, it turned out. She ditched me for some cowboy in Santa

Fe, but I couldn't rightly go back to Nevada, with her or without her. I tried once, near got shot."

"And now you're running my farm?" Sam inquired.

"He's helping out," Annie said. "Sam, I near went crazy till Dallas showed up. You know I don't know anything about cane, and Dallas worked a couple of years as assistant overseer on a cane farm in New Orleans. And anyway, I've got to have him, so that's that. And you haven't exactly been a choirboy yourself, so you just stop it, and—" Her eyes suddenly overflowed with tears. "Oh, Sam, I got to tell you, I meant to right off, but we got on to—Sam, your gran died. It was peaceful, in her sleep, but we didn't have any way to get you word."

Sam bowed his head and stared at the stone floor. "Oh, Lord," he said finally. "And I didn't even get to see her before—I killed her, Annie, I know it."

Dallas backed off again, toward the door.

"You did not," Annie said. "The PGs killed her if anyone killed her. She died the night after the trial, and I'm not going to try to tell you I don't think that brought it on. The doctor said her heart just stopped." She wiped her eyes. "We buried her up on the terrace where you planted the sandalwood trees—the spot you said would make a good burying ground. Tim was there, and all the hands, and we sang 'Amazing Grace.'"

Sam blew out a long breath. He looked up, not at Annie or Dallas but at the wall, as if he could look through it to something. "How's Eden taking it?"

"Real hard," Annie answered. "She's been a little better the last couple days, though. She's helping out like a trooper in the house. She's ordering all the groceries now, and she's real serious about it, asking me what things ought to cost and all. She helped me pack you a basket." Annie held it out. "Those weasels out there went through all of it, looking for a hacksaw or I don't know what. They made a mess, but it'll still taste good."

"Cardboard would taste good to me now," Sam said. As he took the basket, his hands shook with the effort of not ripping off the cover and wolfing down what was inside then and there.

"We still can't find Hoakina," Annie said. "But Tim's looking for him."

"Time's up, lady." A jailer shoved the cell door open so that it caught Dallas in the shoulder. "You too, bud. Out."

"We just got here," Annie protested.

"Fifteen minutes. Warden's orders."

"Oh, Sam." Annie held him to her. "I'll come back as soon as I can. I'll keep the farm running somehow, I promise. If Dallas can stay awhile, it'll be a blessing."

"Uh-huh," Sam said. He looked at Dallas over her shoulder. "Footloose, is he?"

"Always has been, but he's got a good heart. And he's a good friend."

"Yeah? Who to?" Sam muttered under his breath.

After they had gone, he turned his full attention to the food, stuffing himself with chicken, pie, and mangoes before his thoughts turned back to Dallas McCall. He wiped his greasy hands on the tatters of his pants and then tossed the bones in the corner for the rat. Footloose men had to settle down sometime. And just how good friends had these old friends been? Feeling frustrated and angry, he got up and furiously shook the iron bars on the door.

IX

New York, April 1895

Janessa lay on her back on the parlor settee. Her fingers explored her abdomen. "Charley, where's my stethoscope?"

Charley, knotting his tie, came in from the bedroom. "Will you quit that? You know you aren't supposed to be treating yourself."

"I feel funny," Janessa said.

Charley cocked his head. "You look fine—as big around as a barrel with another month to go, but fine. Funny how?"

"Achy," Janessa said. "Tight across here." She rubbed her stomach. As Charley watched, the baby kicked. He could see the movement plainly through Janessa's dressing gown. "The kid's bouncy today. What do you want with the stethoscope?"

"Just bring it," Janessa said. She rubbed her hand over her abdomen some more.

Charley got the stethoscope from Janessa's bag in the bedroom and started to put it to his own ears.

"Give me that!" She held out her hand.

"I told you you're not—"

"I'm not treating anything," Janessa said, exasperated. "I'm just listening." She pressed the stethoscope to her belly, then wrinkled her brow while Charley fidgeted. Finally she handed it back to him. "Tell me what you hear."

Unnerved, he knelt on the floor to listen. His eyebrows shot up.

Janessa poked him in the shoulder. "You hear it, too, don't you? I think there are two of them."

Charley put the stethoscope down. "Can you feel two heads?"

"I think so, but it's hard to tell. They keep moving—or it does. Or whoever's in there."

Charley put his hands palms down, fingers splayed, on her belly and felt carefully. "I think the chances are good. You're going to go to bed right this minute and stay there! Do you hear me?"

Janessa heaved herself to a sitting position. "I'll go crazy," she said through gritted teeth. "I'll go completely around the bend. You'll come home and find me knitting overcoats for the birdies, like old Mrs. Simpson down the street does. They'll take me away in a closed carriage."

Charley put his hands on the edge of the settee on either side of Janessa's knees so that his face was only a few inches from hers. "Twins are almost always early. They're a drain on the mother. An eight-months child isn't as strong as a full-term one. A thirty-four-year-old primipara mother isn't as strong as a woman in her twenties. A—"

Janessa glared back at him, blue eyes to gray ones. She grunted and clasped her hands across her middle. "You're too late, Charley boy. I think I'm in labor."

"I told you to go lie down!" Charlie wailed.

"I don't think a few minutes would have done much good," Janessa said, teeth gritted as another pain ground its way from her left side to her right.

Charley closed his eyes for a moment. "I've always found hysterical fathers to be ludicrous," he muttered. "God keep me from turning into one." He went into the hallway and cranked the telephone over. After a female voice requested his number, he said, "Get me Dr. Schilling. Two-eight-two."

The voice grew chatty and disappointed. "Oh, now, the doctor got called out half an hour ago. Some poor little mite burned itself with lye. I don't know how parents can be so careless. What on earth *is* the world coming to? I might be able to find him for you, though. He might stop off by the dry-goods store later. His wife was saying he wasn't to forget the washing soda."

"Please." Charley silently blessed the busybodies of the telephone system. "This is Dr. Lawrence. Ask him to come round as soon as he can. My wife's in labor."

"Oh, the poor thing." The voice was all concern. "She's early, isn't she? I had nine, one after the other. Wouldn't do it again for any amount. My husband's dead now, of course."

Charley tried to think of a suitable reply to that, but she rang off to locate Dr. Schilling. Charley called a coworker to say he would not report to Ellis Island, then went back and found Janessa putting a kettle of water on the stove.

"Get into bed!" Charley seethed.

"Hmmph!" Janessa marched to the armoire where she kept the linens and took out an armful of clean sheets. "My mother had me on a cornhusk mattress in a log cabin, with nobody to help but Aunt Walini."

"Your mother was twenty-two!" Charley yelled.

Janessa dropped the sheets and balled her hands into fists. "If you tell me again how old I am, I will hit you with something! I'm a doctor. I studied obstetrics. I know as much about it as you do. More maybe, since you haven't ever managed to have a baby personally."

"Neither have you, yet."

"Well, I'm about to, if you'll just let me alone." Janessa walked across the room, winced, and grabbed the back of a chair for support as another pain started. They were excruciating. They wound from one side to the other and then settled at the base of her spine, making her want to double over. "Men always think they know everything," she said, gasping.

Charley tried to put his arms around her. "Honey, I'm sorry. I just think you ought to be in bed."

"I'll do better standing up for as long as I can. Let gravity do some of the work. *Oowww!*" She wrapped her arms around herself. "Charley, I may forgive you for this pregnancy by next week!"

"Now wait just a minute," Charley said, stung. "Having a baby was your idea, too."

"I am not," Janessa said through clenched jaws, "entirely rational just now. And it was not my idea to have *two* babies."

"Well, if they're fraternal twins, it's your own fault," Charley told her. "Two eggs."

Janessa looked at him balefully. "There must be *some* way to pin this on you. Go away while I think of one."

Charley took a risk and got close enough to stroke her forehead. "Poor dear. Do you want a cold cloth?"

"Nooo!" Janessa wrapped her arms around her middle again and paced into the kitchen, with Charley at her heels. "I want you to quit cosseting me and let me do what I'm supposed to be doing. My mother—"

Since cosseting her was all that Charley could do under the circumstances and since he felt frustrated to be deprived even of that, he lost his temper. "Your mother! I'll get you a cornhusk mattress and a goddamn tepee for the backyard if that's what you want!"

Janessa looked at him frostily. "That won't be necessary."

The whistling teakettle on the stove began to shriek, and Janessa let out a long breath that seemed to steam with the kettle.

Charley gave up the battle. "Then I'll be in the parlor if you need me," he said, and retreated.

In the parlor he nearly bumped into Dr. Schilling, who was shedding his coat and hat. "I rang the bell," he said, "but nobody answered. You two were really going at it."

"We didn't expect you so soon," Charley said, embarrassed. The shrieking kettle was suddenly stifled in the kitchen, and he thought Janessa was listening.

"Luckily I wasn't but a block away," the doctor said. "Sounded to me as if I was in the nick of time, too. Charley, you know better than to try to treat your own family." He grinned broadly. "No man's a god to his wife when she's in labor."

"Hardly ever the rest of the time, either," Charley muttered.

"Sit down. Smoke a cigar. Read the paper. Pretend you're not a doctor." Schilling headed for the kitchen.

Charley waited for an explosion, but it didn't come. He heard a murmur of voices, and once he heard Schilling say, "*You* pretend you're not a doctor, too."

Charley picked up the morning paper, sat down, and tried to concentrate on the *World's* account of Spain's attempts to quell the revolt in Cuba. The *World* was plainly on the side of the insurrectionists. In Charley's opinion, Joseph Pulitzer, the publisher, was making it his campaign to get the United States into a war over it. Feeling irritable, Charley put the paper down and listened, but no sound came from the bedroom into which Dr. Schilling had finally managed to lure Janessa.

Charley discovered that his hands were shaking. What if something happened to Janessa? How would he ever get along without her? She was too much a part of him—partner and lover both. As a sedative he tried to read the *World's* financial column, explaining William Jennings Bryan's proposal for free silver coinage. That served only to infuriate him, and finally he got up and started pacing.

The bedroom door was closed, and there wasn't much else to the house. Charley began to understand why Janessa had felt so enclosed in it. There weren't but a few steps from the kitchen to the parlor, and back the other way to the dining room. A short hall offered doors to Charley and Janessa's bedroom and to the second bedroom, which had been fitted out as a nursery. At the end of the hall were a bathroom and a minuscule cubicle, which would be the nursemaid's bedroom. Janessa had found an Irish girl, a niece of Nurse Eileen Riley's of the Hospital Service. Kathleen was seventeen and accounted not to be the flighty sort.

I suppose we'll need her early now, Charley thought. And maybe another set of everything. He stuck his nose in the nursery doorway. Another crib, another twelve-dozen diapers. And he bet they'd have to pay Kathleen Riley extra to wash all those diapers, too.

"Well?" Janessa demanded. Her nightdress was soaked with sweat, and her hair was plastered in damp waves to her forehead. "Well?"

"It's a girl," Dr. Schilling said, exhibiting a tiny red-faced infant who appeared to be consumed with fury at having been hauled out from where she had been so comfortable.

Schilling held her up, cleaned out her mouth and nose, and encouraged her with a mild smack on the bottom to fill her lungs. The doctor cut the cord and washed the blood from the baby.

"I know it's a girl, Richard," Janessa said impatiently. "I meant, is there another? *Owww!* Mother of God and all the saints! God*damn* it!"

"Stoic, aren't you?" Schilling remarked. "She's got company, just as you thought."

He laid the baby in the clean bassinet, which was ready beside the bed. Then he pressed his hands down on Janessa's belly and felt the new contractions ripple across it. "That's a good-sized baby for a twin," he commented. "No wonder you're experiencing discomfort."

"I am not experiencing discomfort!" Janessa shouted at him. "I am in pain!"

"You've only been in labor for a few hours," Schilling said calmly. "Some women take ten or twelve, or more."

Janessa propped herself up on her elbows. "You try it sometime," she snarled.

"Not my function in the biological scheme. You'll have to address your complaints to God. Push now."

Janessa pushed. "When I get up"—she gasped—"I am going to kill you."

"If you aren't civil, I'll send you a whopping bill. Here it comes. . . . Well, what do you know, one of each. You've got a boy."

Janessa flopped back on the pillow. "Let me see."

The doctor cleaned the baby, then laid him beside his sister. They stared at each other with startled, unfocused eyes.

Richard Schilling left at nightfall, muttering "washing soda" to himself. He obviously had not forgotten the errand for his wife. Janessa, clean and perfumed and with a baby at each breast, received Charley in the bedroom. "I'm embarrassed" was her first remark.

"Does that mean you've decided not to have me castrated?" Charley inquired.

"I won't ever be unsympathetic to a patient again," Janessa said ruefully. "I'm sorry I yelled at you. But that *hurt*."

"You didn't think it was going to?"

Janessa looked at him sideways. "I always figured I was too tough a customer to let labor pains bother me."

"Oh. Bad planning."

"Yep." She sighed with satisfaction. "I'm fine now, though. I love you."

"I love you, too." Charley kissed her. "All three of you. Which is which? I can't tell with their britches on."

"This is Mary Lavinia, and this is Brandon Tobias."

"That ought to keep everyone happy," Charley said. The babies were named for their four grandparents. "Are you sure you don't have a yearning for a Dominic or an Esmerelda?"

"Nope. I suppose we'll have to have another son, though, to name after your stepfather." She sighed happily. "I have a yearning for dinner, though. I'm starving."

"I'm not surprised. I'll bring you something."

"Put Mary Lavinia in her crib. She's full." Janessa put the baby over her shoulder. Mary Lavinia gave an enormous belch and began to snore.

"Dainty," Charley said. He tucked the baby into the bassinet. When he returned, he had Kathleen Riley with him. She had blue eyes in a round face lightly splashed with freckles. She wore a serviceable blue serge skirt, and her brown hair was pinned up under a mud-colored felt hat with a pink rose. She wore a nursemaid's apron and a determined expression. This was her first job.

"Of course I don't mind coming early," she was saying. "To tell the truth, it's a pure pleasure not to be sharing a room with me three sisters, and them always borrowing me things. A room of me own seems like a plain miracle."

Janessa supposed it would. The Rileys had come from Ireland ten years before. Eileen had paid her way through nursing school by scrubbing the floors of the school every evening. Her brother Patrick, Kathleen's father, worked on the elevated railway and supported eight children thereby; but the children were expected to support themselves as soon as they could and send some money home to the family as well.

"We'll have to up your wages a little to compensate for the double work load," Janessa said. She and Charley couldn't really afford the increased wages and expenses if she didn't get back to work, but no woman should be expected to wash two dozen diapers a day on top of housework for a dollar a day—except somebody's wife, of course. Wives did it for free. Janessa would be doing it for free if she stayed home.

Was she unnatural, she wondered, as even her grandmother Eulalia had hinted, in not wanting to stay home? For wanting to go back to practice? Plenty of women who had enough money, she thought grumpily, paid a housekeeper just so they wouldn't have to do everything themselves. That seemed to be all right with society, so long as the women didn't actually go out and earn money. That seemed to be what horrified people.

Janessa grinned wearily at Kathleen. It wouldn't horrify Kathleen. The women in Kathleen's family *all* worked. No one had given them a choice.

The next day Charley bought another set of infant paraphernalia. Janessa got up and washed her hair and spent the rest of the day playing with the babies. The minute Charley wasn't looking, she had checked them over from top to bottom and could find nothing wrong.

She guessed their weight at nearly six pounds apiece—
big for premature babies—and their lungs seemed to be
fully developed, judging by the volume they could
achieve when frustrated. They were obviously fraternal
twins since they were of different sexes, and Janessa
couldn't decide whether they were going to resemble
each other much or not. Mary Lavinia was as bald as an
egg, but Brandon Tobias had enough hair for both.

"Isn't she supposed to have some place to put a
bow?" Charley asked.

"Shame on you, Dr. Lawrence," Kathleen said
indignantly to Charley. "She'll have hair soon enough."

Janessa smiled at the babies dotingly.

By the end of the week, she was pushing them in
their pram.

By the end of the month, still doting, she was
nonetheless restless and bored to tears with the conversation of the other mothers also pushing their prams in
the park.

By the middle of June, to the vociferous shock and
horror of a number of people whose business it wasn't,
she had gone back to work.

Janessa confined her practice to the morning hours,
and Kathleen gave the babies a bottle at lunchtime.
Working part-time was enough, however, for Janessa to
feel she was in the world again—and to give her a taste
of the miseries that Charley had been wading through at
Ellis Island for six months.

An unending stream of the hopeful, the bewildered,
and the terrorized passed by the Marine Hospital Service doctors. The immigrants prayed simply to be unno-
ticed. When they saw Janessa they would smile in
relief—she looked less threatening than did the male
doctors. Then they regarded her with trepidation when
they realized that she was a doctor, too.

The federal government had removed the responsibility of examining immigrants from corrupt state
authorities five years before, when horror stories printed
in Pulitzer's *World* had finally forced a long-overdue
Treasury Department investigation. The new, many-

windowed castle on Ellis Island, with its blue slate roof
and picturesque towers, looked like a modern watering-
place hotel, and it could process five thousand immigrants a day. The capricious corruption of the state-run
Castle Garden had been replaced with the impersonal
and ironclad rules of federal regulation. The enforce-
ment of those rules, however, sometimes held enough
misery to send Janessa home weeping and longing to be
a housewife again.

Her workday began at 5:30 A.M. when the doctors
boarded the Immigration launch to meet any incoming
vessel. Their business was to examine the immigrants for
disease and physical handicaps. Hospital Service doctors
had no jurisdiction over state quarantine laws; the
physicians were not allowed on board any ship arriving
from foreign countries until the vessel had been released
from quarantine by the state officials. Until the clearance
was given, Hospital Service doctors were sometimes
forced to sit aboard their launch for hours. Woe to the
doctor who went aboard early, for the physician was
likely to be quarantined for two weeks with the ship if
there was contagious disease aboard.

When the state officers had finally released the ship,
the Immigration doctors used the hour-long passage up
the bay to examine cabin-class passengers in the most
polite and genteel manner possible. American citizens
were not to be examined, and new doctors were reminded repeatedly to inquire about nationality before
remarking on a person's possible deformities. Offended
passengers in the first-class accommodations were likely
to have the capacity and income for making trouble.

Cabin passengers went on to dock in Manhattan.
Steerage passengers, however, were herded onto the
customs wharf for the ferry to Ellis Island. They disembarked grasping their baggage. Everything they owned
was tied up in suitcases fastened with rope, or in seabags
and wicker baskets. Down quilts and pillows were
clutched to their chests, and children were held by the
hand. Too often there were fewer in a family than when
it had sailed from Europe. The disease rate aboard ship

in steerage was appalling, the conditions an invitation to typhoid and to epidemics of measles and scarlet fever. The children, with their lower level of immunity, were especially vulnerable.

The steamship companies guaranteed their steerage passengers as "vaccinated and deloused and vermin free" and gave them a certificate to prove it. By the time the passengers reached America as much as a month later, the vaccination was all that still held good. Lice could be dealt with by a haircut and turpentine, but other, worse, things were grounds for sending an immigrant back to Europe. The steamship companies, responsible for providing the newcomers with a free return passage if they were rejected, employed their own doctors to engage in a battle of wits with the Immigration doctors. More than one incoming soul had his head soaked and scrubbed by a ship's physician to disguise a case of favus, a contagious skin disease.

Steerage passengers—the adults dressed in their black suits and bright beribboned costumes ordinarily saved for church, the children scrubbed—made their way on board the Ellis Island ferry, to the urging of interpreters who knew thirty-seven ways to yell "Quick! Hurry up!"

Pressed against the boat rail, the newcomers dreamed of a happy future. They watched the Statue of Liberty standing across the water a half mile to the south and gazed at the New York skyline just to the north.

At Ellis Island, a broad sand pit just above sea level, they were divided into groups of thirty—the number of names on each page of a steamship company's manifest—and tagged with the letter and number of the page on which they could be found. Then they made their way from the baggage room on the first floor to the registry room above, up a steep double staircase where examiners and doctors lurked as terrifying as dragons.

Here the hopefuls would learn whether they would be allowed to take their chances in this beckoning country—there was no sure road to riches despite advertisement—or whether the island was all they would ever experience of America. Some two percent were rejected and sent back.

To Janessa the new arrivals seemed like human cattle, herded at the doctor's whims, clinging to their dignity as they clung to treasures they had refused to leave in the baggage room—a doll, an embroidered pillowcase, a guitar, a silver menorah. Immigrants and officials alike were battered by the constant din of voices in myriad languages, from frightened children, bewildered parents, and immigration workers always bellowing, "Hurry! Hurry! This way!"

The Hospital Service doctors joked about the "six-second medical," but they weren't far off the mark. Armed with sticks of chalk, they watched for anything that might be contagious or render the victim likely to become a public charge. A ceaseless stream of immigrants climbed the stairs under the doctors' eyes—a Polish woman in a babushka, an Italian with cardboard suitcases tied with rope, Cossack soldiers with sheathed swords, dark-hatted Armenian Jews, Gypsies from the kingdom of Serbia. Like workers at a conveyor belt, the doctors would reach out and mark a sleeve or coat front: *E* for the woman with red-rimmed eyes, suspected of trachoma; *L* for the lame; *H* for the man with potential heart problems; *K* for hernia; *Pg* for the unmarried woman who might be pregnant; *X* for the mentally retarded; *X* within a circle for the insane.

The immigrants passed by so quickly that any potential malady was marked, and the unfortunate carrier was singled out for further examination. Those who escaped would move on, sometimes separated from a family member by that single devastating chalk mark.

At the top of the stairs more inspectors chivied them into a maze of iron-railed aisles and pens, where their eyelids were turned inside out with a buttonhook by a doctor looking for trachoma. Examiners perched on high stools and peered at scalps for favus and, aided by interpreters, shot questions at the bewildered newcomers.

Afraid of singling themselves out for any kind of

official notice by making trouble, immigrants often threw up their hands. When asked to verify their names, they agreed to the spelling on the ship's manifest—even if that version was hopelessly misspelled and missing half its syllables. Not even the most imperturbable of inspectors had much patience with Grzyszczyszn and Andrjuljawierju.

A Russian Jew, told that some people changed their own names upon arriving, asked a clerk what would be a good name to use in America. The clerk, snickering, suggested Rockefeller, and the Russian spent the next hour attempting to commit that name to memory. When an inspector finally asked for his name, he sputtered irritably, "Shoyn feggessen!" which is Yiddish for "I have already forgotten." He became known from that moment as "Sean Fergusson."

After being named, renamed, and sometimes stripped utterly of a former identity, they were peppered with further questions. Correct answers, carefully rehearsed, must be given. "Who paid for your passage?" "I did!" If passage had been paid by the steamship company or a future employer, the newcomer was suspected of being a contract laborer and sent back.

"How much money do you have?" "Twenty-five dollars." (The minimum required to prove the immigrant would not be a charge on the public purse. There was no need to mention that the twenty-five dollars had been rented for the sum of one dollar from a traveler who actually possessed so much wealth or that the money would be passed down the line several times over.)

"Do you have a job in America?" "No." (A tricky question to answer because contract laborers were excluded, but so too was anyone who looked as if he couldn't get a job.)

"Are you a polygamist? An anarchist? A woman of low repute? Who is meeting you?" An unescorted woman was not permitted to leave the island until called for by her male relatives. A "picture bride," to retain her respectability, often married her husband before leaving the island. Or, less frequently, upon first laying eyes on her intended, a disappointed picture bride opted for deportation instead.

In the midst of all this chaos, the kitchen somehow managed to feed everyone soup and sandwiches and more startling fare, bananas and Fig Newtons. The dormitory staff housed those detained for political or medical reasons. The expense was underwritten by the steamship companies, which were supposed to have weeded out anarchists and the feebleminded before they left Europe. Whole families might be housed on the island—men in one wing, women and children in the other—while the fate of one of their number was decided. For most people, the process took five hours. For the derailed, it could be months.

What medical problems could be cured were treated in the infirmary—measles and dysentery and typhoid, from which many recovered to be released. Most of the victims were children, terrified by their parents' absence. Don't Kiss the Children signs in the infirmary warned the tender-hearted on the nursing staff.

When a problem could not be cured, the person was deported. It fell to the Hospital Service doctors to render the decision. During Janessa's first week on duty, she stared in helpless bewilderment at a fifteen-year-old Croatian boy with a white X chalked on his coat. No telling what had prompted the doctor on the stairs to mark him as possibly retarded. Some strangeness in his expression? A slightly open mouth? The interpreter informed her that the child could neither read nor write, but that was useless as a test—neither could the rest of his village. The boy shuffled his heavy boots on the floor and stared pleadingly at Janessa.

"What day do you go to church?" she asked him.

"Sunday."

"Can you name the other days?"

He did, or named something.

Janessa took out a flat wooden picture puzzle of an ocean liner in full steam. She dumped the rectangular pieces on the desk and mixed them up, then pushed them at the boy. "Make the picture right."

He looked at her blankly for a moment, then turned the pieces this way and that, poking them with broad fingers. He had thick nails, newly cut and cleaned. Two pieces bumped together, making part of the picture. The boy smiled suddenly and exclaimed something to the interpreter. His fingers flew, pushing the rest into their proper places. "Boat!" he said proudly. "Boat to America!"

Janessa sighed with relief when he passed the test. She wouldn't put her hand on a bible and swear he wasn't retarded, but she didn't think so.

"Cleared," she pronounced. "Next?"

They passed through endlessly, tearing at her heart. In view of her seniority in the service, she had quickly been promoted from conducting six-second medicals on the stairs to a cubicle like the one Charley inhabited, a ten-foot square with a desk, an examining table, and an eye chart on the wall. But Janessa thought she would almost rather be back on the stairs, with her feet swollen and her head aching, than be required to make the final decisions here.

The door opened, and a puffy-eyed child with an _E_ on her blue flannel coat was thrust through the door. Beyond it a woman cried and railed in Yiddish. Janessa's heart sank.

"Don't be afraid." One of her stock phrases. After a week she could say it in Yiddish, Italian, Russian, Polish, and Armenian. The little girl couldn't be more than six, and she had trachoma. Janessa carefully turned the eyelid down, taking note of the thickening of the lid and the roughened condition of the cornea. The child stood obediently, but the woman outside was still wailing while another female tried to soothe her.

Oh, God, Janessa thought. Trachoma was highly contagious, stubborn to treat, and often impossible to cure. It was responsible for fifteen percent of the blindness in United States institutions, and clinics in big cities were overrun with cases. There was no reprieve from a diagnosis of trachoma. The girl would have to be sent back.

Janessa shook her head at the nurse who had brought the child.

"The mother's outside," the nurse said. "It might be easier on her if you see her."

Janessa winced. She felt sick to her stomach.

"Please," the nurse said. "She's scared. She speaks a little English. I speak Yiddish."

"All right."

The woman who came in wore a heavy black skirt and basque, high-button boots, well scuffed but painstakingly polished, and a cameo at her throat. Her hair was hidden under a black scarf. The older daughter with her wore a dress of lumpy brown wool, beneath which rustled the hem of her best embroidered petticoat. A watch on a chain hung around her neck, and her hair, like her little sister's, framed her face in two thick plaits. Janessa thought the older girl was about sixteen.

"Your little girl has trachoma," Janessa said to the mother. "I'm sorry, but there is nothing I can do. She cannot stay here." *And she's probably going to be blind.*

"No! No! What are we to do? Oh, God, have mercy on us!" The mother began to shriek with despair, and the adolescent girl put an arm around her while the little one clung to her skirt, still bewildered, not quite aware that she was the cause of the trouble.

"Where is your husband?" Janessa asked, hoping he wasn't already in America, waiting for a family who couldn't join him.

"Dead." The mother was sobbing now. "My Isaac died on the boat, and they threw his body in the water. Where will we go?"

"Where did you come from?" Janessa asked.

"Moscow, but the Cossacks forced us to go," the older girl said. "Then we were in Kamenets, then in Polotzk with my aunt. Then we came here."

"Can you go back to your aunt?"

The mother lifted her head and rubbed her hand across her face. "My Isaac was a watchmaker. They burned his store. He spent all we had on our passage. How am I to earn money in Polotzk? How are my girls to marry a Talmud scholar like my Isaac? Or even a peasant who can't read? How?"

Janessa's stomach knotted up again. It was always the children who tore at her. She had two fat babies at home in their clean nursery in their safe house, while hollow-eyed, lice-infested children passed by her every day in this other life.

"Did you have relatives expecting you here?" she asked.

"My Isaac's second cousin Itzel. A grocer. What good is he now?"

"Would Itzel be willing to lend you money to start again?" Janessa asked.

"In Polotzk?" The woman shook her head grimly. "You do not understand, American Doctor. We are Jews. We will be lucky to stay alive in Polotzk."

Janessa bit her thumb and did what she was not supposed to do. "What is your name?"

"Anna Poliakov. This is Rachel, and Sophie."

"Mrs. Poliakov, you and both girls are detained for further examination. The nurse will show you to the women's dormitory."

X

Rachel Poliakov went to sleep to the sound of her mother's weeping, a noise that had been a constant in her ears since Isaac Poliakov had died on the boat. Rachel had never heard her mother cry before, and now the woman wouldn't stop.

It was silence rather than sound that eventually wakened Rachel—her mother had finally drifted into sleep. As long as she could stay unconscious she would be anesthetized from the knowledge that it had all been for nothing. The money spent, the officials bribed, and the seemingly endless miles spent in railway cars more suitable for cattle . . . the terror of the guards at each country's border, the capricious demands for new or different papers or more money . . . then three weeks in steerage, huddling on a bunk above vomit-covered decks. The family tried to close their noses against toilet facilities that barely worked, bathed in ocean water that trickled from rusty faucets, and struggled to stay alive until America—all of it had been for nothing. Now her mother and sister and she would endure the voyage again, but in reverse, and not with hope but with despair at the end of it. Again they would face the murderous intentions of ignorant peasants who blamed the Jews for their own poverty because they must blame somebody.

Rachel sat up and rubbed her eyes. The voyage and the terror had crept into her dreams, so it was a relief, at least for now, to be in this clean dormitory room where no one would come with torches, guns, and clubs because she and her family were Jews. Rachel thought that maybe not everyone who stayed in this dormitory room had liked it. There were drawings—the work of the bored and outraged waiting for their cases to be decided—on the walls. In the blue chalk that the doctors used, someone had drawn a wreath of flowers with a bird inside, and another had scratched a cross and a Latin prayer. But someone else had carved in Russian with a penknife: "Curse you, America, with your much money that took me away from my home!"

She looked at little Sophie, sleeping curled beside their mother, and wondered how her bad eyes had gotten past the medical screenings up to this point. She had been examined by so many doctors, marked and tagged like livestock all across Germany, Switzerland, and France, inspected by the steamship company and by the Jewish immigration assistance committees who had been only slightly less frightening than the border authorities.

The American doctor had looked nice, but she wasn't going to change her mind. *A woman doctor,* Rachel mused. That was odd. It was very important to Jews to be educated, but it was the boys who went to school. Maybe Americans were different. Everything else here seemed to be different.

The only other person in the room was a woman whose features were Negroid but whose skin was the color of tea mixed with milk. She morosely traced with the tip of one finger the outline of something on her knee. Her skirt was pulled up, and she muttered at the knee as she rubbed it. Rachel craned her neck. It looked to her like ringworm. She wondered if the woman was trying to make it go away with a spell. Would prayer work on trachoma if you were devout enough? she wondered. Rachel knew she wasn't devout enough and so didn't try.

It was late afternoon, and the sun came through the window in long yellow bars to pool on the floor. In the dust Rachel could see the patterns of many feet: high-heeled shoes and children's boots and one pair of oddly pointed slippers. She was trying to trace their comings and goings with her eyes when the door opened and the American woman doctor came in.

"Don't be afraid." She said it carefully in Yiddish and then handed Rachel a piece of paper. On it in Hebrew characters was written: "That is all the Yiddish I know. Do you speak any English?"

Rachel flicked a cautious glance at her mother, then said, "On boat. A little." The little had been gleaned from an English sailor, and her mother had not approved.

"I want to examine you." The doctor held up her bag and pointed at Rachel.

Rachel cocked her head suspiciously, wary out of habit. "Why?" There seemed to be an unspoken understanding between them that they should whisper so as not to waken her mother.

"I can't tell you until I'm through."

Rachel mimed bewilderment. "Wait. Later."

The doctor took out her stethoscope and pointed at Rachel's chest. The girl unbuttoned her dress while the woman with ringworm, taking no notice of them, went on crooning her spell.

Rachel wriggled because the stethoscope was cold, but she stood obediently while the doctor listened to her heart and lungs, looked at her eyes (gently, using her fingertips and not the buttonhook), and peered into her nose, mouth, and ears.

"Be still." The doctor ran her hand down the front of Rachel's woolen dress, feeling through the cloth for the contours of her belly. She seemed relieved, but she looked Rachel in the eyes. "You have to tell me the truth. Is there any chance that you could be pregnant? Baby?" She pointed at Rachel's stomach.

"No!" Rachel said, indignant. She slipped a glance at her mother. If her mother even heard the doctor suggesting—!

The doctor smiled. "I have to ask," she whispered. "It's the rules."

Rachel nodded. That was understandable. Who knew what kind of people came through here to America? She had heard that the Irish, for instance, were very immoral.

"I have to leave now," the doctor said. "But I'll be back to talk with you and your mother."

She left, and Rachel sat down on the bunk and swung her legs over the side, making patterns on the floor with the shadow of her boots, moving them over the prints of all those other feet. She stared at the crooning woman and tried to make out the lyrics, but the woman cast her such a venomous glance that Rachel looked away immediately. She had never seen a Negro before. She felt a certain sympathy for the woman. She had heard that they were treated worse than Jews.

It was difficult for Rachel to imagine that anyone could be treated worse than Jews. In Moscow a cordon of policemen, firemen, and Cossacks had surrounded the Jewish settlement in the Zaryadye quarter of the city and ransacked it, dragging everyone from their beds to jail for being in Moscow illegally. After that the Poliakovs had gone to live in Kamenets in the Pale of Settlement, and then in Polotzk, also in the Pale, where an aunt was already living. In Kamenets, Rachel's brother had been beaten to death on his way home from the rabbi's school. In Polotzk, her father's shop had been set afire, all his watches and clocks smashed into a rubble of tiny gears and glass. Her father had been burned trying to put out the flames before they consumed the upper story, and the burns had become infected, leaving his face and arms twisted.

Bereft of his son, his livelihood, and even the face he had once worn, Isaac Poliakov had packed up his wife and daughters and spent his last remaining savings to go to America. His sister, Rachel's aunt, had refused to come, more frightened of the devil she did not know than the one she did. Maybe she had been right, Rachel thought. Isaac had died of blood poisoning on the voyage, probably the result of his burns. How did anyone ever know the right thing to do?

The hours passed. At dinnertime she and her mother were allowed to go down to the dining room;

Sophie had to eat in the infirmary and then remain there until the Poliakovs could be put on a ship. Rachel didn't know why Sophie had been allowed in the dormitory before but wasn't now. She wanted to find someone to ask, but her mother grabbed her arm.

"No! Sit down. You'll make more trouble for us."

"What more trouble can I make?" Rachel asked. "They're sending us back, aren't they? What could be worse than that? And Sophie is frightened." The nurse who had come for her had been kind but insistent.

"Maybe they forgot her. Maybe next they'll remember us. Sit and be quiet and eat."

Rachel bit into a sandwich of boiled beef and white bread while her mother gulped down soup, muttering that she knew it wasn't kosher.

"We have to eat, Mother," Rachel said. "We can't starve to be kosher. Why do we have to be different from everybody else anyway?" she demanded rebelliously.

"If your father were alive to hear!" Anna Poliakov snatched one of Rachel's braids and tugged it hard.

Rachel realized that her mother had to act angry, or the tears would start again.

After they had eaten, they found the American woman doctor waiting for them outside the dining room door. The nurse who had come for Sophie was with her. Anna stiffened.

"Dr. Lawrence wants to talk to you," the nurse said.

"It's all right, Mother," Rachel whispered.

Anna looked as if she didn't believe it, but she followed the nurse and doctor into the examining room. In Russia, when people in uniform told you where to go, you went or they beat you. Sometimes they did both. That these two were women could not outweigh their uniforms.

"I want to talk to you about Rachel," the doctor began.

"Rachel?" Anna said after the nurse had translated. "My Rachel has done nothing!" She whipped her head around toward Rachel. "Have you bothered this doctor?"

She turned to Dr. Lawrence. "There is nothing wrong with my Rachel!"

"Hush. I know. That's what I am trying to tell you. Rachel is healthy. If she wants to, she can stay."

"Alone? By herself? Second Cousin Itzel has seven children, and six are daughters. He will never—"

"I know," the doctor said wearily. "I know. I talked to Second Cousin Itzel. I'm offering to look after Rachel myself. I'll find work for her and take responsibility for her."

Rachel stared. *Leave Mother?*

"On the slight chance that Sophie's eyes can be cured, you might be able to join Rachel later," the doctor said.

"Mother?" Rachel whispered.

"You stay!" Anna spun suddenly back toward Rachel. "Better you should stay here than go back. You're too old to go back. The Cossacks . . . Eli Antin's daughter, raped and left to die in a field—you stay!"

Rachel felt as if the floor were tilting under her feet. "What about you?"

"We'll make do. We'll go to your aunt in Polotzk. When Sophie's eyes are well. . . . Put your hair up so you look older, or you'll never get a job."

"Mother—"

"You do as you're told." Anna held her hand out to Dr. Lawrence. "Thank you, Doctor. I thought I took my family to safety here in America. Now—I will settle for just one of them."

"Rachel can stay here in the dormitory," the doctor said, "until I have found her a place."

"A place with Jews," Anna demanded.

"Of course. Nurse Cohen will help me. I'll speak to a rabbi and the United Hebrew Charities."

Anna nodded. Her hands trembled. *"Mach sholom mitt die unshtanden."*

"We must make peace with the circumstances," Nurse Cohen translated.

"Janessa, have you lost your mind?" Charley looked as if he thought it possible, even probable. "I've been in a tizzy ever since I got home. Kathleen said you came in and went out again but didn't say where, and the babies were screaming blue murder. And now I find out you've been down on Hester Street!"

"I want to find that girl a place," Janessa said, preoccupied. "I spoke with a Jewish grocer, but he wasn't any help. He's afraid he's going to get stuck with another girl to marry off."

Kathleen clicked her tongue as she handed Janessa a baby to nurse. "Dirty people they are, and no Christian charity."

"Kathleen— Oh, never mind." Janessa gave it up. She was too tired to try to install religious tolerance in her nursemaid. Anyway, Kathleen ought to hear what Rachel had to say about the Irish.

She turned to her husband instead. "I couldn't bear it. Safe in my nice clean house with a maid and my babies and no one coming in the night to torment me. When I was a kid I wanted to crawl into a hole because people spat on me at school for being an Indian. *These* people, Charley, have had their house burned over their heads and their children murdered."

"You got a touch of this at Quallatown," Charley said, "when we worked with the Cherokee and you found out you were related to half of them. Why does being secure make you feel so guilty?"

"Not guilty," Janessa protested.

"Oh, yes. Guilty. As if you don't deserve to be warm and dry as long as someone else isn't. You'll break your heart."

"She looks just like that child who died at Quallatown!" Janessa blurted. "The one who died just when we thought the epidemic was over."

"No, she doesn't," Charley said. "She doesn't look a thing like her."

"How do you know?"

"Because she's a Jew from Russia, and that child was a Cherokee."

"She does," Janessa insisted. "There's something about the eyes."

"You mean besides the fact that they both had two apiece?"

"Rachel looks like her to me. Charley, I have to do something. I can't watch this every day and not do something. All these desperate people being sent back, I can hardly bear it."

"You sound like someone pleading to take one kitten home to keep before we have to drown the rest," Charley said, not without sympathy. "How much good do you think it's going to do?"

"In the long run?" Janessa asked. "You mean statistically? None. For me, and for Rachel Poliakov? Quite a bit."

Charley sighed. "Do it then. I just hope you know what you're getting into."

What she was getting into was utterly beyond her experience. Janessa made her way down Hester Street in the company of a friend of Sarah Cohen's from the United Hebrew Charities and a rabbi who found her presence so startling that his eyebrows rose up under his black hat every time he looked at her. Janessa was on her way, armed with these two as artillery, to pay her second visit to Cousin Itzel.

Janessa had lived in poverty. Before her dying mother brought her to her father in Oregon, they had scraped by in Memphis, with midwifery and the doctoring of farm animals. As a doctor, Janessa had worked among the poor Cherokee of North Carolina. But this was a city, where disease and desperation were stacked six stories high. Manhattan's Tenth Ward was known to the public health officials of New York as the "typhus ward" and to the Bureau of Vital Statistics as the "suicide ward."

Tenement buildings leaned, or seemed to lean, over the sidewalks, their iron balconies and fire escapes festooned with washing. And yet, Janessa found something about this street vital and exciting. It transcended the dirt and poverty and possessed a buoyant quality that rose up again almost as soon as it was smacked down.

Janessa's escort, Mrs. Schiff, dodged expertly around the pickle barrels, racks of clothing, and pushcarts that clogged the sidewalk. She and Janessa held their skirts above the flood from an open fire hydrant. Three boys were playing in the water while a city worker tried to turn it off. Shop fronts beneath weathered awnings bore signs in Hebrew, English, and German and sold items that Janessa could not identify. In a way it reminded her of the exotic Chinatown district in Portland, which she had loved so much as a girl.

An old man with side curls, reading a Yiddish newspaper, glared at her from beneath beetling brows. Tired-eyed women in dark shawls argued, shopped, and gossiped, their feet planted firmly on the walk against the buffeting of the crowd. A small boy strained toward the open hydrant as his mother talked. She held him firmly by the hand, not looking at him but not letting go. A girl in a black shawl like her mother's peeked around the side of a pushcart of shoes and stuck her tongue out at him. She noticed Janessa watching and giggled.

"Here we are," Mrs. Schiff announced unnecessarily, turning through the door of the greengrocer's shop. Its awning was a faded green and white, and an orange and white cat was asleep in the front window on a pile of potatoes. Janessa had seen the same cat in the same position two days before. It took no more notice of Janessa than on her last visit, but the proprietor recognized her and began expostulating loudly at the rabbi.

"Please speak English, Mr. Schidorsky," Mrs. Schiff requested. "Dr. Lawrence doesn't understand Yiddish. You're not being polite."

"Mrs. Lawrence doesn't need to understand me," Mr. Schidorsky retorted. "I spoke already to Dr. Lawrence. Now I am speaking to Rabbi Meier." Cousin Itzel was a round man in a green canvas apron and the air of a man much tried. "I have six daughters, Rabbi. The matchmaker hasn't found me a husband for one of them yet. And you expect me to—"

"I don't expect you to do anything," the rabbi interrupted, "except maybe be quiet and listen. What we need is a job for this girl with someone who *doesn't* have six daughters. Someone needing a strong girl from a good family. She is willing to work hard."

"If I knew of one of those," Mr. Schidorsky countered, "I would send one of my own daughters to work for him."

"You were willing to sponsor the Poliakov family on their arrival in this country," Mrs. Schiff reminded.

"That was when Isaac Poliakov was alive. A foot up for a man who can get somewhere, that is one thing; to take on charity for his whole family, that is another."

"Be grateful you don't have his whole family," Mrs. Schiff responded, an edge to her voice. "The younger child is being deported, and the mother, too. And why did *you* come to America, Mr. Schidorsky?"

The grocer threw his hands in the air. "All right. All right. You know why I came. Same reason as Isaac Poliakov wanted to come."

"It is a mitzvah to help the less fortunate," the rabbi informed him. "Now about this Rachel Poliakov. Where is she to go? She cannot live with Dr. Lawrence, good woman though she may be."

"I'm afraid not," Janessa confirmed. "I have no work to give her."

"You are not Jewish," the rabbi pointed out.

"No," Janessa admitted, suddenly realizing that for Rachel to live with her would create a scandal of a degree she hadn't comprehended. Well, thank goodness then, since she didn't have the room. It dawned on her that her very non-Jewishness was putting these people on the spot. Rachel was being rescued from *her* as much as from deportation. "That being the case," she said, taking advantage of her revelation, "I am counting on your help in finding her a suitable place."

Mr. Schidorsky looked with hope at Mrs. Schiff. From the crown of her summer straw, bedecked with silk lilacs, to the hem of her pearl-gray linen suit, it was plain that she did not reside on Hester Street. "Maybe you and your husband—" he suggested.

Mrs. Schiff shook her head. "I have a sufficient

number of housemaids; my husband does not employ females in his firm; and I am not an orphanage. This girl is *your* relative, Mr. Schidorsky. Now, then."

Mr. Schidorsky appeared to feel outnumbered. "I'll find something," he said with the baleful sigh of an unwilling Job. "I'll find something."

"Something *suitable*," Mrs. Schiff insisted.

"With a religious family," the rabbi added.

"Where they'll be kind to her," Janessa said. Experience with members of her own faith had taught her that the two were not necessarily synonymous.

"A suitable position," Mrs. Schiff clarified. "You can't ask for the moon, Rabbi. Nor can you, Dr. Lawrence. Too many immigrants arrive every day. When you live five stories up in a cold-water flat and burn fish crates for fuel, you cannot afford to coddle your children. Rachel Poliakov has been properly brought up. She will know her duty."

Rachel stood, suitcase in her hand, on the sidewalk outside Abel Blum's bakery. She had taken her hair out of its braids and pinned it up in a bun under her head scarf, and put on her best brown wool dress, with black stockings and high-buttoned boots.

"Go on," Mrs. Schiff urged. She gave Rachel a little push. "Don't stand on the sidewalk."

Rachel wished that Dr. Lawrence had come with her instead. New York was so big and so noisy after Polotzk. Mrs. Schiff was as intimidating as the people from the immigrant-aid committees in Germany and France. Rachel peered through the bakery window, and a face peered back at her. It belonged to a young man in his twenties, who was scrubbing the already spotless glass.

"Come *along*," said Mrs. Schiff, and Rachel opened the front door. The young man jumped to hold it for her.

"The glass is clean enough, Aaron. Why aren't you studying?" A woman who, from Aaron's sheepish glance at her, was plainly his mother, came around from behind the counter. Aaron departed reluctantly for the back room and was replaced by another woman, older, with gray hair skimmed back as if in fear that some frivolous tendril might escape and give a false impression.

"I am Mrs. Blum," the first woman said. "And this is my husband's mother, also Mrs. Blum. You are Rachel Poliakov."

They inspected her while Rachel tried not to shuffle her feet. Mr. Blum, who was nowhere to be seen so far, was Second Cousin Itzel Schidorsky's wife's brother. He needed a baker's helper and was willing to take on a girl, who would work for cheap wages. Mrs. Schiff approved since Rachel would be well chaperoned by Mr. Blum's wife and mother. Rachel wondered, but had not dared ask, why this plum job had not been snapped up by one of Itzel's daughters instead.

"Well, come along then. Don't stand like a stick."

Rachel looked over her shoulder at Mrs. Schiff, but she had already vanished, her duty done.

"Come upstairs and change your clothes. You can start by putting *cholent* in the oven. You know what is cholent?"

Rachel nodded. They talked so fast. She hoped she was understanding them correctly. The Blums were German, and they spoke Yiddish with a different accent than the one she was accustomed to.

"Well?"

"It's a stew," she stammered. "In Russia we make it, too. It goes in the oven on Friday afternoon for Shabbes supper." No cooking was allowed on the Sabbath, so cholent was brought by bakery customers to be put overnight in the slowly cooling ovens. That way it would be cooked and warm for eating on Saturday.

Mrs. Blum and Mrs. Blum rolled their eyes at her accent. "Russian," they muttered to each other. As they went up the stairs, the younger Mrs. Blum said, "That skirt is too short," and the elder Mrs. Blum said, "A nice girl does not show her ankles."

They went up two flights of stairs, past a door that opened onto the Blums' sitting room and a family kitchen beyond it. Above that were three bedrooms, but the ladies didn't stop. On the fourth floor was a tiny room with a white iron bedstead and a rag rug. It was furnished no worse than any of the other bedrooms, but Rachel realized with some sense of rebellion that the only bathroom was on the floor below.

"Come down to the bakery kitchen as soon as you've changed," said Mrs. Blum.

"And don't dawdle," said the senior Mrs. Blum. "It's nearly sunset."

Rachel peered out the dusty window. She craned her head in several directions trying to see the sun, but her only view included the eaves of her own building and someone's wet laundry across the alley. By the angle of the light, she decided there were a good three hours to sunset. Rachel thought with longing of kind Dr. Lawrence. Then she looked forward with relief to celebrating the Sabbath in a Jewish house, where she knew what she was eating and that it was all right to eat it.

I stayed in America to make an opportunity, she thought. *So I had better make it.* She changed quickly into a plain dark skirt and a white shirtwaist and recombed her hair. She wasn't used to pinning it up, and the bun wouldn't stay. The face that looked back at her out of the mirror above the clothes chest seemed oddly grown-up, not like hers at all. As she hurried down the stairs, Aaron stuck his head out of the sitting room.

"I'm-I'm glad you're here," he stammered. "Don't mind Mother and Grandmother." He ducked back inside before Rachel could answer. A feminine shadow loomed in the stairwell below her, and she raced on down the stairs.

"Don't run," said Mrs. Blum. "Nice girls don't run."

By sunset it was plain that nice girls didn't do anything the way Rachel did it. But the Blum ladies held hope for her, with sufficient instruction. Mr. Blum seemed not particularly interested in anything other than her stamina, which he tested thoroughly. She carried pan after pan of braided challah loaves to the ovens for baking. He watched her like a hawk to be sure she remembered to pinch off a piece and burn it first. When the challah came out near sundown, the cholent was put in. It was carried in heavy cast-iron pots by housewives coming to buy their Shabbat challah. The pots were arranged in the big brick ovens. The women inspected Rachel with interest. They commented on her as if she were deaf.

"She's too thin."

"That's from the voyage in steerage. Dysentery. They all get it. Itzel Schidorsky says her father was a scholar."

"But no money, and by herself in the world."

"For this she should have to put up with Sonja Blum? It's such a sin to be poor?"

"Such a sadness to lose her father. And the mother and the little girl sent back."

They departed clucking and shaking their heads.

"*Yentas.*" Abel Blum glared after them. "And what are you waiting for? Get their cholent in the oven."

At dinner, however, Mr. Blum underwent a change. He was a thin man, but muscular in the arms, chest, and shoulders from his work. He habitually wore an expression of irritability. That faded with the sunset, and Rachel saw his face take on a look similar to her father's. His life had been one of unrelenting work, but on the Sabbath no work was permitted, and so he could relax without guilt because God required him to rest. He could slip into the comfort of his faith. At the Sabbath table, candlelit and familiar, Rachel thought with a sigh almost of contentment that maybe she was home at last.

Aaron appeared, having returned from synagogue with his father just before supper. The young man spent the meal staring wistfully at her.

After dinner she was permitted to sit with the family in the parlor for an hour, until Mrs. Blum decreed that it was bedtime. That appeared to include Aaron, too, since he stood up.

"I'll walk you upstairs," he said. They were the first

words he had spoken since before dinner, and he looked as if he had been getting up his courage.

"We'll all go," Mrs. Blum announced. "It is time."

Rachel smiled at Aaron, but she thought he was awfully old to be under his mother's thumb like that. He was a very good-looking boy—a man really, twenty-five at least.

There was only one bathroom, and Rachel would have been the last to use it; but Aaron gave her his turn, and Rachel took it, somewhat embarrassed, then went upstairs to undress in the dark and crawl into bed. As she drifted into sleep, she thought she heard Aaron below, arguing with his mother.

By the end of the first week, these furious sotto voce altercations between mother and son had become a nightly ritual. Aaron never worked up the courage to say anything to Rachel, but it was impossible not to hear what he said to his mother, or she to him.

"No money. You can do better."

"She's the one I want."

"Abel, talk to the boy. And the matchmaker just about to find you a nice girl."

"That's what you said last time. But she was squint-eyed, and even then she wouldn't have me."

"No such thing! Your father and I, we told the matchmaker you could do better."

"I want this one."

"You can do better." It appeared to be a litany. Rachel, writhing with embarrassment, put her hands over her ears.

Aaron lost his temper. "I couldn't do better. Nobody who wasn't starving and at their last prayers would accept me because it would mean having to live with you!"

"Aaron Blum, where are you going?"

"Out!" A door banged shut.

The next morning at breakfast, Aaron appeared, looking contrite and sheepish. He set about mixing the dough in the basement and made no comment. Mrs.

Blum spent the early morning conferring with her mother-in-law and heaving deep sighs. Rachel tried to pretend that she didn't notice any of it.

Midmorning Mr. Blum went out to argue with the yeast-company representative over what he claimed was a short shipment. In Mr. Blum's absence Rachel was sent upstairs to tend the counter.

It was a slow day, and she stood by the front window, her nose pressed to the glass, and looked out at the traffic on Hester Street. There was so much going on out there in the world, and so little of it was allowed to penetrate into the depths of Blum's Bakery. She wouldn't marry Aaron even if his mother approved the match, Rachel decided. There was too much else to do. There must be some way to inform Mrs. Blum that she didn't *want* Aaron. Then the woman would stop her infernal sighing.

But if she didn't marry Aaron, what would she do? Her mother and Sophie were gone, she might never see them again. Dr. Lawrence was gone, having abandoned her to the Blums. Sniffling, Rachel pressed her forehead against the cool glass and stared at reflected bagels, bialys, and loaves of bread. The girl was feeling progressively more sorry for herself, lonely and lost and wondering, *Where is the opportunity that everyone said you could find in America?*

Dr. Lawrence and a pleasant-looking man suddenly appeared at the bakery door. Rachel blinked and beamed as if she had wished them up personally. Dr. Lawrence didn't look the same without her uniform, and Rachel sighed with longing over the woman's beautiful blue dress. Her upswept, brown hair was topped by a straw hat adorned with pink velvet roses. It was finer than anything Rachel had ever worn, and it looked so—modern, not like the clothes that Russian women wore for holidays and synagogue.

"This is my husband," Janessa said. "He's Dr. Lawrence, too."

"How do you do?" Rachel said. She had been practicing English with Aaron while they kneaded the tubs of bread dough. She looked with curiosity at Charley. He was wearing a well-cut brown suit and a straw boater. He looked very American, she decided.

Rachel was consumed with a passion to be American, to belong to this country in the same way the Lawrences and Mrs. Schiff did. It wasn't being Jewish she minded; it was being Russian, being old country. The Blums were old country, while Mrs. Schiff emphatically was not.

"How are you getting along here?" Janessa asked.

"I am learning to bake," Rachel said. "Mrs. Blum let me make these." She went behind the counter, put two still-warm, diamond-shaped cookies in a napkin, and offered them to the doctors. Janessa picked one up gingerly in gloved fingers and bit into it. It tasted of onions, sugar, and poppyseeds, and Rachel wondered how the doctors would react to the startling but delicious combination of flavors.

Janessa snapped up the rest of it, while Charley nibbled the edge of his.

"These are wonderful, Rachel," Janessa said. "I'll buy a dozen to take home with me." She watched as Rachel wrapped up the cookies. "What are those?" she asked, pointing.

"Bagels," Rachel said, surprised. Imagine anyone not knowing what a bagel was. She handed Janessa one and watched with interest as the woman tore off a piece with her teeth. Charley was still working on his cookie.

"Interesting," Janessa said when she had managed to swallow one very chewy bite.

Rachel giggled. "Toast it," she suggested, her hand over her mouth. "Then spread it with cream cheese. Or butter."

"Oh," Janessa said.

"I made the challah this week, too," Rachel said.

Mrs. Blum, apparently having heard the voices, pounded up the stairs and was followed by her mother-in-law. She dusted her hands on her apron and surveyed the newcomers. "Can I help you?" Her English was unsteady. "Nice girls don't gossip with customers," she told Rachel in Yiddish. "Go knead the rye bread."

"I am Dr. Lawrence," Janessa said firmly. "We came to see how Rachel was getting along."

"Rachel improves," Mrs. Blum said. Her expression informed them that she took personal credit for that. She jabbed Rachel in the collarbone and pointed at the door behind the counter. "Why are you still here? Now go!"

Rachel heaved an extremely audible sigh and went downstairs. On the top step she turned and, visible only to Janessa and Charley, stuck her tongue out at the Blum ladies' backs.

"We must be going," Janessa said hastily. She towed Charley out of the shop.

"That was a very peculiar cookie," Charley remarked. "I had to gnaw on it with my back teeth."

"Did you see that little devil's face?" Janessa asked, ignoring his remark about the cookies. "That woman's a gorgon. I have an awful feeling this isn't going to work."

"Yep," Charley said. "Now you've done it." He looked at the parcel of cookies Janessa was carrying. "I don't think those are going to grow on me."

"Charley, will you please forget the blasted cookies for a minute?"

"Nope," Charley said. "You got yourself into this, and I don't want any part of it. You can't say I didn't warn you."

"Why on earth would I say that?" Janessa demanded, exasperated. She cast a worried glance back over her shoulder. Mr. Blum—at least she assumed it to be Mr. Blum—was just going into his bakery. He was greeted by a deluge of female voices, and two seconds later he came outside again.

"Oh, dear," Janessa murmured, worried that he might want a word with her. He looked furious.

Rachel, in the cellar, cocked her head upward. Mrs. Blum was arguing with Mr. Blum about seeing the matchmaker again.

"Already I have spent enough for three wives on the

matchmaker!" Mr. Blum exploded before he angrily stomped out of the store.

"Rachel . . ." Aaron was at her shoulder. His face was earnest, his hair and skullcap were powdered with flour. His breath smelled faintly of warm yeast. "Rachel, I am going to talk to Mother again." He covered her fingers with a floury hand.

Rachel backed away. "Aaron, I don't think you should do that—not yet." If she couldn't stave Aaron off, he might actually convince his mother to accept Rachel as his wife. Then, the next thing she knew, she might be the youngest Mrs. Blum, forced to submit to the older women's whims and criticism from sunrise to sunset.

Never, she thought, steeling herself. *Absolutely never*.

XI

Honolulu, April 1895

While Janessa, in the States, was startling the family with the birth of her twins, Sam Brentwood was hanging on to the hope that eventually the PGs would make themselves so noxious in foreign eyes that public opinion would force them to free their political prisoners . . . preferably before those prisoners died of malnutrition or disease or—a common horror in the prison—ended up among the lepers on Molokai.

In April (he had lost track of the days and could only guess at the month) a jailer appeared at the wrong time of day (the hours he knew—all prisoners told time by their meals) and jerked his thumb at Sam to get up.

"Let's move it. Your sentence has been commuted."

"To what?" Sam's fingernails gripped the edges of the stones that paved the floor lest he betray any false hope to the man leering over him.

"To thirty-five years at hard labor." The jailer chuckled. "Not life anymore, just thirty-five years. So let's go."

"Where?"

"To the reef. Didn't you hear what I said? Hard labor."

"They said that last time," Sam said, not getting up. The thought of going out into the open air was overwhelming. He thought perhaps the man was making the offer to torment him.

The jailer lunged at him. "Get up, goddamn it!"

Sam stood. Slowly he picked up his bedroll and tied his comb and thin towel in it. Those were all he owned. His only clothes were the prison garb he was wearing, and inmates were not permitted razors—a barber came and shaved the prisoners when the warden thought of it. The rat sat up on its haunches in the corner and *eek*ed at him.

"'Bye, Mathilda," he told it. The rat had proved to be a female. He didn't suppose that she and her numerous offspring would care much for the reef, even supposing that he wanted to go there with a pocketful of rats.

"Vermin," the jailer said. "Nasty things."

"Fine company," Sam told him. "Better than some."

The jailer looked disappointed that his prisoner wasn't horrified by rats—the rodent population was supposed to be part of the punishment. "Get moving now." He manacled Sam's hands in front of him and shoved him out the cell door and into the corridor.

The hallway was nearly as dark as the cells, but when the men stepped out-of-doors, pain exploded in Sam's eyes because of the brightness, and he quickly clenched them shut. Except to go to his trial, he had not seen daylight since January. He staggered back, his hands across his eyes, and the jailer grasped him by one shoulder and pushed him into a police wagon.

As the wagon rolled along the street, Sam shifted his hands just a little, trying to get used to the glare, hoping to see the world as it went by. A burning blaze of white light was cut across with swimming patches of green, which, he supposed, must be the trees. He could see no difference between road and sky except a faint shift in color. Buildings took on amorphous shapes as the wagon rolled through downtown streets.

He thought he heard someone call his name. He looked around, squinting, but could see no faces among the indeterminate figures beyond the wagon. Annie? Eden? As it rolled on, he looked behind him and forced his eyes open wider, but he couldn't see anyone.

The vehicle jolted on, and Sam concentrated on

opening his eyes in increments. By the time they reached the prison farm, he could look at the gray stone building without being blinded. The edifice proved no uglier than those built as homes by railroad magnates and robber barons in the big cities of the States. It stood upon a coral ridge surrounded by fish ponds, salt marsh, and mud flats in which long-legged birds stalked and then took sudden flight at the wagon's approach. The coral-dusted road was unshaded by trees and flared blindingly in the sunlight.

Sam had toured these facilities in the past, with a group of sanctimonious haoles assessing the treatment of the erring and less fortunate and finding it humane. It was a different matter to be a resident.

When the wagon stopped, the guard climbed down, tugged at Sam, then they both walked to a strangely ornate door set in the wall. Its knocker displayed a British lion in bronze. A guard in a dark uniform passed them in, and Sam noted grimly that the largely Hawaiian prison staff had been replaced by haole guards.

Inside was a courtyard adorned with elaborate stonework in wall and pavement. A series of regimentally arranged flower beds spilled red and gold blooms over their borders.

Out of the golden courtyard, where the prisoners from the infirmary were sunning themselves, the atmosphere was much like that of the Honolulu jail. It was all very pretty and showy—a model prison. But however clean the surroundings, if a man was locked into them, they became claustrophobic and emphasized his helplessness.

The cell into which Sam was put was no larger than the one in Honolulu, and after the open air, its dankness almost choked him. He would rather be outside, breaking up rock on a road crew, than rotting in here, he thought rebelliously. So if the officials thought they were doing him an ill turn, they were wrong. Two prison guards brought him a change of clothes—red and brown divided down the middle like a quartered shield, instead of the stripes of the Honolulu jail—and both men stood watching while he put them on. Then they left him alone. He pounded on the door, shouting after them, but no one came back. Finally he slumped on the cot and willed himself to sleep.

Before dawn, the guards shook the prisoners awake, and Sam saw his fellow inmates for the first time. They eyed one another with faint smiles of recognition and salute across the chow line at breakfast—Lot Lane and his brothers, Robert Wilcox, and Thomas Walker. And Hoakina.

The cook's assistant in the chow line dropped a ladleful of something indeterminate on Sam's plate, but his immediate reaction was one of gratitude. Unlike the Honolulu jail prisoners, they were fed in this place. Wilcox, Seward, and the Lanes ate ravenously, like starving wolves.

After breakfast the inmates were marched in a line into the rear courtyard, which was not so showy as the front, and manacled together, wrist to wrist, under the eyes of a pair of armed guards. Sam stiffened and then made himself relax. If he fought them, they might send him back to his cell. It was too good to be under open sky again to risk that.

They were marched down the coral-dusted road past the mud flats, then unmanacled and set to breaking up rock to be used for roadbed. At first it felt good to swing the pick, to use muscles that had atrophied from idleness, to breathe deeply of the warm, damp air. It felt even better to be among his friends again, not depending upon a rodent for company. But in half an hour the pick grew heavy, and the muscles of his forearms began to spasm. Sam grew afraid that he would inadvertently bring the pick down on his foot. He staggered a little with the next stroke, and the guard prodded him in the ribs with the barrel of his shotgun.

"Keep working, Brentwood."

Sam turned around, snarling. "Get that thing away from me before I twist it around your neck."

The guard stood his ground. "Threaten me again, and I'll put you in solitary."

Sam clenched his teeth. On either side of him the rest were swinging their picks, eyes sliding quickly to Sam and back to the rock. *If we all attacked this son of a bitch with our picks, we could get away,* Sam thought. The others knew it too, he realized. But there was nowhere to go. They would only be hunted down again as they had been after the botched rebellion. Sam's fingers twitched on the handle of the pick.

"Break up the rock, rebel," the guard warned. "Just break up rock and keep your mouth shut. That's how you get along on the reef."

Sam turned his back on the guard and lifted his pick. There was no point in saying he was exhausted. The guard knew it, knew Sam had been confined for months with no exercise, and was having a good time, Sam thought, waiting for him to slip with the pick.

He took a firmer grip and forced himself to raise it slowly and bring it down methodically, his legs braced against the jolt when the point struck the rock. Lift, strike, pause . . . lift, strike, pause . . . Slowly a mindless rhythm emerged that could be achieved despite the tics in his forearms and the sense that his knees were about to buckle. Do it anyway: lift, strike, pause. Lift, strike, pause, let your mind go elsewhere, past the pain, back to the sugar farm, cool in rustling fields of cane. Lift, strike, pause . . .

The guard finally called a halt to give the prisoners water. Sam stared at him dully and lifted his pick twice more before the order made sense to him. Then he stood leaning on the handle, afraid to sit down, knowing he wouldn't rise again if he did. The guard passed around gourds full of water and a calabash of poi. After Sam stuck his fingers into the poi, he left behind a faint streak of pink and tasted blood when he sucked the food off his fingers. He held up his hands, dripping blood and poi, to the guard. The man shrugged, then with a sly grin he pulled a pair of gloves from a canvas bag.

"Guess I forgot to give you these."

Sam put them on, knowing that his raw skin would stick to the padded lining.

At nightfall he had to soak his hands in a bucket of water to get the gloves off, and the prison doctor engaged in a shouting match with the guard when he saw Sam's hands.

The prison physician wrote a letter to the editor of one of the newspapers with Royalist sympathies, who gleefully printed it in toto. No one expected the letter to make any difference in the prison system. While foreign diplomats and the Hawaiian government wrestled over the ultimate fate of the rebels, the prisoners would go on breaking rock.

Foreign journalists were strictly barred from having contact with the inmates, as were those Hawaiian journalists with the "wrong" sympathies. Tim Holt sneaked in disguised as the doctor's orderly, however, and wrote a scathing account of the prison work gang. His article so horrified a group of women in the States that they wrote personally to President Dole, admonishing him for vengefulness.

"Dole hates that," Tim happily told Annie. "Old Dole isn't a bad fellow, and he's getting mighty uncomfortable with being painted as a villain. Rumor has it he's threatened to resign unless Thurston and the rest allow him to grant clemency to the rebels."

"Will they?"

"Eventually. The government wouldn't have the support it has without Dole at its head. If he steps down, all hell will break loose."

"When is eventually?" Annie demanded.

Tim shrugged. "There's no telling."

But the next day they heard that some sentences had been shortened, and Tim advised Annie that a woman who made a sufficient nuisance of herself just now might get some action. "Dole is not an unreasonable man, nor a cruel one," Tim told her. "To be pilloried in the international press as a usurper and a monster is wearing on his nerves."

Accordingly, Annie went immediately to see Sanford Dole.

* * *

The president of the provisional government looked
at Annie as if he had a headache, but she was willing to
bet that the headache was not of her making. While
Lorrin Thurston had been getting more and more shrill
in his demands for punishment for the rebels, President
Dole, battered by public opinion, leaned more and more
toward writing the whole thing off. Annie's presence
simply aggravated an existing condition.

"I need my husband," she said flatly.

"Your husband should have thought of that before
he tried to overthrow the government," Dole remarked.

"He helped *you* overthrow the government to start
with," Annie pointed out.

"And then attempted to reverse the process," Dole
said. "He has found it difficult to make up his mind."

"Perhaps he was disillusioned by his leaders," Annie
retorted. "Since your side has won, you can afford to be
magnanimous. Don't require us to lick your boots. My
husband isn't going to do you any harm if you let him
come home. If he dies out on that rock pile, you will
suffer endless damage. You must be aware that Timothy
Holt, the publisher of the San Francisco *Clarion*, is
Sam's friend. You remember Timothy Holt; he's the one
whose editorials annoy Mr. Thurston so much."

"My good woman," Dole said, irritated, "are you
attempting to blackmail me?"

"Probably," Annie admitted. "I need my husband at
our farm. I heard that you'd shortened some sentences.
Why can't you shorten Sam's?"

"It *was* shortened," Dole pointed out.

Annie snorted. "From life to thirty-five years? You
know that none of those men will survive thirty-five
years at hard labor. Why don't we quit beating around
the bush here? Are you planning on killing those men or
not? It's plain to everybody that hard labor on the reef is
the same as a death sentence."

"You're a very unusual woman, Mrs. Brentwood,"
Dole said. He didn't make it sound like a compliment.

Annie folded her arms. "I am not going to go away,

Judge." She declined pointedly to give him his current title. "I am going to sit here—or, if you have me removed, on your front steps—until I get some assurance that my husband is not going to be abandoned out there. I may get more women to join me," she added.

President Dole was clearly considering the effect on public opinion of a delegation of women, possibly carrying placards, standing on his front steps. He shuddered. "I will take your petition for clemency under advisement," he informed her. "And if you come back here uninvited or make a nuisance of yourself, I'll hand the matter over to Lorrin Thurston."

The next day it was announced that the government, in its infinite mercy, had released all prisoners from their chain-gang labors. All inmates would remain confined until their parole hearings came up, and all rebels would be granted such hearings as quickly as possible.

"Don't stop now," Tim urged her. "Go back and be a pest until you get a parole date. You're on a roll."

She appeared to be, and without incurring Thurston's wrath. Sam was granted a hearing date a week away. Annie was permitted to visit him on the reef.

"You look better," she said, studying his face. The skin was no longer stretched so tightly over the bones, although there was a tic in the corner of his mouth that hadn't been there before. "They say no one's on the chain gang anymore."

"It's reserved for punishment for insubordination now," Sam said. "For not talking sweet to the warden."

"Then talk sweet to him," Annie begged. "You're up for parole, Sam. Don't risk it. Don't get mad."

"What are my chances of getting it?" Sam looked as if he didn't think they were high. The months in prison had made him wary of any hope, any promise.

"Tim says so," Annie said.

"He's still here?"

"He went home yesterday—I think because he was sure they were going to turn you loose."

"More likely because there wasn't any more story," Sam said.

"Don't be so ugly minded. You're suspicious of everybody."

"I've had reason to be."

Annie narrowed her eyes at him. "So now that you're getting out, you can just quit it."

"Has that McCall gone home, too?" Sam inquired.

"No. What's the matter with you?" Annie, perturbed and puzzled, looked at him. Something had happened to Sam since he'd been in prison, some inner barrier put up.

"Just feeling a little territorial," Sam informed her.

"Well, when you tell your pal Dickie to head for his own barn and get out of my hair, I'll see about sending Dallas on his way," Annie said. "Until then, I flat need him. He gives me someone to talk to when I get tired of chatting with precious Dickie about the Four Hundred and Mrs. Astor's new hat."

"Damn it, Annie—"

"You just come home," she said. "Then we'll worry about it."

"I want you to get Hoakina out of here, too."

"After we've gotten you out. I'm not going to push my luck."

"Maybe you just want an excuse to need this McCall," Sam suggested.

"Will you quit calling him 'this McCall' as if he was an Indian tribe or a foreign country? His name's Dallas."

"Chummy," Sam grunted.

Annie stood up. "I'm going home. They'll throw me out of here in a minute anyway. I'll argue with you when you get back."

"You bet you will!" Sam shot after her.

The sea was choppy, and the long trip on the packet from Oahu to the Big Island did nothing to improve her mood.

"Your brother's being paroled in a week!" she shouted at Eden, who could be seen setting the table in the dining room. Then Annie stalked upstairs and slammed her door. She did not come down to dinner.

Dickie Merrill seemed to consider Annie's absence a golden opportunity not to be wasted. He courted Eden all during dinner, praising her beauty, her vivacity, her charm, and attempting to persuade her to take a walk with him in the moonlight.

After Annie failed to appear, Dallas was too preoccupied to pay any attention to Dickie's pushiness, and Eden began to feel cornered. Before, she had considered Dickie to be a nuisance and a joke. This evening, however, he wouldn't let up, and there was something in his importuning that was a little sly or too free. Eden didn't like the way it made her feel.

"I don't see how I could possibly be interested in a gentleman who is also courting my maid!" she said finally in exasperation.

Dickie beamed. He had had too much to drink. "Not at all, my dear. Wouldn't dream of offering *you* any insult. Not when your brother's such a pal of mine."

"That's not what I meant," Eden said. "I meant I—I think you're immoral!"

Dickie appeared stung. "But I just said that I wouldn't treat *you* with anything but propriety. Besides, Sam tells me he doesn't approve of your affair of the heart over Michael Holt. The best thing I could do for Sam is head you my way."

"No, it's not!" Eden said stubbornly. She felt like hitting him, but she didn't want to make trouble. Everything was awful enough as it was.

After dinner she got up and went out in the garden by herself to think. Sam was going to be paroled. . . . Suddenly she felt a hand on her arm and warm breath down the back of her neck. Eden gave a little scream and jumped.

"Didn't mean to startle you, m'dear," Dickie said warmly in her ear.

"Let go of me!" Eden pulled away indignantly. The way he was acting made her skin crawl.

Dickie moved closer again. Eden picked up her skirts and fled back into the house. She ran up the stairs before Dickie could catch her. Annie's door was closed, so Eden ducked into her own bedroom and locked the door. After she had turned the key, she felt very alone—too alone. Annie was preoccupied, and besides, her grandmother had always been the one she could talk to. *Oh, Gran*. Eden sat down on the bed, wrapped her arms around herself, and rocked back and forth, grieving.

There wasn't anything to keep her here now. She couldn't abide Dickie another minute. And Sam would be free soon, so she didn't have to worry about him. His release was her release. But it also meant now or never.

Eden surveyed the contents of her wardrobe. She had already managed to supplement it with two heavy garments purchased surreptitiously and hung well to the back of her armoire. Because it was still spring, she wouldn't have to worry about more heavy clothes for several months. She needed her trunk, though, and she needed to draw her money out of the bank. And she needed an ally. She decided on a combination of bribery and blackmail as a means to the latter.

"Miss Eden, Miss Annie won't like this," Koana informed her as they stood on the steps of the Big Island branch of the Bank of Honolulu.

"And Miss Annie wouldn't like your letting Mr. Merrill into your room at night," Eden hissed.

"I don't!" Koana protested. "Well, once maybe. But he is very nice. He buys me presents and is not jealous like some."

Eden took this to mean that Koana let everyone else in her room at night, too. "Well, I'll buy you a present if you help me."

"Mr. Merrill is going to buy me a silk dress," Koana confided. "Only he hasn't yet."

"Keep working on him," Eden urged. "I'm sure he will." She turned to the two burly Hawaiians who had pulled Koana and her from Aloha Malihini into Pahala.

"You can wait here," she told them. It would have been more private to hitch a pony to the cart, but the large men's presence would be a comfort while she had all her money in her handbag.

Eden took her account book out of her handbag and, with a reluctant Koana in tow, marched up the steps. She presented the book to the teller who bustled forward to help her. The bank was cavernous and plush. A gold and crystal chandelier loomed like the Milky Way above her. It was obvious that they took money seriously here.

"I wish to close my account," Eden informed the teller, a young man with straw-colored hair. His demeanor suggested an acolyte in a temple. He was shocked.

"Close the account? But, Miss Brentwood, you have over nine hundred dollars here. Surely you aren't—"

"Surely I am," Eden said firmly. She allowed herself to look embarrassed. "You know that my brother has been in prison. I'm afraid we're forced to . . ." She let her words trail off, suggesting that poverty was just too mortifying.

"Oh, dear." The clerk was startled. "I had understood that *Mrs*. Brentwood—" He, too, broke off before he committed the sin of speculating aloud on a client's funds. "But you mustn't take this out in cash, Miss Brentwood. I can have your funds transferred to any institution of your choice, or you may write checks on the balance if you wish."

"Cash," Eden said, unmoving. "There are obligations that—" She shuddered delicately. "Obligations that must be paid in cash." If that led the clerk to believe that she was bribing government officials for her brother's benefit, it wasn't her fault.

The clerk's face took on a conspiratorial air. "Of course," he whispered. "Of course." There was no rumor about the government that was too nasty to be true.

Eden emerged from the bank with her nine hundred dollars in her handbag. "I'm going to walk with Koana down to the dry-goods shop," she said to her

burly Hawaiian escorts. Then she would go around the
corner to the steamship office. No need to mention that.

In the dry-goods shop, Eden bought Koana a new
straw hat with silk roses and ostrich feathers. Thus
adorned, Koana stood guard on the steps of the steamship office while Eden purchased two tickets to Los
Angeles, in the most private stateroom available, for
sixty dollars apiece. The second ticket was a pure waste
of money, but Eden knew perfectly well that if the clerks
thought she was traveling unescorted, they might become suspicious and notify Annie. Nice girls of Eden's
social standing did not make ocean voyages alone.

"You and Mrs. Brentwood have a nice trip," the
ticket clerk said, smiling.

"Thank you, we'll do that." With any luck no one
would have occasion before tomorrow to mention to
Annie her voyage to California or the sick sister who
supposedly awaited them there.

When Eden got home, Annie was nowhere to be
seen, so Eden beckoned Koana upstairs with an urgent
whisper.

"Now's the time to get my trunk down from the
attic. Nobody's here."

"What if somebody comes?" Koana looked fearfully
down the hall.

"Nobody's going to come. Annie and Dallas are in
the fields if they aren't here. And Dickie's asleep. He
always naps in the afternoon," Eden said scornfully.

When Koana hesitated, Eden grabbed her by the
arm. "If you don't get up these stairs with me, I'll tell on
you, Koana. I swear I will. *And* I'll take back the hat!"

Koana put a hand up to her hat and backed away a
step. "I can't lift any trunk!"

"It's empty. Besides, you're going to help me lift it
full, tomorrow, and get it in the pony cart."

"No!" Koana wailed. "Miss Annie'll catch me!"

"She won't. The boat sails at seven in the morning,
and I'll be out of here at four."

Soon the trunk was dragged down the attic stairs
and into Eden's bedroom. Koana protested every step of

the way in a terrified whisper. "Miss Annie's going to kill me!"

"Just be quiet and help me pack," Eden hissed. "Now start folding those petticoats."

Koana held one up and admired the hand-embroidered lawn. "I never saw anything so pretty. Just like flowers, all stitched in with a needle."

"You can have it," Eden said desperately. "It's yours. *Now pack the rest!*"

Dinner was eaten in uneasy silence. Annie was tight-lipped. Dallas alternated between a kind of self-disciplined distance and an obvious urge to speak to Annie in private. Dickie Merrill remained blissfully ignorant of these undercurrents but appeared to find Koana's demeanor unsettling. When she acted nervous and was prone to drop spoons, Dickie ran a finger around the inside of his stiff collar and with a worried expression eyed her waistline.

Eden was too preoccupied with her own incipient wickedness to be concerned with her elders. She went up to her room right after dinner, with a speaking look at Koana, which caused the servant to drop another spoon, and this prompted Dickie to lose his appetite for dessert.

Eden got into bed in her underwear, lay awake all night, and at three-thirty got up and dressed. She was sitting on her trunk at four o'clock when Koana tapped on the door.

"Good. I thought you'd chickened out on me."

"I would have," Koana said, "but it's so romantic, you going off to marry Mr. Michael, I just didn't have it in my heart. Like the Good Book says, love conquers all."

"That isn't the Good Book," Eden said. "And you knew that if you didn't show up, I'd come and get you."

Together they wrestled the trunk down the thickly carpeted stairs. Halfway down Eden began to giggle, and Koana looked at her in horror and made shushing gestures. Eden bit her lip. She couldn't help it. It was such a blessed relief to be free at last to go to Michael. Suddenly she thought of the elopement scene in Gilbert and Sullivan's comic opera *HMS Pinafore*, which a traveling troupe had played in Honolulu the year before. She sobered herself with the thought that Annie, like the captain of the *HMS Pinafore*, might appear at the top of the stairs, wielding a cat-o'-nine-tails.

They carried the trunk outside and into the carriage house, where Eden hitched a pony to a cart while Koana crept back upstairs for Eden's handbag and a small carpetbag. By the time she returned, Eden had settled herself on the driver's seat of the cart.

"Now you go back to bed. I've left a note for Annie on my pillow. You can 'find' it in the morning."

"You sure I better not come with you?" Koana asked her. "You bought two tickets, and haole ladies shouldn't travel alone."

"I am positive, thank you," Eden said, contemplating with horror the prospect of being responsible for Koana in the States. "Haole ladies travel alone all the time—just not rich haole ladies."

"Oh," Koana said, disappointed.

"Go back to bed. Don't you dare get up before six." Eden shook out the reins before Koana could offer any further arguments. It might be more respectable to take a maid, but not if that maid was Koana. And everything else Eden was planning was so disreputable that no number of maids could have rendered it respectable.

She put firmly from her mind the certain knowledge that Mike would have said it was disreputable, too. That was exactly why she wasn't going to tell him until she got to New Jersey—which, with luck, she could manage before any telegram of Annie's could arrive. Eden smacked the buggy whip down on the pony's rump and felt grateful for the absence of a transpacific cable.

XII

"She what?" Sam lunged across the cell at Annie, grabbing the bars between them. "She *what*?"

"Koana found the note early this morning," Annie said. "Koana's terrified. She thinks I suspect her of helping."

"Of course she helped!" Sam shouted. "The flighty little trollop hasn't got any morals."

"If she helped, then Eden forced her to," Annie said. "And unless you want to discuss exactly what this escapade makes Eden, you'd do well to leave morals out of this. When I got to the dock, her boat had gone. I caught the next one, but Eden's had already taken on passengers in Honolulu and sailed. She didn't take the interisland packet; she got a ticket on a steamer that was going all the way to the States."

"She picked the fastest thing she could get on," Sam said between clenched teeth. "She'll be sorry it wasn't faster when I catch up to her."

"The warden here seems like a reasonable man," Annie ventured. "He might agree to an early parole hearing. It's only five days away." She twisted gloved fingers together. Sam's face was dark red with fury, and when he unclenched his teeth, he bit off his words like a dog snapping at an outstretched hand.

Sam grabbed his tin jug, in which prisoners were given their daily allotment of water, and ran it back and forth across the bars, making a hellish din. A guard stuck his head around the corner at the end of the corridor. "Cut that out, or we'll tie you up!"

"Get me the warden!" Sam yelled at him.

The guard chuckled. "Get him yourself. Since you're in charge."

"Goddamn you—"

"Will you be quiet?" Annie yelled at him. "They'll throw away the key." She left Sam frothing at the bars and hurried down the corridor to the guard. "My husband's upset," she apologized in a low voice, letting tears well up in her eyes. "His young sister has done something very imprudent, and we fear for her safety. Perhaps you have a little sister yourself?" she suggested.

"No," said the guard.

"A wife?"

"My wife doesn't do nothing imprudent. I'd bust her head if she did."

Annie tried another tack. She fluttered her eyelashes, fringed with tears, and sighed heavily. "I can see that you're a man of strong character. It can be very difficult for a woman alone." She gave another sigh, heaving what she knew to be an attractive bosom. The guard's eyes appeared riveted on it. "If you would ask the warden, I should be *so* grateful." She offered a wan little smile at the end. *Ugh*.

"Well . . ."

The warden allowed Sam and Annie into his office an hour later. Sam appeared nearly ready to explode with suppressed emotion. A muscle beside his eye jumped, and his fingers knotted themselves involuntarily into fists. Finally he stuck his hands in his pockets.

The warden surveyed them from behind a monstrous walnut desk. His office, as gloomy as a cave, was paneled in walnut, and the flowers in a vase on his desk seemed to have trouble holding their heads up in such an oppressive atmosphere. Except for the flowers, the desk was bare until the warden pulled out Sam's folder from a drawer. The warden's eyes brightened momentarily at the sight of Annie, but he didn't appear to like what he saw in the folder.

"Brentwood," he murmured. "Intractable. Insubordinate. Uses foul language to prison personnel."

"Warden." Annie thought it might behoove them to distract the man before he read further. "My husband is scheduled for a parole hearing in five days. Now a tragedy has overtaken us. My young sister-in-law has run away from home. My husband is desperately needed to go find her, before . . ." She paused delicately, letting the warden imagine all the dreadful fates that might overtake an unescorted young female. Privately, Annie suspected that Eden could stave off any of them as long as she was on public transportation. "Her reputation," she whispered, hanging her head.

"A difficult situation." The warden shook his head with a certain ponderous sympathy. His square face was beginning to sag with age, and his jowls gave him the air of a world-weary bulldog. "All the same, I don't conduct the parole hearings, you understand. I merely make recommendations for them. In fact, Mr. Brentwood's was scheduled without my knowledge, by orders from elsewhere." He eyed her with faint irritation at that. "Not my department at all, it would seem."

"You could ask to have it moved up, could you not?" Annie asked him.

"Mrs. Brentwood, it is with great reluctance that I have contemplated paroling your husband at all."

"If you think I was insubordinate before, wait and see what I'm like if you don't let me go find my sister," Sam warned.

Annie elbowed him in the ribs. "Warden, won't you please consider—"

"I will not," the warden said. "Mr. Brentwood can wait five days and abide by the rules, just like the rest of us. If we didn't have rules, then where would we be? We'd have anarchy."

"Can't have that," Sam muttered.

Annie spun around and stamped her heel at him. "Sam Brentwood, I'm trying to help, and so is the warden!"

"No, he's not. He's trying to follow his silly little

rules, for fear the whole social order will collapse if I get out of jail early."

The warden looked up from Sam's file. "The material in here suggests to me that Mr. Brentwood is not a man for whom the government wishes any favors done. Therefore, I am not prepared to do any, since I am a loyal servant of that government."

"Well," Annie hissed at Sam, "now you aren't going to get out of jail early! Can't you ever keep your mouth shut?"

"Probably not," Sam said. "Since the authorities never intended to move my parole date in the first place. I get sick of kissing someone's fat butt just to stay on his good side."

"Sam—"

"And if they don't let me out of here in five days, I'll make them wish they'd never had me in here in the first place." Sam raised his voice. "I'm going to find my sister, and no tin-pot, tin-plate, jumped-up toady of the PGs is going to keep me from it!"

"We are going to keep you from it for the next five days," the warden informed him. "Whether or not a parole is considered after that will depend upon your behavior in the meantime. Guard!"

The heavy door opened, and the guard took Sam by the arm. Annie clenched her fingers in the flesh of Sam's other arm to try to keep him quiet. As they stepped through the door, the warden chuckled almost to himself. "Of course, paroled felons are not allowed to leave the country."

Sam stopped in his tracks. His face flushed dark red, and he took Annie's fingers and detached them from his arm.

The guard pulled at him. "Come along now."

Sam put his face up close to the guard's. "If you're lucky, I won't kill you," he snarled. He shoved the man suddenly so the guard staggered and lost his hold on Sam, who spun around and raced back through the warden's door. It slammed in the guard's face, and they heard the click of the lock.

"Sam!" Annie pounded on the door while the guard threw his shoulder against it and shouted for help. Inside they could hear the scuffling and the warden's voice raised in something between threat and fear, followed by the sounds of furniture crashing against the wall.

Inside the office Sam faced the warden across the big walnut desk. The warden's chair lay on the floor. An overturned table and broken lamp were beside it.

"I'm going to beat your head in, you son of a bitch!" Sam lunged at the warden across the desk and knocked him backward. He raised his fist, and it connected very satisfactorily with the warden's chin. The jowls made a smacking sound, and the warden grunted like a pig as he landed hard on the floor. Sam came after him and hit him in the chest. The warden expelled his breath in a gasp that smelled of onions and bad teeth.

"You'll pay for this!" the warden managed to say. There was blood on his chin.

Sam drew back his fist while he sat on the warden's chest. "I'm going to get my money's worth first." He hit him again and was pounding a brass spittoon against the warden's head when the guards broke the door open.

"Sam!" Annie shouted.

"Get out of here, lady." The guards shoved Annie aside and pulled Sam off the warden. They slammed him against the wall and handcuffed him while he fought them. He was nearly raving. One of the guards pulled his gun.

"No!" Annie screamed, but the guard turned it around in his hand and hit Sam with the butt end of it. Sam slumped forward, and they caught him as he fell.

"Lady, if I was you, I'd get out of here." They dragged Sam into the corridor, and when Annie tried to follow, the guard she had spoken with earlier pushed her back. He wasn't rough, but he was none too gentle.

Annie retraced her steps and looked into the warden's office. The prison doctor was with him. There seemed to be nowhere to go but away before they decided to charge her with trying to aid a jailbreak. She lifted her head and, unescorted, stalked down the corridor. She felt equally furious with Sam and with the warden as she tried not to cry. All she could think of at the moment was that men were unreasonable, that they might as well have been another species, that no woman would behave as either Sam or the warden had done. Sam would be lucky if they paroled him now before he was eighty-five.

Seething with frustration, Annie got into the waiting cart and told the Hawaiian cart boys to take her back into Honolulu. She gave one last furious look at the prison as the cart turned onto the road. The building loomed like a dark cathedral against the shimmering sea. The sun made the coral dust glitter around the cart boys' feet.

A hymn in parody came to mind: "Shall we gather at the river, where bright angel feet have trod?" Annie bit her lower lip. *I am not going to cry.*

In Honolulu she stopped the cart boys outside a stationer's shop, where she bought a box of writing paper, a bottle of ink, and a pen. She asked the merchant to send them with a note of apology to the warden and a request that he see that they were delivered to Sam.

She also enclosed instructions to Sam. He could write Michael Holt a blistering letter, Annie thought furiously as she climbed back into the cart. He had made it impossible for either of them to leave Hawaii by scotching his chance of parole. He had probably put his life in danger as well if the warden chose to complicate matters. Now there would be no tracing Eden until she got to New Jersey. And after that, Annie thought acidly, they had better be grateful if Michael Holt still wanted to marry her.

Sam awoke with his nose against the toe of a jailer's boot. The man had a shotgun trained on Sam's temple. He tried to sit up and discovered that his hands were manacled behind his back.

"I can't get up like this," he snarled.

The guard called another in and kept his shotgun on

Sam while the other man unlocked the handcuffs and locked them again with Sam's hands in front.

"I have to pee."

"Use the bucket."

They waited while he did. It was nearly full, but they wouldn't bother emptying it until it was overflowing.

"Move it, rebel."

"Where are we going?"

"You'll find out when you get there." The first guard jabbed him hard in the back with the shotgun. The officers obviously had orders to make him sorry he'd been born. Without stopping for breakfast they marched him out the back gate, and when a third guard handed him a pick, Sam knew exactly where they were going.

They sat down around him, a triangle of self-satisfied, vindictive faces.

"Start busting rock. You're gonna bust it for a week, and if we don't like the way you do it, you'll get another week."

"We ain't gonna like the way you do it."

Sam raised the pick in manacled hands as the guards shifted silently, guns ready if he tried anything. He lowered the pick. "What if I just tell you to stuff it?"

Their eyes ringed him, gelid and malevolent. "Then you don't get any water."

"And we get to beat on you some till you change your mind." The guard seated in front of Sam now tapped his open palm with a truncheon.

"Won't bother anybody if we kill you by mistake, neither," the voice behind him said. "Now bust up that rock."

"How you holdin' up, Annie Laurie?" Dallas McCall leaned against the wall just inside Annie's bedroom door. His muscular bulk stood out like ball lightning, explosive and forceful against the pale bedroom wallpaper.

Annie was sitting in front of her dressing table. "I'm not holding up any too good," she said, pointing her hairbrush at him threateningly. "And you get out of my bedroom, Dallas."

Dallas grinned. "I ain't gonna jump on you, if that's what you're worried about. I reckon you'd kill me."

"I suppose I would," Annie said complacently. "I'm older, and I got more brains than I used to."

"I come offering comfort," Dallas said. "And to tell you that last batch of sugar we cooked came out near perfect. You ain't gonna lose the farm, at any rate."

Annie's shoulders slumped. "You do comfort me, Dallas, and I rely on you—a whole lot too much, I reckon. I used to think you were too wild to tame, but considering you and Sam and Eden these days, it looks to me like you're the only one with any sense."

Dallas smiled. "I got older, too, honey, and managed to develop a little more control. Can I come in and sit down? I swear to God my intentions are strictly honorable. Doesn't seem quite so much to me like I need to tumble a woman first and talk to her afterward."

"You can come in," Annie said, but she knew damned well the old scoundrel wasn't nearly as over the hill as he pretended.

Across the room was a brocaded boudoir chair, gilded and spindly. Dallas sat in that, testing it gingerly with his weight.

He winced as he lowered himself. "That knee's gonna give out on me sooner or later. Doctors say it's arthritis. Told me I shouldn't have done so much sleeping in the open and general hell-raising when I was younger. Seems like a cheap diagnosis to me. I never thought of arthritis as the wages of sin. Syphilis, maybe . . ."

Annie giggled. "You're lucky you don't have that, you old tomcat." Dallas was such a relief. He was capable of saying anything, and he refused to entertain the notion that she might be too delicate minded to hear it. As a result she could say anything back without pretending not to know all the things that anyone with any brains knew. "Nice" people, of Sam's class, always acted as though their women lived in glass bottles, and they only took the stopper out so they could go to dinner parties or play cards. On top of that, secretly, their ideal wife was the archetypal "lady in the parlor and whore in the bedroom," who could switch, at will, between ice and fire. Annie thought she would like to meet anyone who could do that and not be a nut case.

As Dallas stretched and yawned, his blue eyes crinkled shut. When he opened them, he said, "I told you I was getting old. Annie Laurie, are you happy?"

"This minute?" she inquired. "Are you crazy? Or do you mean in general?"

"I mean in general. You love this guy, when he's not in jail?"

Annie thought about that. Dallas deserved more than an automatic answer, a ritual protest of faithfulness. "Sometimes I want to kill him," she said slowly. "Sometimes I think I was crazy to marry anybody that young." She smiled in wry amusement. "When we first got married, Sam hadn't quite latched on to all that self-control you say you got now. I didn't think I'd care, but it turned out I did. He didn't think *he'd* care I had all the money. Turned out he did."

"He's got money of his own now," Dallas pointed out. "And he's quit helling around, so you say. But I didn't ask you if you'd been through any bad patches; I asked you if you loved him."

"I guess I must," Annie replied. "Sometimes I don't know how I'm supposed to tell. I wasn't in love with him when I married him. It came on gradual, you know? It wasn't like with Eden and Michael Holt. They fell into each other when they were twelve or so, and they've been stuck ever since, like two halves of an oyster shell."

"That being the case," Dallas said, "everybody's going to a lot of trouble to separate them."

"They're too young," Annie said automatically.

"Hmmph. And how old were you when you lit out from your father's farm? Not near as old as Eden."

"I was sixteen, and I had my reasons," Annie said darkly.

"Hell, I know you had. When you told me what

your pa was up to, I nearly went back to Iowa myself and killed him, two years later."

Annie put the hairbrush down. "You never told me that."

"Well, I was flat out in love with you," Dallas said. "'Course I was in so much trouble for running off with a thirteen-year-old, I couldn't have shown my face back there. It was the only thing I could think of to do for you."

Annie closed her eyes. "Well, I'm glad you had the common sense to realize that."

"Besides, you up and married Joe Malone," Dallas said. "After that it seemed a little unnecessary."

Annie looked at him sideways, eyes speculative. "Nobody in their right mind would have married you. And I don't recall your asking me, anyway."

"I didn't," Dallas said.

Annie looked at him full on now. "And you didn't ask me after Joe died, either."

"Would you have done it then?"

She looked sad. "I reckon not. I'd of wanted to, though."

Dallas leaned his elbows on his knees, ran his hands through his hair, thick and the color of dark red earth, but streaked now with gray. He looked at the carpet, not at her, and laced his fingers across the nape of his neck. "I wasn't much of a bet. And I'm a slow learner. I'm awful sorry."

"Oh." Annie blinked back the sudden tears. "Dallas?"

He looked up.

"I could have done better, too. I could have waited instead of marrying Joe."

"Then you wouldn't be rich," Dallas consoled. He got up and sat down next to her on the satin bench. He put an arm around her. It felt comforting and solid to Annie. "Don't you beat yourself up, you hear? We had good times, you and me, maybe all that was coming to us. For a long time after, when I'd get to feeling low and chewing at myself for being a worthless bastard, I'd think of myself as someone you'd love, Annie Laurie, someone who was worth that much. Then I wouldn't feel so bad about myself."

They sat for a long time, staring at their reflections in the dressing-table mirror, images oddly entwined, as if somewhere behind the glass they were eighteen and twenty-one again.

Outside Flagstaff, Arizona

Eden pressed her nose against the window and watched the sun-streaked red rock and the desert roll by outside the Atchison, Topeka & Santa Fe line's Chicago Limited. She bounced a little with excitement in her seat.

The voyage from Hawaii had gone as smoothly as if she had orchestrated it in her mind and all the players were mere figments of her imagination, bound to do her will. She had dressed in her severest dark gabardine skirts and plainest shirtwaists to look as little like a runaway rich girl as possible, and no one had questioned her. It had all been very simple, really. If you dressed like a debutante, Eden had learned, people stared when you went out by yourself. If you dressed like a shop girl, nobody noticed you.

When the steamship had docked at Los Angeles, Eden had had her trunk carted to the train station, tipped the porters what a shop girl would have tipped them, and vanished, unmemorable, into the crowd. She assumed that Mike was back in New Jersey with Mr. Edison, so she bought a ticket to Chicago, with a transfer there for Newark, and finally a day coach to Orange. It cost her another $218, and she stashed the ticket, along with her money, in a canvas belt under her dress. She kept out just enough for her meals at depot stops along the way, and only the page of her ticket that the conductor would want that day. She was proud of her caution and practicality.

The Santa Fe sleeping car was a new one, with gaslights and silver-plated hand railings. The exterior was painted Tuscan red, gilt striped and lettered. The mahogany interior was carved in the Eastlake style of shallow patterns of leaves and birds, and a delicate spider web with a fly caught in its fine-chiseled lines. The Santa Fe provided toilets at each end of the rail car and a separate smoking room for the gentlemen. At night the berths would be made up with cool linen sheets and wool blankets with the Santa Fe Indian-head emblem.

Fascinated, Eden stared as the train pulled out of the desert and headed upward into the beginning of the Rockies.

"It's something, isn't it?" A stout woman who had boarded in Kingman sat down beside Eden. The circuit judge who had had the seat before had gotten off in Kingman to try a case.

"It's beautiful," Eden said, happy to have such a companionable-looking seat partner. The dour judge had expressed his disapproval of what the world was coming to.

"Gives you a sense of awe now, doesn't it? I swear I feel closer to God in the Rocky Mountains than I do anywhere else, and I'm a churchgoing woman. My name's Hester Barlow, but everyone calls me Hattie." The woman held out her hand.

"I'm Eden Brentwood. Are you going far?"

"All the way to Chicago." Mrs. Barlow settled herself more comfortably in the seat. "Going to see my married daughter. She's about to have her first. Make me a grandma." She chuckled indulgently.

"I'm going to New Jersey," Eden said.

"Got a job there?" Mrs. Barlow asked, interested.

"Well . . ." Eden blushed. "Actually, I'm going to get married."

"Do tell!" Plump cheeks crumpled in a motherly smile, and cherubic blue eyes beamed. "I do like a romance. Is he handsome?"

"I don't know," Eden said. "I think so. I mean he

doesn't look like a Gibson man. He's more alive than that."

"Well now, it's what you think that counts," Mrs. Barlow said. "Tell me all about him."

Thus encouraged, Eden, who was dying to tell someone, complied.

Mrs. Barlow patted her hand and told Eden she had the spirit of the pioneers. "My goodness, what a story. You ought to write that up for the magazines. So you ran away from a plantation in Hawaii. Well, well. I thought you looked a bit above the way you was dressed. Oh, don't worry, nobody'll spot it but me. I'm a practiced judge of character. Have you ever traveled alone, hon?"

"No," Eden admitted.

"Well, you'll want to be careful," Hattie cautioned. "For instance, don't leave your handbag on the floor like that. There's all kinds of confidence types working the trains, and they'll snap up a handbag just passing by, and you won't notice till it's past too late."

"Oh, I'm very careful," Eden assured her. "I keep all my money and the rest of my ticket in my money belt. I don't take it off except to sleep."

Hattie patted her hand. "That's my smart girl. It's a long way to New Jersey, though. I hope you've got enough to get you there."

"Oh, yes," Eden said. She whispered. "I brought all I had in the bank."

"Did you now? That was smart. I don't reckon your sister-in-law is going to be likely to send you any more," Hattie said with a conspiratorial grin.

The train stopped to take on coal and water in Flagstaff, and the passengers disembarked for dinner at the depot Harvey House. Most of the Santa Fe trains had dining cars, but the opportunity to eat at a table that was not swaying was inviting—particularly in the mountains, where the next bend might send a hapless diner's steak into the lap of the passenger across the aisle.

Unlike the depot restaurants of old, the Harvey Houses were clean and were often the best restaurants in town. At the telegraph stop nearest to town, the

conductor wired ahead the number of passengers on his
train and their preference for dining room or lunch
counter. A mile or so from the depot the engineer would
toot his whistle. By the time the passengers disembarked, the first course—the same thing for everyone—
was already on the table. Fred Harvey, the genius
behind this system, had made the Santa Fe the most
popular line in the West because it was the only one on
which the travelers could get anything decent to eat.

Eden and Hattie disembarked and followed a white-
coated porter down the lamplit platform. He carried a
big brass gong and banged it solemnly as he walked.

"Just like a parade," Hattie said, chuckling.

The porter led his charges into the Flagstaff Harvey
House, and they took deep, grateful breaths of the
aromas of roasted beef and turkey overlaid with the
cinnamony scent of apple pie. Eden was ravenous, and
she bought the eighty-cent five-course dinner: blue-
points on the half shell; a fillet of whitefish with Madeira
sauce, chosen from a list that also included young capon,
roasted sirloin of beef, pork with applesauce, stuffed
turkey, salmi of duck, English-style baked veal pie,
prairie chicken with currant jelly, sugar-cured ham, and
pickled lamb's tongue. All entrées were accompanied by
seven vegetables; four salads, including a lobster may-
onnaise; a tray of pies, cakes, and custards; and a last
course of cheeses and Harvey House coffee.

"Just like dinner at Delmonico's," Hattie said, digging in. "I bet Mrs. Vanderbilt don't set a better table.
And I remember when all you could get on a railroad
were sinkers, antelope steak, and railroad pie."

"Do you travel a lot?" Eden asked.

"Not so much," Hattie answered. "Just back and
forth some to see my daughter. I just been around a long
time is all, hon."

Eden sipped her after-dinner coffee and waved
away the cheese offered by a pretty, fresh-faced waitress
in a starched apron. "I was starving. I'd better look out,
or I'll be fat before I get to New Jersey." She looked

around. "Do you suppose they have a convenience here?" she whispered.

"Right through that door," Hattie said. "You go on. We got a good ten minutes before the train leaves. I'll make sure they don't snatch up your coffee while you're away." She shook her head. "You young people, always drinking coffee at bedtime. Now it would keep *me* awake all night."

Eden found the toilet, labeled Ladies' Lounge, and wrestled her voluminous skirts and petticoats up around her waist to use it. Like the rest of the Harvey House, the bathroom was sparkling clean—more than she could say for the depot toilets she had encountered—and it was substantially larger than the one on the train. Besides, it was terribly embarrassing to have to walk down the aisle past all those men, who knew exactly where you were going.

When she came back to the table, Hattie had indeed preserved her coffee cup from the efficient waitress who was clearing the rest of the dishes. Eden gulped the last half of it, then she and Hattie reboarded their car just as the conductor was shouting, "All aboard! All aboard for Joseph City, Gallup, Fort Wingate, Albuquerque, Santa Fe, and points east!"

"Joseph City," Hattie said. "That's one of them Mormon towns. They used to have eight or ten wives apiece. They don't so much anymore. Things are looser out here in the territories, but there's some things folks won't stand for. I hear tell it still goes on up in Utah Territory. They practically own the whole place up there." She clicked her tongue in disapproval.

The porters had made up the passengers' berths while they were at dinner. Now Eden climbed into hers, wondering sleepily what it would be like if your husband had five other wives, too. *I'd be jealous,* she thought. *I'd want to poison them all.*

She drew the curtains around her berth, wriggled out of her clothes and into a nightgown, then carefully folded everything and set it at the foot of the bed. She put the money belt under her pillow and raised the

window shade to watch the moonlit mountains go by.
Everything looked black and silver now—straight, dark,
sentinel trees against the massive stone fists of the
Rockies, with a three-quarter moon cupped above them
in the night sky. She looked and thought she found
Orion and the Pleiades but couldn't be sure. Everything
was different here; even the stars were unfamiliar.

The train swayed and swung around switchback
curves as it climbed, wheels clattering out their song.
Eden found that she could put any words to it she
wanted to: Albuquerque . . . Albuquerque . . . runaway . . . runaway . . .

Hattie was right, Eden thought, drowsing through
the first layer of sleep; the coffee wasn't keeping her
awake at all. She was incredibly sleepy. She drifted
deeper, let it take her like a long rolling wave out, out,
and farther out.

"'Night, hon," Hattie said from above her.

Eden woke to daylight streaming through her unshaded window, and then to a strange sensation of
stillness. She peered out, blinking, and then snatched
the shade down. The train was stopped at a platform,
and a cowboy with a red bandanna around his neck was
peering back at her. This must be Santa Fe, she thought
fuzzily. She would have to hurry if she wanted breakfast.
Eden felt under her pillow for the money belt, then
froze.

It was gone. She tore the bed apart, throwing sheets
and pillowcases to the other end, and then into the aisle.
Frantically she scrambled into her clothes and threw the
curtains back. Hattie's berth above her was empty, too,
and the satchel Hattie had stowed in the rack overhead
was not there.

XIII

"Little lady, that money belt's long gone." The Santa Fe depot manager regarded Eden with sympathy, but he exercised considerable caution to avoid implying that the railroad might be responsible. "And old Railroad Lil's long gone, too."

"Who?" Eden kept a protective grip on her handbag and carpetbag, which she had been afraid to leave on the train.

"That woman you say called herself Hattie. Stout lady, looks like somebody's old grandma?"

"You know her?"

"Not to speak to," the manager said. He sifted through a sheaf of dusty papers on his desk. The depot office was nearly full of stacked papers and ledgers and cartons of unknown contents, leaving only narrow channels of navigation in between. "But I have a report here somewhere. We've had the Pinkerton Agency working on it."

"Then you know about her," Eden said. "Then you'll at least replace my ticket?"

The depot manager was horrified. "Certainly not! That ticket is as good as cash. Lil can turn it in anyplace she chooses, and then we'd be out of pocket twice. We can't have that."

"She robbed me on your train!" Eden said indignantly. "You ought to warn people."

The manager slid his spectacles down on his nose and looked at her over the top. "Little lady, the confidence game is older than this railroad. We count on our

211

passengers to know better than to tell strangers where they've got their money hid."

"What am I going to do?" Eden moaned.

"Wire your folks for money," the manager suggested. "You got enough to do that? Never mind; here, the railroad will pay for a telegram." He handed Eden a two-dollar bill.

Eden wanted to tell him that that was a fat lot of use when she was missing a two-hundred-dollar ticket, but she kept quiet. She didn't have but a dollar in her handbag. She got directions to the telegraph office and forced herself to bypass the smell of bacon and pancakes that wafted from the Santa Fe Harvey House. She would eat breakfast when she was sure that Mike could send her some money.

She tried to compose a message that would convey the urgency of the situation and exactly what she was doing in Santa Fe in the first place, but without scaring him to death. She finally decided that that couldn't be done, and she might as well scare him. She was certainly scared herself.

"Here." Eden handed the lengthy message to the telegrapher. "I'll wait for an answer."

She sat down in the dusty telegraph office—everything here seemed to be dusty, she thought, as if the town were silently eroding—and tried to read an old, flyspecked issue of *Scribner's*. The telegrapher clicked his keys and languidly chewed tobacco like a cud.

An hour and a half later, she was beginning to panic.

"Probably nobody home," the telegrapher said when she demanded to know why her reply had not come through.

"Can't you tell them to find him? Ask his landlady where he is? Something?" Eden, distraught, gripped the edge of the telegrapher's counter.

"Lady, we ain't a missing-person service."

Eden haunted the telegraph office for the rest of the morning, clutching her dollar, which was not enough for another wire. At one point she broke down and spent it on lunch at the Harvey House when she couldn't stand waiting any longer. Halfway through lunch she realized that her trunk had gone on without her to New Jersey. With a miserable groan, she put her next to the last dime on the table for a tip and went back to the telegraph office.

"Nope," said the telegrapher.

Eden closed her eyes and blanched so white that the telegrapher said, "Here now, you ain't gonna faint on me."

Eden sat down again, feeling as if she might. Mike could be anywhere. He could be at Mr. Edison's laboratory— Of course! He was still at work! She sighed, relieved. It was two hours later in New Jersey. By five o'clock today at the latest she should have a reply. She stood up again. "I'll come back at closing."

Relieved, she passed the time by strolling through Santa Fe, which was very old and built in Spanish and Indian style, with whitewash and red clay. The houses were adobe, and some had flat roofs that she remembered Mike's aunt Cindy Blake telling her the people slept on. There were ladders leaning against the walls, and as she watched, two black-haired, coppery children chased each other up and down like kittens. An old woman in a black skirt went by with a huge pot on her head, her shadow as black and long as a tree against the low sun.

Dusk turned the surrounding mountains from rose to bloodred. Sangre de Cristo, they were called—Blood of Christ. When the sun had dropped behind the western mountains and the Sangre de Cristo had gone dark except for their tops, Eden returned to the telegraph office. The telegrapher was locking the door. He shook his head when he saw her coming.

"But there must have been an answer!" Eden grabbed his arm as if she could somehow shake it out of him. Above them the last light went out of the mountains, and the platform lights came on at the depot.

"Lady, I'm tellin' ya, if there was an answer I'd have given it to you. What do you think I am?"

Eden took a deep breath. "I'm sorry. I'm just a little

worried." That was putting it mildly. "I have ten cents in my purse, and I haven't had dinner. Do you know where I might find some assistance?" She sounded like someone out of a melodrama, she thought, except that the villain had been a nice little grandmother instead of a dastardly cad in a black coat. She would have recognized the cad at once, of course. That was the trouble—villains shouldn't be allowed to go around looking like someone's kindly nanny.

"Lord God," said the telegrapher. "You might try the fathers at the mission, I suppose."

Eden didn't think the fathers at the mission were a good idea at all. They would be bound to write to Sam and Annie when they found out what she was up to.

"And the Harvey House hires waitresses pretty regular," the telegrapher suggested. "You ever slung hash?"

"Not yet," Eden said. "But thank you. I'll try it." Maybe they would give her dinner, even if they didn't hire her.

But as it turned out, the manager of the Harvey House, a man in his fifties who smelled of peppermints and apple pie, was indeed hiring waitresses. "They get married all the time," Mr. Hope said dolefully, shaking his head. "You have to sign an agreement not to get married for a year," he told Eden.

Eden, who was so hungry that she would have signed an agreement with the devil for a piece of pie, lied earnestly and assured him that she wouldn't.

"Salary is seventeen-fifty a month, plus tips and room and board. Board is in the Harvey House dormitory, and there are rules." He bent a stern eye on Eden. "Ten o'clock curfew; no callers except in the parlor; you have to go to church on Sundays."

Eden nodded. She didn't want callers anyway; all she wanted was to earn enough for a new ticket. She could get a third-class seat on one of the emigrant trains for a lot less than her first-class ticket had cost. She had begun to realize that she might not have a reply from Mike for weeks. Mr. Edison and his staff might still be at the winter house in Florida. Mike had said that some of the other fellows had complained that if Edison was working on something he didn't want to interrupt, he stayed in Florida until the end of May, when the weather was so miserable that even he couldn't stand it anymore or his wife put her foot down.

If that was the case now, she would have no way to contact him. Any letter she wrote would have to make its way across the country, then wait to be barged to Fort Myers. And if a letter had just missed connecting with the monthly barge . . . There would be no telegraph office in that subtropical wilderness, either, she was certain.

Eden thought of giving in and wiring Annie with her first tip money, or Tim Holt in San Francisco, or even Toby or Janessa. The Holts would come to her aid, all right; they would assist her right back to Hawaii. *I won't*, she thought. *I can be a waitress. There's no reason why I can't. Plenty of girls are on their own, and I can use this time to prove that I can live on what Mike earns. Then nobody will be able to say I didn't know what I was getting into. . . .*

"You can settle in tonight and start tomorrow morning," the manager was saying. "And— Miss Brentwood, are you listening to me?"

Eden started. "Yes, of course." What had Mr. Hope said? Bed, that was it. Thank goodness, she would have a place to stay that night. Her stomach growled. "Do you think I might have dinner tonight, too?" she asked.

The dormitory housemother was Mrs. Patterson, a widow in her sixties. She gave the impression of being one who took her duties very seriously. Her goal seemed to be to make her charges as unattractive to men as possible. When Eden wondered what Mr. Patterson had been like, she shuddered, remembering some of the old tobacco-chewing ranchers who had dined at the Harvey House the night before, trying to flirt with the waitresses. Most of the men looked clean only above the shirt collar and smelled like billy goats.

Eden told Mrs. Patterson the same story she had told Mr. Hope, that she had been on her way to New Jersey to visit her cousin and try to find work in the textile mills there, and that she was an orphan. Mrs. Patterson expressed sympathy over this turn of fate. Then she explained to Eden about the uniform of a Harvey girl: "Plain black dress, white apron, white collar with a black bow, black shoes and stockings, hair in a simple puff. No rings or eardrops."

"Yes, ma'am."

"Since your trunk has gone to New Jersey, you may buy what you lack of those items against your first month's wages. Did Mr. Hope advise you of our house rules?"

"I think so," Eden said.

"Ten o'clock curfew, three times late is grounds for dismissal. No gentlemen except in the courting parlor, and no dances or other unauthorized social events except for our own Friday-night gatherings. Evidence of low moral character is also grounds for dismissal."

"Yes, ma'am." Sleepily, Eden let herself be led upstairs and shown the room she would share with three other Harvey girls, who had not yet returned from their shift at the restaurant.

She didn't wake up when they came in, but she jerked awake, startled, when they shook her in the morning.

"Get up, lazybones," said a brown-haired girl with freckles and a round, cheerful face.

"Or old Pat-Pat will chase you out of bed with a broom."

"Welcome to Devil's Island," another one said. She had blond hair, paler than Eden's, piled in a bun on her head, and a long, square-jawed, determined-looking face. She smiled. "I'm Inga Solvison, and that's Lizzie Harris—" She nodded toward the brown-haired girl. "And Isobel Lafourche." A darker-haired brunet said hello in a faint Cajun accent. "I'm not on till tonight," Inga continued. "If you have to buy clothes, I'll take you into town. I know what old Pat-Pat will allow."

After breakfast, which consisted of free run of the Harvey House table, Eden followed Inga into Santa Fe. She sighed wistfully while bypassing the Indian shops, which sold fascinating rugs and turquoise jewelry and heavy fringed shawls. She had the required black shoes and stockings in her carpetbag, along with enough undergarments to get by on. She bought a plain black dress that was the sort of thing a proper housemaid would wear (if they had ever had a proper housemaid, Eden thought, chuckling. Koana wouldn't have been caught dead in that dress) for $2.19, the apron for 25¢, and the collar for 12¢. She added a nickel's worth of black ribbon for the bow and gave the clerk the three dollars that Mrs. Patterson had allotted her for these purchases.

Eden, who was used to ordering her gowns from Paris, had never bought a dress in a shop. She decided that she had better not let the other girls get a good look at her underwear, or the jig would be up—her petticoats had cost about ten times what the dress had, and looked it. Maybe she would say that a former employer had given them to the mother for whom Eden had just made up a lingering death from consumption. This was almost fun. . . .

It was less fun, however, by the time Eden had finished her shift that night. Under the tutelage of Mr. Hope and her roommates, she learned to serve full meals to sixteen people in twenty-five minutes and to polish the cutlery and china in between. A Harvey House permitted no frayed napkins, chipped cups, bent silver, or mixed-up orders. While passengers dug into the first course, a waitress took their drink and entrée orders, and the "drink girl" arrived with coffee, hot tea, iced tea, or milk.

"Now it's this way: right side up in the saucer for coffee, upside down for hot tea, upside down and tilted on the saucer for iced tea, and upside down on the table for milk," Isobel said, moving coffee cups around like a gambler in a shell game. "Got it?"

"I think so." Eden repeated the pattern and got it hopelessly snarled.

"Try again," said Isobel. "It took me a whole day to learn it. Once you get it in your head, though, you won't forget. Mr. Harvey, he don' allow sloppy, him."

"*Doesn't,* Isobel," Mr. Hope corrected, passing through in midargument with a produce supplier.

"Mr. Harvey himself comes here?" Eden quailed. Fred Harvey had been so often quoted to her that he was taking on mythic proportions in her mind.

"Sometimes," Isobel said. "He don' . . . he *doesn't*"—she shot a dark look at Mr. Hope—"ever say when. He just comes. I hear if he sees a table not set right, he pulls it all off on the floor, tablecloth an' all, and the manager he gets a big lecture. Fired, maybe."

Eden blanched. It would be just her luck to serve coffee instead of milk to Fred Harvey.

"Now," said Isobel, "Inga will show you behind the lunch counter. We all work all the stations, so we know what to do wherever Mr. Hope he need us."

Inga took over and educated Eden in the variety of sandwiches offered by the lunch counter and the proper way of fending off male patrons who tried to be too chummy.

"They're worse at the lunch counter," Inga said. "That's where all the cowboys come. You just got to be firm with them, ja?"

"Mr. Hope says everyone gets married in a year," Eden said.

"Ja, what do you think we work here for?" Inga laughed. "Who am I going to find on a farm in Minnesota?"

"Inga's engaged," Lizzie announced, passing by with an armload of tablecloths.

"I'm not," Inga said placidly.

"Lars thinks you are." Lizzie chuckled.

"He's Swedish and I'm Swedish, so he thinks we're engaged," Inga explained. "If I'd wanted to marry Lars Jensen, I could have stayed in Minnesota."

"Is he from your hometown?" Eden asked her.

"No," Inga admitted. "But he might as well be. I want something different. That's why I came here."

The thin shriek of a steam whistle in the distance cut across the conversation. "Here it comes!" Lizzie called, and they scrambled to their places. The Los Angeles Limited would be huffing to a stop at the depot in two minutes.

Eden, carrying steaming plates of oysters to the tables in the dining room, crossed her fingers under the blue and white platter and prayed she wouldn't pour gravy on anyone. The dining room, nearly empty except for a few local ranchers and bachelor businessmen, filled to overflowing within minutes.

Assigned to tables three and four—eight diners apiece—Eden took orders for their entrées and preference in drinks, flipping cups as she went. A small boy in a soot-covered sailor suit watched her and put his cup back in the saucer.

"Don't do that," Eden said, "unless you want coffee instead of milk."

"Billy, just please leave things alone," his mother said distractedly. "Is *that* how you gals tell!" another passenger said. "I always wondered." He looked like a drummer, by the sample case at his feet.

Billy left his cup where it was but began to pour salt on the tablecloth.

After the diners had eaten their meal and been whisked off to their train, Eden discovered that she had $1.50 in tips and a sugar bowl full of pepper.

"How you doing?" Isobel asked as they took clean tablecloths from the linen closet.

"My feet are killing me," Eden whispered. "They feel as if they're on fire."

"Soak 'em in Epsom salts tonight," Lizzie suggested. She piled a stack of napkins on top of her tablecloths. "You don't want to miss the dance Friday night."

Isabel snorted. "For a dance, she's pretty tame, *hein?*"

Lizzie chuckled. "Pat-Pat organizes these dances.

They're about as exciting as a church social. But all the boys come anyway."

Isabel poked Eden. "Customers at your table."

Eden flew back into the dining room and spread the clean cloth and napkins.

"You're new, ain't ya, honey? Take it easy, we're not in a hurry."

"Maybe not, but I'm supposed to be," Eden said frankly.

The speaker laughed. He looked like a cowboy or maybe a ranch foreman, somewhere in his forties, with grizzled hair and a clean red-flannel shirt. The younger man with him had on a blue serge suit with a spotted tie, but the hat he hung on the rack was the same style of broad-brimmed Stetson as his companion's. He ordered the baked veal pie and stared at Eden admiringly while the older man perused the menu. "We ain't got all night," the young one said finally. "We got to get those beeves home."

The older man snorted. "Your dad knows we're on the way. And you ain't growed into a trail boss yet, so just calm yourself. I'll have the duck, honey."

The young man continued to stare at her while he ate, and when he left she discovered a twenty-cent tip. Lizzie, watching her expression, burst into laughter. Eden blushed and put the money in her pocket.

By the end of the week, Eden had discovered why Harvey girls got married so quickly: They were nearly the only respectable single women in town. Besides, Eden imagined that after a year of Mrs. Patterson's strict chaperonage, a Harvey girl would marry anyone.

There wasn't much to do in Santa Fe, and what there was had to pass Mrs. Patterson's inspection and was generally found unacceptable. Church was permissible. A concert in the park was permissible if it wasn't ragtime, which was beginning to be all the rage. Harry Salter's Dramatic Company, presenting *Lady Windermere's Fan*, was not permissible. Actors were all immoral, so who could predict what might go on. And Mrs. Patterson, who prided herself on keeping up with the

New York newspapers, had read some very disturbing things about Oscar Wilde. The Friday-night dance, chaperoned by Mrs. Patterson, was always permissible, but before they were allowed to attend, the Harvey girls were lined up for inspection.

"Put a scarf around your throat, Lizzie. You'll catch a cold. Isobel, is that rouge on your mouth?" Mrs. Patterson produced a handkerchief and scrubbed it across the wriggling Isobel's lips. A faint pink smear appeared on the linen. "What is the world coming to? Go and wash."

Isobel washed, grumbling, and Lizzie draped an organdy scarf in the neckline that Mrs. Patterson had decided was too low. "Catch a cold" was a euphemism. Eden passed muster primarily because all she had had in her carpetbag were a plain skirt and shirtwaist and a brown gingham dress. All her good clothes were in her trunk because she had been traveling in disguise. She looked in the mirror dispiritedly and decided she was more disguised than she wanted to be; but she couldn't afford even another two-dollar dress.

The men who came to the Harvey House Friday-night dance would probably not have noticed had the Harvey girls been wearing burlap. They outnumbered the girls by two to one, and any girl whose feet would stand it after a week of waiting on tables could dance every dance if she so desired. Eden, amused, watched Inga fending off her Swedish suitor to make room for someone more exotic.

"No dairymen, Lars Jensen." Inga pointed a finger at him, poking him in the center of his clean flannel shirt. "No dairymen, no cows. I milked my last cow in Minnesota."

Eden's partner, who was at least three times her age, huffed to a halt as the fiddlers wound up "Skip To My Lou."

A younger man was the next to bow in front of her. "I remember you, sugar." It was the cattleman in the blue serge suit. He smiled at Eden's panting partner. "My turn, Pops."

The man, out of breath, bowed over Eden's hand. "Whoo-boy, I ain't twenty no more, that's for sure. But you dance a fine reel, Miss Brentwood."

He glared at the boy in the blue suit. "You call me Pops again, we'll see how old I am."

The boy threw up his hands, mock afraid. "I'll be good! My name's Don Gilbert, Miss Brentwood. What's your first name? I know I can't call you by it, but I'd just like to know what it is."

"Eden," she said. "Do you live in Santa Fe? I remember you, too. You were taking some cattle somewhere."

"We've got a spread not too far out of town, down by Apache Canyon. Do you dance the waltz, Miss Brentwood?"

He swept her into the swirling crowd, and she found he was a good dancer, far better than the cowboys and drummers who had been stepping on her toes all night. He danced like the planters' sons she knew from Hawaii, and she realized that he, too, came from a privileged background. Don Gilbert had probably been to school in the East and had had a mother who made him take dancing lessons. It made him safe and somehow familiar, part of the world in which she had grown up.

When the dance was over, he fetched her a glass of lemonade and went off to dance with someone else. But first he said, "You save me another waltz, you hear?"

"You watch him," Lizzie whispered in Eden's ear. "He's fast. His daddy owns the biggest spread around here, and Donny Gilbert thinks he runs the world on account of it."

"I can handle him," Eden said confidently.

"Don't let Pat-Pat see you dance with him too often," Lizzie warned. "She's got it in for Donny. Last year a girl thought he was going to marry her, and she was so broken up when he didn't that she had to go away." Lizzie put her mouth close to Eden's ear. "I don't *think* she was, well, you know . . . but nobody was sure."

"Well, I don't *want* to marry him," Eden said. "So I guess I'm safe."

"Just be careful," Lizzie said over her shoulder as she danced into a reel with a teller from the bank. He was Lizzie's favorite, and Eden thought Lizzie herself might be engaged pretty soon. Lizzie held definite opinions, none very good, about cowboys and railroad men. She wanted someone she could rely on and said that if you couldn't rely on a man who worked in a bank, then who could you trust?

"Ja, and so that leaves the cowboys for me," Inga said, watching them, admiring their tanned faces and lithe, muscular arms, the faintly sinuous way they stood, thumbs hooked in their cartridge belts. "Cows are fine so long as they are not cows I have to milk."

Eden laughed. It was fun to watch her new friends being courted and planning their futures. Because hers was certain, because she had Michael, Eden could enjoy being an observer. Isobel had found, or been found by, a railroad brakeman from Auvergne, and they were delightedly chattering to each other in French. It seemed to Eden that these girls who never had any money, who knew that they must work for a living, enjoyed more options than the girls of Eden's class. But she was beginning to sympathize, too, with the restrictions that poverty placed on them. She lived in sight of the depot and heard the hiss of steam, the shrilling of the whistle, and the clatter of the rails in constant chorus. It was maddening not to have the funds to buy a ticket and simply get on a train.

"You look awfully thoughtful, sugar," Donny Gilbert said, and Eden jumped.

"I was daydreaming," she confessed.

"What about? Handsome cattleman coming to sweep you off your feet maybe?" He gave her a self-satisfied grin. He had curly brown hair and bright blue eyes, and his eyebrows quirked up in little inverted Vs. He was adorable, Eden thought, and he knew it.

"No," she said, remembering Lizzie's information about the girl last year, "I was wishing for an ugly cattleman who could dance. Handsome ones are too conceited."

Donny laughed. "I'll pull my hat down over my face. You want to dance with me anyway?"

"I suppose so," Eden said. Donny was really very easy to deal with.

The fiddlers struck up a fast waltz, and Donny knew the words and taught them to Eden while they danced.

"Oh, what was your name in the States?
Was it Thompson or Johnson or Bates?
Did you murder your wife
And fly for your life?
Say, what was your name in the States?"

"Theme song of the territories," Donny said, laughing.

"Like the French Foreign Legion," Eden said. "The men without names."

"Only the territories are a lot handier."

"Are there really very many criminals out here? Men running from the law, I mean?"

"Plenty who're running from something," Donny said. "Maybe not the law. I guess there are quite a few who didn't go so far as to murder the old woman; they just ran out on her."

"Well now, that doesn't make you boys such good bets for husbands, does it?"

Donny chuckled. "You're on to me. Don't believe everything you hear, though."

"I hear you're a heartbreaker. Maybe worse."

Donny's arm tightened a little around her waist. "That scare you?"

"Nope. *I* don't want you."

Donny laughed. "You're something. Say, you want to go to a show with me tomorrow night?"

"Those traveling actors? I'd love to, but we're not allowed," Eden said wistfully.

"Ah, come on. There's a window with a nice sycamore outside it at Patterson's. I bet you know how to climb a tree, don't you?"

"Certainly not," Eden said, wondering how many

other girls Donny had persuaded to climb down that tree.

The waltz ended, and she was scooped up by another eager partner before Donny could argue further. The new boy was a switchman in the rail yard. Not so finely scrubbed as Donny, he was clearly more in earnest.

"You're the prettiest girl here tonight, Miss Brent-wood," he said. "I been watching you all evening trying to get up my nerve to ask you to dance with me."

"Well, now you have." Eden smiled at him but didn't let him hold her too close. This one was likely to fall in love with her, and that would never do. Donny Gilbert was fine to flirt with, but she certainly didn't want to *be* like him and hurt this nice boy's feelings.

The dance ended at midnight, when Mrs. Patterson herded the girls back to the dormitory.

"Convicts on a chain gang," Inga said, laughing, as she and Isobel walked by in lockstep.

That reminded Eden of Sam, and her heart lurched. Then she and the others passed another poster for *Lady Windermere's Fan*. Eden lagged behind, reading it with longing:

The Harry Salter Dramatic Company
Presents
The British Sensation
Lady Windermere's Fan
by Mr. Oscar Wilde
with
The Great Kar-Mi Troupe
Originators and Presenters of
The Most Marvelous Sword-Swallowing Act on
Earth

And below, in smaller type, the list of players:

Douglas Seaberry, actor-manager, as Lord
Darlington
Jill Cabell as Mrs. Erlynne
Catherine Martin as Lady Windermere

Catherine Martin? Eden looked at the poster again. It bore a scene from the play, full of grand gestures and rolling eyes. She supposed that the soulful young woman with the roses could be Cathy Martin. Of course it was. It couldn't be anybody else.

Cathy might help her. She would surely listen sympathetically and give Eden a cup of tea and not send any wires to Sam. Even if Cathy didn't have enough money to lend her any, Eden would gladly settle for a familiar face and the tea.

When Cathy was nineteen, she had run away from the boarding school that she and Eden both attended and gone to New York to be an actress. After the family had quit having hysterics and decided not to drag Cathy home to Oklahoma, Eden's grandmother Claudia traveled to Manhattan, took Cathy under her wing, gave her a taste of theater life, and prepared to wait until the girl tired of it.

Cathy hadn't tired of it, and Eden had spent a charmed season in New York seeing all the plays and getting a glimpse of the sometimes hand-to-mouth but always fascinating life backstage. Cathy's touring the territories meant that she wasn't starring on Broadway yet; but she wasn't a flop, either.

"Hurry up, Eden."

Eden obediently trotted after Mrs. Patterson, but as they neared the dormitory, she looked with new interest at the sycamore tree with which Donny Gilbert was so familiar.

XIV

Her shoes in her hand, Eden slunk down Mrs. Patterson's upstairs hallway and beckoned to Inga to follow. They could hear the housemother downstairs, snoring in her rocker. Mrs. Patterson made it her habit to sit by the front door until ten o'clock every night, and woe betide the girl who thought that that snoring betokened oblivion. Just try to ease past, and Mrs. Patterson would snort herself awake like a watchdog at the gate and bite.

Eden slipped into the bedroom at the far end, where the sycamore grew. She put her finger to her lips when Maisie, a timid girl with a penchant for sweets, who was just getting ready for the late shift, looked around.

"Shhh!" Eden tied her shoelaces together and hung her shoes around her neck.

Maisie's eyes widened. "You'll get caught!"

"We won't if you don't tattle. There are pillows under the blankets in our room, and nobody *there* will tell on us." Eden's expression indicated to Maisie that only a spineless goody-goody would tell.

"Where are you going?" Maisie demanded, excitement warring with disapproval.

"To see a play," Eden said.

Maisie looked uncertain. "It's not nice. Or the man who wrote it isn't. Or something. Mrs. Patterson said—"

"Stuff," Eden retorted. "Mrs. Patterson doesn't know anything about it." She had no more notion than Maisie what was supposed to be the matter with Oscar

Wilde, but she couldn't see what difference it made to his play. But Eden had had experience at boarding school and knew how to deal with Maisie. "If you don't tell on us, we'll both give you our desserts tomorrow" was her parting offer as she slid out the window.

The sycamore was almost in full leaf and cloaked any shadow Eden and Inga might have made against Maisie's lighted window. They had chosen the black uniform dresses as being the least visible. The girls came down the tree from branch to branch with only a slight rustle of leaves and a fleeting glimpse of white petticoats as they dropped to the ground.

The theater was some distance from the dormitory, and they stopped at the corner to put their shoes on and pin their shawls tighter. The desert air was cold at night, and Eden, accustomed to the almost constant temperature of Hawaii, was unprepared for the rapidity with which the desert could rocket from scorching heat to icy cold. After standing and shivering in the long line to buy the tickets, Eden was grateful for the warmth inside the theater, an elaborate edifice of adobe and Spanish columns surmounted by a terra-cotta roof.

Eden and Inga found their places just as the house-lights were going down. When the curtain went up, the woman upon the stage arranging roses in a blue bowl really was, Eden knew, Cathy Martin. Eden watched the play with interest, trying to decide what was so awful about Oscar Wilde.

She whispered as much to Inga, who whispered back, "I don't know, either. But if Lady Windermere and her husband really loved each other, I think that they'd trust each other more."

Eden considered the philosophical implications of that. It was fun to go to a play with another girl and be able to say what you thought instead of having to worry about what your escort thought. Not that Mike wasn't interested in Eden's ideas, but she had a shrewd notion that Donny wouldn't have been. She was glad she hadn't come with Donny.

At intermission the girls drank lemonade in the

lobby and mulled the play over some more. "When men and women don't trust each other," Eden suggested, "it creates an artificial society like the one Lady Windermere's trying to make, in which things are either *done* or *not* done, and anyone who's made a mistake can't ever be forgiven. But all they've done is break the rules that Lady Windermere has dreamed up, in order to stuff everyone into neat little boxes and put lids on them. At least I think that's what Mr. Wilde's trying to say."

"You are a freethinker," Inga said admiringly. "I am, too. That is why I left Minnesota."

"I thought you left because of the cows," Eden teased.

"That, too." Inga laughed.

They put their lemonade glasses down and returned to their seats. Cathy Martin was found standing by Lord Darlington's fireplace, preparing to disgrace herself forever through what Eden considered to be perfect silliness. It was such fun to watch Cathy, though. She was really very good.

Eden thought she recognized Lord Darlington as a young man she had met in Manhattan at a friend's party. She consulted her program. The fellow was listed as Douglas Seaberry, the troupe's actor-manager. He had dark, curling hair and a raffish look just right for a rake. She wasn't certain about Jill Cabell, Mrs. Erlynne, but Eden thought she had met her, too. What fun! She would take Inga to meet them.

As the play progressed, everyone in the cast seemed to be madly explaining, reexplaining, and covering up—when they were not discussing the nature of good and evil or sin and virtue.

"I never heard anybody talk so much," a man in front of them said irritably at the end of it. "Not even a sword duel to put some pepper in it."

Eden and Inga looked at each other in mutual horror. It was Mr. Hope, the restaurant manager. They stood and stumbled over the couple in the seats beside theirs, gaining the aisle before he could stand up. But emanations of pure guilt must have reached him somehow, because Mr. Hope shifted ponderously in his seat and froze at the glimpse of fleeing Harvey House uniforms.

The aisle was suddenly jammed with people, and Eden and Inga were caught in the press. Afraid to look back in case the devil was gaining on them, they forged ahead. At the theater door, they heard Mr. Hope yelling at them to wait.

"Run!" Inga urged.

They set out across the park, tripping over the flagstones in the walk, with Mr. Hope huffing behind them.

"Stop this instant! Who are you? You are dismissed!"

"Rodney! Wait!" Mrs. Hope wailed in the background.

Inga stumbled and turned her ankle. When she tried to stand on it, she looked despairingly at Eden. "It's no use. I can't run."

"You have to!" Eden told her.

"Well, I can't." Inga took a few steps with Eden dancing impatiently beside her. "Walk, yes. Run, no."

Footsteps thudded behind them. Judgment was descending. "Well, how scandalous could the play be if *he* was in the audience?" Eden said indignantly, but that rationale would not cut any ice with Mr. Hope or, for that matter, Mrs. Patterson. Besides, it was after curfew. "You go on, Inga," she said. "I'll slow him down."

"They'll fire you!" Inga wailed.

"They'll fire us both in a minute. I have a plan. Now go!" Eden gave her a shove. "Go on!"

Inga looked at her, wavering. Mr. Hope thundered nearer. In a minute he would be able to see their faces.

"Go *on!*"

Inga picked up her skirts and hobbled into the darkness.

Eden promptly dropped to the ground, feigning the injury that belonged to Inga. "Oooooh! My ankle," she moaned theatrically.

She let Mr. Hope get almost upon her, and then she

rose and hobbled a few steps toward the theater, away
from the direction that Inga had taken.

"You stop this minute!" Mr. Hope shouted. "I know
you!"

Eden put her hands over her face and limped
farther away. She would have been quite proud of
herself if she hadn't been so certain of getting fired. But
she had talked Inga into this. It wasn't fair to let Mr.
Hope fire Inga.

"Stop this minute!" the restaurant manager bellowed.

The theater crowd had thinned somewhat, and his
voice echoed in the darkened park. Eden ran toward the
back of the theater, where an open door split the
darkness with a sharp blade of light.

"Eden Brentwood, I know you!" Mr. Hope reached
out for her shoulder as faces peered through the open
door. His hand grabbed her, but Eden didn't stop. With
a horrible ripping sound the armhole seam tore out of
her dress just as the people in the doorway began asking
one another what was going on. Eden pulled away with
a jerk, and Mr. Hope found himself with her sleeve in
his hand.

"What's going on, here?"

"You, sir! What do you think you're doing?"

Eden produced a pitiful moan.

"This young woman—" Mr. Hope realized he was
on shaky ground.

"This man assaulted me," Eden whimpered. She
sank to her knees, not entirely acting. Her heart was
pounding so hard she thought she was going to faint.

"Who are you, sir?"

"I'm this young woman's employer," Mr. Hope said
furiously. "She is out after hours."

The actors gathered around Eden protectively.
"Obviously a dangerous thing to do," one of them
remarked dryly, with an accusing look at Mr. Hope.

"Now see here!" he defended.

"Go away," another insisted, "or we'll call the
coppers."

"Merciful heaven! Eden." Cathy Martin bent and helped her to her feet.

Mr. Hope gave up. "You're fired!" he said crossly, and stalked off with the furious air of a man who knows he has made himself look ridiculous.

In the background, Mrs. Hope was still shouting plaintively, "Rodney!"

"Eden, *what* are you doing?" Cathy Martin was wearing a quilted wrapper, and her hair was hidden under a scarf. She was still in makeup, and up close it made her eyes even bigger. Somehow she seemed larger than life.

Eden leaned against her shoulder gratefully. "Thank you." She looked around, trying to retrieve her composure.

"He's gone," Cathy told her.

"Of course he's gone," a masculine voice said. "If he'd hung around we'd have beaten him to a pulp. We can still call the police, though. They might catch him yet."

"No, don't do that," Eden sniffled.

"Come along inside and tell me the whole thing before we decide what to do," Cathy said. "You need a wash and some hot tea. And a new dress, I'd say." They had reached the light, and Cathy inspected Eden's two-dollar dress. "Goodness, what a hideous frock. You come along to my dressing room and tell me what you are doing here dressed up like a washerwoman."

Eden sniffled.

Cathy peered at her in the hallway light. "You haven't run away, you little wretch?"

"Well, sort of." Eden dragged the back of her hand across her eyes, and the words came tumbling out. "I'm going to marry Michael, and nobody's going to stop me. But I lost all my money on the train—this awful woman, she seemed so nice—and I got a job. But now I'm fired, and I haven't earned the money for my ticket—"

"Good heavens." They went inside Cathy's dressing room, and the woman pushed Eden into an ancient overstuffed chair with a section of spring protruding from the back. It seemed a haven to Eden, and she curled into it. A kerosene heater in the corner hissed and sputtered, but it gave off a comforting warmth.

She sniffled a muffled "thank you" when Jill Cabell, whom she did recognize from Manhattan, tucked a paisley shawl around her shoulders to cover the torn dress. Other troupe members, curious and sympathetic, crowded in after her. They were in various stages of costume and undress, some still in makeup.

Douglas Seaberry had shed his tailcoat and stiff-bosomed shirt for a smoking jacket of red wool. The evening trousers he had worn onstage, visible beneath the smoking jacket, when seen close up were shiny and threadbare. The man called Maurice, who had played Lord Augustus, was enveloped in something that looked like a priest's cassock, with Turkish slippers sticking out from beneath it. He was wiping cold cream off his face with a rag. Jill had shed Mrs. Erlynne's dress, but the stiff petticoats caused her dressing gown to stand out around her like a bell. She had a towel tied around her neck, knotted at the back, and her hair swept back by a band. A woman in an apron, with her shirtwaist front stuck full of pins and needles, bustled in and gave Eden a cup of tea.

"Now, then," Cathy said. "From the beginning. Slowly, please, and don't skip bits."

Eden told it all between sips of tea, while the gathering tut-tutted and whispered among themselves in little bursts of outrage and sympathy.

"Imagine their saying you couldn't see our show! We can still beat that man to a pulp for you," the sandy-haired young man who had played Lord Windermere said helpfully when she had finished.

"No, you won't, Freddy," Cathy said. "You'll get us all arrested. Eden can press charges over her dress if she wants to."

"Why bother?" Eden said morosely. "It won't get me my job back."

"That's not fair," Freddy protested.

"Whoever told you life was fair?" Jill, who was a

good ten years older than Freddy, looked at him in disgust.

Cathy looked up at Seaberry. "We can't leave her here like this."

"Certainly not!"

They all proffered opinions.

"Just look what's happened to her already, on her own."

Eden's story appealed to all that was best in their theatrical instincts.

"Such a romantic story! Even when I was young, no one ever loved *me* that much!"

"That's because you're such a shrew."

"At least I'm not in my cups before the last curtain's down, like some people."

"See? That's what I mean."

"Stop squabbling. This is important."

"We can't let true love down."

"Certainly not."

They were prepared to adopt her immediately.

"Douglas . . ." Cathy's gaze held Seaberry's.

"I can give you a position as a seamstress," Doug Seaberry told Eden. "Mary-Ann has more than she can manage, trying to keep us all together." He nodded at the wardrobe mistress, the woman in the apron.

"Can you sew?" Mary-Ann asked.

Eden wide-eyed, nodded, startled by this turn of events.

"Given your story, I think it's safe to say you won't run off with a drummer in Topeka like the last seamstress," Mary-Ann said. "So if you want the job, you've got it. But it's a lot of work and no thanks." She glared at Maurice.

"I thanked you," Maurice protested. "I just said the buttons were crooked. It's not my fault the buttons were crooked. They made my waistcoat stick out funny."

"Your stomach makes your waistcoat stick out funny," Mary-Ann retorted. "Buttons or no."

"A congenial, happy family," Seaberry said to Eden.

"Don't mind them, for goodness' sake," Cathy said,

laughing. "We're taking the tour through New Orleans, and then to Savannah and Charleston and up the Atlantic coast to New York. So in a roundabout way we'll get you where you're going. And you can wire Mike from every stop."

"The pay is twenty dollars a month, plus travel, meals, and accommodations," Doug said. "Mary-Ann will work your fingers to the bone. Do you want it?"

"Oh, yes!" Eden said happily. The pay was more than she was earning at the Harvey House, and the work certainly more interesting and probably not much more arduous. At least she could do it sitting down. No tips, she thought wistfully, but every stop would take her closer to New Jersey. "Yes, and thank you!" What fun. Life *was* fun.

"I still think we ought to go punch his lights out," Freddy said.

"Since you're feeling brave, you can take Eden to the dormitory for her bags," Cathy said.

Freddy quailed. "There won't be anything left of me but raw bleeding flesh," he protested. "I've met those Harvey housemothers before."

"We're assuming that the experience will cool your engine some," Doug said. "We are *not* going to get in a brawl with the locals. I'm not going to wire Harry and tell him his whole company's in jail and would he please send bail. Huh-uh."

"Okay, kid. I'll be your knight errant," Freddy said.

"You're about as errant as they come," Cathy said. "Now get out of here while I find Eden a decent dress." She shooed them all toward the door.

An hour later, washed and brushed and in a pink wool day dress of Cathy's, Eden, with Freddy on her arm for courage—or vice versa, she thought—presented herself at the dormitory door. Freddy jumped and ran his fingers around the inside of his collar when the door opened.

Mrs. Patterson peered out at them, in a wrapper of shabby blue wool, her nightcap askew on her head.

Curling papers bristled from beneath it. She resembled a hedgehog.

"Eden Brentwood! Where have you been?" The woman was shaking with rage.

"Out," Eden said. "I've just come for my bags. I don't think I want to stay. I mean, that is, I quit."

"You do not quit," Mrs. Patterson said. "You are fired. I've spoken with Mr. Hope. You are a disgrace to the Harvey House! *Where* did you get that unsuitable dress?"

"This is my cousin's dress," Eden said indignantly. "It's not unsuitable."

"It's flashy," Mrs. Patterson said with pursed lips. "It is unsuitable for a Harvey girl."

"But you just said I wasn't a Harvey girl," Eden pointed out. "Now may I have my bags?"

A crowd of girls had collected in the doorway behind her. Eden could see Lizzie and Isobel, big eyed; Inga, apprehensive; and Maisie, with a Sunday-school look on her face.

Mrs. Patterson glared at Eden, but there was no way to deny her the right to collect her luggage and thus shield the other girls from contamination. Mrs. Patterson braced her shoulders. Perhaps an object lesson could be made. "You may come in," she said. "But that—*man* must remain outside." She made it sound very like "that crocodile" or "that drug fiend."

"Here, now." Freddy was insulted. "I was just escorting Miss Brentwood. You might let a fellow come in. It's darned cold out here."

"My girls have retired for the night," Mrs. Patterson said icily. "You may wait on the porch." She swung the door open for Eden and faced the other waitresses. "Go to bed, girls. And I hope this has been a lesson to us all."

They went reluctantly up the stairs, whispering to one another, craning their necks back at Eden, and wondering what she had done.

Inga, Lizzie, and Isobel pounced on Eden and carried her off to their own room, with triumphant glances at the crowd of girls in the hall.

"Tell all," Lizzie commanded.

"All of it," Isobel said. "Who is that most beautiful man?"

"I owe you everything," Inga said tearfully. "Maisie let me in, and Pat-Pat doesn't know."

Eden, packing, told all.

"Who's the beautiful young man?" Isobel demanded again.

"Oh, that's Freddy. My cousin sent him with me to get my things."

"He's an actor?" Lizzie said, enthralled.

Maisie, just coming into the bedroom, frowned in disapproval. "They're all out there looking at him. Mrs. Patterson has allowed him into the front hall." In the upstairs corridor, a row of backsides in white lawn nightgowns bent over the banister, as the girls peered down.

"Go to bed!" Mrs. Patterson bellowed from below, and the girls retreated from the railing.

"Ask for his autograph," Lizzie called, laughing.

"It is not a subject for levity," Maisie said. "Just because I helped Inga get back inside doesn't mean I condone your behavior. When a young woman goes out wearing one dress, then comes home in another, she has lost her good name. I saw you, Eden Brentwood. You had on your black dress."

After what she had been through, that was too much for Eden. "Why didn't you tell on me then? Your complicity makes you just as guilty as I, bargaining your wicked soul for extra desserts. I'll tell Pat-Pat on *you* if you don't watch out."

"I had hoped that you would come to your senses and step back from the brink before it was too late." Maisie had her own flair for drama.

"Then you're a silly hen," Eden said.

"I?" Maisie was furious. "*I* have not dragged my name in the mud, consorting with actors in who knows what low circumstances." She pointed her finger at Eden and fired the most damning shot she could think of.

"Eden Brentwood, you have disgraced the name of the Harvey House!"

Eden started to giggle.

"Don't you laugh at me. You are a low trollop and a—"

Inga advanced on Maisie. "You get out of this room, Goody Two-Shoes, before I yank your ears off."

"You take one ear. I take the other," Isobel said.

"Don't! Don't you touch me!"

It was a standoff. Maisie couldn't tell on Inga at this late date. She departed with a sniff.

Eden buckled her carpetbag and put on her hat. She kissed her roommates. "It's been wonderful knowing you all," she said. "I hope to see you again." After all the acting she had done tonight, Eden knew she meant every word of her good-bye.

"I think you're brave," Lizzie said.

Inga's eyes glowed. "I think it's romantic. Just like books."

"Maybe we see *you* on the stage," Isobel said.

In the hall below, Freddy was waiting for her with the look of a trapped elk, while the housemother stood, arms folded, at the foot of the stairs.

"It's been grand, Mrs. Patterson," Eden said. "Thank you so much for your hospitality. Do come and stay with me sometime."

They swept out with the panache of the young and saucy. At the door Freddy, who wasn't much older than Eden, turned and raised his arm. "Farewell, you secret, black, and midnight hag!"

All in all, it was not a peaceful departure.

XV

Cross-country, April to June, 1895

It was like traveling with the Gypsies, Eden decided—colorful, fascinating, and frequently uncomfortable. She acquired a certain sympathy for the "highborn lady" who ran away with Gypsy Davy in the song and slept with him on the cold, cold ground. Not that it ever came to that, but the hotels where the troupe stayed were of the serviceable kind, and the dressing rooms that the local theaters provided varied from adequate to insufficient. When there weren't enough dressing rooms to go around, squabbles invariably resulted over who had to share with whom and whose billing rated them better than they had been given. Mary-Ann and Eden and the wardrobe would be packed into the smallest of these, and only the warming weather as they went farther east freed them from having to sew with their gloves on.

Now that she was on the road and could not be found and brought home, Eden wired Annie to assure her that she was all right, among friends, and well taken care of. By the time the wire made its way by ship from Los Angeles, Eden would be long gone from New Orleans.

She worked hard at her new job. There was always clothing to be mended, and she and Mary-Ann frequently fixed torn curtains and drops as well. The Kar-Mi Troupe of Sword Swallowers, who traveled with the company as the opening act, were theoretically on their own; but the lone woman among them was the only one who could sew, and she did so unhandily. As a result Eden and Mary-Ann took pity on them when Doug wasn't looking and tidied up their costumes. The Kar-Mi Troupe painted their faces to look Oriental and wore harem pants and short Turkish jackets, but they were really Americans.

The troupes traveled together in the same railroad car, with the stagehands and a scenery painter as well as Eden and Mary-Ann. Often they would leave at night after the last performance and arrive at dawn in the next city. They traveled by day coach in seats that reclined but didn't convert into beds. Eden, dozing and drifting half-asleep as the train rattled eastward, would rest her head on her carpetbag while Freddy or Jill or a sword swallower snored next to her.

She listened to the voices around her as the sleep-less found things to occupy them. When Jill and Maurice were wakeful, they played gin and complained about the food. The stagehands played poker and drank and when they got too drunk, they sang "Railroad Bill" loudly until Doug came and took their bottle away. Doug would sit with the light turned low and go over receipts and expenses. Sometimes Cathy would sit behind him and rub his shoulders. Eden wondered if there was some-thing romantic growing between them, but she decided that if there was, it hadn't quite jelled yet. In the enclosed society of the company, love affairs were inev-itable, and when they went bad they caused trouble. Doug, as an actor-manager, couldn't afford to cause trouble.

When the train stopped, the baggage had to be unloaded, along with crates of flats and props to be hauled by wagon to the theater. Eden craned her neck out of the carriage to stare at unfamiliar locales. Doug, meanwhile, fretted over whether the sets were going to work here or if they would have to be changed to fit the stage. If that occurred, all the actors' movements had to be reblocked to fit the size of the stage.

In New Orleans the theater was in the old French

Quarter. Enthralled, Eden stared at wrought-iron lace-work balconies clinging to tall houses, some well kept and spruce with new paint, others sagging and crumbling.

In the short period that Eden lived in Santa Fe, Isobel, a firm believer in ghosts, had told her about the white-haired wraith with fiery eyes who haunted the French Opera House. Isobel had also talked about her cousin Orestia, who had "married twice as old as herself with a man" who took her from the Bayou Caillou to live in the city, where she was unhappy. Eden imagined her imprisoned behind one of those balconies, face pressed against the beautiful latticework to catch a bit of sunlight.

At night, when the French Quarter glowed with lights, lively tunes from a ragtime piano spilled from an open doorway, and there seemed to be an ongoing street party. Cathy ordered her to stay in the theater.

"New Orleans is a high-living town," Mary-Ann said, biting off her thread in agreement.

The next day, when Eden had a free hour, Freddy hired a hack and took her on a tour. He showed her the little white houses on Rampart Street, where white planters still kept quadroon mistresses. A high-living town indeed, Eden thought. She filed it all away, the good and the bad and the things she wasn't supposed to know about. She telegraphed Michael again from New Orleans, thinking he might have returned north, but received no answer.

She returned to the theater to find Cathy morosely contemplating a bouquet of pink roses and a card inscribed with extravagant French compliments.

"Stage-door Johnnies," Cathy said irritably. "Hot air and fast talk. I'd take what you have with Michael any day."

"If I could find him," Eden muttered.

"Here, find this instead." Mary-Ann appeared with Lady Windermere's evening gloves, which were missing buttons.

"Don't worry, Eden," Cathy said absently. "He'll come home."

Meanwhile, Michael, oblivious to anything but his growing desire to strangle his employer, was in Fort Myers, Florida, living on the edge of a swamp. At this moment he was lying facedown on the floor of what felt like a Turkish bath, with nameless insects crawling down his neck.

A perplexed housemaid sat on an inverted tin washtub at the other end of the Turkish bath—which was really a wooden shack of Michael's own construction, with an unreliable skylight that leaked when it rained and an Edison dynamo to power electric lights on stands.

"I got sheets to wash," the housemaid reminded him.

"Just another minute, Leona," Michael murmured. He was trying to rig a heavy camera so that it could be raised slowly from the floor while the film ran through it.

"What do you want to take pictures of my feet for anyway?" she asked.

"I don't want to take pictures of your feet," Mike explained. "I want to start with your feet and go up to your hands, doing the wash."

"What's the matter with my face?"

"Nothing's the matter with your face," Mike said, tinkering with the camera. "You have a fine face." He sat up, brushing a millipede off his shirtfront. "But the story I want to tell is about work, making something clean. Your feet, braced against the floor, show that. And your hands in the tub. The face isn't important."

The housemaid looked as if it was important to her.

"It's hot as the dickens in here."

"I know, Leona. I'm uncomfortable, too." Fort Myers was about the soggiest place Michael had ever been. William Dickson, a longtime Edison employee, had built a studio in New Jersey for the moving-picture camera. The studio's roof could be peeled back, and the turntable foundation could follow the sun. Mike had begged and pleaded to have it dismantled and shipped to

Fort Myers along with the other tons of assorted baggage that had been barged up the Caloosahatchee River to this retreat in the wilderness, but Edison had balked because of the studio's size. The balmy climate of Florida, he said cheerfully, did not necessitate such protection. The balmy climate of southwestern Florida was so muggy, however, that even when it wasn't raining the camera jammed after fifteen minutes in the open, and moisture condensed on the film.

So Michael had cobbled together his own imitation of Dickson's studio, smaller and hotter inside than the original. The studio in New Jersey was sheathed in black tar paper and nicknamed the Black Maria by Edison's crew because of its size and lack of comfort. After five minutes in Mike's studio, a fellow slave of the inventor's had christened it Baked Maria and declined ever to set foot in it again.

"All right, let's try it." Mike mopped his face and motioned the housemaid off her washtub. He poured it full of water from the wooden bucket and dumped soap flakes in, then stirred them up with his fist.

"You're gettin' me wet!"

"I want suds, big thick ones."

"I think you're crazy," Leona said. "I think all you Yankee boys are crazy."

"I know it, darlin'," Mike said. "Just put those shirts in and wash 'em, okay?"

Mike fixed the camera on her feet and flipped the electrical switch that fed the film through it. The maid was barefoot, and her callused feet were thick, with squared-off toes and thick nails. She stood with her feet braced on either side of the washtub, and her dark, heavy skirt swayed just above the ankles as she bent and scrubbed.

The lever that lifted the camera worked this time, and Mike raised it slowly to the edge of the tub. Suds spilled, and bubbles floated gently through the humid air. The girl's hands, strong and square like her feet, lifted and beat the shirts against a scrub board in the tub. There was a rhythm to it, as hard and ponderous as the tide. He stopped the camera just under her chin. The soap bubbles hung in the air and contrasted nicely with those muscular arms.

"Hey, Holt! The old man says to get your tail into the lab!" The door swung open, and a shaft of light split Mike's carefully illuminated scene.

"Goddamn it, Willis!" Michael stopped the camera. "Do I have to put a lock on the door? How many times have I asked you to knock?"

"Cheery, aren't you? When the old man says hop, I don't hang around to ask if you're receiving." Willis looked at Mike's model. "I thought the old man wanted some cooch girl."

"He wants an Arabian dancer," Mike said. "Thinks it'll appeal to the kinetoscope trade. But Arabian dancers are hard to find in these parts. He'll have to take what he gets."

"Well, he sure doesn't want this one with a load of wet wash."

"This is art," Mike said. "Or it was till you opened the door. Get out of here. Tell him I'm coming." Leona was taking her shirts out of the tub. "Thanks anyway, honey."

"Where's my dollar?"

"Here." Mike dug in his pocket.

She departed with the wet shirts under her arm. Willis followed, shaking his head. "You're crazy, Holt. Nobody pays for art in a kinetoscope parlor. Cooch girls, yeah."

Mike grinned after him, then started packing up the camera. He was hoarding this film—and a lot more that Edison didn't know anything about. If he weren't so determined to wring every bit of knowledge he could out of Edison and William Dickson, he would have been long gone. As it was, he was about willing to swim the seventy miles up Florida's Gulf coast to Sarasota just to get out of Fort Myers.

There wasn't any way to get to Fort Myers except by barge up the Caloosahatchee, and there wasn't anything there when you arrived—except Edison's complex of houses and laboratories and a modest community of people who, in Mike's opinion, must all have been crazy to live there. Edison's complex consisted of two houses just alike, which had been built in Maine ten years before and shipped to Florida on four sailing schooners; a "honeymoon cottage," the original building, which now housed his unfortunate assistants; botanical gardens into which Edison stuck beehives and every tropical oddity he could lay his hands on; and chemical and electrical laboratories. The twin white-frame houses with their red roofs were palatial in the context of Fort Myers. The honeymoon cottage was less so and provided an atmosphere conducive to Spartan dedication to work.

A cowpath bisected the grounds, bordered by an avenue of queen palms barged up from Cuba, which were waiting for the cowpath to grow into a thoroughfare. The gardens contained such menacing items as an African sausage tree, which grew foot-long fruits shaped like clock weights and dropped them on unwary visitors, and a South American dynamite tree, which grew tomato-shaped fruit that exploded.

The twin houses were connected by a covered breezeway. Only one house contained a kitchen because Edison disliked the smell of cooking food. He didn't mind eating the food; he just didn't want to sleep in the same house with the aroma. The house with the kitchen also served as a guest house; the barge came upriver only once a month, and Mr. Edison and his guests found it difficult to put up with one another in the same house for that length of time.

Mrs. Edison, who had to have some hobby besides putting up with her husband, was a bird lover. She planted birdhouses on poles along the dock to keep them from cats. When she found a sick bird, she nursed it back to health in a set of special cages. When she found a dead one, she had it stuffed and exhibited in a glass case on the front porch. On state occasions when the laboratory assistants were invited to dine with the family, Michael found the stuffed peacock on the plate rail in the dining room a little unsettling.

"Is the old man crazy?" was the question that most assistants had to ask only once. That he was a genius was undoubtable; but he was irascible, deaf, and volatile.

Mike's enthusiasm was beginning to waver. He had managed to film one short moving picture, which Mr. Edison thought was salable. It did not feature dancing girls but was a comedy piece in which Fred Ott, Edison's handyman, capered and sang and then fell off a ladder. It was burlesque, Mike thought disdainfully. Burlesque, Edison maintained, was what sold. All his kinetoscope films were simply translations of what one might see on a stage, shot with a static camera, like viewing vaudeville through a window. Mike had heard of film shot by the Lumière brothers in France, taken on the street with a portable camera, and this concept captivated his interest.

He tried explaining this to Fred Ott, when the handyman appeared to reclaim the washtub, the absence of which had been noticed by Mrs. Edison.

"I don't get it," Ott said shrugging. "Inside, outside, what's the difference?"

"It's the difference between life and a photograph," Mike replied.

"These *is* photographs," Ott said.

"They're *moving* photographs. We don't have to be so limited in our subject matter."

"Our stuff moves. I sure as hell moved off that ladder. Near cracked my skull."

"Look at it this way," Mike said. "What we've been shooting is what would happen on a stage. It's artificial. Everything moves from side to side. There's no depth. The Lumière brothers shoot on the streets. People come closer, then they move away. They're alive."

"I think you're as crazy as the old man," Ott grumbled. "Only trouble is, you ain't a genius, and you ain't rich. You better just do it the way he says."

"He's *wasting* it," Mike fumed, frustrated.

"You think you can do better?" Ott, huffing, dragged the washtub to the door and poured out its contents.

"You wait till I get some backers for my own company. Then you watch my smoke."

"Mebbe," Ott allowed. "In the meanwhile, you better smoke on over to the laboratory."

Disgruntled, Mike put the film box under his arm and headed first for the honeymoon cottage. Halfway across the road, Edison spotted him.

"Holt! What do I pay you for?"

"Coming!" Michael yelled. *You don't pay me enough to put up with you.*

He ditched the film box in the cottage and sprinted for the electrical lab. Inside, the boss was standing in front of a phonograph, apparently biting it.

Three assistants were gathered around him in attitudes of studied expectation. Edison couldn't hear a phonograph from two feet away, but he claimed—with seeming veracity—that he could sense the vibrations through the nerves of his teeth. He looked up, champing his incisors together as if casting about for something else to bite.

"Terrible sound. Awful. Who recorded this?"

"I did," Mike admitted. "It was an experiment, to go with the new film. I thought—"

"I *don't* pay you to think! I think enough for every man working for me. All I want *you* to do is what I tell you."

"Yes, sir." Mike resisted the urge to grind his own teeth.

"Hmmph." The inventor had a strong-featured face under thick brows and a high-domed forehead, which connoted either intelligence or a receding hairline, depending on how you looked at it. He combed his hair down over his forehead, in vaguely the same manner as Napoleon Bonaparte. "It sounds like ducks paddling in a pond. Splash-splop." He snorted with disgust. "Forget about it. You don't have time to play with film. I want you to work on the storage battery."

Michael groaned. The storage battery was Edison's obsession. So far they had run nine thousand experiments, and it still didn't work. Mike was willing to

concede that a storage battery would be a boon to
mankind; he just didn't want to try another nine thousand times to produce one.

Charlie Dally smiled sympathetically at Mike from
the glass-blowing table across the room. Dally provided
test tubes, light bulbs, vacuum bottles, and any other
glass apparatuses to order. When Edison wasn't looking,
Dally blew little glass animals and glass orchids, like the
real ones that clung spiderlike to the trees in the
botanical garden. Mike had a glass orchid packed away,
which he was saving for Eden.

"Storage battery," Edison said again. "Here are my
notes to work from. I didn't hire you for moving pictures."

Yes, you did, Mike nearly said, but the issue wasn't
worth arguing about. If Edison decided he hadn't said
something, then he hadn't said it, even if he had.

Mike gave up and went to lift a beaker from the
wooden rain tank that provided pure water for the lab.
The battery used a diluted solution of sulfuric acid. Mike
wiped his brow. It was stiflingly hot in the lab at the end
of May, nearly as bad as in the film studio. Nobody could
figure out why the old man hadn't packed up for New
Jersey yet, but nobody had the nerve to ask, either.

Mike fiddled gingerly with the battery acid and
thought wistfully of his half-finished film. He had to have
something completed to show prospective backers before he jumped ship and lost the use of Edison's equipment. The picture, as he imagined it in its completed
form, was about real people doing their real work. It told
a story of sorts, moving back and forth between the
washerwoman and an old cattleman in Fort Myers
braiding a rope, then catching a loose cow with it. In the
last segment, as yet unfilmed, the cattleman would put
on the washerwoman's clean shirt, and leading the cow,
they would walk together down the dirt road under the
palms.

Sweat dripped into Mike's eyes, and he began to
feel panicky. Even the old man wouldn't put up with this

heat for much longer. Mike *had* to get that last scene before they went north again.

Accordingly, he sneaked out of the cottage at four in the morning in his long johns. The film he had shot the day before was in his pocket. He glided past Charley Dally, who slept near the door. Dally had a terror of burglars but didn't awaken when Mike slipped out. Maybe Charlie was only attuned to people coming in.

Because Edison had a habit of working all night, Mike approached the lab cautiously. The building was dark, and he slipped in and felt his way to the darkroom at the far end. Before he worried about the next shot, Mike wanted to develop the previous day's film and make sure that Willis hadn't spoiled it by opening the door.

Mike closed the darkroom door and locked it before he turned on the red light and poured developer and fixer into pans. He took the folded film out of its box, and as he ran it through the developer, he peered at it anxiously. When it looked right, he rinsed it in the fixer and held it up. Except for the last few frames, it was fine, and he thought he could do without those.

Mike stood for a moment, staring at it, entranced as always. Motion pictures operated on the principle that the human eye did not react as fast as the frames of film could be cranked through a camera. The shutter opened and closed as each frame was exposed, producing a series of slightly changing images that seemed to move when viewed quickly enough. As a child Michael had painstakingly drawn flip books by hand on pads of paper; but this was real, the mass entertainment of the future. Mike knew it with the same surety that his cousin Peter Blake knew about automobiles: They were coming; it would happen.

As he waited impatiently for the film to dry, he kept one ear cocked for sounds of movement in the lab. By the time he packed the film back in its box, the first faint glimmers of dawn were hanging in the air among the exotica of the botanical gardens. Now for the washerwoman, the shirt, the old man, and his cow. Mike was going to play hooky. If it got him fired, at least he would have the film.

When he was on his own up north, he would need to locate someone to build him a decent projector. Edison was wedded to the kinetoscope, which he had patented. It showed the film in a little box. To Mike's frustration, Edison steadfastly refused to tinker with enlarging projectors. "Pigheaded old devil" had become a synonym for Mr. Edison in Mike's vocabulary. When someone else patented an enlarging projector, Mike thought, the old man was going to be sorry. William Dickson had wanted to build one, too, and produced a fair try at it a few years before. But Edison had ditched the project after that.

Now he loaded the heavy camera, fresh film, and one of his own clean shirts onto a handcart and lay in wait for the housemaid as she emerged from the main house. Her apron was full of chicken feed. He popped out at her from behind one of Mr. Edison's more sinister botanical specimens, and startled, she dropped the feed.

"Now look what I done! What you think you're doing, jumping out at people like a ha'nt?"

"Come on, Leona. I'll give you another dollar."

Suspicious, she put her hands on her hips. "Come on where?"

"Just down the road a piece."

She eyed him dubiously.

"One hour, that's all. You'll be back before anyone's up, and then I'll help you feed the chickens."

"Well . . ."

"Come on. And help me push the cart."

He lured her down the cow path half a mile to where the cattleman had his shack. They caught him just as he was going out. The cowman also demanded another dollar.

"I'm paying you people more than Edison pays me," Mike grumbled, but he handed it over.

"An' a dollar for the cow."

"Where's she going to spend it? I'll give you fifty cents."

The cow's wages agreed upon, Mike picked his spot for the camera and set it up. This camera was his own, a present from his father. It was hand cranked and thus portable, unlike the Edison camera, which was powered by electricity. (Edison held firm to the conviction that anything that could be run by electricity should be.) The trick here was to match the speed of his cranking to the preset speed of forty-six frames per second at which the indoor shots had been taken.

"What the hell difference does it make?" the cowman demanded as Mike cranked the camera, filmless, for a few minutes to get the rhythm.

"Because it's all going to be projected at the same speed," Mike explained. "If you don't shoot it at the same speed, half of it's going to look normal, and the other half's going to look like a bunch of jackrabbits."

They nodded, accepting the logic.

"All right. Let's do it."

Miraculously, he got the shot on the first try, which was fortunate, because upon his return he found that Mr. Edison had become aware of the temperature in Florida at the end of May and Mike's absence with Edison's handcart and Mrs. Edison's housemaid.

XVI

New Jersey, June 1895

Michael paid the cabman outside a dingy rooming house on Spring Street in West Orange. He referred to it as his apartment house, and his mother, Alexandra, called it "that dump you live in." Alexandra's assessment was closer to the mark. Shingles hung dispiritedly from the edge of the roof, and the paint would have been peeling—had there been any paint left to peel. Its single advantage was that its rent was cheap. Michael had returned from his truant morning in Fort Myers to be greeted not only by the news that the Edison Company was moving north again, but that he was fired and could find his own way back to New Jersey. Only Mrs. Edison's intervention had gotten him a ride on the barge as far as the train station in Sarasota.

Mike picked up his bag in one hand and his camera box in the other and went carefully up the steps, which had given way on one side during his absence. His landlady greeted him at the door.

"Heard you was fired," she said.

"I'm still solvent," Mike told her, and wondered how in the world she could have known that. He longed to move into better accommodations, but frugality was going to be of primary importance for a while.

The landlady wore a dingy housedress and bedroom slippers. Her hair was in curlpapers, probably because it was too much trouble to brush it out. "Rent's due next week," she reminded him. "See you pay it on time."

On a silver platter, you old besom. "Don't worry, Mrs. Higgins. I'll pay it."

As he went upstairs, he wondered with what and for how long. Forced to find his own way home, Mike had stopped in Washington to visit his parents—and to sponge a few decent meals and any old, cast-off clothes of his father's and Tim's he could snag. Alexandra had pleaded with him to come back home. Maybe he should have, he thought. But if he was going to find backing for his fledgling company, he should remain close to the theatrical investors in New York. At least he had something to show them. And when Toby wasn't looking, Alexandra had given him a hundred dollars. He hadn't been too proud to take it, either.

Mike unlocked and opened his door, sending a pile of telegrams and a letter from Hawaii across the dusty floor. He stood stunned, then dived for them.

The first one, grabbed at random, was a telegram from New Orleans. It said only that Eden was there and asked him to wire her back right away. He looked at the date and groaned. His heart pounding, he snatched up the next one and the next. They all said the same thing on varying dates and from various cities—Abilene, Shreveport, Baton Rouge. At last he came on the one from Santa Fe and became truly terrified. Stranded with no money.

Mike blanched, envisioning all the things that might have befallen her. Why had she sent the telegrams to New Jersey? he wondered. Hadn't she gotten his letters from Florida? Frantically he read them again, trying to sort them by date, and came on the one from Amarillo, Texas, the first stop with the Salter company's tour. She was with Cathy Martin. Mike didn't know whether to be relieved or unnerved at the thought of his darling traveling with actors. He rather liked actors but considered them erratic of habits and amorous by nature—not the people he would have chosen for his adored Eden to spend time with. And Cathy Martin, by family reckoning, was wild and feckless. Oh, God . . . where was Eden now?

Mike opened the letter last, supposing it to be from
Eden, apprising him of this foolhardy plan. Why hadn't
he been here to dissuade her from it? He cursed himself
until he read the first few lines and then discovered that
the letter was from Sam, and Sam was doing all the
cursing necessary.

"If you don't find her and send her back, when I get
out of jail I'm going to shoot you" was the mildest thing
Sam had to say. Mike found himself a little relieved that
Sam was still in jail.

And since Eden obviously hadn't known that he was
delayed in Fort Myers, why hadn't Mrs. Higgins had the
telegrams forwarded there? She knew where he was.
Mike went roaring down the stairs, clutching a fistful of
yellow sheets.

Mrs. Higgins was sweeping the front steps with a
broom but making very little headway. "I see you found
'em," she said grimly.

"Why didn't you forward these?" Mike yelled.

Mrs. Higgins tucked her snuff more firmly under
her upper lip. "Not my business to pay all that postage.
Nor yet no telegrams." She sniffed. "Gettin' telegrams
from females asking for money."

"You *read* them?"

"I keep a respectable house here!" Mrs. Higgins
snapped. She swept an empty potted-meat tin off the
porch and into the dejected geranium that was trying to
claw out an existence in her flower bed. "I don't hold
with such goings-on. If you've ruined some girl, you're
gonna have to move."

Mike felt his temper overflowing, and the tightness
in his chest meant that he was going to lose it. He had
finally learned that the squeezing sensation didn't beto-
ken an incipient heart attack, only fury. He was about to
scream at Mrs. Higgins when a telegraph boy came
whistling up the dirty street on his bicycle.

"Got another one," he told Mrs. Higgins.

"Give it to him." She jerked her thumb at Mike.

Mike bounded to the edge of the porch and
snatched it before the boy had gotten off his bike. "Give

me that! Why didn't you forward these things? I left a forwarding address at the post office!" He tore it open, then squinted in the sun at the pale letters.

MICHAEL HOLT, 364-D SPRING STREET, ORANGE, NEW JERSEY MICHAEL ARE YOU HOME YET STOP IN SAVANNAH NOW STOP ARE YOU EVER COMING HOME STOP WHAT DO I DO IF SAM FINDS ME STOP LOVE STOP EDEN BRENTWOOD WESTERN UNION SAVANNAH GEORGIA

"Savannah!" Mike yelled. "She's in Savannah! Why the hell didn't somebody *find* me?"

"I just deliver 'em," the telegraph boy said. He held his hand out. "You gonna give me a tip? I got places to go."

"I'll give you a place to go." Mike grabbed him by the throat. "You little weasel, you could have found out where I was! You could have asked this woman here. Get out of my sight! You want a tip, I'll give you a kick in the backside!" He let the boy go and lifted a foot to make good on it. Mike chased the boy ten or twenty yards as he pedaled frantically down Spring Street, and then came back in stiff-legged fury.

"I've got to go send a wire," Mike growled at his landlady, who had watched the proceedings with a stolid lack of interest.

"You ain't bringin' no woman here," she informed him.

"I wouldn't dream of it," Mike snarled. He slammed the front door and stalked up the stairs.

In his room he got Alexandra's hundred dollars out of his bag and stuck it in his pocket. That ought to be enough for Eden's fare and his own into New York. He could camp at Janessa's house until he found something there. Work, for instance.

He dashed down the stairs again, shouted at Mrs. Higgins that he would be back for his bags, and got out his own bicycle, which was his only method of transportation.

I have to find a decent room for Eden, he thought,

pedaling. His digs at Mrs. Higgins's consisted of a rusty iron bedstead, a gas ring, and a desk made of a board and two packing crates. He wouldn't bring Eden to this rattrap, even if the old beldam would let him.

At the telegraph office, he encountered the messenger boy again, looking aggrieved. Mike ignored him, went inside, and wired seventy dollars to Eden.

Michael arrived on Janessa's doorstep at dinnertime with his trunk, a leather traveling bag, his bicycle, and his camera.

"You can't stay here," Janessa informed him after he had played with his niece and nephew. "There isn't any room." She set him a place at the table. "And you can't rent a room and take Eden to it. That would be indecent." She put a bowl of hot lamb stew in front of him. "And you can't just get married without any notice." She gave him a glass of milk and a napkin. "You're going to have a decent wedding in a month's time. And you are going to wire Dad and then write to him and ask for the money to get started on. And if you're too pigheaded to do that, I'll do it for you. Is that clear?"

"Yes," Mike said meekly through a mouthful of stew.

"And Charley agrees with me, don't you, Charley?"

"I expect so," Charley said. His mouth twitched in amusement, but he made no further comment. He could see Kathleen in the kitchen, her head craned over her shoulder like an owl's, listening in fascination.

"And what are you going to do about Sam?"

"You mean I get to decide something?" Mike asked her.

"Michael . . ."

"I'm going to write and ask for his sister's hand," Mike said, and started laughing in spite of himself. "He's still in jail, thank God."

"Ah, the poor man." Kathleen stuck her head through the doorway, a baby bottle in one hand. "And what's he done?"

"Started a revolution," Mike answered.

Kathleen's eyes widened, but she nodded approvingly. "And so he should. You have to stand up to the government then, or they'll lay you low every time. Me brother was the same way, rest his soul."

"That will do, Kathleen. I think I hear the twins crying," Janessa said firmly, since Charley showed signs of losing his composure entirely.

"Kathleen on the subject of politics is always a revelation," Charley murmured after she had departed.

"You shouldn't laugh at her," Janessa chided. "Her family has had a very hard time."

"If you don't laugh, you're doomed," Charley said.

"Well, I'm not laughing," Janessa told him. "We'll be lucky if any of the Brentwoods speak to us again. Michael, how could you?"

"I didn't," Mike protested. "Eden did."

"We wonder what Eden sees in you," Charley informed him.

"My dashing good looks," Mike said. "My savoir faire. My carefree acceptance of unemployment and total financial ruin." He felt a little drunk with relief to be eating lamb stew in his sister's dining room, in this heaven of warmth and family, out of Mrs. Higgins's boardinghouse. "The palatial suite I'm going to rent for her as soon as I figure out how to pay for it."

"Not with you in it, you're not," Janessa warned. "Absolutely not."

"I'm not that stupid," Mike told her. "Why do you think I want to get married right away?"

Janessa put her hands on the table opposite him and bent over, eye to eye. "I *know* why you want to get married right away."

Mike blushed.

"However. That child is going to have a decent wedding, with a wedding dress and a reception and flowers and—"

"All the trimmings," Charley said. "Candles, organ music, flower girls, fat old aunts to give you toasting racks. Look on the bright side, old man. You're broke. If you don't have a proper wedding, no one will give you wedding presents."

"Charley!"

"Mercenary." Mike shook his head. "In light of my current circumstances, I guess I'd better do it."

Janessa surveyed them affectionately. "You're disgraceful, both of you. Come along, Charley, and open that bottle of champagne you've been saving."

> "Hail the bridegroom, hail the bride!
> When the nuptial knot is tied—"

The Harry Salter Dramatic Company, chanting Gilbert and Sullivan and with a laughing Eden in their midst, capered down the railway platform at the Savannah depot. Cathy Martin held a pink parasol over Eden's head, and Doug Seaberry had a handful of rice, which he tossed into the air to rain over the parasol. Jill Cabell wore a hat with enormous ostrich plumes, and Freddy led the chorus, dancing backward at their head.

The Kar-Mi Troupe gamboled behind them, turning cartwheels and swallowing swords to the obvious apprehension of other passengers.

> "For happy the lily
> That's kissed by the bee—"

They swirled Eden up to her railway carriage and pelted her with flowers as she climbed the steps. She found her seat and threw the window open, laughing at them. Cathy handed her a bunch of roses, and Doug Seaberry swept off his hat and bowed. As the train jerked into motion, they danced backward in formation, Freddy waving his arms wildly in time to the final chorus.

> "But happier than any,
> A pound to a penny,
> A lover is, when he
> Embraces his bride!"

"Good-bye!"

"Good-bye!"

"Invite us to the wedding!"

The hissing steam chuffed into a roar, and the train picked up speed.

"Mercy," said the lady in the seat next to Eden. "Who was that?"

"Friends," Eden said. "Lunatics. Bridesmaids." She looked at the lady dubiously, remembering the last time she had been lured into conversation. She didn't have anything to steal this time, of course.

She settled back in her seat and thought with a little start, *I'm going to get married.* Her imagination picked up speed along with the train as she tried to feel what that would be like, how it would be to be with Mike all the time. At night . . .

She blushed. Nice girls weren't supposed to think about that sort of thing, but Eden didn't know any nice girls who didn't. How could anyone help but think about it? It had felt so good when Mike held her and kissed her. But then she thought about the time she had seen a stallion at Aloha Malihini mounting a mare, its powerful muscles moving under its glossy skin, its teeth in the female's neck. And she had caught a fleeting glimpse of . . . something. Having been given a classical education, Eden had seen statues, but the male organ hadn't looked as innocuous on the stallion as it had on Michaelangelo's "David."

Eden thought with revulsion about Dickie Merrill, his hot breath in her ear, and what he did with Koana, and then about Mike doing the same thing with her, which seemed altogether different. She and Mike almost had made love, she remembered, two years ago in Hawaii. But then they hadn't, because Mike had stopped. What would it be like now? *I'm going to find out,* she thought, shaken. She conjured Mike's image in her mind's eye quite deliberately and took stock of her reactions. Her body, she discovered, was quite ready to find out.

The woman beside her patted her hand. "You'll just

make the prettiest bride, sugar. And don't you let your new husband scare you off." She looked at Eden with maternal concern. "There's things a woman has to do for a man that we don't like; but the men, well, they need it. It's in their nature, being closer to the beasts. You remember that, and it'll help you understand him."

"I'll remember," Eden said. She turned her face to the window, and a small, secretive smile curled her lips.

Eden anxiously scanned the crowd at Grand Central Station as she looked for Mike, afraid she wouldn't see him, assuring herself over and over that she would recognize him. It was so hard to tell what anyone looked like from a photograph, and she had not seen him for two years. And then there he was, unmistakably Michael, and yet a face changed as strikingly as a kitten's grown into a cat's. Mike had always been thin, but Eden's immediate impression was that he had grown thinner. And then she saw that it was only in the face. If Mike had had any puppy fat to lose, it had been in cheeks and chin. Now his face appeared oval instead of round. And he had chosen a year when every other man was shaving his whiskers—in the mode of Charles Dana Gibson's idealized man—to grow a mustache.

They stood on the platform, twenty feet apart for a frozen moment, with a herd of people lowing like cattle between them. It lasted only an instant while she absorbed the change in his face. And then she was walking swiftly through the herd, and then she was in his arms, face tight against his chest, listening to his heart pound.

"Eden. Oh, my Eden." He bent his face and kissed her, and the mustache was both unfamiliar and oddly comforting. She had her carpetbag in one hand and her pocketbook in the other, and she dropped both of them, one by one, and wrapped both arms around his back. Mike hooked his ankle through the strap of the pocketbook and put a foot on the carpetbag, but he didn't stop kissing her. He was wearing a summer straw hat, and it kept bumping the brim of Eden's until, still kissing, finally they reached up and took them off. They looked at each other, eyes wide with delight. A second later they clung to each other and kissed again.

Finally Mike stood back and said, stumbling over the words, earnest and as nervous as she was, "Come on. I think we're a bottleneck here." He stopped and picked up her bags. "Don't ever turn your back on anything for a minute in this place. New York pickpockets can darn near steal your shoes while you're wearing them."

"Thank you." They turned their talk to practicalities to give their hearts a chance to stop pounding. Eden felt charged with electricity and possibility. Her reaction to seeing Michael was so intense that if she did not calm down, she thought she would explode. "You've gotten taller," she said, measuring her eyes against his chest. She had been at eye level with his chin two years before. Now it was his top shirt button.

"A little," he said. He stood still again, just staring at her. "Oh, God, you're beautiful."

How did you tell a man that he was beautiful, too, Eden wondered, and make it sound like a compliment? She couldn't think of the words, so she just smiled and stroked his cheek with her gloved fingers. She was getting used to the mustache. She touched it. "I like it."

Mike grinned sheepishly. "I just wanted to prove I could grow one. I was shaving only about once a week the last time you saw me. But if you think it makes me look like an anarchist, I'll get rid of it."

"It makes you look adorable. It's not as if it was something awful, like muttonchop whiskers."

"Never. I promise you."

They went on, arm in arm, acutely aware of each other's physical presence, determined not to be obvious about it, Eden out of years of a proper upbringing, and Mike, she assumed, for fear of frightening her. It was the upbringing that gave way first.

"I think we ought to get married as soon as we can," she whispered.

"So do I," Mike agreed morosely, "but Janessa's put her nose into the business and says we have to wait a month and invite everybody in the family so as to be no more scandalous than necessary. I've never known Janessa to be such a busybody. It must be the effect of motherhood. She's got leftover maternal instinct, and she's passing it on to everybody else."

"Well, then we'll wait," Eden said. "I'm not going to start out by crossing your family. I've already got mine on the warpath, I expect."

"I'll let you read a letter I got from Sam," Mike said ruefully, "if it hasn't gone up in flames of its own accord."

Eden bit her thumb and looked at him dubiously. "Where are we going to live? Oh, Mike, I meant to bring enough money to get us started on! I am *so* stupid!"

"Because you trust people and someone took advantage of it? Don't worry, we have a place to live—or *you* do. I found a suite at the Chelsea Apartments on Twenty-third Street. They're a little down at the heels, but the neighborhood is decent."

"I'm sure I'll love it."

"A tenants' association oversees it. Wait till you meet the neighbors. Dad lent me the money for the first few months' rent, and I've found a job running a magic-lantern show for an old boy named Ira Hirsch down on lower Broadway. He'll let me sleep in the back of the theater until we get married. So we're all set." He grinned, and then because they couldn't stand it any longer, they kissed again.

The Chelsea Apartments, when Eden and Michael tore themselves out of each other's arms long enough to catch a hack and get there, loomed over a big stretch of Twenty-third Street between Seventh and Eighth avenues beside a bookie's parlor, a left-wing bookstore, a vaudeville theater, and a restaurant where good, cheap lobster was served by surly waiters.

The building had been financed in the early eighties by a group of artists who had managed simultaneously to come into some money and agree upon how to spend it. It was one of the first cooperative apartment houses in the city. But the population had moved north in the last ten years, and Twenty-third Street, which was once considered classy, had fallen on hard times. The red brick front was still imposing, however, and the entrance was guarded by a doorman who shooed away loitering derelicts and was wise enough to know them from the tenants.

The apartment that Mike had rented had been partitioned from twelve rooms down to four and was on the ninth floor. It featured a balcony overlooking Twenty-third Street, and the flowery iron railing matched the main staircase. Eden, remembering New Orleans's French Quarter, fell in love with the railing. In one neighboring apartment lived an artist who wore the first thing he stumbled upon in his closet in the morning. His walls were frescoed with smoky, visionary paintings depicting the circles of hell and were inhabited largely by wraithlike fiends who turned out to have the other tenants' faces. On the other side of Mike and Eden's apartment was that of a composer who owned a snake and a fluctuating menagerie, which, from time to time, included a pair of doves, a cockroach-eating gecko, and an ill-tempered skunk named Phoebe, who bit female visitors.

Mike had decorated the rooms with an assortment of furniture acquired in the secondhand shops on the Lower East Side. His acquisitions included an enormous mahogany bed whose veneer had peeled beyond repair. The neighboring artist had solved that by painting it white and picking out and painting the curlicues of the remaining trim with lavender and rose. Eden adored it and was thrilled with the minuscule kitchen with its secondhand icebox, the equally minuscule bathroom with its marble floor, the stained-glass transom, the daily parade of odd-looking residents in the hallway, and the roof, where tenants watched the stars and grew tomatoes and strawberries.

Janessa came to see it and could barely drag an enthralled Charley away. Alexandra, placated by a contrite note from Eden and a wedding invitation, came up on the train to see the apartment and said "Good heavens."

Eden wired Annie and wrote decorous notes to all her other friends and relations announcing her upcoming wedding. Thus she soothed the feelings of anyone whom it was still possible to placate.

Annie wrote back immediately with immense relief. She also enclosed a thick packet of Mike's letters, which had apparently been opened by the PGs but deemed harmless and finally forwarded in one bundle to the plantation. Annie verified what Mike had already told her—that Sam was still in prison. "Don't come home again," Annie wrote. "There isn't anything you can do but wait for this government to give in. I want only the best for you, darling. I wish I could dance at your wedding, but I can't leave Sam."

Eden felt uneasy and feared for Sam's well-being. In an effort to keep herself distracted, she scrubbed, cleaned, and painted more furniture, watched the swirling images of the magic-lantern show with Mike from the projectionist's booth where he slept at night, and had dinner with him afterward in strange foreign restaurants where whatever she ordered turned out to be a surprise.

On the walk home one evening they paused to kiss passionately under streetlights and were encompassed by the roar of the elevated railway. Outside Eden's door in the Chelsea, they managed with growing difficulty not to give in to a mutual urge for Mike to spend the night. He had grown older in more than years, and if his physical presence had rocked Eden before, it was a temptation that burned her to her fingertips now.

Eden would cheerfully have taken him in and drawn him into her bed, if he had tried at all to convince her. But he was obviously holding himself back. He had promised himself, he told her. He seemed to think it would be wrong, and she couldn't quite explain why it wouldn't. Besides, she was a little afraid, and the excitement and the fear together were oddly pleasurable.

Janessa had taken over the wedding plans, under orders from Alexandra, who said that Eden was too young to be reliable and Mike too— Alexandra had paused in her instructions, and Janessa had supplied, "Too Bohemian?"

"That's it," Alexandra said. "There's a snake living across the hall from them."

In the daytime Eden visited Janessa and Kathleen and the babies on Staten Island and comforted herself with the knowledge that this was how it would be for her soon—Mike to come home every night to her and someday to her babies, and the easy companionship that lay at the heart of a marriage. She could kiss him—or do anything else she felt like—any time she wanted to then, she thought with the slow, secret smile that crossed her lips whenever she thought of him.

Eden was cuddling Mary Lavinia and searching her soft pink scalp to see if she was ever going to get hair.

"You're under Alexandra's instructions not to invite the neighbor's snake to the wedding," Janessa told her, laughing.

"But I thought I might wear it," she murmured, "for a boa."

"It *is* a boa," Janessa said.

The door bell rang, and Janessa picked up her notes from the caterer again and took Brandon Tobias onto her lap as Kathleen passed through the parlor to answer the bell and deposited the baby en route.

"Maybe that's the florist's boy," Janessa said. "I asked for samples."

They waited to see who the visitor was, and when Kathleen returned, Janessa's eyes widened, and she said, "Oh, Lord," before she could stop herself.

Rachel Poliakov stood on the hearth rug, her suitcase in her hand.

"I quit," Rachel said firmly.

Janessa pressed her hand to her forehead. "What happened? Eden, this is Rachel Poliakov, Rachel, this is my sister-in-law—almost—Eden Brentwood."

"Aaron Blum wants to marry me," Rachel announced.

"But, Rachel, that's wonderful."

"So what's wonderful? A mama's boy with *two* mamas, and I have to live with them yet? At the bakery there is Mrs. Blum *and* Mr. Blum's mother. I would rather stay unmarried."

"Oh, dear." Janessa, who had met the Blums, was not unsympathetic. "Couldn't you tell him no?"

"Already I told him no," Rachel answered. "His mama tells him no also. Over and over she tells him no, very loud with shouting, until Mr. Blum leaves the bakery and doesn't come back for a week, not even for the Sabbath. So all the yentas are in and out of the bakery every day, and they tell me what a nice boy is Aaron, what a catch. Then Mrs. Blum tells Aaron he is dead to her and locks herself in her bedroom to sit *shivah* for him. And all this time I am doing the baking with Aaron, and he is standing up to his mother for the first time in his life, but what a time. Then Mr. Blum comes home in a week with the matchmaker and a rabbi and takes Mrs. Blum's bedroom door off the hinges."

"So you left?" Eden asked. "Oh, I think that's brave."

"I don't know from brave," said Rachel. "But at least I am not married to Aaron. Aaron maybe I could have stood, but not his mama."

"But, Rachel, have you thought about what you're going to do now?" Out of the corner of her eye, Janessa could see Kathleen regarding Rachel with dark suspicion.

"I thought someone might need a nursemaid," Rachel said. "Already I have taken care of my little sister, and my brother who died."

"Rachel, dear, I have a nursemaid."

"Sure and she isn't needin' another!" Kathleen, outraged, snatched Brandon off Janessa's lap.

Rachel looked at Kathleen thoughtfully. "So how many babies are there?" She lifted two hands, gesturing at both.

"No heathen foreigner is going to mind me darlings!" Kathleen crossed herself and tried to pick up Mary as well.

"Stop it!" Janessa said. "You'll drop them." She took Mary herself because Eden looked so fascinated with this scene that the baby was beginning to slide off her lap. She gave Mary to Rachel with a look at Kathleen that told her to mind her tongue. "Hold her and let me think."

Rachel cuddled Mary and sang a little song to her in Yiddish. Mary smiled and poked chubby fingers at Rachel's face.

"And what's that you're singin'?" Kathleen demanded.

"A lullaby," Rachel said haughtily.

Kathleen muttered and crossed herself again.

Rachel glared at Kathleen and said something else in Yiddish, which was clearly not a lullaby.

Janessa looked at Eden, who couldn't do anything except bite her lip to refrain from laughing.

"Maybe just till after the wedding," Janessa said faintly. "I *can't* face tackling Mrs. Schiff about another place until then."

"What'll Charley say?" Eden whispered.

"Lord knows," Janessa said. "He may disappear for a week, too. He told me not to get involved." She put her fingers to her temples. Kathleen and Rachel glared at each other over her head. Janessa looked up at Rachel. "I don't keep a kosher kitchen," she said. "We aren't Jewish."

"God will forgive me," the girl said. "We are commanded not to keep kosher if we are starving."

"You aren't starving," Janessa pointed out.

Rachel adopted a tragic look. "I will be if you send me away."

"We eat pork."

Rachel blanched a little at that. "Then I will buy something else, at a kosher store."

"The Jews drink the blood of Christian babies," Kathleen announced, glowering at Rachel as if she might bite Mary at any moment.

"We do not!"

"I was told so."

"That is because Irish are superstitious and not educated," Rachel said loftily. "It is Christian priests who drink blood."

"That is the blood of our Lord!" Kathleen said furiously. "Anyway, it's wine."

"And they think it turns to blood and drink it anyway?" Rachel made a disgusted face.

"Jews killed our Lord," Kathleen accused, and crossed herself again.

"Christians killed my brother!" Rachel shouted.

"Jesus *was* Jewish," Eden offered helpfully.

"Maybe you had better stay out of this," Janessa suggested. She looked at Kathleen and Rachel. "I could use some help until Eden's wedding. Rachel, this is not a permanent position. I have Kathleen already, and she does an excellent job." She gave Kathleen a look of praise intended to mollify her, if possible.

"I could cook," Rachel suggested. "I am a good cook."

"Mother of God! She'll poison us all," Kathleen protested.

"*Stop it!*" Janessa was so loud that both girls stared at her. "Fine, Rachel, you can cook. And take care of the babies on Sunday while we are at church. Kathleen, you will cook on Saturdays and mind the babies while Rachel is at synagogue. And I don't want to hear another word about it."

"Where is she going to sleep?" Kathleen inquired suspiciously.

"With you. Consider it a trial sent to test you."

Charley, informed of these arrangements, said he considered it a trial sent to test him.

"Think of it as an education in cultural differences," Janessa muttered through the foliage emerging from a bucket of florist's samples. "Rachel may prove to be a blessing. Kathleen can't cook anything but corned beef, and I haven't time to prepare meals right now. What do you think of the pussy willow?"

"What?"

"In sprays on the altar, with some delphinium in front."

"Charming. Janessa, have you lost your mind? There's an air of menace in that kitchen that could explode into physical violence."

"I've never seen anyone so intolerant," Janessa said, distracted finally from her bucket. "You'd think Kathleen would be more understanding: The Catholics have been persecuted dreadfully at times."

"Rachel's just as bad," Charley said. "Nobody likes anybody who's different. As a species we seem to be suspicious by nature. You aren't going to institute universal brotherhood by forcing Rachel and Kathleen to share a tiny bedroom."

"At the moment I would settle for common civility. Kathleen has her side of the room plastered with holy cards from church. And Rachel put a mezuzah on the doorpost, and now Kathleen hurries by it as if it might bite her. The worst of it is, I know Rachel did it to annoy her. She said that looking at somebody's heart with thorns in it was depressing her."

"I can understand that. Rachel's a rascal, but I'm beginning to like her."

Charley changed his tune about her cooking, too, when they sat down to a meal of roasted chicken and carrots, with a plate of something that looked like large ravioli. Bitten into, they proved to have a filling of shredded meat and onion.

"Those are *kreplach*," Rachel explained.

Kathleen poked hers with a fork as if to ascertain that it was dead. "She boiled all the pots and silverware first," she announced.

"They were dirty," Rachel said.

"They were not!"

"Not clean," Rachel said. "*Trayf*. Not *kashered*. She'd been cooking milk with them."

"Sure and what's wrong with that?"

"If I cook, I cook as kosher as I can," Rachel said. "Mrs. Lawrence wouldn't let me buy another set of dishes." She eyed her plate disapprovingly.

"No, I think that would be going a little too far," Charley said.

"I was going to make a nice pudding," Kathleen said with a sniffle. "*She* wouldn't let me."

"Pudding is *milchik*. You cannot have dairy with a meat meal." Rachel adopted a martyred air. "But I won't complain when you cook, not even on Shabbat. Not even if I can't eat your food."

"Let's just eat this," Charley encouraged. "I think I've acquired a taste for kreplach."

"We haven't said grace," Kathleen reminded him.

Charley put his fork down. "Maybe we'd better." Kathleen opened her mouth, but Charley said firmly, "*I'll* say it." He tried to think of something that wouldn't be incendiary, and settled for, "O Lord, make us grateful for *all* food and for the diversity of mankind. And *remind* us about it now and again, okay?"

XVII

Eden peered over Mike's shoulder as he threaded his newly spliced film around the spools of the projector. Ira Hirsch, a blocky, balding man with a pince-nez and the pessimistic expression of an insomniac basset hound, leaned, arms folded, against the wall of the projection room.

"You're the fourth person this year who claims he can project kinetoscope film," he remarked. "But all we got was a bunch of blurry people waving their arms and some burned film." He looked toward Eden. "Now your boyfriend wants me to hire him so he can get me out of bed at midnight because he set fire to my theater?"

"I'm not going to set fire to your blasted theater," Mike said. "Just wait till you see it. I'm letting you in on the ground floor on this, Ira. You ought to be grateful."

"I ain't."

"I'm sure it will work, Mr. Hirsch," Eden said devotedly. She patted the machine as if it were an extension of Michael.

"No wonder he wants to marry you," Hirsch said gloomily. "I got a wife wants me out of the magic-lantern business. Thinks it's déclassé."

"*You* are délassé," Mike muttered. "Volcanoes and undraped women. She's probably embarrassed. This is art."

"So who pays for art? There! See? I told you it didn't work."

The projector had jammed as soon as it was turned

271

on, and they heard the sizzle of frying film. Mike slapped the switch off.

"It's torn, damn it. I don't have the loop right. Just be quiet, will you?" He clipped out the damaged film, respliced it, and tried again, threading it with care. The projector was the invention of a young American named Thomas Armat, who had hit on a principle that solved the problem of Edison's projector and every other one Mike had tried. Film run in a continuous loop past the light resulted in blurry, dim images. Sharper pictures were created by intermittent motion, in which each frame stopped for a fraction of a second in the projection gate. But that ripped the film unless a small loop was provided to take off the tension just before the gate. A cooling system was also required to prevent the film from catching fire while it stood briefly stationary in front of the lamp. Film was extremely volatile, and more than one aspiring projectionist had had his projector, as well as his hair, go up in flames.

Thomas Armat had solved these problems, so Mike firmly believed, with the Vitascope. Armat was also negotiating a deal with Thomas Edison to market it, and Mike had spent nearly his last cent on an Armat projector before the jaws of the Edison Company closed around it and tripled the price. Just before Michael had left Fort Myers, a certain amount of industrial spying and ten dollars slipped to Fred Ott had led him to the Armat projector—and also explained why Edison hadn't felt like fooling with his own.

Ira Hirsch, however, was of the opinion that it was money down a rat hole, and dragged from his house at midnight on a Sunday night, he said so loudly.

"Hush," Mike said. "You'll see."

Holding his breath, he flipped the switch again, and this time the film ran faultlessly. The washerwoman's arms moved through clouds of floating bubbles; the cowman's hands in close-up braided rawhide thongs as leathery as his fingers. When the cow lumbered toward the camera, Ira yelped.

"Gotcha!" Mike said triumphantly. "Try that with a magic lantern."

Washerwoman and cowman disappeared down the dusty road with the cow switching her tail behind them.

"Lemme see that again," Ira said.

Mike rewound the film and ran it again. This time Ira watched like a hawk. "Maybe you've got something here. I like that it tells a story. Who wants to watch clowns and pies in the face over and over? Could you make a longer one?"

"Sure, if I had the money. I need backers, Ira, and a theater that's set up right."

"A theater I got. Backers I don't know about. It's too new."

"Everything's new sometime. And who makes the most money? The guys who get in there first. I could make you rich, Ira."

"You could also make me a laughingstock," Ira said, but he looked thoughtful. "We'll see. Maybe I'll bring one or two fellows around tomorrow night or the next."

On Wednesday night, after the last magic-lantern-show patrons had left, a different audience assembled. They were all men, and they settled in a blue cloud of cigar smoke into the seats in front of the screen. Mike had rounded up some men, and Ira had invited the others: distributors of celluloid film, vaudeville producers, promoters of dime shows—no representatives of the legitimate stage, but men who had already dabbled in entertainment that played to mass appeal or in the technology of photography.

"And quit calling it art," Ira warned Michael, "or you'll scare them off."

Arms folded on their chests, the men watched in stolid silence. Eden, meanwhile, bit her nails. The film was only two minutes long. When the last frame had run through the projector, Mike turned up the houselights.

"Turn 'em off. Run it again," a voice commanded. No one else said anything.

Mike ran it again. He waited.

"Lights!" the same voice said.

The men were arguing with one another by the time he got out of the booth.

"It's got potential."

"Potential to bore 'em to death. Who wants to see cows?"

"What do you want?" Ira demanded. "Bearded ladies? This is class, not some dime-show flimflam."

"You weren't bored when that cow jumped out. I thought you were gonna bust a gut."

"Make a tiger jump out like that, and you'll pack the house."

"Better yet a pretty lady, not too many clothes."

"Gentlemen!" Mike stood in front of them and spread his arms for silence. "This is an experimental film, a prototype. I can produce a moving picture ten minutes long with all the excitement and pretty ladies you want."

"They got to have clothes," one celluloid film distributor said.

"Some clothes," a dime-show man agreed. "And she's got to be a looker." He eyed Eden thoughtfully. "How about you, honey?"

"Only if it's a lot of clothes," Eden said firmly. Mike looked about to defend her honor, so she made a shushing motion at him. "You see, Mr. Deyel," she continued, "this is a new form of entertainment. People will come because it's unlike anything they've ever seen. If we give them a wholesome show that they can bring their families to, we'll sell a lot more tickets."

"A class act, you mean?"

"Exactly," Eden said sweetly.

"She's got a head on her shoulders," Ira said. "You listen to her."

By the end of the night, Mike had four backers and a contract that allowed him a month to produce a ten-minute film. He was also forced to pay an exorbitant interest rate on his borrowed funds.

"You did all right, kid," Ira said.

"All right?" Mike protested. "I got skinned. And you did some of the skinning."

"Just make good on it," Ira said, "and next time you'll have the clout to cut a better deal. That's how it works. Besides, I got to replace you, don't I?"

"That won't cost you much, you old skinflint."

Ira chuckled. "You swim with the sharks, kid, you learn to bite. Next time bite 'em good."

"Don't think I won't bite you."

"Sure you will." Ira slapped him on the back and gave his other arm to Eden. "Come on. I know a restaurant that stays open late. I'll buy you dinner and a bottle of wine. We'll celebrate."

Ira's bottle of wine stretched to three in a restaurant with oilcloth on the tables and a band that played Greek music. The threesome ate moussaka and stuffed grape leaves. When the other patrons got up to dance, whirling across the floor in line, hands on each other's shoulders, they joined in, clumsily at first, laughing and tripping.

"Rats. I was just getting the hang of it," Mike said when the music ended.

"Hoo boy! I got to sit down." Ira puffed back to the table, and they joined him.

Mike laid his cheek against Eden's. "You're something, you know?" he whispered. "I was going to strangle Deyel for insulting you, but you didn't seem to want me to."

"You wanted the contract, didn't you?" Eden asked practically. "And I don't mind. I can handle people like Mr. Deyel." She could, she had found. Maybe it was the result of her stay in Cathy's troupe. Or maybe it was just being with Mike again. Nothing felt as if it was too much for her now.

"She's something all right," Ira said. "You hang on to this woman, Holt. She's got a head for the business. You, you're too young to know."

"She's younger than I am," Mike protested.

"Nope," Ira disagreed. "Not in some ways."

* * *

In the morning Mike had a headache from the wine and remembered how much retsina tasted like turpentine; but he didn't remember its having bothered him the night before. He crawled off the cot in Ira's projection room and went looking for a warehouse with good light. A studio was the first thing he needed. He stepped out into the early morning sunlight, and the headache vanished.

I have a production company! he thought, elated. He also had specific orders from his backers—keep the story straightforward. How the hell could anyone tell what was going on, they had wanted to know, when one second you were looking at a washerwoman and the next at a cow? The audience wouldn't understand, they said. It made the picture jump when you hitched it together like that. No conjuring tricks. And more girls. He wanted to make money, didn't he?

He did, desperately. He couldn't be dependent upon his father forever. And despite Eden's cheerful acceptance of the Bohemian squalor of the Chelsea, Mike didn't much want to feed her on beans. Nor did he want her supporting him, even if Sam would turn loose of her inheritance and let her.

By the end of the day he knew he had miscalculated at least one element of his plans.

"There's no such thing as a warehouse with good light," he complained to Eden.

Eden, wearing an apron borrowed from the artist next door, was in their suite at the Chelsea, painting an end table.

"Pyotr is such a nice man," she said of their neighbor. "He's painted us into his third circle. And I've been thinking about your studio. Come along." She got up and led him down the hall and into the unreliable but elegant brass-doored elevator. They went clear to the top floor, where a number of artists kept light-flooded studio aeries.

"All of these are occupied," she said, "but look." She drew him out onto the roof through a studio whose door stood open. "This is Pyotr's," she said as Mike raised his eyebrows. "He won't care."

On the roof Mike saw that there was plenty of open space among the gardens. "We can build movable flats," Eden continued. "The kind Cathy's troupe uses. And Pyotr says we can come through his studio if we let him paint us while we're working. He's fascinated by moving pictures."

Mike thought Pyotr might also be fascinated by Eden, but he decided that Eden could stave the artist off. And if Eden couldn't, Mike could. Besides, the roof was free.

"Oh, honey." He put his arms around her. "What would I do without you?"

"Work for that nasty Mr. Edison," Eden said primly.

"Never again," he told her.

Mike kissed her, just losing himself in the feel of her. She sank hungrily into his arms. Mike got a grip on himself. The wedding was just a week away. He thought he could last that long—barely.

In the next week Mike worked off his excess amorous energy by scouring the city for actors and stagehands who were willing to work on a roof for long hours and low pay. These turned out to be not as hard to come by as he had feared. There were always theater people out of work. Janessa introduced him to a Hungarian refugee who had once painted flats for the opera and to two Turks who had been village carpenters. Cathy Martin, recently returned to New York, sent Mike so many out-of-work actors that he had to tell her to stop.

Then he realized he had made one more miscalculation. He had assumed that he had a leading lady in his betrothed, and the first thing he did after lugging his camera to the roof of the Chelsea was put Eden in front of it. She was beautiful, and she did not, as Cathy pointed out with a touch of legitimate-theater snobbishness, have to be an accomplished actress for a ten-minute moving picture.

But when he developed the film in the darkroom he

had converted from their apartment's only closet (Eden sighed and went and bought a secondhand wardrobe cupboard), it was awful. It was dreadful. He couldn't believe it was Eden.

"Michael, you aren't going to use that!" Eden looked with horror at her image flickering on the parlor wall.

"I must have focused it wrong," Mike said. "Come on. We'll try again."

They tried again; they tried it three times, in fact. Pyotr came in from next door, and frowning, suggested, "Is needing better light maybe?"

They tried better light.

Pyotr shook his head at Eden. "Is dreadful. You do not let him do this to you."

"I didn't do it," Mike protested. "The camera did it. I don't know why. Here, look at these." He handed Pyotr a photograph of Eden, delicate and lovely, smiling ethereally.

"Well," Eden said, biting her lip, "that took three sittings to get. I wouldn't send you the ones from the first two. They were awful."

Mike sighed. "The camera just doesn't like you. I don't know why it is."

"I rarely have good pictures taken," Eden told him. "I thought maybe if it was moving, I might look better. These are even worse, though. Something happens to my face. I look like a turtle."

"Honey, I'm sorry." Mike spread his hands. "I just can't use you."

"You certainly can't," Eden agreed. "I won't let you."

By the day of their wedding, Mike still didn't have a leading lady. He had auditioned several in front of the camera, having learned from his experience with Eden to make a test film; but none of them was right. Many were photogenic but not exactly what he wanted. It worried him when he could remember to worry about it. The closer the wedding had gotten, the more he hadn't been able to think of anything but Eden.

"He's a wreck," Janessa said, seated beside Charley, with Kathleen and Rachel holding a baby apiece, in the pews of Trinity Church. "Poor Mike. He's like a terrified deer. Charley, what are you doing?"

Charley was craning his neck around. "I'm looking at the other guests," he said.

Everyone else in the family was looking at him, too. Toby's eyebrows had shot up nearly under his hair. Since Eden had little family left except for Sam and Annie, who could not attend, and Rob and Kale Martin, who were Cathy's parents and Eden's cousins, the Harry Salter Theatrical Company occupied two rows. They had turned out in their finest, some of it raided from the company's wardrobe department. They stood out, like a row of flamingos in a well-bred New York dovecote, as they eagerly awaited the ceremony. Behind them in a phalanx of rectitude were elderly friends of Eden's late grandmother Claudia.

"There's Mrs. Meigs," Janessa whispered. "She looks as if she's about to burst her corset."

"I'd be more inclined to attribute her expression to dyspepsia," Charley said, studying her, "brought on by disapproval and nerves. It can't be comforting for her to have that bizarre fellow just behind her in the pew. Where on earth did Eden find him?"

Janessa suppressed a giggle. "That's Pyotr, the artist who lives next door. He looks like someone out of a novel by Dostoevsky."

For Eden's wedding Pyotr had chosen a style of frock coat with a nipped waist and a velvet collar, which had not been in fashion since the forties—nor had his hairstyle, which was quite long about the ears. In place of a cravat he wore a scarf of hand-dyed silk in alternating bands of magenta and rose. Mrs. Meigs sat ramrod straight, apparently to keep her spine as far away from Pyotr as possible.

On the groom's side, the Holts, Blakes, and Lawrences—with the exception of Tim, who was to be best man, and Peter and Frank Blake, who were serving as ushers—were ensconced in the front row. The whole clan had gathered, including Mike's grandmother Eulalia, who had traveled from Oregon with the Madrona Ranch's foreman, White Elk, and his Chinese wife, Mai, to take care of Eulalia on the train. Although Annie and Sam were absent, Annie had written Eden that they both wished her to be happy, not to pay any attention to any message to the contrary from Sam, and that Sam was all right but still in prison. She had also sent five hundred dollars and a cookbook for a wedding present.

Everyone in the family wondered whether Annie's letter was written to sound more reassuring than Annie really felt. When consulted, Tim said that he thought Sam was probably all right, but political pressure was the only way he and the other rebels would be released from prison. That, Tim warned, was always a lengthy process. The unspoken question was whether or not Sam would survive long enough for that to do him any good. Tim's report of prison conditions had been frightening. Annie had written to Tim about Sam's assault on the warden. Everyone realized that if Sam were to annoy the warden again, or even alienate the wrong guard, he could be worked to death. Nobody had much confidence that Sam could keep quiet and behave indefinitely. He hadn't so far.

With Sam unavailable, Toby had asked Eden, of whom he was extremely fond despite his misgivings about the marriage, if she would like to have him walk her down the aisle. But Eden had said no, she had gotten to New York by herself, so she thought she would walk herself down the aisle. Alexandra had worried about how it would look, but Tim and Janessa had come in on Eden's side.

"She's saying she's her own woman, Mother," Tim had said. "That it's *her* decision to marry."

"It certainly was," Alexandra murmured.

"I don't blame her," Janessa said. "Who wants to be handed over like a parcel?"

"Your father walked *you* down the aisle," Alexandra pointed out.

"So he did. But if Dad hadn't been available, I

wouldn't have gone looking for a substitute just to have somebody."

"Oh, very well." Alexandra gave up on that point, considering herself fortunate to have prevented them from being married by a justice of the peace and thus scandalizing everyone on both sides of the family. Apart from the fact that such a decision would have appeared suspicious, the family liked weddings and would have felt terribly deprived if denied the celebration.

The organist, who had been playing softly in the background, suddenly sat up and took notice as Tim and Mike appeared at the altar. She launched into the strains of the Wedding March from *Lohengrin*—Eden's one apparent concession to convention—and the guests turned to watch the bride come down the aisle.

Cathy Martin came first, as Eden's sole bridesmaid, in a gown of blue taffeta that made her look like a water nymph. Her hair was crowned with bachelor's buttons, and she carried a posy of them done up in a silver holder.

There was a general intake of breath as Eden appeared, and a second when it registered that she was unescorted. Eden sailed serenely past the disapproving, pausing to smile at Ira Hirsch, who beamed at her from behind his pince-nez. Deciding to start her married life in practical fashion, she had picked a silk gown she could wear later to garden parties. She wore a crown similar to Cathy's, but the bachelor's buttons were interspersed with white rosebuds, and a heavy lace mantilla fell over her shoulders. Pyotr sighed audibly as she went by.

Mike, waiting at the altar, appeared suddenly older than he had before. Maybe it was the expression on his face when he gazed at Eden, or perhaps it was his mustache. Or maybe it was simply that everyone, including his mother, was forced to view him from a new angle, to see the sick child and the rebellious boy overlaid now with the man.

Mike's and Eden's eyes locked and held until finally the minister coughed gently for their attention.

"Dearly beloved—"

Tim and the Blake brothers were looking suitably

pious, considering the fact that they had been teasing
Mike with a feigned search for the wedding ring ten
minutes before. Cathy Martin looked out the corner of
her eye at Doug Seaberry in the front row. Mike and
Eden were still gazing at each other and had to be
prodded by the minister to say "I do" at the proper time.
The cleric, having forgotten his notes, was clearly off his
stride. He asked, "Who giveth this woman to be married
to this man?"

Eden said quite firmly, "*I* do."

The couple looked so absolutely sure of themselves
and so blazingly in love that when the ceremony was
over, there wasn't, as Ira Hirsch put it, a dry eye in the
house.

The reception was set up on the roof garden of the
Chelsea, and the wedding party jammed the corridors
and elevator, sweeping along with them, Alexandra
noticed, some residents who hadn't been at the wedding. They spilled out onto the roof in a flood of several
languages and much champagne. Mike and Eden posed
with the cake, and a photographer took their picture.

A band had been hired to play dance music, but
after an hour of decorous waltzes, the musicians were
dismissed by Pyotr, who produced both a balalaika and a
friend with an accordion. After that the evening got
livelier until it was, Tim said, the "damnedest wedding
reception" he'd ever been at. As the sun dropped down
into the Hudson River to the west, Pyotr, arms raised
like a conductor, was teaching a Russian wedding dance
to a line of capering participants.

Rachel and Kathleen, nursemaids not guests, had
been sitting dutifully to one side. But when Rachel
heard the music, her eyes lit up, and she looked
pleadingly at Janessa. "Oh, I know this! This we danced
at home. Is it all right if I dance, also?"

"Of course." Janessa took the baby on her own lap.
"I've had quite enough dancing. I have a stitch in my
side."

Rachel ran happily to the line of dancers and slipped
into place.

"Ah!" Pyotr exclaimed gleefully when he saw that she knew the steps. "Pretty Russian lady, come help me teach this." He held out his hand, and Rachel spun over to him.

"Hey!" Mike's eyes locked on Rachel. He nudged Eden. "Who's she?"

"Rachel Poliakov," Eden answered. "She's your sister's current headache. I told you about her."

"But I haven't seen her before. What do you think of her, darling? In front of a camera, I mean?"

Eden resigned herself to a lifetime of her husband's asking her what she thought of other women's looks. "She might be just right. She had on an ugly old head scarf the last time I saw her, but she does seem to have blossomed."

"I want to talk to Janessa. Come on." He tugged her away from the dancers.

When asked for her opinion, Janessa said, "For starters, you absolutely have to keep her away from that crazy Pyotr. I promised Rachel's mother that I'd find her a place with a nice Jewish family. Acting in a moving picture is *not* what she had in mind."

"I'll guard her virtue with my life," Mike promised. "Just let me do a film test on her."

"Well . . ."

"I'll be there, too," Eden said. "If it works out, then she'll have a job."

"For how long?" Janessa wanted to know. "I don't need to tell you the time estimates that Dad is putting on this venture of yours."

"You don't have to," Mike said with a grin. "Dad already has. Aw, come on, Janessa."

Janessa thought about Rachel sharing a room with Kathleen for even one more week, while each tried to put the evil eye on the other and complained about the cooking. "All right, you can test her. But if it works out, you have to find her a respectable place to stay. And that doesn't mean with young Rodya Roskolnikov over there. Is that clear?" Janessa looked at her watch. "And would you two please go away somewhere? None of your guests is going to leave until you do, and I have to get these babies to bed."

"Maybe Rachel will take up with Pyotr, and he'll quit mooning around after you," Mike whispered, nuzzling Eden's neck. With only three weeks left to produce the moving picture that was promised to his backers, Mike and Eden had decided to put Annie's five hundred dollars in a bank and postpone a honeymoon. Accordingly they had retreated to Eden's suite at the Chelsea—now *their* suite—and locked the door. They put a chair under the knob as a precaution against any unauthorized pranks their reception guests might devise when drunk enough.

"We promised Janessa that we wouldn't let that happen," Eden responded. "And quit worrying about Pyotr. He's just being artistic. If I threw myself at him and said 'Take me, I'm yours,' he'd probably run screaming into the night."

"I wouldn't bet on it," Mike said. "So don't try it, huh?"

"Certainly not," Eden said. "What would I want with Pyotr?"

They looked at each other uncertainly. Now that the time had come, they were nervous. It mattered too much. It was why they had stayed so long at the reception.

Eden swayed toward him again, and Mike's grip around her waist tightened. His lips slid down her neck and encountered the tip of her whalebone collar. "I can't get at you in this thing," he muttered. "Do you mind if I undress you? Are you shy about that?"

Eden thought about it for a moment. "Not with you," she decided.

So he did, lovingly unhooking, unbuttoning. His heart pounded in his throat. "Oh, God, I love you so much!"

He kicked off his shoes and pulled at his own shirt studs and the buttons of his trousers. Eden watched him, eyes wide, gaslight flickering on their bare skin.

Then he picked her up and carried her to the carved bed with its gaudy, painted flowers.

Eden awoke the next morning in the big double bed she had slept in alone for a month . . . and the previous night with Mike. She stretched languidly and looked at his sleeping face. His red hair was tousled, and the droopy mustache fluttered a little as he breathed. He was inexpressibly dear to her. She snuggled down under the blanket and laid her head on his bare shoulder. Last night had been fun, almost as much fun as she had hoped, and Mike had said it would get even better. Making love was certainly far more fun than the motherly woman on the train from Savannah had predicted. Animals indeed, Eden thought sleepily, deciding that she already knew a lot more than the woman on the train did. People were animals anyway, weren't they, biologically speaking? Darwin said so, Eden thought fuzzily, drifting into sleep again. It would be a shame not to take advantage of it. Mike's collarbone proved uncomfortable for sleeping on, so she turned over, and Mike woke enough to cuddle against her back, spoonlike, one arm around her, his hand on her breast.

They woke together an hour later when the sun was fully up. Their neighbors, stymied by the chair jammed against the door, had the happy thought of introducing the composer's snake via the transom. It liked to be warm, and so it got into bed with them.

"I'll kill them!" Mike shouted, dancing naked out of bed while Eden, giggling uncontrollably, jumped out on the other side. It wasn't a very big snake, and they hauled it out of the bed covers by the tail and dumped it in the hall. Mike slammed the door and climbed up on the chair to lock the transom. "I should have thought of that," he muttered. "I must have been drunk."

Eden giggled again. She looked vaguely like the Statue of Liberty, wrapped up in the sheet she had snatched off the bed for decency's sake. "You were preoccupied," she suggested.

Mike looked at her. The sheet had begun to slip,

and her tangled gold hair made a feathery cloud around her to her waist. "So I was," he said softly. "Oh, God, you're so beautiful." He tugged experimentally at the sheet, and Eden turned, barefoot on the faded carpet, and let him unwrap her.

They got back into bed again and didn't get up until midafternoon.

XVIII

That afternoon Eden and Mike took the ferry to Staten Island and presented themselves a little self-consciously at Janessa's house to collect Rachel Poliakov.

It was Sunday, and Charley, Janessa, Kathleen, and the babies had returned from their various church services. Charley was looking a little hollow eyed—the aftermath of attending services with two babies. He wouldn't have gone at all if Janessa hadn't chivied him out of bed because Toby, Alexandra, Sally, and the whole contingent from the Madrona were planning to meet them at church. Since the whole family was going to be there, the twins went, too, instead of staying at home with Rachel.

Now Charley eyed Mike with a grin. "You look chipper, pal. Get any sleep?"

"Enough," Mike said. "We didn't go to church. We figured the wedding would last us until next week."

"It'll take me a month to recover from that reception." Charley groaned. "What was that thing we were dancing at the end? I feel like a horse walked on me."

"It is called Korobushka," Rachel said. "In Russia we dance it often, for happy times." She did a few quick steps.

"You had a good time, didn't you, kid?" Charley smiled at her. He sat down carefully in a chair and groaned again. "Lord, you Russians are sturdy people."

"She's younger than you are," Janessa soothed. "And you were showing off." She looked from Rachel to Mike. "All right, I explained it all to Rachel, and she's

287

willing to take the film test. She can go with you for the rest of the day. Have her back by ten."

"With both glass slippers," Mike said. "I promise."

"Hell of a honeymoon," Charley said after they departed with an exuberant Rachel between them.

"They'll manage," Janessa said. "I never saw anyone look so happy. Eden and Michael have done the right thing, no matter what the rest of the family thinks."

"Oh, I agree," Charley said. "But I'll be interested to see what they do with your foundling."

"Maybe she won't come back," Kathleen said hopefully.

"There," Eden said. "Take a look."

She held up the mirror, and Rachel stared at her reflection, fascinated at a face she wasn't sure she knew at all. Eden had put her knowledge of theatrical makeup, gleaned on the road with the Harry Salter Dramatic Company, to work for the camera. The face that looked back at Rachel was as vivid as a Renaissance portrait— her dark, liquid eyes outlined carefully in kohl; her cheeks and chin and narrow, straight nose accented with greasepaint. Her face seemed to leap from the mirror with an urgent if overdrawn beauty.

Rachel touched her scarlet lips apprehensively. "This the rabbi won't like," she said. Nice women, regardless of ethnic origin, didn't paint their faces.

"The rouge won't look like that on film," Eden assured her. "It doesn't even look like that on stage. And film is black and white."

"Is making you look very beautiful," Pyotr said, lounging in a window seat to watch. They were using his rooftop studio because the light was good. "Like—" He waved his hands. "Like Madonna in icon." It dawned on Pyotr that Rachel was Jewish. "Or something." But Pyotr's restrictive Russian Orthodox upbringing was part of the reason he had left Russia. Since he met Rachel, he had been trying to assuage her natural distrust of him. "I am an artist," he said. "I know."

"Let's see if the camera knows," Mike said, practically holding his breath. If Rachel didn't work out, he didn't know what he was going to do; he had tried all the other females he could find. He might be forced to put a dress on Pyotr!

He had Rachel stand on the rooftop, the skyline behind her, the breeze just ruffling her hair, which Eden had dressed into a soft Psyche knot that accentuated Rachel's slender neck. Her face was young, big eyed, and earnest. Mike had her mimic great joy, then despondency, and then fear. When she faltered, stiffening, he told her ruthlessly, "Think of Cossacks. Think of a burning house."

Pyotr was offended, but the technique worked on Rachel. Beautiful and terror-stricken, she stared into the camera, hands held out as if to ward off something unseen.

"Now she is not coming near me ever," Pyotr muttered.

"She isn't supposed to," Eden retorted.

"Now think of love," Mike suggested to Rachel. "Think of the man you could love."

Pyotr smiled hopefully, but Rachel wasn't looking at him. No one knew what she was looking at, but her face lit up.

"Oh boy, this is great!" Mike used the last of the film, then rewound it in the camera. "You wait here. I'll be right back!"

They drank sticky tea, brewed by Pyotr in a brass samovar and sweetened with cherry preserves, and waited. Rachel in her makeup looked as exotic as a Gypsy, and Pyotr got out his sketch pad.

"I put you in my hell," he said. "On my wall. In first circle because you are so beautiful. Is compliment," he added when Rachel looked startled.

"It sure is!" Mike came galloping back, waving still-wet film. He held it up to the light. "Look at this! Just look!"

Rachel stared. "That is me?"

* * *

"So now you have your moving picture," Ira Hirsch said. "So now we talk business." The theater owner had come to the Chelsea for a private showing and was more impressed than he was admitting to.

"What business?" Mike asked. "We show it; we make money; I pay you back; I get a better interest rate next time."

"Money." Ira threw up his hands. "You talk like it's a sure thing. I been in the magic-lantern business a long time, I know the public. Trust me." Eden brought him a cup of tea, and Rachel put a plate of cookies on the table. Ira had demanded to meet Rachel. "Thank you, beautiful ladies."

"What exactly are we discussing here?" Mike demanded.

"Publicity," Ira explained. "Public interest. A gimmick."

"This form of entertainment is absolutely new," Mike said. "How much more public interest can you get?"

"Like hell it is. Excuse me, ladies. People have been watching Edison's filmstrips for years now—people sneezing, silly dancers . . ."

"You mean we need to show this is unlike Mr. Edison's?" Eden asked. "Make them *expect* something different?"

"That's it!" Ira said. "I tell you, Michael, you hold on to this one. She knows the business already, and she just got in it."

"Well, what do you have in mind?" Mike thought that Ira's advertisements for his magic-lantern shows already encompassed all the superlatives that could be crammed onto a poster.

"This lady, for instance." Ira regarded Rachel over his pince-nez. "Her I can use."

"Her photograph?"

"No, you dimwit." Ira looked at Mike as if despairing of his intelligence. "Her. Who knows about her? Nobody. She's a mystery—a mystery woman. Glamour,

you see? That's what we want! But not like the theater.
More mysterious. These motion pictures, they're illusion. They're magic. When I get through, every girl in
New York is going to want to do her hair like—what's
your name again, little lady?"

"Rachel Poliakov."

"Umm. No. First we change her name."

"Why?"

"It's foreign," Ira said. "It's Jewish. Trust me, I
know the disadvantage."

"You didn't change yours," Mike said, defending
Rachel.

"And I'm not a beautiful woman, either," Ira retorted. "For businessmen, Jewish is okay. Also for
comedy acts. But not for leading ladies."

"Change me to what?" Rachel demanded, wrapping
her arms around herself. She looked taken aback, as if
her whole self might be snatched away.

"Not you, sweetheart. Your image. They aren't the
same. You'll learn. *You* stay Rachel Poliakov. But the
lady on the screen . . . let's see. It needs to be part
you, maybe, Rachel . . . Rochelle. Rochelle is good.
Poliakov I can't do anything with." He snapped his
fingers, thinking. "Names. Family names. Give me some
more family names."

"Schidorsky," Rachel said.

"Never."

"Blum?"

"Blum? Bloom? No."

"Blossom," Eden said suddenly.

"Rochelle Blossom," Ira looked at Rachel. "Stand
up. Turn around, Rochelle Blossom. Like a fairy name.
Like flowers. We put her against a background of roses
on a poster."

Rachel stopped turning. "Rochelle Blossom," she
said to herself. It sounded strange and magical, as
ephemeral as the image on the film. The name would
come to life only with the switching on of the projector
lamp, then would fade with its dying. Rachel Poliakov
could still exist. And Rachel Poliakov wouldn't have to

marry Aaron Blum. That was important. "With me it's all right," she said. "If Michael says."

"What about your rabbi?" Mike asked, already used to Rachel's considering that gentleman's opinion of proper conduct.

"Maybe this he'll like better than my real name," Rachel said frankly. "So no one knows I'm Jewish."

The Rochelle Blossom who flowered in the poster created by Pyotr—who was willing to subvert art to commerce when he needed rent money—could have been any nationality or none at all, a girl from who knew where. Smoky eyes looked out from a cloud of pale roses and gave off an air of both innocence and knowledge. Although it was not customary to use the name of the actors who appeared in the various short filmstrips that were beginning to be shown by other entrepreneurs, Ira ruled against custom. ROCHELLE BLOSSOM! the poster trumpeted in large type. It said nothing else about her except the further attribute, DIRECT FROM FAME ON THE CONTINENT! "So we fudge a little," Ira said, shrugging.

For the audience she was anyone they might choose her to be. Ira, by unspecified skulduggery and bribery, had managed to be interviewed by a reporter from the *Tribune*. However, Ira firmly refused to discuss the picture's star. The reporter was thus thoroughly hooked. He indulged in so much speculation on the origins of the "mystery girl" that Ira, waving the paper, came dancing and cackling up the stairs of the Chelsea.

"Already everyone wants tickets," he enthused, chortling. "We got two weeks till we open. The house is going to be packed!"

At Ira's further insistence, not even the other backers knew anything more about Rachel or anything about the picture itself, other than the title. After some deliberation, Mike and Ira had agreed on *The Homecoming*, which, as Ira pointed out, had a nice wholesome sound and covered a lot of ground. "You tell them anything more, they'll spill the beans," he insisted.

"People got no sense when they start talking to reporters."

The backers, grumbling, agreed to remain in the dark, but Mike knew they would be there on opening night, waiting to see what he had done with their money. *The Homecoming* was to open the bill at the Atheneum Theater, thus renamed by Ira who felt it had more class than Hirsch's Music Hall.

"We'll see how it plays," said Mike, who was beginning to get nervous. "If it's a sellout, we're on our way. Here's to the Eden Motion Picture Company." He was pleased with that name.

"Of course it will sell out," Eden loyally assured him.

"It may just as well lose him his shirt, too," Toby said to Alexandra in Washington, perusing Mike's latest letter. "How could he invest everything into such a harebrained scheme?"

"It's what he wants to do, dear," Alex said. "He's happy." She bit her lip and didn't mention the fifty dollars she had sent Michael "just in case." Alexandra didn't have any more faith in motion pictures than Toby had, but she did harbor a secret fear of Mike overtaxing his heart by worrying about money. Mike had written back to her saying that he would give her the check on opening night, to which they were invited, but thanks for the insurance.

"We *are* going, aren't we?" Sally asked. "I want to stay in the Chelsea this time. I love the Chelsea."

"I'm not at all sure there are any empty apartments or that the management rents them by the week," Alexandra said. Privately she was of the opinion that the management might very well rent them by the night and that the Chelsea was a wholly unsuitable environment for Sally, who was precocious enough.

"We're going if I can get away," Toby said. "And I imagine I can. Washington's pretty quiet in August. It all depends on whether Mr. Olney has a conniption fit."

"Over your leaving?" Sally asked. "I thought Mr. Olney didn't like you."

"He doesn't." Toby chuckled. "But I was given to him by the President, so he has to work with me." Toby had been assigned a post as assistant secretary of state and special adviser to Secretary of State Olney, who absolutely didn't want his advice. "I meant a conniption fit over Cuba. Olney's determined to get us entangled in that. I'm supposed to be the counterweight."

"Why doesn't Mr. Cleveland just fire him?" Sally inquired. "I don't think anybody likes him much, do you?"

"Let us say that his personality is somewhat caustic and leave it at that."

"Alice says he wrote a dreadful letter to the prime minister of England about our will being law on this continent and that Canada and Mexico didn't like it at all."

Toby blanched. "How in hell does Alice know about that? And don't you dare repeat it to anyone else."

"Theodore I would suppose," Alex said. "He really doesn't pay attention to what he says in front of that child—much like some other people I could name. Sally, you mustn't ever repeat things your father tells you about politics."

"Yes, ma'am." Sally did not appear squelched at all.

"Theodore . . ." Toby groaned. "He's a sound man in most respects, but he's bound and determined to get us into a war with Spain. I suppose that brings him in on Olney's side for the moment."

"Is that what Mr. Olney's letter was about?"

"Not exactly," Toby replied. "Great Britain and Venezuela are in the middle of a boundary dispute over the line between Venezuela and British Guiana. They've been at it since 1814, but now someone's found gold in the area, which gives it, shall we say, more immediacy."

"What makes it our business?" Sally demanded.

Toby and Alexandra exchanged glances. "Out of the mouths of babes," Toby remarked.

Alexandra took Sally by the shoulders. "It's time for

bed," she said firmly, "if you want me to put your hair in curlpapers. And I want you to promise me that you will not discuss this conversation with *anybody*. Including your father. He has a headache."

"If women could vote," Sally said rebelliously, "I could get elected, and then I could discuss things."

"*That*," Alexandra said, "you may discuss with your father."

"Maybe I'll be a suffragist when I'm grown." Sally went off with Alexandra to have her hair curled.

Toby hid his grin until Sally and Alex had left the room. If women could vote, he'd be willing to bet there would be fewer silly letters sent and fewer wars started.

The women's right to vote wasn't a proposition he felt like putting to Richard Olney in the morning, however. Olney was armed with the latest editions of the Hearst and Pulitzer papers and dropped them on Toby's desk with the air of Moses producing the Ten Commandments. "The people of America are behind the efforts of the people of Cuba to counter Spanish imperialism," he announced.

"With American imperialism?" Toby inquired. He glanced at the newspapers. "Irresponsible journalism," he said, then snorted. "I suppose I ought to mention that your correspondence with Lord Salisbury appears to be public knowledge, at least in some circles."

Olney narrowed his eyes. "I stand by my letter."

"Canada and Latin America probably don't," Toby commented. "And have you any idea of the consequences of alienating Great Britain?" *Or do you want to get us in a war with them, too, you blasted fool?*

Olney glared at him. "Allow me to remind you of how very unwelcome you are in my department, Mr. Holt. And that any dissemination on your part of privileged information will be grounds for my going to the President with my complaints."

"I'm not the one who's been writing inflammatory letters," Toby remarked benignly. "Nor did I disseminate them. I—stumbled upon that information."

"Then I do not expect to see it printed in the San Francisco *Clarion*," Olney said stiffly.

"I have no idea what you can expect to see printed in my son's newspaper," Toby said. "But that particular piece of foolishness won't come from me. Frankly, I'm embarrassed by it."

"The *Clarion* is a disreputable newspaper and disloyal to the government of the United States," Olney snapped. "I haven't forgotten its coverage of the illegal strike by the Pullman workers. There was irresponsibility for you."

"Neither has the city of Chicago forgotten that you sent the army in there as if it were an occupied country," Toby shot back.

"I acted with the full authority of the President."

"Then the President was ill-advised." Toby wasn't going to give any ground here. Olney had been attorney general at the time, and Toby privately considered his overreaction to have been responsible for the loss of lives and the millions of dollars in property burned when the army's presence had escalated an already tricky situation. The country was still feeling the reverberations of those labor strikes.

Now Cleveland had made Olney secretary of state. But because the President was a firm believer in the principle of checks and balances, he had also stuck Toby Holt in the same department to temper Olney's hotheadedness. Toby was finding it very trying to attempt to balance Richard Olney. Sometimes he thought everybody in the world was going crazy, and it might be simpler just to go back to being a gentleman farmer in Oregon and let other people deal with Olney.

"Perhaps we might discuss a situation on which I believe we see more clearly eye to eye," he said instead. "I'm sure you're growing increasingly concerned over the refusal of the government of Hawaii to release its political prisoners." *Since you're so concerned with public sentiment*. Public sentiment in the States was becoming vehement in that cause.

"I believe you have a personal interest in that situation, too," Olney said suspiciously.

"My daughter-in-law's brother has been sentenced to thirty-five years of hard labor," Toby said. "And I *don't* have a personal interest in Cuba—or Venezuela, either. And I *don't* write my son's newspaper." *And I don't think you've got a brain in your skull.* "The situation in Hawaii is somewhat different, however. The United States has been invited into that conflict, beginning with the illegal use of our marines to topple the monarchy and then by the current government's request for annexation. It would be greatly to our advantage to do so before some other country does it first—but not if we appear to be receiving stolen goods."

Toby was aware that supporting annexation was *not* a popular position in the States. Public sentiment was for restoring the monarchy, or at least for installing a democracy elected by free ballot. And public sentiment also feared that if Hawaii was annexed, statehood would be the next request. Americans were terrified of "foreign races" overrunning their government. All in all, Americans wanted to think of Hawaiians as happy islanders in their idyllic kingdom, not as fellow citizens. Pragmatic politicians, of whom Toby was one, perceived the situation differently. Without backing from the United States, Hawaii wasn't strong enough to hold out for long against Russia or Japan. The islands were far too conveniently placed in the middle of the Pacific and had far too useful a harbor.

"Of course our own party is not entirely in agreement on the issues of political prisoners or annexation," Toby murmured, prodding Olney a little harder. "Our colleagues would be greatly relieved, of course, were Hawaii to clean its own house before annexation was considered."

"I do not require that you lecture me on the obvious," Olney snarled.

"I'm refreshing your memory," Toby said mildly. "Since your energies are somewhat overtaxed at the moment with interfering in matters that do *not* concern us."

Olney stopped glaring at him and sat down behind his desk. "You have the tact of a buffalo, Holt," he said grumpily. "No wonder you didn't get reelected."

Toby chuckled. "And now you wish I had. Maybe we could stop crossing swords for the moment and stick to the Hawaiian question. My recommendation, for your unbiased consideration, is that we increase pressure on the Hawaiian government. We would be most ill-advised to annex the islands under the existing situation. But annex them we must."

Olney was silent, thinking. Toby suspected that it was costing Olney a good deal to admit that Toby had a point, even though he also suspected that Olney held the same opinion on the Hawaiian question.

"It's an election year, next year," Toby said softly.

"Hmmm." Both men knew that 1896 was going to be an important but unpredictable year politically. Cleveland was in his second term, but the terms had not been consecutive. Some Democrats were outraged over his handling of the labor issue and unemployment relief. Whether the party would nominate him again was chancy. And whomever they did nominate would have Cleveland's administration's record to deal with during the campaign. It all added up to a bundle of doubt. Soothing the American political conscience over the treatment of Liliuokalani, who was popular in the American imagination, and the treatment of jailed citizens in Hawaii were important to the party's future success.

"I'm sure," Toby murmured, "that the President would be gratified if you and I could reach an accord on *some* issue."

"I'd be gratified myself," Olney said. "You're a nuisance. Oh, all right. We're in accord on this. I'll speak to the President and to Minister Willis."

Richard Olney spoke to President Cleveland, who spoke to Minister Willis, who spoke to President Dole. After everybody had spoken to everybody else, Sam still remained in jail, and Liliuokalani remained imprisoned in her small room in the Iolani Palace.

The queen received a letter signed "Citizens of the Cherokee Nation," asking how many American volunteers it would require to overthrow the PGs and put her back on her throne. The offer was a spiritual comfort but not a practical solution, as Liliuokalani was well aware that the Cherokee Nation had not been able to keep the United States government from stealing its land.

President Dole, meanwhile, received a letter from the women of Texas, declaring themselves on the side of the deposed queen. The Chicago *Times Herald* ran a scathing article on "that ridiculous little oligarchy called a republic." The San Francisco *Clarion,* whose publisher did not agree with his father's political long view, called for the establishment of a constitutional monarchy and referred to the PGs as "bandits in business suits, missionaries' boys gone bad, who found sugar and land grabbing more profitable than Bible thumping, and are now hiding their delinquency behind pious platitudes."

As the roar of American disapproval increased, a harried Dole was rumored to be threatening to resign unless his government allowed him to follow a course of leniency with the prisoners. He gave orders that Prince Kuhio, an imprisoned relative of the queen, was not to wear prison clothes; Kuhio, however, refused to take them off. As long as any other Hawaiians wore prison stripes, he said flatly, so would he.

The queen was allowed no visitors, and the vengeful PGs even took to examining gifts of food and flowers sent to her, "presumably for a file or a six-gun," as Theresa Wilcox said acidly.

The queen retaliated by having some of her musical compositions sent to sympathizers in the States, where the songs became quite popular. "Aloha Oe" was among them, but so was "The Queen's Prayer," a spiritual chant asking divine forgiveness for her enemies, a sentiment that raised Dole's blood pressure immeasurably.

Forty-five Hawaiians received conditional pardons. And in Honolulu, anyone not in jail was engaged in arguing the matter. The PGs, possibly hoping to strike back at the United States, sent a diplomatic negotiator to Japan. Alarmed by the prospect of being "swamped by an influx of coolie immigrants," a group of haoles who had previously opposed annexation by the United States now began to support it.

Hawaiians loudly refused to countenance that idea, and the government now found itself looking uneasily over both shoulders. Someone found more guns in a flower bed, or claimed he had. Someone else was suspected of passing secret messages. The rate of arrests picked up again, drawing in those merely suspected of sympathizing with people already in jail.

To Sam's best knowledge, no one had suggested any pardon for him, nor were they likely to. By the time he received Annie's message about Eden's safe arrival in New York and her marriage to Michael Holt, it was a relief to him not to have to worry about her safety. That his sister was better off out of Hawaii was not arguable. Sam lived in terror that Annie might be arrested, and he was torn between relief that Dickie Merrill and Dallas McCall were still with her for protection, and unease over how far McCall's "protection" might extend.

Sam had lost nearly thirty pounds since his arrest. After he lay down at night, with the bone-deep ache in his limbs from splitting rocks, minutes or hours might pass before the oblivion of sleep claimed him. He worried about Annie during that feverish half-waking dream state. At night he dreamed of murder and woke in the morning, not remembering the dream but feeling sick to his stomach.

At last he was given a letter from Eden, which had been opened and read and held back by the warden for two weeks. A grinning jailer allowed Sam to ready only three lines and then prodded him with a bayonet out of his cell.

Sam tried to read as he limped down the corridor, but the jailer prodded him again. "Move it. That letter ain't going anywhere."

Sam bit his lip and found himself willing to plead. "Please . . . it's from my sister."

"So what? You're goin' out to earn your keep now. Maybe I'll let you look at the letter during your rest break. If you get one."

Sam quickly stuffed Eden's note in his prison shirt before the guard decided to take it away. He walked heavily, dully, hardly seeing the inmates in the other cells as he passed. Sometimes there would be new faces, of the recently arrested; but they all looked alike to him. They watched him go, faces pressed in silent sympathy to the bars. Sam was the only prisoner on the reef who went to the rock pile every day. Everyone knew why. The guards had bets as to whether the warden would keep him at it until the work killed him.

Except for Annie's messages—which were so few and far between that Sam suspected that the majority were not allowed through to him—he had no knowledge of the world outside the reef. His days were an endless motion of pick and sledgehammer and rock. No one did anything with the rubble he produced; its only purpose was to torment him.

The rock breaking became rhythmic, his body an automaton that could still feel pain. He thought that he was dying, but sheer, stubborn fury kept him alive. Sometimes his weariness and anger would boil over, and he would fight with other prisoners over half-imagined causes, until most of the other men, sympathetic but wary, kept out of his way.

Hoakina watched his former employer from a cautious distance, for fear that the warden might learn that Hoakina had been Sam's foreman on Aloha Malihini and, out of spite, set Hoakina to work on the rock pile, too. Someone was aware of that relationship, Hoakina thought, or he would have been freed by now. Most of the little fish had gone already. Someone knew, but who? Hoakina was afraid to ask.

He watched as Sam deteriorated, as his eyes developed an unsteady glitter, as his muscles twitched so badly that when he ate, he couldn't hold the spoon—that is, on those rare occasions when the guards allowed him to be fed in the chow line and not in his cell.

"He is not going to make it," Hoakina said quietly one morning when Sam rose, dragging his chains, and then fell, tripping over nothing visible.

The guards kicked him onto his feet, and Sam spun around, snarling at them, teeth bared. The guards, looking frightened, raised their truncheons. Sam picked up his chains and stumbled past the silent prisoners still at their breakfast.

"He will make it," Lot Lane predicted.

"His body will make it," another Lane brother murmured. "It is his mind I am not sure of. I saw someone on the edge of madness once. Now I have seen it again."

They cast glances around them, wary of being overheard by guards. Any speculation on the fate of other prisoners was considered "treasonous."

"You're wrong," another man, a burly Scot, said. He had arrived in the islands by jumping ship from a whaling schooner off Maui thirty years before and was now in prison for armed robbery. "That one has the balls to beat the bastards if they don't kill him outright."

Ordinarily the political prisoners and the criminal convicts kept their distance from each other, each in his own closed society. But this man stood high in the pecking order of the prison, and even the politicals respected his position and his knowledge. If he chose to eat with them, they heard what he had to say.

"He's learning, you see," the Scot explained, wolfing a plate of beans and poi. "He's making 'em a little too afraid of him to kill him."

"The way he picks fights, he'll be lucky if one of the convicts doesn't kill him," Hoakina said sadly.

"Not unless I'm the one that does it," the Scot said. "The others think he's crazy, so they leave him alone." Madness was nearly as respected as power. "I know different, see, but that's because I know more than the rest of you stupid bastards."

"How do you know he isn't mad?" Lot Lane asked softly.

"Because, look you, he doesn't trouble *me*. Brentwood may be crazy on the edges from the beatings he's taking, but not down in the core of him where a man survives." The Scot wiped his mouth on the back of his hand. "Still and all, the government's breeding a bad thing in him, keeping him at those rocks. He'll be dangerous when he gets out."

"So will we all," Lane said.

"But not like this one. This government's a pack of fools. They've taken a good citizen and turned him into a man I'd be easy to have at my back. And I'm thinking they didn't mean to do that." He pushed himself from the table and stood, towering over the seated politicals.

Lot Lane stood, too, towering a little larger. "We have little in common, but if you help Sam Brentwood stay alive, I'll see that you get some tobacco."

"No man on the reef takes a quarrel to a killing unless I say to," the Scot growled.

"That's what I mean," Lot said evenly. "I've watched you. You keep order among your own. What if Brentwood's not as stable as you believe?"

The Scot spat on the floor. "Then maybe I'll take your baccy for insurance."

He strode off into the exercise yard with the rest of the criminal convicts.

Hoakina looked after him. "I am afraid of that one," he said frankly.

Lane laughed gently. "You might well be, my friend. But all the same, if tobacco buys Brentwood a bodyguard, we'll keep up the acquaintance."

"What did he mean," Hoakina asked, "when he said they'd made Mr. Brentwood a man he'd be easy to have at his back?"

"That they've turned him into a convict," Lane explained.

"A convict? We are all convicts," Hoakina muttered dolefully.

"Not like that one," Lane said. "The Scot meant that

the PGs may have turned our friend from a rebel into a criminal, a man he'd be willing to trust as an accomplice—a man outside society now . . . one of his own."

"Never!" Hoakina darted a furious glance at the door to the exercise yard. "Mr. Brentwood is not capable of such a thing!"

"I am not at all sure," Lane said, "what Sam Brentwood may be capable of now. If I were the PGs, I would not want to find out."

XIX

A lieutenant of the Citizens' Guard and three troopers moved through the rows of darkened cane. They padded quietly, like hounds on the hunt when the quarry was near and still unsuspecting. It was the same quarry they had been hunting all year, and they had acquired a taste for it.

The cane fields of Aloha Malihini whispered enticingly to them. This was Sam Brentwood's plantation. Any quarry caught in these fields would be better received by the authorities than most. They had no concrete evidence, but that did not matter. Annie Brentwood was known to be a friend of Liliuokalani's. She was the wife of Sam Brentwood. That was reason enough to be in her fields. The guards intended to frighten her into giving herself away. Only the fact that she was a woman had kept her out of jail this long.

The four guards stopped, watching the lights of the house. Mrs. Brentwood had two men staying with her, the lieutenant knew. This in itself was evidence of degenerate moral character, and everyone knew that rebels condoned heathenism. That was why the queen had been deposed. It might be that the two men were involved, too.

The lieutenant went ahead purposefully, signaling to one of his troopers to follow. The other two stayed behind with the crate that they had carried up from the Pahala road, where they had tethered their horses. A well-armed fourth trooper had stayed behind to guard the mounts. Once, the lieutenant had had his horse stolen by rebel sympathizers while he was arresting a traitor. He had had to walk his prisoner back, to the jeers of the arrested man's neighbors, and had earned a chewing-out from the captain in the bargain. The lieutenant knew better now.

He pounded on the door and yelled, "We know you're in there. You can't hide!"

When Annie opened the door, a square of light spilled out onto the porch and onto the lieutenant's shiny boots and pinched face. She looked up at him. "No one's hiding," she said. "What do you want now?" She was still wearing black for Claudia and because of general misery. The clothes hung on her thinning frame. Dallas and Dickie stood behind her.

"I have orders to search your house."

"You searched it before," Annie said tiredly. "You aren't going to do it again. You'll frighten my servants."

"Maybe your servants have a good reason to be frightened," the lieutenant suggested. "Maybe you're hiding something."

"What?" Annie demanded. "What could I possibly be hiding?" Her mouth twisted. "The rebellion is over. Now get off my porch."

"You're in very serious trouble, Mrs. Brentwood. You'd better get out of my way."

Dallas took her hand. "Let the damn fools in," he whispered. "It's easier."

Annie grudgingly backed up a few paces. Dickie moved out of the troopers' way with alacrity.

"Where were you at four o'clock last Tuesday?" the lieutenant snapped over his shoulder as he marched into the first-floor library, with his trooper at his heels.

"Last Tuesday?"

"Don't be evasive!" The lieutenant began riffling through Annie's desk. "Where were you?"

"That's my private correspondence and the farm bills!" she protested. "Leave them alone!"

The lieutenant threw them onto the floor, then pulled more papers from the pigeonholes above the desk. "You refuse to admit where you were?"

"I don't know where I was!" Annie said. "Let me think. I was here on the farm."

"Where on the farm?"

"At the south camp." She tried to snatch the flying papers. "No, maybe I was up here. We were cooking sugar."

The lieutenant tilted the desk and shook its entire contents onto the carpet. He didn't bother to read them. Next he went to the bookshelves, pulled books out, and flipped through them quickly. He spun around, a volume of poetry in his hand. "You'd better think clearly, Mrs. Brentwood. Are you sure you weren't in Honolulu?"

"I was in Honolulu two weeks ago."

"What day?"

"Wednesday. No, Thursday."

"Why did you say Wednesday?"

"Because I can't remember. Let me look at my date book."

"No. Suspects are not allowed to rehearse their testimony." As Annie reached for her date book, the lieutenant grabbed it and put it in his pocket. "Where were you at noon on Wednesday? And at quarter of five on Friday? I warn you, Mrs. Brentwood, this is serious."

"This is harassment," Dallas said. "You watch your attitude, buddy boy."

"And who are you?"

"Name's McCall. I wasn't around for your little unpleasantness, and I can prove it. Since I got here, Mrs. Brentwood's mostly been with me, running this farm, since you morons arrested her husband and her foreman. Now just what are you trying to get at?"

Annie, driven nearly to tears, had her hands to her head. The lieutenant seemed satisfied for the moment. He left the library without answering and started up the stairs. Koana saw him and fled shrieking.

The lieutenant turned through the doorway of Annie's bedroom and began to search through her bureau drawers.

Annie followed. "Stay out of my things!"

The lieutenant tossed chemises and rolled stockings onto the floor. He emptied Annie's jewelry box onto the bureau top. The trooper pulled dresses from the wardrobe while Annie batted at his hands.

Dallas started to intervene and then stopped, looking with suspicion at the lieutenant. He turned abruptly, went quickly back down the stairs, pulled a shotgun out of its rack in the ruined library, and strode purposefully out the front door.

The moon wasn't up, and the cane moved menacingly in the darkness beyond the front yard. Dallas looked toward the sugarhouse, but there was no sign of movement there. He cocked his head, listening, trying to distinguish any human movement from the rustling of the cane. Then he heard it—just a faint *clink* and a splash from the cane field where the irrigation ditch ran past the road.

Dallas glanced back toward the house. Annie's voice and the lieutenant's still came angrily from the top floor. Dickie Merrill was visible, hovering uncertainly in the hallway beyond the open door. Dallas went back up the porch steps and caught Dickie by the collar.

"Come with me."

"Where?" Dickie looked with apprehension at the shotgun.

"Out," Dallas said. "Just keep your mouth shut."

"I don't want to get involved."

"You're involved, Dickie boy. Now move it." Dallas dragged him out the door.

"What are you going to do? You'll make trouble," Dickie protested.

"You betcha."

Dallas let go of Dickie's collar, but since it was clear that he would bring Dickie by force if he had to, the young man followed down the dark road. He looked from left to right with quick, nervous jerks of his head.

Dallas moved silently, his steps light despite his arthritic knee. The shotgun was cradled in the crook of one arm. A hundred yards down the road he stopped and motioned for Dickie to stand still. A low murmur of voices could be heard from the cane field, and then Dallas caught the faint chink of light from a shielded lantern.

He shot the bolt on the rifle. The voices stopped in midmurmur at the ominous sound and lapsed into silence.

"Get outta there with your hands up," Dallas ordered, "or I'll blow your butts clear to Oahu."

After another moment of uneasy silence, two faces peered out at him through the cane.

"Move it!" Dallas shouted.

Two troopers of the Citizens' Guard eased out, hands high, and stood in the road. Their boots were caked with damp earth. One fellow had apparently slipped in the irrigation ditch and was wet to the knee. His eyes widened. "Rebels," he breathed.

"Protective home owners," Dallas corrected, smiling dangerously. "What are you boys up to here?" He noted that their service pistols were still holstered on their belts. "Hard to dig a hole with a gun in your hand, ain't it, boys?"

"We're looking for contraband," the first trooper blustered. "You're under arrest."

"Who's got a gun on who?" Dallas inquired. "Dickie boy, supposing you just slide over and take those pistols."

Dickie hesitated, then scuttled over and gingerly lifted the pistols out of their holsters.

"Attaboy." Dallas dropped the pistols in the irrigation ditch behind him. The weapons sank with a *plop* in the wet muck. "Now slide on into the cane there, Dickie, and see what kind of contraband these boys were looking for."

"I don't want to have anything to do with this," Dickie protested. "I'm not involved."

"You will be," Dallas threatened, "if you don't hop."

Dickie sidled into the cane. He gave a startled exclamation, then stuck his head out through the leaves. "There's a box of dynamite in here!"

"Well, well," Dallas said with mock surprise. "Bend the cane back and let me take a look."

Dickie flattened the cane stalks and held up the lantern. A wooden box sat beside a shallow hole. The troopers' abandoned shovels lay beside it, blades encrusted with newly dug earth.

Annie, eyes flaming, surveyed the shambles of her bedroom. The lieutenant glanced at his watch as if waiting for something, while the trooper looked out the bedroom door and into the hall. Once, he paced to the bedroom window and peered out.

Annie, fists balled together, stood in a pile of torn silk and trampled clothing. The sheets had been pulled from the bed, and the mattress and pillows slit with a knife. "Are you satisfied?" she asked, near tears. "Are you going to steal everything I own, or did you just come here to ruin it?"

Again the lieutenant checked his watch, then flicked a glance at the window. As he looked back, his eye lit on a ring among the tumbled jewelry on the bureau. He snatched it up. It was a little signet with a crest in onyx. "Where did you get this?"

"That was a present," Annie said icily, "from the queen."

"She's not to be called that!"

"From Mrs. Dominis, then. Two years ago."

"A code message," the trooper suggested hopefully. "Signal for rebellion."

"Everyone who knows me has seen me wear that ring for the last two years," Annie snapped.

"We'll see about that." The lieutenant put the ring in his pocket and appeared very relieved to have found something. He was looking at his watch again when a commotion erupted in the hall downstairs. His eyes lit with happiness.

"What have you found, men?" The lieutenant strode to the balcony.

Dallas McCall looked up at him. "A couple of sneak

thieves masquerading as troopers," he said evenly. "With a box of dynamite."

The lieutenant, drawing his pistol, ran down the stairs with Annie right behind him. "Those are my men! Put up your weapon!"

Dallas still held the shotgun in the crook of his arm. Behind him Dickie appeared to be trying to flatten himself into the woodwork. The troopers looked sheepishly at their boots.

"That hole wasn't but half dug," Dallas remarked. "And that box didn't have any dirt on it. And get your pistol out of my face before I make you eat it."

"He snuck up on us, Lieutenant," one of the troopers apologized.

"That's right. And now I'm gonna sneak you all to the Pahala police. I reckon all this searchin' was just a diversion." He gave a disgusted look at the mess in the library.

The lieutenant took a deep breath. "Perhaps my men were a little carried away in attempting to do their duty." He shot them a look that boded them no good, then he spun around to face Annie. "Mrs. Brentwood, perhaps you can tell me where that box came from."

Annie had regained her composure out of sheer outrage. "You brought it with you!"

"That's only a rebel's word against a member of the Citizens' Guard."

"Supposing we put all these guns away," Dallas suggested, "and talk like reasonable folk. Now I caught your boys red-handed, and Mr. Merrill here was with me."

Dickie blanched. "I'm not involved. I'm a United States citizen. I'm just here on a vacation."

The lieutenant apparently gave up on the dynamite, but not on his lacerated pride. "You arrived in the islands before the rebellion," he snapped at Dickie. "We know these things."

"He found the dynamite," one of the troopers said sullenly. "We never saw it, Lieutenant."

Dickie looked panic-stricken. "It was right there in

the cane field! I never saw it before! I don't know anything about it! Maybe it *was* there before. I don't even know Sam Brentwood that well. I mean, I knew him in New York. I just came out here for my health. I—"

"I thought you two were old friends in New York," Dallas said helpfully.

"No! I mean, not for very long. And I didn't know him well. I didn't know Mrs. Brentwood, either. I only stayed on to help out, but I'm leaving tomorrow and—"

"What knowledge do you have of Mrs. Brentwood's activities?" The lieutenant closed in.

"None! None at all! I make it a point not to know. If she's up to something, I didn't know about it. She probably *is* up to something, but I didn't know!"

"Sit down, Mr. Merrill. We want to talk to you."

"I'm a United States citizen. You'd better not trifle with *me*, my good man. I have influence. I have money. I have— McCall, tell them I didn't have anything to do with it."

Dallas lost his temper. "Didn't have anything to do with what? Lieutenant, this man here may know more than we thought."

"Dallas—" Annie began.

Dallas quickly shook his head at her. "I think you've been taken advantage of, honey. Mr. Merrill here may be a spy. We'd better find out."

A gleam in her eye, Annie studied Dickie. "Oh, Dallas, do you think I've been taken in?" She swayed a little as if about to swoon. "Nursed a serpent in my bosom? After eating my food and enjoying my hospitality and not helping out with the farm one whit? Oh, Dickie, how could you?"

"Now see here!" Dickie bobbed out of the chair into which the lieutenant had maneuvered him.

The lieutenant barred his way, pistol still in his hand. Dickie, panicked again, ran around like a rabbit, careening this way and that until he slammed into a table and rebounded to crash entirely by accident into the lieutenant. The pistol discharged, putting a hole through

the ceiling. The shot reverberated as if someone had
struck a heavy gong in the still night.

In a moment they heard hoofbeats pounding up the
road. The sound stopped directly outside, and another
trooper breathlessly hurled himself through the front
door and stared wide-eyed at the gathering in the foyer.

An overturned table and shattered glass littered the
floor, and in the middle of the chaos, the lieutenant, who
had decided to take what he could get, held a struggling
Dickie by the arms.

On the balcony above them, Koana reappeared,
screamed, and threw her apron over her head.

"Mount up," the lieutenant ordered, looking nearly
as rattled as Dickie. "We're taking this one in. Assault on
a government official. He may have additional evidence."

Koana screamed again as the troopers dragged
Dickie outside and put him on a horse. Dallas and
Annie, arms folded, watched them go.

"He keeps the code in his underwear, Lieutenant!"
Dallas shouted after them, and then doubled up with
laughter.

"Dallas, that was wicked," Annie said, trying to
suppress her own laughter but failing badly. "Oh, mercy!
What will they do to him, though?"

"Feed him on bread and water," Dallas predicted.
"Torture him with thumbscrews. Deprive him of gin. Aw
hell, Annie Laurie, they'll let him go in a couple of days
when they figure out he's too dumb to be a spy."

"I don't know. . . ." Annie said dubiously. "They're
pretty stupid themselves." She looked around in dismay
at the ruin of her house.

"They ain't gonna hurt him," Dallas sputtered.
Tears of laughter rolled down his cheeks. "Barring
maybe in the pocketbook. If he keeps on yelling about
how much money he has, they'll slap him with a fat fine."
He clutched his sides. "Lord God, but that did me
good."

A moaning wail above them drew their attention to
Koana, who was hanging over the balcony. "My Mr.

Merrill!" She threw her arms wide and then beat her breast. "They have taken him!"

Annie went upstairs. "Koana, stop that! He isn't your Mr. Merrill, or at least he isn't supposed to be. I warned you about that."

Koana continued to howl. "He promised me! He promised—!" She let out another hiccuping wail.

Annie looked at her suspiciously. "Stop that this minute! Koana, you didn't! He promised you what?"

"Owwwwooooo! Auwe! Auwe!"

"*Koana!*"

Koana lifted her head, dark eyes staring out in mournful bereavement. "My dress! My silk dress like the haole ladies. He hasn't bought me my dress! And now he can't because he's in jail! Owwwoooo!"

"Maybe the lieutenant'll buy the dress for her," Dallas suggested the next morning. "Seeing as he's deprived her of her true love."

"Don't you even suggest it," Annie warned. They had finally persuaded Koana into bed the night before by threatening to fire her. She was up and about her duties in the morning, still sniffling dolefully. "And you stay away from her, too."

"I got me a girl," Dallas said mildly.

"No, you don't." Annie put her hat on. She was dressed in a traveling suit. "I have to see Sam, if they'll let me in. I've got to tell him about Dickie."

"Reckon he might be happier not knowing," Dallas commented.

"Reckon he might," Annie agreed as she walked out the door. "But I got to tell him."

Dallas sighed as he watched her cart disappear down the road. He smacked his fist into the doorpost again and again until it hurt. "Aw hell, Annie Laurie," he said to empty air. "What the tarnation are you doing here anyway?"

Annie looked so haggard after the steamer voyage from the Big Island that the warden grudgingly permitted her in. And when she saw Sam, Dickie's dilemma didn't seem nearly so funny as it had the day before. She stared at Sam and was appalled at the change in him just since her last visit.

"So Dickie's in jail," Sam said. "That was very clever of you and Mr. McCall. You're having a good time without him, I trust?"

"Sam, don't be ridiculous." Annie tried to breathe without smelling the stench in the cell.

"Who's ridiculous? You look like a hag. Is it guilty conscience, or have you just been staying up all night with McCall?"

"You look awful, too, honey," Annie said, trying to be conciliatory. "Oh, baby, I'm trying to get you out of here."

"Keep trying," Sam said. "It'll give you something else to do."

"You haven't made it any easier," Annie said. "The warden says you're intractable. He nearly wouldn't let me in."

"Oh? Well, I'll try to be tractable," Sam said bitterly. "While I'm out breaking up rock and worrying about who my wife's sleeping with."

"That's not fair! I'm not sleeping with anyone!"

"Then why did you try so hard to get rid of Dickie?"

"I didn't try very hard." Annie looked at him wearily. They were both almost too exhausted to fight with each other. "That parasite was so anxious to make sure they knew *he* wasn't involved, he was ready to sell me down the river. And then where would your damn farm be? On account of you I can't even get Hoakina released. And all your precious Dickie has done for months is eat my food, drink your liquor, and say he doesn't know anything about farming, but he thinks he'll have another gin rickey. And as for Dallas McCall, if you want to have a home to come home to, you leave me alone about him. I need him."

"All my fault, eh?" Sam lay back down on the filthy mattress, trying to turn to some place on his body that didn't hurt. "Had a change of heart in your politics, have you?"

Annie stamped her foot in helpless fury. "No, Sam, not my politics. I stood by you, and I thought you did a brave thing. I *admired* you for it. But it's over. We lost. The revolt failed, and we have to give it up and go on. If you don't stop fighting it, they'll never let you out."

"Am I to understand that that would bother you?" Sam looked at the ceiling, not at Annie.

"Understand what you damn well please," Annie said. "I've told you how I feel."

"Then get Dickie out of jail" was all Sam said. He turned his face to the dirty wall.

After Annie had gone, he lay there silently, and eight months of accumulated tears slid over his face. They had dried by the time the guards came to take him out to the reef again.

"Please believe me." Annie was speaking to the chief of the Honolulu Police, to whom the Citizens' Guard lieutenant had delivered his prisoner via interisland packet. "Dickie Merrill is an old friend of my husband's, and other than that they haven't anything in common except a taste for liquor. Dickie hasn't got the energy, much less the inclination, to be a rebel. All he wants to do is go back to New York."

"So he has said." The police chief's mouth twitched in spite of himself. "I understand, however, that you and Mr. McCall here gave evidence against him."

Dallas looked sheepish. Although he was not exactly feeling contrite, he was unwilling to cause Annie any more trouble. "Naw," he said. "That lieutenant just sort of went off half-cocked. I expect you know what civilians are like when they get a chance to wear a fancy uniform."

The police chief sighed. He did indeed.

"And I guess we were pretty steamed about the mess the lieutenant made of Mrs. Brentwood's house," Dallas added.

"Searching for contraband is serious business," the chief said.

"So is planting it," Dallas remarked. "Like I said, he got a little carried away."

"I'd be more than willing to have *you* search my house," Annie said sweetly. The invitation cost her some effort. She had no love for the PG police. "I'm just trying to keep the farm running until my unfortunate husband has served his time."

"Well, the Big Island's not exactly my jurisdiction," the chief pointed out. "Furthermore, Mr. Merrill is charged with assaulting the lieutenant."

"I'm sure there's a fine for that," Annie suggested, tucking her hands around her purse. "I'd be glad to pay it, since the business was my fault in some ways. But you know there has been so much dreadful publicity in the States about the situation here. Those of us who felt a loyalty to Mrs. Dominis also feel loyal to Hawaii. We must go on and try to make a productive situation of this new government, since it is the people's will."

Dallas coughed. He didn't add anything, but he regarded Annie with admiration for her ability to lie through her teeth when necessary.

"I'm afraid that if Mr. Merrill isn't released, stories will appear in *all* the New York newspapers. He comes from a socially prominent family there."

"So he says," the police chief remarked.

"It might be embarrassing to have the matter come to a trial," Annie suggested.

"'Prominent American playboy philanthropist held captive in Honolulu prison,'" Dallas murmured. "You'd hate to have Americans reading that at the breakfast table."

"So I should." The police chief actually smiled at Annie, although there was something faintly wolfish in his expression. "I have to tell you, Mrs. Brentwood, you're barking up the wrong tree here. *I* don't want the fellow. His incessant whining is keeping all my prisoners awake at night. I'm going to give him to you on the condition that you pay his fine and put him on a ship for the States." He gave Annie a level look. "But that doesn't get *you* off the hook. You're still under suspicion as a rebel, and you're going to stay that way. Next time, they may find real evidence. I'm not at all sure it isn't there. We may just send somebody more—professional to look over the situation." His expression said plainly that the Citizens' Guard was getting to be an embarrassment. It was equally plain that he wasn't going to admit it.

"Feel free," Annie said grimly. "Perhaps you'd like to do it real soon, before I straighten up my house."

The police chief folded his arms. "That'll be up to the Council of State. Just remember you're under observation."

"How could I forget?" Annie snapped. She got a grip on her temper and said more evenly, "And what is Mr. Merrill's fine?"

"Two thousand dollars," the chief of police said.

"*What?*"

"Now look here—" Dallas leaned forward.

"Take it or leave it."

"Two thousand dollars!" Annie said furiously as she and Dallas, with Dickie walking between them, left the police station. "And going into the chief's pocket, I'm sure!"

"You can bet on that," Dallas said. "I hope old Sam thinks you're worth it, Dickie boy."

Dickie was pale and unshaven, and his clothes looked very like those of a man who had ridden facedown across a trooper's horse's rump. But once outside the jail, he regained some bluster. "I'll have you sued, McCall! You'll hear from my lawyers as soon as I get home!"

"Stuff it," Dallas grumbled, pushing him up the gangway of the packet.

"Defamation of character and false imprisonment!" Dickie shouted.

"Keep it up, and we'll take you back to the police," Dallas suggested.

Annie put her hands to her head. "Dickie, just be quiet."

It was not a particularly pleasant voyage, and after they reached the Big Island, Dickie, who had suffered from seasickness, was angrier than ever. Fortunately, to Annie's thinking, he was also too ill to talk. His skin was pale green and beaded with sweat, and he didn't recover his voice until the cart rolled to a stop outside the big house at Aloha Malihini.

Then he looked gloomily at the gaily painted sign above the door and muttered, "Aloha Malihini. 'Welcome Stranger,' my foot." Clutching his stomach, he headed toward the stairs.

"Maybe you should take a nap," Annie suggested.

Dickie straightened his shoulders and managed to say haughtily, "I am going to pack my bags," before he stumbled into his bedroom. They heard him throwing up in the washbasin.

Koana, eyes bright, peeped around the corner of the hall and nipped up the stairs and into the room behind him.

Annie started to go after her, but Dallas laid a restraining hand on her arm. "Let her have him. It'll give him something to take his mind off his troubles."

"Not if he's as sick as he looks." She and Dallas both burst out laughing. Then her amusement faded, and she put her hands to her head again.

Dallas slipped an arm around her. "Annie Laurie, you got to take your jokes where you find 'em. All that gets us through this life is laughing."

"I suppose," Annie allowed. "Dallas, I'm exhausted."

"I'll make you some tea," he offered. "And you come sit on the porch swing for a spell, and I'll tell you a story that'll amuse you some, about me and a trail boss and a poker game in Kansas City."

Half an hour later, Annie was asleep on the porch swing, with her head on Dallas's chest. He smiled, cuddled her closer, and went on with the story, telling it softly, as if it were a lullaby. "So the trail boss says, 'Well, I got four aces, too, an' mine are all out of the same deck.' And the dude in the green hat, he just throwed his cards down on the table and left." He looked closely at her to make sure she was really asleep. "And I do love you, Annie Laurie, and what the hell do you want with this Brentwood guy?"

Voices came through the upstairs window, and Annie stirred. Dallas carefully cocked his head up to listen, then chuckled softly.

Annie opened her eyes. "What is it?" she asked fuzzily.

"You just wait."

Koana's melancholy wail floated down from the window. "Oooowaaa! You are going away! You promise me! You say you loved me! When my cousin Hoakina hears of this—"

They couldn't hear Dickie's response, but in a moment his feet hit the stairs, and when he emerged onto the porch, he resembled a rabbit with a determined bobcat after it. "The next boat's in two hours," he said. "Get me on it."

In the hallway Koana sat down on his packed luggage and wailed.

Dallas got the buggy out, and after wresting the handles from Koana's fingers, they loaded Dickie's bags into it.

"You aren't coming!" Dickie told her.

"I too come!" She climbed in and sat. "And I follow you if you put me out."

The thought of Koana running after the buggy and howling was too much for Annie. "Just get in," she told Dickie.

They drove into Pahala with Koana weeping noisily in the back of the buggy. As they slowed for the traffic in Pahala, she pointed and began to wail again. "You don't love me! Oooowwwaaa!"

Dallas drew rein outside the clothing establishment that had drawn her eyes.

"If you stop here, I'll miss my boat," Dickie protested.

"You want to buy your ticket while she's carrying on like this? You promised her, lover boy, so get in there and do it."

Koana's eyes brightened, and then she had another happy thought. "I go to New York with you. There are many dresses in New York."

Dickie's eyes widened in horror. He jumped out of the buggy and shot into the dress shop.

The steamer in Honuapo Bay was just hauling in its boarding plank when Dickie leaped on it, ticket in his teeth and bags in his hands. "I'll sue you, McCall!" were his parting words.

Koana, clutching her silk dress like the haole ladies wore, waved at him, tearfully smiling.

"Have you heard?" Beatrice Sessions, the Hawaiian wife of Harvey Sessions, who owned the farm next to Aloha Malihini, was just stepping off an incoming packet. She pulled her two small children to a halt, then caught Annie's arm. "Annie, have you heard? The government has granted a conditional pardon to the queen!"

Annie caught her breath. "When?" If the PGs had pardoned Liliuokalani—

"Yesterday. The Council of State released her on parole. Prince Kuhio, also. Harvey won't approve," Beatrice said, "but I am so happy for her, and I knew you would be, too."

"What about the others?" Annie held her breath. She could see Dallas standing a few feet away, with Koana. He was listening.

Beatrice's face fell. "Forty-seven others," she said. "Sam?"

"Not Sam. Oh, Annie, I'm so sorry. I had hoped—"

"I know. Thank you, Beatrice." Beatrice bustled on, herding her children ahead of her through the passengers. Annie found Dallas at her side. She felt bone weary, too drained and sad to move. "I don't think they'll ever let him out," she whispered.

The emotions on Dallas's face chased between relief and sympathy until he gave up trying to hide them. "I don't know what to say, darlin'. You know why."

They stood still for a moment while the crowd on

the dock surged around them, buffeting them like the rolling surf against the rocks.

Dallas took her hand, and she let it stay in his. She stared at Dickie's steamer disappearing in the bay. Now there were just the two of them in the house. . . .

XX

New York, August 1895

"The screen's not right."

"The screen's fine," Ira Hirsch said for the seventh time as Mike adjusted it for the eighth time.

Mike clung to a ladder and fidgeted with pulleys. A fine shower of dust and pieces of an old swallow's nest came down from the accumulation of ages that nestled in the rafters, powdering his hair. "No, it's too high." Mike batted a tendril of dry grass from his mustache. "The audience will be craning their necks."

"The screen's where I always hang it." Ira got a push broom. "So stop shaking everything loose."

Mike muttered something under his breath and lowered the screen by two inches.

"Let him alone," Eden said. "He's nervous."

"*He's* nervous," Ira muttered, sweeping. "Now *I* got to tinker with the rest of the show. Already I readjusted everything twice."

"I'll get you a cup of tea," Eden offered. "You drink it and wait till he comes down. Then we'll hide the ladder. *Then* you can adjust the lantern slides."

The Homecoming was only the first item on Ira's bill for the evening. A song and dance team, a comedy turn, and a magic-lantern show of fireworks and a haunted castle—with ghosts dangling in midair—filled the rest of the bill.

Eden pushed Ira down in a seat in the front row and trotted backstage, where a kettle burbled on a gas ring.

323

Making tea and soothing opening-night nerves seemed to be her function this evening, she decided as she ladled tea into Ira's ancient pot. But that was all right; someone had to do it. Eden crossed her fingers and whispered a little prayer. Mike's whole family and all the backers would be there. Eden didn't think she could bear it if he was humiliated in front of them. She felt fiercely protective of him and certain of his talent at the same time.

The backstage greenroom and corridors and the dingy dressing rooms were unnaturally still. Then something chirped at her, and Eden listened, motionless, waiting for the thin note to grow louder. There was a cricket in the greenroom walls. It liked to be near the gas ring, which radiated warmth. The notes trilled again, mellow and merry, a private overture. Crickets were lucky, Eden thought. People were not allowed to whistle backstage, she had learned from Cathy Martin, but crickets were considered good luck.

Eden took a biscuit from a tin and crumbled it near a crack in the wall on the chipped enameled table that held the gas ring. The Hawaiians made offerings to the goddess Pele in her volcano. If Eden in her way wished to do the same for the resident sprite of the Atheneum Theater, she saw no harm in it. She had by now lived long enough with artists to be able to find God in a cricket or anywhere else He should choose to appear. She chirped back at it, a little sound between tongue and teeth that was not a whistle, and took Ira his tea.

By seven o'clock the theater was no longer muffled in watchful silence but awake and breathing to the patter of footsteps and the rising and falling of voices behind its stage. The comedy turn, in their shared dressing room, squabbled sotto voce; the song and dance team limbered up—a swift, unseen spatter of steps on bare floorboards.

While Ira and his new projectionist arrayed their store of magic in the projection room, Mike stood before the moving-picture projector, checking and rechecking spools and sprockets, coaxing it into precision. He looked slim and elegant in evening dress, but Eden could see the tension in his eyes and in the finely drawn lines at their corners.

In the orchestra pit the musicians in their tailcoats tuned up. Mike's family and the newlyweds' friends from the Chelsea were expectant and hopeful in the front row. The backers were in the last row, where they could watch the audience's reaction.

Charley and Janessa had brought Rachel Poliakov, escorting her like a pair of watchful duennas. Kathleen had stayed at home with the twins, happy in her restored privacy. With Rachel's first wages, Eden had found her a room in a respectable boardinghouse with a Jewish landlady. Rachel was dressed in her best outfit, her face scrubbed. Eden winked at her as she passed by to take her seat just behind them.

Eden saw with satisfaction that Ira's publicity campaign had done its work. The house was packed, and the audience was mostly families, middle-class New Yorkers with well-tended children. The houselights dimmed, and the audience rustled and shuffled and shushed itself into silence as the orchestra began to play. These were musicians whom Ira regularly used, and they were adept at fitting their music to the action of the show. Where there was no dialogue, there must be music, sad or sweet or rollicking, to cue the audience to the proper mood.

The screen lit up, a flare of white light that caused the startled audience to jump. The opening scene was Mike's pride, shot on Ellis Island itself with Charley's connivance—a whole population of new Americans spilling into the country, faces that many of the theatergoers knew, faces that could have been themselves or their parents or grandparents. The audience reaction indicated that they felt as if they, too, were standing on the dock of the island, in the path of the throng of eager, hopeful, frightened immigrants, who clutched seabags and suitcases, feather beds and babies. The mob was pushing, jostling, and hurrying past the camera, almost into the audience's laps.

After the immigrants swept past, the scene changed, to what appeared to be a hall in the interior of the immigration building. It was actually a set on the roof of the Chelsea, illusion made truth by the reality of the opening. There was only one person before the camera now, a dark-haired woman, her face lit with joy. She leaned forward on tiptoe, taking one step and then another. Then a man in a Greek fisherman's cap and pea coat stepped into the frame and caught her in his arms.

The audience, enthralled, sat on the edge of their chairs, as if to meet the pair, and explained to one another, grasping the idea: "She's just off the boat, see? He's her brother."

"No, you thickhead. Nobody kisses their brother like that!"

"Where are they now?"

"Hey, I know! That's Twenty-third Street!"

To give his story a definite location, one with which the audience was well acquainted, Mike had spliced scenes of Manhattan in between the scenes he had shot on the rooftop.

At Ira's demand he had leaned heavily toward melodrama: The girl from the Old Country, come to join her intended husband, meets a rich man and has to choose between them. The scenario offered Rochelle Blossom the opportunity to emote sufficiently to compensate for there being no dialogue. To the audience's satisfaction, she returned, disillusioned with high society, to her first love. In the final scene, the camera lingered on Rochelle, with her immigrant husband standing behind her chair, and her baby in her lap (Brandon Tobias, borrowed for the afternoon)—the ideal family portrait. The orchestra played "Home Sweet Home."

The houselights came up, and a piercing whistle sliced through the orchestra's tear-jerking rendition. It was followed by another and another until the bandleader gave up. He stood and bowed, but nobody paid any attention to him.

"Show it again! Show it again!"

The audience began to stamp their feet while clapping and hooting and yelling up to the projection booth.

The song and dance team, Mirella and Manuel, waited in the wings for their turn. Where was the drop that was supposed to be coming down, painted with their names and a scene from a Spanish village? The team glared upward at the projection booth. But the houselights dimmed again, and the screen stayed uncovered.

"Of all the nerve!" Mirella poked her husband in the chest. "Are you just gonna let 'em get away with it? I've never been so insulted."

Manuel appeared dubious, but he hunched his shoulders, shoved his hands into his pockets, and went through the wings to the stairs that led to the projection room. His wife and he were supposed to have second billing. To run the first act twice demoted them to third. In the touchy world of the theater, that was a fighting matter. He straightened his Spanish hat, adorned with red bobble fringe around the edges. As he opened the projection-room door, he tried to look like a man to be reckoned with.

"Now, Fred," Ira said as he came in (Manuel was no more Spanish than Mirella was), "we're just gonna show it once more, and then we'll put you on."

Below them, feet stamped in rhythm to the chant: "Show it again! Show it again!"

"That ain't in our contract," Manuel said.

"Sure it is," Ira said. "I ain't putting another act in ahead of you; I'm just repeating the first one."

"It's the same as—" Manuel said stubbornly.

"Naw, it's not." Ira peered downward at the audience. "But if I don't show the film again, they'll riot. Then where's your 'Spanish Serenade'?"

"Ready," Mike said from behind the projector.

They ran it again, with Manuel lurking, furious, into the corner, and then when the audience wouldn't stop shouting, once more after that.

"You can go on now if you want to," Ira told Manuel.

"But I ain't gonna be responsible for what the audience will do if they get you instead of what they want."

By this time all the backers had crowded into the projection room, to slap one another on the back, congratulate themselves on their perspicacity, and clog the room with cigar smoke. When the film had ended for the fourth time, the audience permitted the rest of the program to continue. Mike turned the projection room over to Ira's new man and settled in beside Eden in a trance of relief to watch Mirella and Manuel.

After the evening's entertainment was over, the newlyweds went, with the backers and Mike's family and such of the Chelsea residents as trailed after them, to Ira's favorite Greek restaurant, where they gloated and congratulated one another some more. They introduced Toby Holt to retsina, a favor for which, they warned him, he would not be grateful the next morning.

"Damnedest thing I ever saw." The backers muttered among themselves, drinking wine, casting clouds of blue smoke over bowls of olives and feta cheese.

"Newspaper reporters were there. Did you see?"

"The audience went nuts."

"Just count the money."

"But will it last? Will they go for the next one? We gotta figure out what turned the trick."

"Hell, I can tell you that," Ira said.

"Always you can tell. But you ain't always right."

"This time I am. We gave 'em a way to get inside it, that's what we did. I remember as a kid, looking at this picture in a museum. There were all these people having a picnic on the banks of a river. Kids running around, dogs, some kid had a kite. I wanted to be at that picnic so bad I couldn't stand it. I squeezed my eyes shut and held my breath, trying to make it happen, trying to get *in*. So that's what this new picture did—made it a story, not just a bunch of silly stuff. A real story with people the audience cares about. Then we put it right in the audience's lap, practically jumping off the screen at them, so they have a chance to jump, too—you know, jump *in* it. That's what we did. We let 'em in."

"*Who* let 'em in?" Mike asked over his shoulder, but he laughed. If Ira wanted to take credit for Mike's innovations, he could. Ira had come up with the money men.

"What about the next one?" one of the other backers demanded, staunchly prepared to believe in the fickleness of the public.

"Just wait till you see the papers tomorrow," Ira said, satisfied. "Just wait."

So they waited, and danced a little, and drank some more retsina. At midnight they pounced on a passing newsboy working the all-night saloons. Ira and Mike bore three copies of the *Tribune* back in triumph. "A New Gimmick Altogether" the headline said. Below it, the *Tribune's* reporter, not its regular theater critic, launched into an assessment:

> One of the pleasures of living in New York is that we get to be the first to try out a hot idea, and last night we saw one. The moving picture at the Atheneum is no carny trick. It's the real goods. It tugged the heart, delighted the eye, and introduced a new comet in the night sky—the mysterious Rochelle Blossom.

"Hot damn!" Ira hooted. "Hot diggety damn!"

In the meantime, the audience, clutching playbills adorned with that haunting face, had made their way home. And every female between the ages of twelve and twenty went to sit in front of her mirror, trying to coax her hair into Rochelle Blossom's style and frame lips and eyes into the same yearning glance.

Aloha Malihini, October 1895

Annie Brentwood surveyed the outlines of the sugarhouse and the home camp offices hulking against a fat moon. It didn't feel like October to her; it never did. There ought to be leaves scuttering across the road or making bat shapes on the moon. There ought to be crispness in the air and the smell of wood smoke, someone warming his toes and a pot of broth on the hearth. Annie looked upward into the mountains. The high terraces of Mauna Loa were veiled by a faint, thin mist.

It was almost Halloween. Maybe the night marchers would come, she thought. Did Hawaiian ghosts believe in haole holidays? Maybe they would come on invisible horses, hoofbeats rushing on the wind. Tonight she would welcome any company. She felt alone now in this strange land that she had loved so much at first. She felt bereft and hungry for any familiar being, some piece of home.

She went into the camp office and sat down at the desk to wait for Dallas. He had gone to Oahu with a load of sugar to deliver to the factor in Honolulu. Niall Tevis, a Downtown man, preferred dealing with Mrs. Brentwood's apolitical overseer to consorting with a self-proclaimed friend of Liliuokalani's. The PG government spied on its own adherents with the same paranoia with which it watched the Royalists. Dallas would catch the last packet back after a morning with Tevis.

When she heard Dallas's horse and his familiar whistle at last, she forced herself not go to the door to meet him.

Dallas came through the door whistling "Who's the Pretty Girl Milkin' the Cow?" He grinned widely and held out his hand, palm up, balancing a notebook full of receipts. "I got a fair price and a bit more," he said, "in case you were worried."

"I *was* worried," Annie said frankly. She took the receipts and inspected them. "I don't know what the PGs might take it into their heads to do."

"Sugar doesn't know who boiled it," Dallas told her. "And the money men don't cut off their noses to spite their overfed faces." He kissed her cheek before she could stop him. "Now suppose you break out the whiskey bottle and pour me a drink for being your faithful hound?"

"Faithful, my eye," Annie said, but she got out the bottle.

"I have been, as faithful as a man can be," Dallas declared, "ever since I got to these blessed isles. And all for love of you." His voice softened. "And it's damn near killing me, I want you so bad."

"Dallas, don't."

"We got to sometime."

"No, we don't," Annie said, pouring the whiskey.

"You ain't gonna make it go away by saying it ain't here. Not even on a witchy night like this."

He came toward her and stood very close, not touching her but near enough for her to feel his warmth and take in the smell of him. She handed him his whiskey in a glass, and he set it on the desk. Suddenly, with violent clarity, she could remember the way his hair had smelled as they were lying in bed after they made love. She had pillowed his head on her bare breast, and her arms had encircled his young back. She could remember the way his shoulder blades had fit into the crook of her arm.

"We got to sometime," Dallas said again. Now his hands rested on her forearms. They were big hands, battered hands, marked with calluses and old scars from an ore pick and a carpenter's hammer, a cane knife and lariat—a lifetime of tools, of earning a living. They hadn't been any less marred when he was twenty-one.

"I must be something to you, Annie Laurie. I know I still am."

His voice was low in her ear, and it seemed to pull down a dome of distant air and the past around them, desert dry and thick with sage. Enveloped in the past, she could smell a hint of coming snow and felt the warmth of being wrapped in a buffalo-skin robe as she and Dallas sat in front of a pinecone fire.

"What am I to you?" he asked. "You got to cough it up sometime. Run me off, Annie Laurie, or let me in."

"I'm afraid to let you in," she said finally. "You might stay."

He nodded solemnly. "There's always that."

She saw in her mind's eye a picture of bare toes sticking out from the buffalo robe, warming at the fire. Her naked limbs under it were twined with Dallas's, and they were exultant in the sheer joy of being young.

"I'm not young now, Dallas."

"So you ain't. Me neither. But I know what I want a sight better'n I did."

Annie wished desperately that she did. "I left Sam once," she said, "for running around on me. How can I square it if I go and do the same to him?"

"I dunno," Dallas answered. "I reckon you're gonna have to wrestle that one yourself. I ain't gonna let you off the hook by telling you it won't count. It'll count, all right."

How like him. Annie shook her head ruefully and buried it in his chest. Truth-telling had been a kind of reverse virtue with Dallas. He'd always told the truth, whether or not she wanted to hear it.

"I ain't proposing a fling here," Dallas said. "I should have hung on to you when I could. Come with me, and I'll be your lifetime partner, Annie Laurie. I swear it."

"I'm married, Dallas." It seemed such a silly thing to say; it was painfully obvious to them both.

"That can be undone. I'm ready to get married, I swear I am. But if you don't want to go through a divorce, I'll live with you any way you want." His fingers stroked her back. "I'll stay by you and be your lifetime man."

"You were never anybody's lifetime man," Annie retorted. "And I'm not ready to talk about that."

"Got to sometime," Dallas said yet again. He leaned his face against her hair and swayed gently as if they were dancing, and sang under his breath.

"O 'twas on a bright mornin' in summer,
When he first heard her voice singin' low,

And he said to a colleen beside him:
Who's the pretty girl milkin' the cow?"

Annie's eyes instantly overflowed with tears. "Don't you know anything else?" She began to cry into his shirtfront.

"Hush." Dallas stroked her hair, then nuzzled her neck and ear with his lips. "I thought you liked it."

Annie sniffled. It had always been his favorite song. He'd been whistling it when she met him, whistling and methodically beating a bent wagon axle straight, his hair just the color of a new tile roof in the April sun. He had been halfway from Carson City to Virginia City with a wagon, one mule, and the clothes on his back.

So long ago! They had been so young! Something within her ached to have that back, poverty and all. And something else in her just plain ached for Dallas. He had been the first man she really loved, even though she had known he wasn't a good bet. What if she could have him now, after all? Would she leave Sam for him? She would think about that later.

Sam owed her, she decided, just this once, what with all the tomcatting Sam had done, and all the lies he had told her, and the way he was acting now. Maybe she could forgive him better, finally lay it to rest, if she hadn't tried to be little Saint Annie herself. But maybe that was just an excuse for giving in to the good way it felt to have Dallas's hands stroke her breast and feel him pressed against her and remember what his bare skin felt like.

They clung together, forgetting to argue, kissing greedily. Dallas reached out to extinguish the oil lamp that burned on the desk.

"Miss Annie! Miss Annie!"

They flung themselves apart, gasping for breath. Koana came running up the path from the big house towing someone by the hand. "They let him go! Hoakina's come home!"

Annie turned and ran down the steps. Her heart was pounding. She could feel Dallas behind her on the porch even though he didn't follow. The air was full of him.

Hoakina was thin. His eyes were darkly wary and held a fear that hadn't been in them before. His wrist bones stood out like drawer knobs. He was dressed in a blue work shirt and new blue jeans, prison issue. They smelled of sizing.

"I'm home, Miz Brentwood," he said.

"And Mr. Brentwood?" Annie whispered.

Hoakina shook his head. "I don't know. There were ten of us, but not him."

Annie took a deep breath. "Thank you, Hoakina. I'm very glad you're safe. You go and rest now. Let Koana fix you some food."

The cousins turned back down the road toward the big house, Koana with an arm around Hoakina. "I got a silk dress," she confided. "Now you are home, you can take me to parties."

Dallas chuckled. Annie turned to him slowly. She was still breathing hard, and her stomach seemed to be tied in a knot. With Hoakina back, she had an overseer for Aloha Malihini again. In a few days Hoakina would be strong enough to work. And then she and Dallas couldn't hide behind the farm's need of him.

She could see by his face that he saw what she was thinking. "Time to fold 'em or bet, darlin'. This hand's about played out." He leaned in the doorway, silhouetted by the nimbus of the oil lamp. He held his hands out to her and stood waiting.

November, 1895

Sam's body felt strangely light to him. He balanced on the deck of the packet as if his weight might not be quite heavy enough to keep him down on the boards. The warden had let him go. The jailers had come to his cell that morning with no more explanation than they had given him when he was being marched to the rock pile or the chow line or any other destination. They simply prodded him out of bed with bayonets and shoved him down the corridor.

They marched him to the showers and handed him new denim jeans and a chambray shirt. After he was dressed, they hauled open the prison gates, and when he stood stunned and staring, they shoved him through them.

"Your wife's been notified."

The gates slammed shut behind him.

But Annie hadn't come for him. Was she still at home? he wondered. He waited for a while and then begun to walk, finally catching a ride in a fisherman's cart. His banker had looked pleased to see Sam and gave him the cash with which to go home.

"I heard they had let the last ones loose. Goodwill gesture for the holidays." The banker winked. "The United States raises a powerful lot of hell when it sets its mind to."

Sam was silent. The bank's plush carpet had felt luxurious under his feet. He wanted to take his shoes off and stand on it. He stared blankly at the banker. "What did you say?"

"Never mind," the banker said jovially. "I can tell your mind's on getting home. It's been a bad year, but bygones ought to be bygones now." He grinned. "You'll be wanting to get back to the little woman, I'm sure."

"Yes. Have you seen her?"

"Not for a couple of weeks. Won't she be surprised?"

"Yeah."

Now Sam stared at the water curling under the steamer's prow. Would she be at Honuapo Bay? he wondered. He looked down at his hands grasping the rail. They were battered, the knuckles red and scabbed, never quite healed.

The sun was falling into the water behind him. Sam turned and saw it as the steamer cut into the bay. It looked brazen, as if the water might boil when the sinking sun touched it. Another steamer passed them, coming out of the bay—a big ship, one of the transpacific fleet, bound for San Francisco or Los Angeles probably, or maybe even north to Portland.

Would Annie be at home at all? he wondered as he disembarked, carrying nothing. Then he hired one of the cart boys who waited at the docks.

The sun was gone beyond Mauna Loa when the cart boy sent the horse up the road to the big house. No lights were on, and Sam caught his breath. He paid the cart boy, and when he turned around again, he saw that a lamp had flowered in the kitchen window. He tried to let the breath out, but it wouldn't come. Was it only Koana?

He walked slowly, not really wanting to go in to find that Annie had gone. Then the door opened, and Annie stood framed in it.

Sam stumbled, knelt in the dirt, nearly nauseated with relief.

In a moment she was beside him and helped him to stand. "What's wrong, honey?"

"The food was mostly rotten. Half the time I can't keep anything down." *I thought you'd left me, Annie*.

"Come in. Thank God you're home." They didn't know how to embrace each other and did it awkwardly.

"They told me they'd notified you that they were letting me go. Where were you?"

"I didn't know. Nobody told me anything." She measured his waist with her arms. "Oh, baby, you're so thin!" She looked him in the eyes. "Sam, I put Dallas on the boat."

"Just now?"

"Just now."

He stood, arms hanging at his sides, trying not to clutch at her and burst into tears. "You planning on going anywhere yourself?"

"No."

He dropped his head in relief. Eyes closed, he drew a deep breath. The air smelled of sugar and of the oranges on the hill and of Annie's toilet water. "Good," he said finally.

"That's all?" Annie asked. "That's all you want to know?"

"If you're staying it is," Sam said. He put an arm around her and turned her toward the house. In the thickening twilight, the sign above the door was unreadable, but he knew it letter for letter: Aloha Malihini. *Welcome Stranger*.

Author's Note

The Holts would never have been possible (or nearly as much fun to write) without a host of fine people. I particularly want to thank Tiba Willner of Ojai, California, who came to America in steerage when she was six years old and has wonderful stories to tell. Also, at Book Creations, the following: Laurie Rosin, senior project editor and a good buddy for many years; Marjie Weber, a copy editor who always knows when a sentence has gone on way too long; Judy Stockmayer, who knows things like when long distance telephone service became available; and Betty Szeberenyi, Book Creations' librarian, who can find out anything.

For the reader interested in knowing more about the immigrant experience, I recommend *Gateway to Liberty* by Mary Shapiro and *Strangers at the Door* by Ann Novotny.

A fine memoir of the Public Health Service at the turn of the century is *An American Doctor's Odyssey* by Victor Heiser.

For those interested in the "Americanization" of Hawaii, and the events I have fictionalized here, I recommend *The Islands* by W. Storrs Lee and *An Island Kingdom Passes* by Kathleen Dickenson Mellen.

The best-selling saga of the Holt family
continues with

THE HOLTS:
AN AMERICAN DYNASTY

Volume Six

For an exciting preview of this book, to be
published in July 1992, turn the page. . . .

*Frank Blake, Cindy and Henry's son, has per-
formed so well at military academy that his parents have
rewarded him with a trip to New York City. There,
Frank's eyes are opened to the misery of recent immigrants living on Manhattan's Lower East Side. The
innocent seventeen-year-old returns home to Washington, fired up to work for social reform.*

"And ninety-four percent of our taxes are spent in
protecting property and not in protecting life!" Frank
fixed earnest blue eyes on his father, sitting across the
heavily laden dinner table. "So the means of production
must be given back to the people!"

Henry Blake swallowed carefully. "Let me see if I
grasp this." He unclenched his hands from the arms of
his chair, to which they had unaccountably locked
themselves.

"It's simple really, sir. The socialists are trying to
bring a new form of justice for the poor, based on
scientific thought, not on a mishmash of charity and
religion."

"And what is wrong with religion?" Henry managed
to inquire. Cindy had stopped chewing in midbite.

"Oh, nothing, sir. As a form of comfort and a moral
imperative it is invaluable. But in the hands of the upper
and middle classes it becomes a tool to keep the poor
subservient."

"You are aware, I suppose," Henry said dryly, "that

you yourself are a member of the upper end of the middle class."

"Absolutely. That's why I feel my obligation so strongly. This is the next logical step for America."

"What's a socialist?" Midge, Frank's younger sister, asked, fascinated.

"A misguided reformer who is convinced that everyone should own everything equally so that nobody will be poor," Henry said with an edge to his voice.

"And what's wrong with that?" Frank demanded.

"Well, it doesn't allow for advancement through personal initiative, dear," Cindy ventured.

"It also cancels out your education, this house, your mother's and sister's comfort, and everything else I have worked all my life to ensure!" Henry snapped. "I have been poor, incidentally, and I did not find it necessary to deprive everyone else of their wealth in order to make my own way in the world!"

"You were adopted by Grandpa Lee," Frank pointed out stubbornly. "That's when you quit being poor."

"Frank!" Cindy looked shocked. "That is disrespectful."

"It's true, though, isn't it?" the boy insisted.

Henry was furious. "I was sixteen when I was adopted, and what your grandfather gave me was the understanding that hard work and attention to my studies would make the difference in my life. You will apologize immediately."

"No, sir," Frank said. "I didn't mean to be disrespectful, but those slum children didn't even have a chance to study. And they already work sixteen hours a day."

"The ones that aren't thieves," Henry growled.

"You'd steal, too, if you were hungry."

Cindy looked from her son to her husband and was horrified at the sudden anger that burned in both their faces. Henry dropped his fork with a clatter on his plate. "I have never taken what was not mine. Nor has anyone in this family. *Apologize!*"

Clearly Frank wasn't going to. His face was almost as bewildered as it was stubborn. "I thought you would understand," he said in a low tone.

"I understand that you are ignorant and not too old for a whipping," Henry retorted.

Frank's cheeks were flushed. "When your real father was killed, how did you eat until Grandpa Lee found you?"

"I went hunting," Henry said. His voice was loud, as ominous as gunfire. "I am not required to justify myself to a child!"

"What should they hunt in New York?" Frank asked grimly. "Rats?"

"I've had enough of this!" Henry shouted.

"Henry, wait!" Cindy leaned forward as if to block them from each other. "Frank, you don't understand. If you want to help the poor, the way to do it is to go to school, prepare yourself to be a leader of this country. I know you have seen terrible things—"

"He's seen a bunch of anarchists preying on the poor, telling them the world owes them a living! *Socialists.*" Henry spat the word out as if it were a disease. "They want to destroy everything this country stands for."

"This country was built on revolution," Frank insisted. "When a situation is intolerable, revolution is the only answer. That's in the Declaration of Independence."

"Don't you dare compare patriots like Thomas Jefferson and George Washington to sneaking, sniveling rioters! You need a good dose of reality!" Henry was shouting.

"I got one!" Frank shouted back. "I saw what *you* never let me see before—starving, oppressed people whose only function is to be slaves to the rich. They're worse off than the Negroes before the war. And we bring them over here by the boatload to work for us for nothing."

"These people are *free*! They came here of their own free will!"

"Because *we* promised them a better life! And then what do they get?"

"They get a better life than they had in Europe, I can tell you that!"

Midge looked terrified. Their faces, hard and bitter and hostile, were nearly unrecognizable. She burst into tears.

Neither Frank nor Henry even noticed her. Frank leaned across the table, knocked over the salt cellar, and shouted at his father, "I suppose they should be grateful because we starve them and oppress them but just not quite as badly as their old government did?"

"Be quiet this instant!" Henry sounded honestly bewildered through his anger. "Your mother and I have given you everything. You have an honorable future, a family tradition. I won't have you spouting the theories of this treasonous riffraff—"

"Who's riffraff?" Frank asked furiously. "Anyone who doesn't wear blinders to what's going on? Anyone who doesn't shut up and do what he's told?"

"You will do what you're told!" Henry demanded. "If I hear one word from you about this when you get back to school—"

"I'm not going back."

"*What?*"

"Frank—" Cindy smacked her fist down on the table. "Frank, how can you even say such a thing?"

"I'm not going back," Frank repeated. "I'm not going to march around a parade ground all day while people are suffering."

"You don't know anything about suffering." Henry stood and threw his napkin down on the table. "You don't know anything about *life!*"

"Whose fault is that?" Frank shouted. "You picked my school. You picked my friends. *You* decided I was going to West Point! *You* decided it was my duty to turn into some kind of imitation of you and Uncle Toby!"

"Frank, how can you say that?" Cindy asked, hurt. "You know you love school. Maybe it was a mistake to send you to New York. You're so young."

"You mean you should have waited until I was as narrow-minded as you," Frank snapped. "Until I could look at all the suffering and not care!"

"How dare you speak to your mother that way?" Henry's anger went over the edge. "You ungrateful puppy! If you want to see life, then go see it. But don't expect any help from your mother and me."

"Henry, no!" Cindy turned to him, horrified. Midge shrank into her chair.

Frank stood too. "Very well," he said icily. "That will be fine." He kicked his chair back out of his way, sending it flying into the wall. "I don't want your help! And don't expect me back."

Father and son stood glaring at each other in bitterness and betrayal, and then Frank turned on his heel. He snatched his greatcoat from the hall tree in the foyer, then the front door banged behind him.

Midge burst into sobs and ran from the room. They heard her flying footsteps on the stairs, and then Henry and Cindy were left alone with each other.

Meanwhile, Frank's older half brother, Peter, has come into the rest of his sizable inheritance from his mother, the baroness Gisela von Kirchberg. After conferring with family friend Edward Blackstone, a man with the Midas Touch, Peter decides to invest heavily in Coastal Oil, a small but promising company in California. Peter moves to the Ojai Valley to learn about Coastal's operations and to protect his investment. He unavoidably becomes entangled in the board of directors' infighting.

Sanford Rutledge, the Coastal Oil president and general manager, was locked in a power struggle with William H. Kemp, the former president and the most powerful of the other directors. They fought over everything until the board meetings took on the atmosphere of a perpetual dogfight. Peter's investment gave him enough clout to swing votes, and Rutledge and Kemp had begun to lie in wait for him, lurking around corners to expound their opinions and to demand his vote: Rutledge wanted to move operations to a new refinery on the San Francisco Bay, at a location fancifully named Oleum. Kemp wanted to stay put.

An oil company, Peter knew, drilled where the oil was, and the best wells that Coastal Oil had sunk were high in the mountains between Ojai and Santa Paula. Unfortunately the refinery in Santa Paula was more than decrepit.

Rutledge dug in his heels every time any repairs were proposed to the Santa Paula operation. Kemp fussed and fumed about the expenses of shipping crude oil north to Oleum, yet was stubbornly willing to spend any amount to shore up the most dilapidated sections of the Santa Paula operation. Peter's concern was that most of the refinery workers in Santa Paula couldn't afford the move to Oleum, and the company certainly would not be willing to pay their way.

Peter mulled over these pieces of the puzzle as he rode back to his lodgings in Santa Paula. Black clouds were boiling up over the mountains. Peter pulled his slicker off the back of his saddle just as a cold rain sheeted down around him. He struggled through the folds of yellow oilskin, then gave his hired horse a good kick. He had no intention of standing under a tree until the rain let up.

The storm caused a concern, never far from Peter's mind, to intrude his thoughts. Where the hell was Frank? Was he out somewhere, soaked and miserable in a rainstorm? Cindy, he knew, was frantic. How could Frank have done anything so idiotic and put his family through such pain? Sure, Dad could be stiff-necked, but that was no excuse for Frank's running away.

Rain sloshed over the brim of Peter's hat and down the neck of his slicker. He shivered miserably, as cold as he imagined Frank to be. The hell with him. He was probably lolling on a beach somewhere, warm and fat and not giving a damn that the family was in an uproar. Damn stupid kid. Peter's hands clenched angrily on the reins. Frank ought to be thrashed, and it was a shame that Dad hadn't done it. And where *was* he?

Horse and rider were soaked by the time they came down the mountain into Santa Paula, just as the rain let up and the sun came out in a splash of brilliant yellow.

The horse snorted suddenly and swiveled its ears. Peter turned in the saddle at the clatter of a gasoline engine behind them. He grinned. Here was progress—the automobile had arrived in Santa Paula. Better yet, it was a Blake. The motorist, as soaking wet as Peter, beamed from behind the tiller, obviously pleased with the stir he was making.

Peter's horse jigged at the smoke and noise.

"Get used to it," Peter advised the horse. He followed the Blake, curious, and saw the car turn in at the gates of the Coastal Oil refinery several blocks away. By the time Peter tied up his horse, the driver was talking to the refinery's office manager.

"None?" The driver's expression was peevish.

"Not a drop." The manager shrugged. "Sorry, bud. We only refine gasoline once a week, on Thursdays."

"This *is* a refinery, isn't it?" the motorist demanded. Pipes and tanks looming behind them made the question rhetorical and sarcastic. "Well, I'm not sitting here till Thursday."

"We don't get much call for it," the manager said.

"'A plentiful supply of good, cheap fuel,'" the driver, obviously quoting from the Blake Company's sales brochure, muttered as he passed Peter. He cranked the Blake over and chugged away.

Peter headed for the refinery office. "What do you mean, we don't have any gasoline for sale?" he demanded.

"We don't sell enough to make it worthwhile, Mr. Blake," the manager apologized.

"What exactly *do* we sell here?" Peter demanded, exasperated.

"Fuel oil, lamp oil, kerosene," the manager answered. "And asphalt," he added.

"I'll let you know when I invent a motor car that can run on asphalt," Peter said.

"Maybe you ought to talk to Mr. Rutledge and Mr. Kemp," the office manager suggested. "I don't set the refinery schedule."

"Oh, I intend to."

Infuriated, he mounted his horse again and headed back into town.

Two blocks down the muddy main street, a crowd had gathered to watch as a farmer in bib overalls maneuvered a pair of mules into position. As Peter drew abreast he was appalled to see that the farmer was hitching the mules to the front of the Blake.

"Get a horse!"

"He's got mules now. He don't need no horse!"

The crowd of wags on the sidewalk slapped their thighs hilariously while the much-tried driver of the Blake, out of gasoline, stood with arms folded and attempted to ignore them. Peter reined his horse around them and was immensely grateful that he hadn't been the one to sell the man his Blake.

He returned his horse to the livery stable and walked to the furnished cottage he had rented. The cottage came with a Mexican gardener who spent his time moving plants around according to some undisclosed plan and understood not a word Peter said to him, and a cleaning woman who came once a week, muttered something about bachelors, and told Peter not to put his feet on the sofa. Unfortunately the cottage did not include laundry services.

He shucked off his wet clothes and threw them into an already overflowing hamper. When he was dry, Peter picked up the hamper and set out to find a laundry.

The sky looked threatening, and he pushed his way through the door of the "Fine French Laundry" on Alvarez Street just as the clouds opened. A red-haired girl in a white canvas apron came from the back room when she heard the bell over the door.

"Put the basket on the counter, and let's see what you've got."

Peter decided that the "French" was a frill for elegance's sake. She sounded American to him, maybe with a touch of Irish. Her hair was pinned into a knot on her head, but the steam made stray tendrils curl appealingly around her face. Peter thought she was awfully pretty.

She seemed to notice that he did. "You're new here, aren't you?" she asked, sorting his shirts. "You work in the oil fields?"

"Not exactly," Peter said. "I, uh, I own part of the company."

She peered at his clothes more closely. "I guess you do."

Peter peeked uncomfortably at his custom-made laundry. "My name's Peter Blake," he said, trying to sound friendly.

"I'm Peggy Dulaney," she said, stuffing his shirts into a canvas sack. "You going to be a regular customer, Mr. Blake? I'll give you your own bag if you are."

"I expect I'll be here for a while."

She wrote "P. Blake" on the bag with a laundry marker and tossed the sack onto the pile behind the counter.

"Do you own this place?" he asked.

"I run it," Peggy said. "Me dad owns it, such as he is." Her lips compressed in annoyance. "Wherever he is."

Peter looked at her longingly. She was the first pretty woman he had met here, and he was cold and lonely.

She cocked her head at him. "Your shirts'll be ready Wednesday."

Peter looked at the floor, embarrassed. He couldn't think of a reason to stick around. "I—I like a little starch in them," he said, feeling foolish. "But not too much."

"Right you are."

The door banged open again, jangling the bell, and a man came in, shaking water from him like a dog. He looked about forty-five, burly, and red in the face. He stomped behind the counter and reached for the till.

Peggy tried to slap his hand away. "You've had enough."

He pushed her away. "It's cold out there. I need a bit to warm me up."

"You're pickled already." Her lips tightened as she watched him stuff a handful of bills into his coat pocket. "There won't be enough to pay the girls."

"There's plenty." He glared at her, and then at Peter for good measure. "Plenty if you were out hustling work instead of mooning around with the men." He glared at Peter. "Who the hell are you?"

"This is Mr. Blake," Peggy said. "He's from Coastal Oil."

"Well, get back out to the field and leave my daughter to the wash, damn you. We got a livin' to earn."

"He's an owner," Peggy told him sharply. "You're stinkin' drunk."

"Don't sass me, or I'll clip you one." Dulaney glowered at them both. "I'll be back for dinner. It better be hot." Head down, he slammed out the door.

Peggy, biting her lip, looked at Peter. "That was my Pa," she muttered.

Peter wondered where her mother was, if Peggy Dulaney had any defense against that old devil. Or if Peggy was her mother's defense. He couldn't think of any way to ask that didn't make him sound like a do-gooder trying to tell the poor how they ought to live. He'd known a bunch of that type and could never understand why the poor didn't throw rocks at them.

"I guess you need to get back to work," he said.

Peggy snorted. "Somebody'd better." She picked up a pile of laundry bags and marched around the partition. Her whole back was rigid with embarrassment.

Peter stood for a moment in the empty room and then went out into the storm. There was a grocer's on the corner, and Peter ducked in to see if he could wait out the rain in there. Maybe he'd try cooking his own dinner tonight instead of going to a restaurant. He wasn't much of a hand at it, but it was something to do.

He peered around the grocery shelves, trying to think what he could manage to cook. A fat black and white tomcat was asleep on sacks of rice in the window. At first Peter thought it was stuffed, but then it opened one green eye. Peter hefted a sack of rice, and the cat stretched and spread out its toes, claws extended.

"That's Hiram," the woman behind the counter said. "He's a fine mouser."

"I'll bet he is," Peter said. He didn't mind a little cat hair in his rice; it was preferable to mouse droppings. In a country grocery, one or the other was inevitable.

"What can I do for you?" The woman was round and motherly looking.

"I was trying to decide what I could cook without burning it," Peter confessed.

"Well now, rice is easy. Twice as much water as rice. Boil it about twenty minutes. I could give you a nice fresh chicken to go with it. I raise 'em myself."

Peter smiled, glad to have someone friendly to talk to. "That would be great."

"You just wait here, Mr. Blake." She disappeared into the back of the store, and Peter heard a door open and close. He wondered how she knew his name. In a few minutes he heard a furious squawking and then a thud and silence. Apparently the chicken was extremely fresh.

She came back in a few minutes with the headless carcass—already gutted, he hoped. She poured a pot of water that was already hot from the kettle on the potbellied stove and dipped the chicken in it by the feet.

"How do you like Santa Paula, Mr. Blake?" She was perched on a chair now, expertly plucking feathers.

"Uh, very much," Peter replied.

"Are you planning to live here permanent?"

"Well, not forever," Peter said. "It's a nice town, though."

"You're not seeing us at our best in all this rain." She hesitated, peering at him over the chicken, her fingers automatically yanking feathers. "Mr. Blake, tell me: Is it true they're closing down the refinery?"

"I don't know," Peter said honestly. "I'm new on the board, and—"

"Mr. Blake, we got to have that refinery. Can't you make 'em see the light?"

"Well, it's a business decision," Peter said. "The new facility at Oleum is much better equipped." He felt like a cad.

"My husband's a boiler tender," she said. "We couldn't make it without his pay. Us nor half the folks that buy from us here." She shook feathers off her fingers. "We're doin' about all we can now, what with the store and the chickens. I just don't know . . ." Her words trailed off, and she bent her eyes on the half-plucked chicken. "I know I shouldn't be putting you on the spot like this, but you looked so friendlylike."

"It's all right," Peter said, embarrassed.

She finished plucking the chicken in silence, then rinsed it in the pot again. "You want the feet?"

"No," Peter said. "Not at all."

She disappeared into the back room once more, and Peter heard the hatchet *thunk* twice. She emerged with the dressed chicken and began wrapping it in butcher's paper. "No point in havin' the feet if you don't use 'em," she said. "I make soup with them. Sometimes I give 'em to Hiram for a treat. He likes 'em."

Back at his cottage, Peter looked dubiously at the chicken. Plucked and naked, it looked reproachful to him. He found a Dutch oven in his kitchen cupboards, put the chicken in it with a cup of water, and gratefully set the lid on it.

The cast-iron stove was wood fired, and as black as soot. Peter opened the firebox to see how the fire he had laid was doing and discovered that it was about to go out. He never had gotten the hang of building a fire in a stove.

He thought wistfully of Peggy Dulaney, who would probably have got this old wood stove whipped into shape in nothing flat . . . and for a hell of a lot more appreciative audience than her old man. Of course Peter knew he couldn't invite a nice girl to dinner and expect her to do the cooking, or even invite her to dinner at his house without a chaperone, not in Peter's world. He suspected, however, that Peggy's world might be different.

She had a competence about her that he liked. He pictured her shapely, muscular arms bent over a laundry tub or building a stove fire. He could invite her out to a restaurant. He'd bet she didn't get much chance to eat in restaurants.

The fire began to smoke suddenly, billowing around the firebox door. Peter swore and yanked it open with a potholder. It wouldn't do to get her hopes up, of course. She'd have to understand he wasn't serious, just looking for a friend. It would probably be better not to do it at all. . . .

He managed to cook the chicken and boil the rice. He discovered that two cups of rice turns out to be about six cups after it was cooked, enough to last him until doomsday. He took a plate to the kitchen table, with his notebook on Coastal Oil's finances, and settled down to something he did know—figures. The chicken wasn't too bad, with liberal additions of salt and with his notebook to distract him from the fact that the bird was burned on the bottom. So was the rice. Peter tried chipping it out of the bottom of the pot and finally filled the thing with water and set it out on the back porch.

He went back moodily to his figures and hoped he hadn't given himself indigestion. Kemp and Rutledge were going to do that for him on their own.

From the creator of WAGONS WEST

The

HOLTS

An American

Dynasty

OREGON LEGACY
An epic adventure emblazoned with the courage and passion of a legendary family--inheritors of a fighting spirit and an unconquerable dream.

❑ 28248-4 $4.50

OKLAHOMA PRIDE
America's passionate pioneer family heads for new adventure on the last western frontier.

❑ 28446-0 $4.50

CAROLINA COURAGE
The saga continues in a violence-torn land--as hearts and minds catch fire with justice...and indomitable spirit.

❑ 28756-7 $4.95

CALIFORNIA GLORY
Passion and pride sweep a great American family into danger from an enemy outside... and desires within.

❑ 28970-5 $4.99

Available at your local bookstore or use this page to order.

★ WAGONS WEST ★

This continuing, magnificent saga recounts the adventures of a brave band of settlers, all of different backgrounds, all sharing one dream— to find a new and better life.

- ☐ 26822-8   **INDEPENDENCE! #1** $4.95
- ☐ 26162-2   **NEBRASKA! #2** $4.95
- ☐ 26242-4   **WYOMING! #3** $4.95
- ☐ 26072-3   **OREGON! #4** $4.50
- ☐ 26070-7   **TEXAS! #5** $4.99
- ☐ 26377-3   **CALIFORNIA! #6** $4.99
- ☐ 26546-6   **COLORADO! #7** $4.95
- ☐ 26069-3   **NEVADA! #8** $4.99
- ☐ 26163-0   **WASHINGTON! #9** $4.50
- ☐ 26073-1   **MONTANA! #10** $4.95
- ☐ 26184-3   **DAKOTA! #11** $4.50
- ☐ 26521-0   **UTAH! #12** $4.50
- ☐ 26071-5   **IDAHO! #13** $4.50
- ☐ 26367-6   **MISSOURI! #14** $4.50
- ☐ 27141-5   **MISSISSIPPI! #15** $4.95
- ☐ 25247-X   **LOUISIANA! #16** $4.50
- ☐ 25622-X   **TENNESSEE! #17** $4.50
- ☐ 26022-7   **ILLINOIS! #18** $4.95
- ☐ 26533-4   **WISCONSIN! #19** $4.95
- ☐ 26849-X   **KENTUCKY! #20** $4.95
- ☐ 27065-6   **ARIZONA! #21** $4.99
- ☐ 27458-9   **NEW MEXICO! #22** $4.95
- ☐ 27703-0   **OKLAHOMA! #23** $4.95
- ☐ 28180-1   **CELEBRATION! #24** $4.50

Bantam Books, Dept. LE, 414 East Golf Road, Des Plaines, IL 60016

Please send me the items I have checked above. I am enclosing $_____ (please add $2.50 to cover postage and handling). Send check or money order, no cash or C.O.D.s please.

Mr/Ms _____

Address _____

City/State _____ Zip _____

Please allow four to six weeks for delivery.
Prices and availability subject to change without notice.   LE-9/91